Curtis Sittenfeld is the author of the ~~international~~ best-seller *American Wife*. Her first ~~novel was a New York~~ *Times* bestseller and was longli~~sted for the Orange~~ Prize. Her second novel was *The Man of M*~~y Dreams~~. Her books are translated into twenty-five languages. She is married, with a little daughter, and lives in America.

Praise for *Prep*

'*The OC* meets Donna Tartt's *The Secret History* with flashes of *Clueless* . . . Sittenfeld's strength is in making the experience feel universal . . . Everyone will wince with recognition at the horror of being a teenager. It's great to relive it all, now that it is happening to someone else' *Observer*

'Straightforward, serious, funny . . . There is so much that is right about this book. Sittenfeld captures the hothouse atmosphere of boarding-school, the way you see even people you *don't* like in their underwear . . . Mostly, however, it's Lee's voice that makes all this worthwhile' *London Review of Books*

'Curtis Sittenfeld shares with Salinger a knack of capturing, in effortless prose, a teenager mindset . . . It feels important . . . Most vitally of all, it feels like adolescence' *The Times*

'You don't have to have attended an elite Massachusetts boarding school to find yourself reliving your adolescence in Curtis Sittenfeld's *Prep* . . . Even the Cross Sugarmans (major crush) and Aspeth Montgomerys (long legs, super popular) of this world will cringe with recognition at the book's fine-knit accuracy and detail' *Vogue*

'*Sweet Valley High* as written by George Eliot. Sittenfeld is a pin-sharp observer, and in *Prep* she needles away at class, race and character . . . A highly accomplished novel' *Independent on Sunday*

'Any feelings of nostalgia for adolescence should be dispelled by the exacting intimacies of this first novel . . . hilarious and excruciating . . . In the end, Lee's incisive vision of herself and others is her downfall but also – as this richly textured narrative suggests – her greatest gift' *New Yorker*

Also by Curtis Sittenfeld

THE MAN OF MY DREAMS
AMERICAN WIFE

Curtis Sittenfeld

PREP

BLACK SWAN

TRANSWORLD PUBLISHERS
61–63 Uxbridge Road, London W5 5SA
A Random House Group Company
www.rbooks.co.uk

PREP
A BLACK SWAN BOOK: 9780552776844

First published in 2005 by Random House, an imprint of The Random
House Publishing Group, a division of Random House, Inc., New York, and
simultaneously in Canada by Random House of Canada Limited, Toronto

First published in Great Britain in paperback in 2006 by Picador, an
imprint of Pan Macmillan Ltd
Black Swan edition published 2010

Addresses for Random House Group Ltd companies outside the UK
can be found at: www.randomhouse.co.uk
The Random House Group Ltd Reg. No. 954009

The Random House Group Limited supports The Forest Stewardship
Council (FSC), the leading international forest certification organisation.
All our titles that are printed on Greenpeace approved FSC certified paper
carry the FSC logo. Our paper procurement policy can be found at
www.rbooks.co.uk/environment

Typeset in 10/12.5pt Giovanni Book by
Falcon Oast Graphic Art Ltd.
Printed in the UK by CPI Cox & Wyman, Reading, RG1 8EX.

2 4 6 8 10 9 7 5 3 1

For my parents, Paul and Betsy Sittenfeld;
my sisters, Tiernan and Josephine;
and my brother, P.G.

CONTENTS

PREP

1

Thieves

I THINK THAT everything, or at least the part of everything that happened to me, started with the Roman architecture mix-up. Ancient History was my first class of the day, occurring after morning chapel and roll call, which was not actually roll call but a series of announcements that took place in an enormous room with twenty-foot-high Palladian windows, rows and rows of desks with hinged tops that you lifted to store your books inside, and mahogany panels on the walls—one for each class since Ault's founding in 1882—engraved with the name of every person who had graduated from the school. The two senior prefects led roll call, standing at a desk on a platform and calling on the people who'd signed up ahead of time to make announcements. My own desk, assigned alphabetically, was near the platform, and because I didn't talk to my classmates who sat around me, I spent the lull before roll call listening to the prefects' exchanges with teachers or other students or each other. The prefects' names were Henry Thorpe and Gates Medkowski. It was my fourth week at the school. and I didn't know much about Ault, but I did know that Gates was the first girl in Ault's history to have been elected prefect.

The teachers' announcements were straightforward and succinct: *Please remember that your adviser request forms are due by noon on Thursday*. The students' announcements were lengthy—the longer roll call was, the shorter first period would be—and filled with double entendres: *Boys' soccer is practicing on Coates Field today, which, if you don't know where it is, is behind the headmaster's house, and if you still don't know where it is, ask Fred. Where are you, Fred? You wanna raise your hand, man? There's Fred, everyone see Fred? Okay, so Coates Field. And remember—bring your balls.*

When the announcements were finished, Henry or Gates pressed a button on the side of the desk, like a doorbell, there was a ringing throughout the schoolhouse, and we all shuffled off to class. In Ancient History, we were making presentations on different topics, and I was one of the students presenting that day. From a library book, I had copied pictures of the Colosseum, the Pantheon, and the Baths of Diocletian, then glued the pictures onto a piece of poster board and outlined the edges with green and yellow markers. The night before, I'd stood in front of the mirror in the dorm bathroom practicing what I'd say, but then someone had come in, and I'd pretended I was washing my hands and left.

I was third; right before me was Jamie Lorison. Mrs. Van der Hoef had set a lectern in the front of the classroom, and Jamie stood behind it, clutching index cards. "It is a tribute to the genius of Roman architects," he began, "that many of the buildings they designed more than two thousand years ago still exist today for modern peoples to visit and enjoy."

My heart lurched. The genius of Roman architects was my topic, not Jamie's. I had difficulty listening as he continued, though certain familiar phrases emerged: *the aqueducts, which were built to transport water . . . the Colosseum, originally called the Flavian Amphitheater . . .*

Mrs. Van der Hoef was standing to my left, and I leaned toward her and whispered, "Excuse me."

She seemed not to have heard me.

"Mrs. Van der Hoef?" Then—later, this gesture seemed particularly humiliating—I reached out to touch her forearm.

She was wearing a maroon silk dress with a collar and a skinny maroon belt, and I only brushed my fingers against the silk, but she drew back as if I'd pinched her. She glared at me, shook her head, and took several steps away.

"I'd like to pass around some pictures," I heard Jamie say. He lifted a stack of books from the floor. When he opened them, I saw colored pictures of the same buildings I had copied in black-and-white and stuck to poster board.

Then his presentation ended. Until that day, I had never felt anything about Jamie Lorison, who was red-haired and skinny and breathed loudly, but as I watched him take his seat, a mild, contented expression on his face, I loathed him.

"Lee Fiora, I believe you're next," Mrs. Van der Hoef said.

"See, the thing is," I began, "maybe there's a problem."

I could feel my classmates looking at me with growing interest, Ault prided itself on, among other things, its teacher-student ratio, and there were only twelve of us in the class. When all their eyes were on me at once, however, that did not seem like such a small number.

"I just can't go," I finally said.

"I beg your pardon?" Mrs. Van der Hoef was in her late fifties, a tall, thin woman with a bony nose. I'd heard that she was the widow of a famous archaeologist, not that any archaeologists were famous to me.

"See, my presentation is—or it was going to be—I thought I was supposed to talk about—but maybe, now that Jamie—"

"You're not making sense, Miss Fiora,' Mrs. Van der Hoef said. "You need to speak clearly."

"If I go, I'll be saying the same thing as Jamie."

"But you're presenting on a different topic."

"Actually, I'm talking about architecture, too."

She walked to her desk and ran her finger down a piece of paper. I had been looking at her while we spoke, and now that she had turned away, I didn't know what to do with my eyes.

13

My classmates were still watching me. During the school year so far, I'd spoken in classes only when I was called on, which was not often; the other kids at Ault were enthusiastic about participating. Back in my junior high in South Bend, Indiana, many classes had felt like one-on-one discussions between the teacher and me, while the rest of the students daydreamed or doodled. Here, the fact that I did the reading didn't distinguish me. In fact, nothing distinguished me. And now, in my most lengthy discourse to date, I was revealing myself to be strange and stupid.

"You're not presenting on architecture," Mrs. Van der Hoef said. "You're presenting on athletics."

"Athletics?" I repeated. There was no way I'd have volunteered for such a topic.

She thrust the sheet of paper at me, and there was my name, *Lee Fiora—Athletics*; in her writing, just below *James Lorison—Architecture*. We'd signed up for topics by raising our hands in class; clearly, she had misunderstood me.

"I could do athletics," I said uncertainly. "Tomorrow I could do them."

"Are you suggesting that the students presenting tomorrow have their time reduced on your behalf?"

"No, no, of course not. But maybe a different day, or maybe—I could do it whenever. Just not today. All I'd be able to talk about today is architecture."

"Then you'll be talking about architecture. Please use the lectern."

I stared at her. "But Jamie just went."

"Miss Fiora, you are wasting class time."

As I stood and gathered my notebook and poster board, I thought about how coming to Ault had been an enormous error. I would never have friends; the best I'd be able to hope for from my classmates would be pity. It had already been obvious to me that I was different from them, but I'd imagined that I could lie low for a while, getting a sense of them, then reinvent myself in their image. Now I'd been uncovered.

I gripped either side of the lectern and looked down at my notes. "One of the most famous examples of Roman architecture is the Colosseum," I began. "Historians believe that the Colosseum was called the Colosseum because of a large statue of the Colossus of Nero which was located nearby." I looked up from my notes. The faces of my classmates were neither kind nor unkind, sympathetic nor unsympathetic; engaged nor bored.

"The Colosseum was the site of shows held by the emperor or other aristocrats. The most famous of these shows was—" I paused. Ever since childhood, I have felt the onset of tears in my chin, and, at this moment, it was shaking. But I was not going to cry in front of strangers. "Excuse me," I said, and I left the classroom.

There was a girls' bathroom across the hall, but I knew not to go in there because I would be too easy to find. I ducked into the stairwell and hurried down the steps to the first floor and out a side door. Outside it was sunny and cool, and with almost everyone in class, the campus felt pleasantly empty. I jogged toward my dorm. Maybe I would leave altogether: hitchhike to Boston, catch a bus, ride back home to Indiana. Fall in the Midwest would be pretty but not overly pretty—not like in New England, where they called the leaves *foliage*. Back in South Bend, my younger brothers would be spending the evenings kicking the soccer ball in the backyard and coming in for dinner smelling like boy-sweat; they'd be deciding on their Halloween costumes, and when my father carved the pumpkin, he would hold the knife over his head and stagger toward my brothers with a maniacal expression on his face, and as they ran shrieking into the other room, my mother would say, "Terry, quit scaring them."

I reached the courtyard. Broussard's dorm was one of eight on the east side of campus, four boys' dorms and four girls' dorms forming a square, with granite benches in the middle. When I looked out the window of my room, I often saw couples using the benches. the boy sitting with his legs spread

15

in front of him, the girl standing between his legs, her hands perhaps set on his shoulders briefly, before she laughed and lifted them. At this moment, only one of the benches was occupied. A girl in cowboy boots and a long skirt lay on her back, one knee propped up in a triangle, one arm slung over her eyes.

As I passed, she lifted her arm. It was Gates Medkowski. "Hey," she said.

We almost made eye contact, but then we didn't. It made me unsure of whether she was addressing me, which was an uncertainty I often felt when spoken to. I kept walking.

"Hey," she said again. "Who do you think I'm talking to? We're the only ones here." But her voice was kind; she wasn't making fun of me.

"Sorry," I said.

"Are you a freshman?"

I nodded.

"Are you going to your dorm right now?"

I nodded again.

"I assume you don't know this, but you're not allowed in the dorm during classes." She swung her legs around, righting herself. "None of us are," she said. "For Byzantine reasons that I wouldn't even try to guess at. Seniors are allowed to roam, but roaming only means outside, the library, or the mail room, so that's a joke."

I said nothing.

"Are you okay?" she asked.

"Yes," I said and began to cry.

"Oh God," Gates said. "I didn't mean to upset you. Here, come sit down." She was patting the bench beside her, and then she stood, walked toward me, set one arm around my back—my shoulders were heaving—and guided me toward the bench. When we were sitting, she passed me a blue bandanna that smelled of incense; even through the blur of my tears, I was interested by the fact that she carried this accessory. I hesitated to blow my nose—my snot would be on

16

Gates Medkowski's bandanna—but my whole face seemed to be leaking.

"What's your name?" she said.

"Lee." My voice was high and shaky.

"So what's wrong? Why aren't you in class or study hall?"

"Nothing's wrong."

She laughed. "For some reason, I don't think that's true."

When I told her what had happened, she said, "Van der Hoef likes to come off like the dragon lady. God knows why. Maybe it's menopause. But she's actually pretty nice most of the time."

"I don't think she likes me."

"Oh, don't worry. It's still so early in the school year. She'll have forgotten all about this by November."

"But I left in the middle of class," I said.

Gates waved one hand through the air. "Don't even think about it," she said. "The teachers here have seen everything. We imagine ourselves as distinct entities, but in their eyes, we merge into a great mass of adolescent neediness. You know what I mean?"

I nodded, though I was pretty sure I had no idea; I'd never heard someone close to my own age talk the way she was talking.

"Ault can be a tough place," she said. "Especially at first."

At this, I felt a new rush of tears. She *knew*. I blinked several times.

"It's like that for everyone," she said.

I looked at her, and, as I did, I realized for the first time that she was very attractive: not pretty exactly, but striking, or maybe handsome. She was nearly six feet tall and had pale skin, fine features, eyes of such a washed-out blue they were almost gray, and a massive amount of long light brown hair that was a rough texture and unevenly cut; in places, in the sunlight, there were glints of gold in it. As we'd been talking, she'd pulled it into a high, loose bun with shorter pieces of hair falling around her face. In my own experience, creating

17

such a perfectly messy bun required a good fifteen minutes of maneuvering before a mirror. But everything about Gates seemed effortless. "I'm from Idaho, and I was the biggest hayseed when I got here," she was saying. "I practically arrived on a tractor."

"I'm from Indiana," I said.

"See, you must be way cooler than I was because at least Indiana is closer to the East Coast than Idaho."

"But people here have been to Idaho. They ski there." I knew this because Dede Schwartz, one of my two roommates, kept on her desk a framed picture of her family standing on a snowy slope, wearing sunglasses and holding poles. When I'd asked her where it was taken, she'd said Sun Valley, and when I'd looked up Sun Valley in my atlas, I'd learned it was in Idaho.

"True," Gates said. "But I'm not from the mountains. Anyway, the important thing to remember about Ault is why you applied in the first place. It was for the academics, right? I don't know where you were before, but Ault beats the hell out of the public high school in my town. As for the politics here, what can you do? There's a lot of posturing, but it's all kind of meaningless."

I wasn't certain what she meant by *posturing*—it made me think of a row of girls in long white nightgowns, standing up very straight and balancing hardcover books on their heads.

Gates looked at her watch, a man's sports watch with black plastic straps. "Listen," she said. "I better get going. I have Greek second period. What's your next class?"

"Algebra. But I left my backpack in Ancient History."

"Just grab it when the bell rings. Don't worry about talking to Van der Hoef. You can sort things out with her later, after you've both cooled off."

She stood, and I stood too. We started walking back toward the schoolhouse—it seemed I was not returning to South Bend after all, at least not today. We passed the roll call room, which during the school day functioned as the study hall. I wondered if any of the students were looking out

18

the window, watching me walk with Gates Medkowski.

It was nighttime, after curfew, when Dede made the discovery. She had just finished laying out her clothes for the next morning. Every night, she set them on the floor in the shape of an actual person: shoes, then pants or else tights and a skirt, then shirt, then sweater or jacket on top of the shirt. Our room was not large—though three of us shared it, I'd heard that in other years it had been used as a double—and Dede made no concession to this fact. For me and our other roommate, Sin-Jun Kim, the arrangement of Dede's clothes necessitated as much stepping around as if a real body were on the floor. But we had not objected during the first few days of school and now Dede's pattern was established.

The night of Dede's discovery, our room was quiet except for the low sound of her stereo and the clicking open and shut of her dresser drawers. Sin-Jun was reading at her desk, and I was in bed already. I always climbed into bed when I got sick of studying—I wasn't sure what else to do—and lay there under the sheets, facing the wall, my eyes shut. If someone came by to see Dede, they'd enter the room speaking in a normal voice, then see me and whisper, "Oh, sorry," or else, "Whoops," and I would feel strangely flattered. I sometimes pretended I was in my bed in South Bend and that the sounds of the dorm were the sounds of my family—the flushing toilet was my brother Joseph, the laughter in the hallway was my mother talking on the telephone to her sister.

Since our meeting the previous week, I'd often found myself thinking of Gates Medkowski. Before roll call, I watched her, and a few times, she'd looked right at me. When we made eye contact, she smiled or said, "Hey, Lee," before turning away, and I usually blushed, feeling caught. I didn't necessarily want to talk to her again because I would probably be awkward, but I wanted to know things about her. I was considering whether or not Gates had a boyfriend when Dede exclaimed, "What the fuck!"

Neither Sin-Jun nor I said anything.

"Okay, I had forty dollars in my top drawer this morning. and it is *not* there right now," Dede said. "One of you guys didn't take it, did you?"

"Of course not." I rolled over. "Did you check your pockets?"

"It was definitely in my drawer. Someone stole money from me. I can't believe it."

"Is not in drawer?" Sin-Jun said. Sin-Jun was from Korea and I was still unable to gauge exactly how much English she understood. Like me, Sin-Jun had no friends. and also like me, she was generally ignored by Dede. Sometimes the two of us walked together to the dining hall, which was preferable to walking alone.

Though Dede took pains to separate herself from Sin-Jun and me, leaving earlier than we did for morning chapel or for meals, she herself was not exactly cool. At my junior high she would have been royalty, but here she was, apparently, neither rich enough nor pretty enough to be truly popular. Even I recognized that if you compared Dede to the best-looking girls at Ault, her nose was a bit round, her calves a bit stocky, her hair a bit, well, brown. She was a follower, literally a follower—I often saw her scurrying behind two or three other girls. The strenuousness of her efforts made me feel embarrassed for her.

"I already told you it's not in my drawer," Dede said. "You didn't borrow it, did you, Sin-Jun? Like take it and plan on paying me back later? It's okay if you did." This was a notably kind remark on Dede's part.

But Sin-Jun shook her head. "No borrow," she said.

Dede exhaled disgustedly. "Great," she said. "There's a thief in the dorm."

"Maybe someone else borrowed the money," I said. "Ask Aspeth." Aspeth Montgomery was the girl Dede followed most enthusiastically. She lived down the hall, and I assumed Dede considered it a stroke of singular misfortune that she had been assigned to live with Sin-Jun and me instead of with Aspeth.

"Aspeth would never borrow money without asking," Dede said. "I need to tell Madame what's happened."

This was the moment when I actually believed that the money had been stolen, or at least I believed that Dede believed it. The next night at curfew, after calling out our names and checking them off the dorm list, Madame Broussard said, "It is with great displeasure that I must tell you there has been a theft." Madame—our dorm head, the head of the French department, and a native of Paris—peered around the room through her cat's-eye glasses, which were either (I wasn't sure which) outdated or retrohip. She was in her early forties, and she also wore stockings with seams, tan leather high heels with an ankle strap fastened by one leather-covered button, and skirts and blouses that emphasized her small waist and not-small backside. "I will not say how much money it was, nor will I say from whom it was taken," she continued. "If you know anything about this incident, I request that you step forward. I remind you that stealing is a major disciplinary violation and as such is punishable by expulsion."

"How much money was it?" asked Amy Dennaker. Amy was a junior with a hoarse voice, curly red hair, and broad shoulders, and she scared me. I had spoken to her only once, when I was waiting in the common room to use the pay phone and she walked in, opened the refrigerator, and said, "Whose Diet Cokes are these?" I had said, "I don't know," and Amy had taken one and walked up the stairs. Maybe, I thought, she was the thief.

"The amount of money is not pertinent," Madame said. "I am telling you of the incident only so you may take precautions."

"What, you mean like locking our doors?" Amy said and people laughed. None of the doors had locks on them.

"I urge you not to keep large sums of money in your rooms," Madame said. "If you have ten or fifteen dollars, that is enough." She was right about this—you didn't need cash at

Ault. Money was everywhere on campus, but it was usually invisible. You caught a glimpse of it sometimes in things that were shiny, like the hood of the headmaster's Mercedes, or the gold dome of the schoolhouse, or a girl's long, straight blond hair. But nobody carried wallets. When you had to pay for a notebook or a pair of sweatpants at the campus store, you wrote your student ID number on a form and, later on, your parents got the bill. "If you see any unfamiliar persons in the dorm," Madame continued, "you may report it to me. Are there other announcements?"

Dede's friend Aspeth raised her hand. "I just want to say that whoever is leaving pubic hair in the bathroom sink, could you please clean it up? It's really gross."

Aspeth made this announcement every few days. It was true there were often short wiry black hairs in one of the sinks, but, clearly, Aspeth's complaints were achieving nothing. It seemed like maybe she just liked to make them because they established her firmly in opposition to pubic hair.

"If that is it," Madame said, "then curfew is complete." Everyone rose from the couches and chairs and the floor to shake her hand, which was by then a ritual I had become used to.

"If we started a vigilante group, would the student activities committee give us funding?" Amy asked in a loud voice.

"I do not know," Madame said wearily.

"Don't worry," Amy said. "We'd be peaceful vigilantes." I had seen Amy in action before—she did imitations of Madame that consisted of clutching her chest and crying out something like *Zut alors! Someone has sat upon my croissant!*— but I was still surprised by her joking. In chapel, the headmaster and the chaplain spoke of citizenship and integrity and the price we had to pay for the privileges we enjoyed. At Ault, it wasn't just that we weren't supposed to be bad or unethical; we weren't even supposed to be ordinary, and stealing was worse than ordinary. It was unseemly, lacking subtlety, revealing a wish for things you did not already have.

Climbing the stairs to the second floor, I wondered if it was possible that I was the thief. What if I had opened Dede's drawer in my sleep? Or what if I had amnesia, or schizophrenia, and couldn't even account for my own behavior? I didn't think I had stolen the money, yet it also did not seem impossible.

"We'll get to the bottom of this *tout de suite*," I heard Amy say as I reached the top step, and then someone else, someone standing much closer to me, said, "That bitch is crazy."

I turned. Little Washington was on the steps behind me, I made a noncommittal noise, to acknowledge her comment, though I wasn't even sure if she meant Amy or Madame.

"The mouth on her," Little added, and then I knew she was referring to Amy.

"Amy likes to kid around," I said. I wouldn't have minded sharing a moment with Little at Amy's expense, but I feared doing so in the hallway, where we could be overheard.

"She ain't funny," Little said.

I wanted to agree—less because I actually did agree than because I'd recently been considering trying to become friends with Little. I had first noticed her one night when we returned from formal dinner at the same time; just inside the common room, she said to no one in particular, "I gotta get these shoes off because my dogs are *barking*." Little was from Pittsburgh, the only black girl in the dorm, and I'd heard that she was the daughter of a doctor and a lawyer. She was a star in cross-country and was supposed to be even better at basketball. As a sophomore, she lived in a single, which normally carried a stigma—a single implied you didn't have any friends close enough to share a room with—but Little's blackness made her exist outside of Ault's social strata. Not automatically, though, not in a negative way. More like, it gave her the choice of opting out without seeming like a loser.

"The stealing is weird, huh?" I said.

Little made a dismissive noise. "I bet she's glad it happened. Now she gets to be the center of attention."

23

"Who?"

"What do you mean who? Your roommate."

"You know it was Dede's money? I guess there aren't any secrets in the dorm."

Little was quiet for a few seconds. "There aren't any secrets in the whole school," she said.

I felt a flip of uneasiness in my stomach; I hoped she wasn't right. We were standing outside her room, and it crossed my mind that she might invite me in.

"Do you like it here?" I asked. This was the problem with me—I didn't know how to talk to people without asking them questions. Some people seemed to find me peculiar and some people were so happy to discuss themselves that they didn't even notice, but either way, it made conversation draining. While the other person's mouth moved, I'd try to think of the next thing to ask.

"There's good parts about the school," Little said. "But I'm telling you that everyone's in each other's business."

"I like your name," I said. "Is it your real name?"

"You can find that out yourself," Little said, "Prove my theory."

"Okay," I said. "And then I'll report back to you."

She didn't object; it was like permission to talk to her again, something to look forward to. Though, apparently, she would not be inviting me in—she had opened her door and was about to step inside.

"Don't forget to hide your money, I said.

"Yeah, really." She shook her head. "Folks are messed up."

All of this was still in the beginning of the year, the beginning of my time at Ault, when I was exhausted all the time by both my vigilance and my wish to be inconspicuous. At soccer practice, I worried that I would miss the ball, when we boarded the bus for games at other schools, I worried that I would take a seat by someone who didn't want to sit next to me, in class I worried I would say a wrong or foolish thing. I

24

worried that I took too much food at meals, or that I did not disdain the food you were supposed to disdain—Tater Tots, key lime pie—and at night, I worried that Dede or Sin-Jun would hear me snore. I always worried someone would notice me, and then when no one did, I felt lonely.

Ault had been my idea. I'd researched boarding schools at the public library and written away for catalogs myself. Their glossy pages showed photographs of teenagers in wool sweaters singing hymns in the chapel, gripping lacrosse sticks, intently regarding a math equation written across the chalkboard. I had traded away my family for this glossiness. I'd pretended it was about academics, but it never had been. Marvin Thompson High School, the school I would have attended in South Bend, had hallways of pale green linoleum and grimy lockers and stringy-haired boys who wrote the names of heavy metal bands across the backs of their denim jackets in black marker. But boarding school boys, at least the ones in the catalogs who held lacrosse sticks and grinned over their mouth guards, were so handsome. And they had to be smart, too, by virtue of the fact that they attended boarding school. I imagined that if I left South Bend, I would meet a melancholy, athletic boy who liked to read as much as I did and on overcast Sundays we would take walks together wearing wool sweaters.

During the application process, my parents were mystified. The only person my family knew who had gone to boarding school was the son of one of the insurance agents in the office where my mother was a bookkeeper, and this kid's boarding school had been a fenced-in mountaintop in Colorado, a place for screwups. My parents suspected, in a way that was only honest, not unsupportive, that I would never be accepted to the places I'd applied; besides, they saw my interest in boarding school as comparable to other short-lived hobbies, like knitting (in sixth grade, I'd completed one third of a hat). When I got in, they explained how proud they were, and how sorry that they wouldn't be able to pay for it. The day a letter

25

arrived from Ault offering me the Eloise Fielding Foster scholarship, which would cover more than three quarters of my tuition, I cried because I knew for certain that I was leaving home, and abruptly, I did not know if it was such a good idea—I realized that I, like my parents, had never believed I'd actually go.

In mid-September, weeks after school had started in South Bend for my brothers and my former classmates, my father drove me from Indiana to Massachusetts. When we turned in the wrought-iron gates of the campus, I recognized the buildings from photographs—eight brick structures plus a Gothic chapel surrounding a circle of grass which I already knew was fifty yards in diameter and which I also knew you were not supposed to walk on. Everywhere there were cars with the trunks open, kids greeting each other, fathers carrying boxes. I was wearing a long dress with peach and lavender flowers and a lace collar, and I noticed immediately that most of the students had on faded T-shirts and loose khaki shorts and flip-flops. I realized then how much work Ault would be for me.

After we found my dorm, my father started talking to Dede's father, who said, "South Bend, eh? I take it you teach at Notre Dame?" and my father cheerfully said, "No, sir, I'm in the mattress business." I was embarrassed that my father called Dede's father sir, embarrassed by his job, embarrassed by our rusty white Datsun. I wanted my father gone from campus as soon as possible, so I could try to miss him.

In the mornings, when I stood under the shower, I would think, *I have been at Ault for twenty-four hours. I have been at Ault for three days. I have been at Ault for a month.* I talked to myself as I imagined my mother would talk to me if she actually thought boarding school was a good idea: *You're doing great. I'm proud of you , LeeLee.* Sometimes I would cry while I washed my hair, but this was the thing, this was always the thing about Ault—in some ways, my fantasies about it had not been wrong. The campus really was beautiful: the low, distant, fuzzy mountains that turned blue in the evenings, the perfectly rectangular fields, the Gothic cathedral (it was only Yankee modesty that made them call it a chapel) with its stained glass windows. This beauty gave a tinge of nobility and glamour to even the most pedestrian kind of homesickness.

Several times, I recognized a student from a photograph in the catalog. It was disorienting, the way I imagined it might be to see a celebrity on the streets of New York or Los Angeles. These people moved and breathed, they ate bagels in the dining hall, carried books through the hallways, wore clothes other than the ones I'd memorized. They belonged to the real, physical world; previously, it had seemed as if they belonged to me.

In big letters across the top, the signs said, *Drag yourself out of the dorm!!!* In smaller letters, they said, *Where? The dining hall! When? This Saturday! Why? To dance!* The paper was red and featured a copied photograph of Mr. Byden, the headmaster, wearing a dress.

"It's a drag dance," I heard Dede explain to Sin-Jun one night. "You go in drag."

"In drag," Sin-Jun said.

"Girls dress as boys, and boys dress as girls," I said.

"Ohhh," Sin-Jun said. "Very good!"

"I'm borrowing a tie from Devin," Dede said. "And a baseball cap."

Good for you, I thought.

"Dev is so funny," she said. Sometimes, just because I was there and because, unlike Sin-Jun, I was fluent in English, Dede told me things about her life. "Who are you borrowing clothes from?" she asked.

"I haven't decided." I wasn't borrowing clothes from anyone because I wasn't going. I could hardly talk to my classmates, and I definitely couldn't dance. I had tried it once at a cousin's wedding and I had not been able to stop thinking, *Is this the part where I throw my arms in the air?*

The day of the dance—roll call and classes occurred even

on Saturday mornings, which was, I soon learned, a good detail to break out for people from home, to affirm their suspicion that boarding school was only slightly different from prison—neither Gates nor Henry Thorpe was at the desk when the bell went off announcing the start of roll call. Someone else, a senior girl whose name I didn't know, rang the bell, then stepped down from the platform. Music became audible and students stopped murmuring. It was disco. I didn't recognize the song, but a lot of other people seemed to, and there was a rise of collective laughter. Turning in my seat, I realized the source of the music was two stereo speakers, each being held in the air by a different senior guy—there weren't enough desks for everyone in roll call, so juniors and seniors stood in the back of the room. The seniors seemed to be looking out the rear doorway. A few seconds passed before Henry Thorpe made his entrance. He wore a short black satin nightgown, fishnet stockings, and black high heels, and he was dancing as he approached the desk where he and Gates usually stood. Many students, especially the seniors, cheered, cupping their hands around their mouths. Some sang and clapped in time to the music.

Henry pointed a finger out, then curled it back toward his chest. I looked to see where he'd pointed. From another door at the opposite end of the room, the doorway near which the faculty stood, Gates had appeared. She was dressed in a football uniform, shoulder pads beneath the jersey and eye-black across her cheekbones. But no one would have mistaken her for a guy: Her hair was down, and her calves—she wasn't wearing socks—looked smooth and slender. She, too, was dancing, holding her arms up and shaking her head. By the time she and Henry climbed on top of the prefects' desk, the room was in an uproar. They came together, gyrating. I glanced toward the faculty; most of them stood with their arms folded, looking impatient. Gates and Henry pulled apart and turned so they were facing opposite directions, Gates swiveling her hips and snapping her fingers. Her unselfconsciousness astonished me. Here she was before a room of more than three hundred people, it was the bright light of day, it was *morning*, and she was dancing.

She gestured toward the back of the room, and the music stopped. She and Henry jumped down from the desk, and three seniors; two girls and a guy, climbed the three steps to the platform. "Tonight at eight o'clock in the dining hall . . ." one of the girls said.

". . . it's the eleventh annual drag extravaganza," said the other.

"So get ready to party!" shouted the guy.

The room erupted again into wild cheers and applause. Someone turned on the music, and Gates grinned and shook her head. The music went off. "Sorry, but the show's over," she said, and students booed, but even the booing had an affectionate sound to it. Gates turned to the three seniors next to her. "Thanks, guys." She picked up the clipboard where the names of the people who'd signed up to make announcements were listed, and said, "Mr. Archibald?"

Mr. Archibald stepped onto the platform. Just before he spoke, a guy from the back of the room yelled, "Gates, will you dance with me?"

Gates smiled a closed-mouth smile. "Go ahead, Mr. Archibald," she said.

His announcement was about soda cans being left in the math wing.

Gates passed the clipboard to Henry.

"Dory Rogers," Henry called, and Dory said the Amnesty International meeting had been switched from Sunday at six to Sunday at seven. During the five or six other announcements, I found myself waiting for more theatrics—I wanted to see Gates dance again—but it appeared the show really was over.

After Henry had rung the bell, I approached the platform. "Gates," I said. She was putting a notebook in her bag and didn't look up. "Gates," I said again.

This time, she looked at me.

"Your dancing was really good," I said,

She rolled her eyes. "It's always fun to see people make fools of themselves."

"Oh, no, you weren't making a fool of yourself. Not at all. Everyone loved it."

She smiled, and I understood that she had already known everyone loved it. But she hadn't been asking for a compliment, as I myself was whenever I said something self-effacing. It was more like—this dawned on me as I looked at her—she was pretending to be regular. Even though she was special, she was pretending to be like the rest of us.

"Thanks," she said. "That's nice of you, Lee."

In the evening, a giddy energy swirled in the courtyard and inside the dorm itself. Boys from the nearby dorms appeared in our common room—boys weren't allowed upstairs except during visitation—and summoned certain girls. Aspeth, I was not surprised to see, was a popular choice, and Dede often trotted downstairs along with her. They brought purses and nail polish and bras that they fastened, amid lots of shouts and laughter, right over the boys' T-shirts. I was doing laundry, and as I traipsed between the basement and the second floor of the dorm, I observed the progress of the festivities. The thought of a boy wearing my bra over his T-shirt was horrifying—the empty cups sagging, the fabric straining, or, even worse, not straining, around his rib cage, the fact that when he removed it he'd be able to see the exact size and might leave it on the floor of his room, stepping on it as he climbed into bed. But perhaps my horror stemmed from the fact that, as I was fast realizing, I did not own particularly pretty bras. Mine were beige cotton with a beige bow between the cups; my mother and I had bought them over the summer at JCPenney. These other bras that emerged were satin or lace, black or red or leopard-spotted, bras of the sort that I had thought only adult women wore.

After the dorm cleared out—even Sin-Jun went to the dance with a mascara mustache—I studied Spanish vocabulary words for a while, then went downstairs to the common room to read the old yearbooks that lined one shelf. I loved the yearbooks; they were like an atlas for the school. The ones in our common room went back as far as 1973, and in the past few weeks, I'd nearly worked my way to the present. Over the years, the format hadn't changed: candid shots in the front, then clubs, sports teams, dorms, entire classes. For, say, that year's tenth grade, there was a general write-up of the notable events that had occurred between September and June and a little joke about every person: "Can you imagine Lindsay without her curling iron?" Then came the best part, the seniors, each of them with their own page. In addition to the standard expressions of gratitude to family members, teachers, and friends, and the sometimes-nostalgic, sometimes-literary, sometimes-incomprehensible quotations, they were filled with pictures. Many of the boys' pictures were action shots from games; many of the girls' showed them with their arms around each other, sitting on a bed or standing on a beach. Girls also had a fondness for including photos from childhood.

You could figure out, if you had the inclination and the time, who in a given year was friends with whom and who had dated whom, and who had been popular, or athletic, or weird and fringy. The graduated students began to feel like distant cousins—I learned their nicknames, their sports of choice, which sweater or hairstyle they'd worn on repeated occasions.

In the three most recent yearbooks, I found several photos of Gates. She played field hockey, basketball, and lacrosse, and she'd lived her freshman and sophomore years in Elwyn's dorm and her junior year in Jackson's. Her sophomore year, the little joke about her was, "The crystal ball predicts that Henry and Gates will buy a house with a white picket fence and have twelve kids." The only Henry at Ault was Henry Thorpe, who I knew was currently going out with a prissy-seeming sophomore named Molly. I wondered if Henry and Gates had really dated and, if so, whether any tension of either the good or bad sort lingered between them. When they danced together at roll call, it had not seemed like it.

It was at the end of the yearbook from Gates's junior year, which was the newest one, that I came across the picture. The final section, after the seniors' pages, contained photos of graduation: the senior girls in white dresses, the boys in white pants and navy blazers and boaters. There were pictures of them sitting in rows at the ceremony, a picture of the graduation speaker (a Supreme Court justice), pictures of the seniors hugging each other. Among these—I was not looking for her here and might easily have missed it—was one of Gates by herself. It showed her from the waist up, in a white short-sleeved button-down. She wore a cowboy hat, and her glinting hair fell out from under the brim and spilled over her shoulders. The picture would have been in profile, but it appeared that the photographer, whoever it was, had called her name just before snapping the shutter and she'd turned her head. She might have been simultaneously laughing and protesting, saying something like, *Oh, come on!* But saying it to a person she liked very much.

I stared at the picture for so long that when I looked up again, I was surprised to see the nubbly orange couches and cream-colored walls of the common room. I had forgotten myself, and I had forgotten Ault, at least the real, three-dimensional version in which I, too, was a presence. It was a little after ten. I decided to check in early with Madame and go to bed, and I put the yearbooks away.

In the upstairs bathroom, Little stood before one of the sinks in a pink bathrobe, rubbing oil through her hair.

"Hey," I said. "How was the dance?"

She made a face. "I wouldn't go to no drag dance."

"Why not?"

"Why didn't *you* go?"

I smiled, and then she smiled, too.

"See?" she said. "But your roommate sure was excited about it. If I lived with that girl, I'd have slapped her by now."

"She's not that bad."

"Uh-huh."

"You play varsity basketball, right?" I said.

"Yep."

"So you're on the team with Gates Medkowski, right?"

"Sure am."

"What's Gates like? I'm just wondering because she's the first girl ever to be a senior prefect, isn't she? I know that's a pretty big deal."

"She's about like everyone else here."

"Really? She seems different."

Little set the bottle of oil on the counter and leaned in close to the mirror, peering at her skin. Then she said, "She's rich. That's what Gates is. Her family has a whole lot of money." She stepped back and made a face in the mirror, sucking in her cheeks and arching her eyebrows. It was the kind of thing I'd have done alone but never in front of another person. But I kind of liked the fact that Little's attention to me was sporadic; it made me feel less inhibited.

"I thought Gates was from a farm," I said.

"A farm that's half the state of Idaho. Her people grow potatoes. Bet you didn't think such a nasty little vegetable could be worth so much."

"Is Gates good at basketball?"

"Not as good as me." In the mirror, Little grinned. "You ever find out about my name?"

"Not yet," I said. "I'm conducting an investigation, but all my leads have been dead ends."

"Yeah, right. I'll tell you why. It's because I'm a twin."

"For real?"

"Yep. I'm the baby, so you can guess my sister's name." She was quiet, and I realized I really was supposed to guess.

"This might be too obvious, but is it Big?"

33

"Got it on the first try," Little said. "Give the girl a prize. I'm bigger than Big now, but these things stick."

"That's really cool," I said. "Where does Big go to school?"

"At home. Pittsburgh. You ever been to Pittsburgh?"

I shook my head.

"It's different from here, I'll tell you that much."

"You must miss Big." Knowing Little had a twin, even a twin who was far away, made me wonder if she didn't need a friend.

"You got any sisters?" Little asked.

"Just brothers."

"Yeah, I got a brother, too. I got three brothers. But that's not the same." She stuck her bottle of oil into her bucket—on the first night in the dorm, Madame Broussard had given us all buckets for our toiletries—and turned toward me. "You're not bad," she said. "Most people here, they're not real. But you're real."

"Oh," I said. "Thanks."

When she was gone—on the way out, she said, "G'nighty"— I pulled my toothbrush and toothpaste from my own bucket. When I stuck my toothbrush under the faucet, I noticed that in the sink next to mine, the one where Little had been standing, there was a sprinkling of short, coarse black hairs. So they were head hairs, Little's head hairs. With a paper towel from the dispenser, I wiped them away.

The next theft was a hundred-dollar bill Aspeth's grandmother had sent for her birthday. It had been in her wallet, which had been on top of her desk. We found out on Sunday, the night after the drag dance. I learned the amount and the owner of the money not from anything Madame Broussard said at curfew—again, she was stony-faced and discreet—but from Dede, who was outraged.

"It's like my friends and I are targets," Dede said when we were back in our room. "We're being discriminated against." She leaned over and set a red cashmere sweater on the floor,

34

on top of black pants. When she was upright again, she wrinkled her nose; "Something stinks in here."

I sniffed the air, but I was pretending. She was right—it did stink. It had stunk for several days, and at first I'd thought I was imagining the fishy odor, but it had become more pronounced. When Dede and Sin-Jun were out of the room, I'd smelled my armpits and between my legs, then my sheets, then my dirty laundry. The fishiness hadn't increased in any of these places, but it hadn't decreased either. "It does smell kind of weird," I said.

"Hey, Sin-Jun," Dede said. "Take a whiff. It smells bad, right?"

"Take a whiff?"

"Smell the air," I said. I mimed inhaling deeply. "Our room smells funny," I said. "Not so good."

"Ahh," Sin-Jun said. She turned back to the papers on her desk.

Dede rolled her eyes at me.

"Maybe it's coming from the bathroom," I said. This seemed unlikely.

Dede opened the door to our room and stepped into the hallway. Then she walked back in. "No, it's this room," she said. "It's definitely this room. What food do you guys have in here?"

"Only that." I gestured toward the shelf above my desk, where I kept a jar of peanut butter and a box of saltines.

"What about you, Sin-Jun?" Dede said.

Before Sin-Jun could respond, I said. "Why are you assuming it's us? It might be you."

"I'm not the one keeping an entire grocery store in here," Dede said, and it was true that Sin-Jun had several packages and containers beneath her bed and in her desk and closet.

"But you don't know that it's food," I said. "Maybe it's your shoes." I picked up my bucket.

"What are you doing?" Dede said.

"Getting ready for bed."

"You're not going to help me look?" Dede's mouth hung open in surprise, or maybe indignation, and I had a strange temptation to stick something in it—the bristle-free end of my toothbrush, or my own finger.

"Sorry," I said.

As I left the room, before the door shut, I heard her say, "Yeah, I can tell."

It became December. (*I have been at Ault seventy-eight days.*) Once, Little and I spent a Saturday night, while everyone else was out, playing Boggle in the common room as Sin-Jun looked on. Another time, just Little and I watched a crime show on TV, and she made popcorn that burned, but we ate it anyway. ("I'm still kind of hungry," I said afterward, and Little said, "Hungry? My stomach and my back are touching.") There were two more thefts, which Madame announced at curfew. I wasn't sure whose money it had been, but it hadn't been any of Dede's friends'. The smell in our room intensified; it became a stench, and I worried that even if it wasn't emanating from me, I carried it on my clothes and skin. Sometimes in class or even outside, leaving chapel, I'd get a flash of it. When people came by the room, Dede made embarrassed jokes or flat-out apologies.

The week before Christmas vacation, I was walking through the mail room during the morning break when I saw Jimmy Hardigan, a senior, slam his fist against the wall. Then I saw Mary Gibbons and Charlotte Chan, also seniors, hugging. Charlotte was crying. Usually, the mail room was noisy at morning break, but now it was quiet. I wondered if someone had died—not a teacher or a student, but a member of the administrative staff perhaps.

I approached the wall of gold, windowed mailboxes. You knew you had mail because you saw it in profile, leaning diagonally against the wall of your box, and years later, after I was gone from Ault, I dreamed sometimes that I saw that skinny shadow.

36

My mailbox was empty. I glanced to my right and saw Jamie Lorison from Ancient History. I could hear his heavy breathing. "Jamie, why is it so quiet?" I asked.

"The seniors just heard back from Harvard, the ones who applied early. But everybody's striking out this year."

"No one at all has gotten in?" Long ago, before Ault had taken girls, the boys would go to the headmaster's house the day before graduation and on a slip of paper they'd each write *Harvard, Yale,* or *Princeton*; the school they wrote was the one they'd attend.

"Only two so far," Jamie said. "Nevin Lunse and Gates Medkowski. The rest got deferred."

I felt a swelling in my chest, a rise of breath. I scanned the mail room, hoping to congratulate Gates, but she wasn't there.

I finally spotted her in the dining hall that night. It was regular dinner, not formal dinner where you had to dress up and sit at assigned tables. As I set my plate in the dirty-dishes carousel, I saw her in the food line. My heart pounded. I wiped my mouth with the back of my hand, swallowed, and walked toward her.

I was less than ten feet away when, from the opposite direction, Henry Thorpe appeared. "Lay it here, Medkowski," he said.

Gates turned.

"That's right," Henry said. He was holding up one hand. "Gimme five, you rock star."

Gates slapped her palm against his. "Thanks, man."

"How do you feel?" he asked.

Gates grinned. "Goddamn lucky."

"Forget luck. Everyone knew you'd get in."

The casualness of their interaction made me understand I could not approach her, not in such a public setting. Even in complimenting Gates, my own neediness would rear up. I decided to make her a card instead, and then I could stick it in her mailbox, or leave it off at her room.

Back in the dorm, switching between blue and red markers

for each letter, I wrote *CONGRATULATIONS, GATES!* Then I wrote *Good luck at Harvard!* With a purple marker, I drew stars. The sheet of paper still looked a little bare, so I added vines in green, weaving them around the words. Then I had to sign my name. I wanted to write *Love, Lee*. But what if she thought that was weird? My name alone seemed curt, and *Sincerely* or *Yours truly* seemed formal and dorky. I held the blue marker above the paper, hesitating, then signed it *Love, Lee*. I'd leave it in her dorm, in an envelope outside her door. That way, she'd likely be alone when she found it.

The next night was formal dinner, and most people showered in the gym after sports practice, then went straight to the dining hall. I saw that if I hurried, I'd have time to return to my room, get the card, and drop it off; I didn't like to get to formal dinner too early anyway, because then you stood around.

Just before I reached the courtyard, I broke into a jog. It was getting dark so early that no one would see me and wonder why, in a skirt and navy flats, I was running. Broussard's was quiet. I skipped up the stairs to the second floor. When I opened the door to the room, Dede slammed shut a drawer and whirled around, and then I realized—I was preoccupied enough that I'd never have realized this otherwise, and I noticed it only because of the frantic quality of the gesture— that she was not standing in front of her own dresser; she was in front of Sin-Jun's.

"This isn't what you think," she said.

I stepped backward, and she stepped forward.

"I'm just trying to figure out where the smell is coming from," she said. "It has to be Sin-Jun. Because it's not us, right?"

"If you think it's her, you should have asked if you could look through her things."

"I don't want to offend her." Dede's tone was impatient. "Lee, obviously I'm not the thief if I was the first one who was stolen from."

We regarded each other.

"Oh, come on," she said. "You think I would steal from myself?"

I continued to back out of the room.

"Are you going to tell Madame?" she said. "There's nothing to tell. I'm not lying, Lee. Don't you trust me?"

I still said nothing, and she lunged toward me, gripping my upper arms. My heart jumped. Standing so close to her, I could smell her perfume, I could see the tiny hairs that were growing back in her eyebrows. If only I'd known before this moment that she plucked her eyebrows, I thought, I could have gotten her to teach me how. Then I thought, no, we'd never been that kind of roommates.

"Let go of me," I said.

"What are you planning to do?" Though I could tell she was trying to sound firm, her voice was uneven. "Are you going to say something?"

"I don't know." I tried to shrug away from her, but her grasp was tight.

"What do you want me to do to prove I'm telling the truth?"

"Let go," I said again.

Finally, she withdrew her hands. "I'll tell Madame myself I was looking in Sin-Jun's dresser," she said. "Then will you believe me?"

I let the door shut without answering her.

I hadn't yet left the dorm when I realized I'd forgotten Gates's card. I decided to skip dinner—I could hide out in the common room phone booth until I knew Dede had gone to the dining hall, then sneak back upstairs. Also, this way I'd have time to decide what to do about having caught her.

The phone booth was hot and smelled like dirty socks, and my pulse was wild. I wanted to do jumping jacks just to get rid of my roiling energy. Instead, I sat on the chair inside the booth, the soles of my shoes against the seat, my knees bunched up in front of me with my arms around them.

After the thought of the picture popped into my head, it was like knowing that as you sit in the living room, cake is in the kitchen. All you have to do is fetch it. *Don't*, I thought. *Dede will hear you moving around.* Then I thought, *But she won't know who it is.* I peered out the phone booth's window, which was streaked with fingerprints, slowly pushed open the door, and crept across the common room to the bookshelf. With trembling fingers, I pulled down the most recent yearbook and crept back to the booth.

The picture was exactly as I remembered it: her cowboy hat; her unruly hair, her smart, perfect face. Opening to the page it was on was like taking the first bite of cake, knowing the whole slice awaits you. If Dede would just leave, I could take the yearbook upstairs, I thought. It wasn't like I would gaze at it endlessly. I just wanted to know it was mine, to look at when I needed to. I wanted to get in bed and turn out the lights; in the dark, I would be alone in my head, and I could have imaginary conversations where I made funny remarks and Gates laughed, but not in her being-nice-to-a-freshman way. It would be a laugh that meant she respected me and knew that I was like her.

I heard someone descend the stairs, so I waited, then went to the window, hunching down and peering over the sill. It was Dede. I lifted my blouse and stuck the yearbook in the waistband of my skirt—I seriously doubted it would be missed since I'd never seen anyone besides me look at any of them. Upstairs, I placed it on the shelf in my closet, underneath a sweater. As much as I wanted to, there was no point in going to bed, because Dede and Sin-Jun would return from dinner within the hour, flicking on lights and talking. Plus, I still needed to deliver the card.

It was folded into my dictionary, where I'd left it the night before. I unfolded it and set it on the desk. The second *N* in *CONGRATULATIONS* had smudged. I licked my finger and pressed it against the smudge, which made it worse. I wondered why I'd written *Good luck at Harvard!* That was stupid; it made it seem as if she were departing immediately, when she'd be at Ault for another seven months. The stars and vines looked, suddenly, like the efforts of a nine-year-old. And *Love*—love? Who was I kidding? We hardly knew each other. I picked up the card and tore it into long strips, then ripped the strips into thirds. The pieces of paper fluttered in the trash can before they settled.

I thought of Dede, her panicky denials, her fingers gripping my arms. I wanted to talk to somebody about what I'd seen, but everyone was at dinner. I picked up one of Dede's celebrity magazines and lay on my bed, trying to read. The world outside Ault seemed strange and irrelevant, and I had trouble paying attention to the articles. Before long, I had set aside the magazine, removed the yearbook from my closet, and was looking at Gates's picture again. When I heard voices outside, I hurried to the bathroom to avoid Dede's return and hid in a stall for ten minutes. Then I went straight to Little's room. "Am I bothering you?" I asked when she opened the door.

"I don't know yet, do I?" She was wearing glasses and a gray sweatsuit.

"Can I come in?"

She stood aside to let me enter. I sat on her desk chair, though she hadn't invited me to, and she sat on her bed, her legs crossed in front of her open textbooks and notebooks. I had never been inside Little's room, and it was stark, without posters or tapestries or photographs. The only personal touches besides her bedspread and books were a clock radio on the windowsill, a plastic bottle of lotion on the dresser, and a small teddy bear at the foot of the bed. The bear wore a pale purple sweater; looking at it, I felt a plunging sadness that entirely eclipsed the suspicion and irritation I felt toward Dede. But the sadness was too large for me to understand, and then it passed.

"You won't believe what happened," I said. "I know who the thief is."

Little raised her eyebrows.

41

"It's Dede."

Little's eyebrows sank and scrunched together. "Are you sure?"

"I caught her red-handed. She was going through Sin-Jun's dresser."

Little murmured, "Dede Schwartz," then nodded. "I believe it."

"It's so creepy," I said. "It makes her seem like a pathological liar or something; the way she made sure she was the first one whose money was stolen."

"I knew I didn't like that girl. What did Madame say?"

"I haven't told her yet. Dede begged me not to."

"But you saw her digging around in Sin-Jun's dresser."

"Exactly."

"If you don't turn her in, she'll just keep doing it."

"I know. I don't get why she would steal, though. She gets a huge allowance from her parents."

"You try to understand a lot of folks here, all you'll do is give yourself a headache."

"Can I sleep in your room tonight?" I asked.

Little hesitated.

"It's okay," I said. "I don't need to." I stood, embarrassed. "I have to see Dede sooner or later, right?" When I left the room, Little made no effort to stop me.

I hid again in the bathroom, this time in the corner shower, which was known to have low pressure and thus was never used. I still hadn't changed out of my formal dinner clothes, and sitting on the blue tiled floor in my skirt felt odd and unclean. Once I heard the bathroom door open and Dede call, "Lee? Lee, are you in here?"

Before curfew, I went downstairs and found Madame. I opened my mouth to tell her about Dede, but standing in the entry of her apartment, I could feel the seriousness of the accusation, how much it would alter both my own life and Dede's. I wasn't ready yet.

"I'm going to bed," I said. "Can I check in early?"

42

I shook her hand, then returned to the bathroom.

At the infirmary, six rooms containing only beds lined either side of the hallway. There was also the room where the nurse sat and where you had your temperature taken when you first came in, the TV lounge, and the kitchenette with a poster featuring nutrition trivia. Among other facts, the poster informed readers that eating chocolate released the same chemicals in the brain as being in love. From time to time during the years I was at Ault, I'd be at a lunch table, either listening to or participating in a conversation about any number of topics, and someone would say, "Did you know that chocolate releases the same chemicals in the brain as being in love?" And other people at the table would say, "I think I've heard that, too," or, "Yeah, I remember reading that somewhere." But you could never remember where until you were back in the infirmary; sick or faking sick, the rigidity of a normal day having given way to some long, pale, vaporous unfolding of hours: You slept, you ate pudding and toast, you watched daytime TV with other students who'd also ended up in the infirmary on this day, whom perhaps you were friends with or perhaps you'd never spoken to before.

This was my first visit to the infirmary. The previous night, I'd returned to my room after midnight, when I knew Dede and Sin-Jun would be asleep. At dawn, I rose, pulled on jeans, and left the dorm without even brushing my teeth. If I could just have another day to sort things out, I thought as I walked through the cool, still-dark morning, then I'd be able to decide how to turn Dede in.

The nurse took my temperature and assigned me a room, and I fell deeply asleep. When I awakened, the yellow light of late morning was shining through the shade, and I could hear the TV. I stepped into the hall in my socks.

A mousy sophomore girl named Shannon Hormley was in the lounge, and so was a senior guy, Pete Lords, one of the two boys who'd been holding a stereo speaker the day Gates had danced at roll call. They both looked up when I entered the room, but they didn't say hello, so neither did I. I sat down. They were watching a soap opera. On-screen, a woman in a blue sequined dress said into a telephone, "But with Christophe in Rio, I simply don't see how that's possible." I wondered who had selected the show. Already, I wanted to get up and leave, but I thought that doing so this quickly might seem peculiar. I glanced around the room. On the table next to my chair, several pamphlets were fanned out. *I'm considering suicide*, one said across the top. The next said, *I was a victim of date rape*, and the third said, *Am I gay?* Something in my stomach tightened. I averted my eyes, then glanced at Shannon and Pete to see if either of them had been watching me read the pamphlets. It seemed they hadn't.

I pretended to become absorbed in the show while I waited for them to leave. When they did—Shannon, disappeared after half an hour, then Pete lumbered into the kitchenette—I grabbed the third pamphlet and darted back to my room. *Women who identify themselves as lesbians are sexually attracted to and fall in love with other women*, the pamphlet said. *Their sexual feelings toward women are normal and appropriate for them. These feelings emerge during childhood or adolescence and continue into adulthood.* There were questions you could ask yourself: *When I dream or fantasize sexually, is it about boys or girls? Have I ever had a crush on or been in love with a girl or a woman? Do I feel different from other girls?*

I tried to imagine kissing Gates: We would be standing, facing one another, and then I would step forward. I might have to get on tiptoe, because of her height. I'd tilt my head so our noses didn't smash and press my mouth against hers. Her lips would be dry and soft; when I parted mine, she'd part hers, too, and our tongues would slip against each other.

The scenario neither disgusted nor excited me. But maybe this was because I was trying not to be excited. I continued to read the pamphlet: *The first time I touched my girlfriend's breasts, it felt like the most natural thing in the world—Tina, 17.* I

44

thought, *Tina, 17, where are you now? Are you still seventeen, or are you an adult? Do your neighbors or coworkers know your secret?* I could picture her in Arizona, say, or Oregon, but I doubted she lived in New England. As far as I knew, there were no gay people at Ault. In fact, I had met a gay person only once in my life and that had been at home—he was our neighbor's son, a guy in his thirties who'd moved to Atlanta to work as a flight attendant.

I imagined placing my fingers on the mound of Gates's breast. And then what? Would I clutch it? Move it around? The image was absurd. But if I didn't want to touch her, I wasn't sure what I did want. I stuffed the pamphlet in my coat pocket, out of sight, and wished I hadn't taken it.

When I returned to the room in the early evening, Dede was sitting on her bed, clipping her fingernails. She jumped up when she saw me. "Where have you been? I have something to show you." She pulled my arm, leading me back out of the room. We stopped in front of the giant trash can in the hall, and the same stench from our room filled the air. "Look," Dede said and pointed. Dry, stringy, wax lay on top of newspapers, an empty potato chip bag, and the remains of a potted plant. The wax was yellowy-orange and perhaps a foot long. "It's squid," Dede said. "Dried squid. That's what stinks. It was in Sin-Jun's closet. Isn't that the grossest thing you've ever seen?" Dede seemed happy, no longer desperate. "I asked Sin-Jun if I could look around, and she said fine, and I found it. I told you that's all I was looking for."

"It's food?" I asked and when Dede nodded, I said, "Where's Sin-Jun now?"

"On the phone with her mom, I think. She feels bad, but she should because it's disgusting."

"Did you tell her you were looking through her dresser earlier?"

"Lee, you need to get a grip about that. If you try to turn me in, you'll just embarrass yourself. Why don't you wait and see if Sin-Jun complains that anything is missing? If she doesn't, I think that clears my name."

"Nothing will be missing," I said. "I'm sure you put it back!" Oddly, now that I was starting to believe Dede was innocent, I felt more free to accuse her.

"Okay, Nancy Drew." She leaned in. "Let me tell you something. You don't need to be such a freak. It's your own fault. If you didn't do stuff like this, maybe we could be friends."

"Gosh, Dede." I made my voice earnest, like a girl's from a 1950s sitcom. "Could we really?" It felt good to be unpleasant; I was relieved to find I still had an aptitude for it, underneath my Ault-induced meekness and sentimentality.

Dede shook her head. "I feel sorry for you!"

She went down the hall, fingernail clippers in hand, and I presumed she'd gone to discuss my freakishness with Aspeth. I hung up my coat and lay on my bed, on top of the covers. Then I remembered the pamphlet in my coat pocket. I retrieved it, and when I saw the idiotic title—*Am I gay?*—a bitterness rose in me. *No, you're not gay*, I thought. *You're a pamphlet.* I wanted to burn it.

I heard the doorknob turn, and I pulled open the top drawer of my desk and shoved the pamphlet inside. I assumed Dede was back with fresh insults, but it was only Sin-Jun.

"I so sorry about squid," she said.

"It's okay!"

"I was bad roommate!"

"It's really not a big deal," I said. "Don't worry."

"You're not here today," she said.

"I was in the infirmary."

"You have sick?"

"Sort of. Yeah."

"I make tea for you."

"That's okay," I said. "But thanks."

"No tea?"

"Not now."

46

She seemed disappointed, and I thought that I should have accepted the offer, but the moment had passed.

It was in Spanish class, just after lunch, that I remembered. Terror passed through me. The pamphlet was in my desk, in the top drawer—the most obvious place imaginable! The thief would be looking for cash, but how much more interesting, how damning, this would be.

Twenty minutes were left in class. I tried to calm myself with math: If nineteen of us lived in Broussard's, and if four thefts had occurred over the last six weeks, then the likelihood was slim, it was infinitesimal, that one would occur between now and the end of sports practice, when I could get back to the dorm. But already one of the thefts had been in my room. And anyway, how could I rely on numbers, their cold impartiality? What did numbers care if everyone at Ault thought I was a lesbian?

Fifteen minutes were left in class, then ten, eight; five, four, two. When the bell rang, I bolted from the schoolhouse. I would be late to biology class next period, if I didn't miss it altogether, but having my name reported to the dean seemed a small price to pay for hiding the pamphlet.

Hurrying across campus, outside when most everyone else was in class, I thought of the day I'd left Ancient History and felt a tenderness toward my earlier self. Things actually hadn't been so bad then. At least, they hadn't been so complicated.

I cut through the courtyard, past the empty granite benches where I'd met Gates. It was a windy, overcast day, and when I opened the door to Broussard's, the handle was cold.

This is the part I think about the most often: the timing of it. Sometimes I wonder about the accidents that happen to a person—car crashes, falling tree branches, fires in the night—and I wonder, were they avoidable or were they destined? Once they've decided to occur, will the bad coincidences of your life seek you out, their shape changing, their

47

consequences staying the same? Or maybe their shape doesn't even change; maybe they hold form, waiting for you as patiently as turtles.

Little emerged from our room just as I was about to enter. It was as if she had anticipated my arrival and was opening the door for me, except that once it was open, she did not step aside deferentially, and we almost collided.

We stood there for so long without speaking that I thought we might not speak at all. But that kind of silence would happen only in a movie; in real life, it's so hard not to clutter the significant moments by talking.

"Their families are loaded," she finally said. "They don't need the money."

"But it's theirs. It's not yours."

"Yeah, and I see how they throw it around. They don't like dinner, they order pizza. Cross-country warm-ups cost seventy dollars? No problem."

"But stealing is wrong."

"You're gonna act like you don't understand? Don't even try to pretend you're one of them."

"What's that supposed to mean?"

"It means I can see with my own two eyes you're not paying your way here."

"You don't know that."

"Sure I do."

"Even if I'm on scholarship," I said, "which I'm not saying if I am or not, how would you know?"

She shrugged, then said, "Your comforter."

"My what?"

"Your bedspread. Whatever you want to call it. It's not flowered."

I was not sure how she'd known which bed was mine, but she was right. My comforter was reversible, red on one side, blue on the other. So that was one of the clues; I'd have to remember.

"But *you're* not on scholarship, are you?" I said.

She stared at me. "Of course I am. It costs twenty grand a year to go here."

"But isn't—isn't your dad a doctor and your mom a lawyer?"

She almost smiled, but it turned into a snicker. "What, like *The Cosby Show*?"

I looked at the floor and wondered if she hated me. I wanted to ask, *How could you think you wouldn't get caught? Or were you hoping you would?* But nothing indicated that she had been.

"Listen," she said, and I looked up. "I'm gonna stop. I just needed a little cash until Christmas break, you know? And the way it's happened, it's good for both of us."

I was incredulous. "How would it be good for me?"

"Your roommate," she said, but still I didn't understand. "She'll be out of here by tonight."

So Little had stolen Sin-Jun's money this time; her plan actually wasn't a bad one. And I was supposed to help. Before, I'd have done so unwittingly, believing when I turned Dede in that she really was the thief. Now, because I'd know it wasn't Dede but could pretend to have proof, I'd be doing so on purpose.

"You didn't think I took from you, did you?" Little said.

I glanced away.

"I'd never take from you. Damn, girl." Her voice was cheerful; maybe if I hadn't been able to see her, I'd have bought the act. But her eyes were full of unspeakable longing and sadness. As we stood at the threshold watching each other, I felt a sense of recognition so profound that I almost believed I would keep her secret.

49

2

All School Rules Are in Effect

AFTER MADAME BROUSSARD checked us in at curfew, the common room cleared out except for Dede, me, and Amy Dennaker, who was inside the phone booth; she kept laughing and saying, "Shut *up!*"

I looked down at my notebook. "Okay," I said to Dede. "What's the reproductive pattern for the protist *Euglena*?"

"Binary fission," Dede said.

"Right." In my head, I repeated, *binary fission, binary fission, binary fission*. It astonished me that Dede, who seemed to expend most of her energy grooming herself and trying to be ingratiating with people more popular than she was, retained such information effortlessly while I was averaging a C in biology. It was not clear to me how I'd arrived at this juncture gradewise, because before entering Ault, I'd never received lower than a B plus in any class. Either Ault was a lot harder than my junior high had been, or I was getting dumber—I suspected both. If I wasn't literally getting dumber, I knew at least that I'd lost the glow that surrounds you when the teachers think you're one of the smart, responsible ones, that glow that shines brighter every time you raise your hand in class to say the perfect thing, or you run out of room in a blue book during an exam and have to ask for a second one. At

Ault, I doubted I would ever need a second blue book because even my handwriting had changed—once my letters had been bubbly and messy, and now they were thin and small.

"What about for bacteria?" I said. "What's the reproductive pattern called?"

"For bacteria, it's binary fission and conjugation. It can be—"

"What are you guys doing?" Amy Dennaker had emerged from the phone booth and was regarding us with more interest than usual. The month before, in February, Amy had scored a hat trick in the ice hockey game against St. Francis and then, in the third period, broken her nose. This made her, to me, even scarier. "If you're studying for tomorrow, don't bother," Amy said.

Dede and I looked at each other. "We have a biology test," I said.

"No, you don't." Amy grinned. "You didn't hear it from me, but tomorrow is surprise holiday."

"What's that?" I said, and at the same time, Dede said, "That's awesome. Are you sure?"

I turned to Dede. "What's surprise holiday?" I said.

"How do you know?" Dede asked Amy.

"I can't reveal my sources, And you can never be totally positive. Sometimes, if Mr. Byden thinks too many students know, he'll cancel it. But look at it this way: It can't be on a Wednesday because of sports, it's not usually on a Monday or a Friday because it would be lame if it was just attached to the weekend, and it's almost always before spring break. So that leaves Tuesday and Thursday, and the boys' basketball game against Overfield was rescheduled for next Tuesday. Next Thursday, some presidential speechwriter dude is coming to speak fourth period. And the week after that is the week before spring break. You never know for sure until you see the green jacket, but basically, process of elimination says it's tomorrow."

Dede was nodding. Apparently, she had heard about the green jacket.

"Here's another thing," Amy said. "Alex Ellison has a history paper due tomorrow, but he told people at dinner that he hadn't even started it."

"Why does that matter?"

"Alex rooms with Henry Thorpe, and since Henry is one of the senior prefects, he would know for sure. The prefects are the only students who find out ahead of time. And Henry would definitely tell Alex."

"Would Henry be allowed to tell?" I asked. Both Dede and Amy looked at me as if they had forgotten my presence.

"No," Amy said. "But so what?" She seemed to suddenly remember who I was: a dorky freshman she didn't know very well, sitting with my only slightly cooler roommate. Clearly, she had not meant to be this generous with her time or her information. "Do what you want." she said. "You guys can study all night long if it floats your boat."

I waited until she had disappeared up the staircase, then turned to Dede. "So are you going to explain this to me or not?" I still didn't particularly *like* Dede, but there was no one I felt closer to at Ault. Back in December, Little Washington had been asked to leave less than twenty-four hours after I talked to Madame Broussard, and when we gathered in the common room for curfew you could feel the difference, the new emptiness. Little herself was gone—her parents had come to get her and, just like that, her room was cleared out—and so was the suspense of who was stealing, or when it would happen next. Around two in the morning, I was having such bad stomach pains that I went into the bathroom, sat on the floor by the toilet, and stuck my finger down my throat. Nothing emerged, but I gagged a few times, then leaned over the bowl, considering the toilet from this angle—the calm water, the curving porcelain. I had been there for about twenty minutes when Dede pushed open the unlocked stall door. "Could you leave me alone?" I said, and she said, "You did the right thing. You didn't have a choice."

In the common room, Dede said, "Surprise holiday is an

52

Ault tradition. Once a year, classes get called off to give us a break."

I thought of my C in biology and wasn't sure I deserved a break.

"When you see the green jacket at roll call, that's when you know," Dede continued. "Mr. Byden might be making an announcement and he'll take off his jacket, and the green jacket will be on underneath, or someone will jump out from under the prefects' desk wearing it. Something like that."

"So we don't have our test?"

"I guess not. At least until Friday."

"Then we don't need to study."

"Well." Dede bit her lip. "We probably should just to be safe."

"I'm tired," I said.

"If we study now, we won't have to tomorrow."

I looked at her—she was so responsible. It was as if I were seeing a version of myself from a year before, the version who had convinced my parents to let me go to Ault, against their better judgment, by saying it would be a first-rate educational experience. Now I was a different person, someone unlike Dede. She could study because she approached her life straightforwardly. But I was living my life sideways. I did not act on what I wanted, I did not say the things I thought, and being so stifled and clamped all the time left me exhausted; no matter what I was doing, I was always imagining something else. Grades felt peripheral, but the real problem was, everything felt peripheral.

"I'm going to bed," I said. I left Dede in the common room, peering at her biology notes.

At breakfast, Hunter Jergenson recapped a dream she'd had involving space aliens, which prompted Tab Kinkead to ask if maybe it hadn't been a dream after all but an abduction, and then Andrea Sheldy-Smith, who was Hunter's roommate, told a long story about how she had accidentally used Hunter's toothbrush, and Tab said to her, "So basically you guys have made out?" I was constantly amazed at the ridiculous topics raised by other people, especially by other girls, and I was equally amazed by the enthusiastic responses their ridiculousness elicited. Of course, maybe being ridiculous was the point—the way they didn't give off the painful feeling that something was at stake.

No one at the table brought up surprise holiday, and I felt a growing suspicion that either Amy had been wrong or—this possibility had occurred to me in the middle of the night—she had duped us. At chapel, Mr, Byden spoke about the importance of humility, and I scrutinized his expression for a sign that there would be no classes. He did not give one. Generally, I liked chapel: the rickety straw seats, the dim light, the impossibly high arched ceilings, the sound of the organ when we sang hymns, and the wall in back where the names of Ault boys who had died in wars were carved into the stone. But today I was restless.

At roll call, I could feel an extra sense of anticipation, a chatty exuberance. At the desks around mine, no one was studying, as people usually were before and during the announcements; everyone was talking and there were loud, frequent bursts of laughter from every direction. Aspeth Montgomery, the blond, mean girl for whom Dede functioned as an acolyte, was sitting on the lap of Darden Pittard, who was our class's cool black guy; Darden was good at basketball and from the Bronx and wore a gold chain and rugbies that pulled across his muscular back and broad shoulders. (The other black guy in our class, who wasn't cool, was Kevin Brown—Kevin was a skinny chess whiz who wore glasses, whose parents were both professors at a university in St. Louis.) I saw Darden make fish lips at Aspeth, as if to kiss her, and then I saw her take his face in her hand, her thumb on one cheek and her index finger on the other, and pretend to scold him, and as I watched, I thought that probably, almost definitely, today was surprise holiday. How could it not be?

Henry Thorpe had to ring the bell three times before people were quiet enough for roll call to start. The first announcement, from Mrs. Van der Hoef, was that anyone going on the Greece trip in June needed to make sure their parents had sent in the five-hundred-dollar deposit. Then a junior boy whose name I didn't know said he'd left his math notebook in the library and if you saw it, please give it to him. The third person to go was Dean Fletcher, who ambled up to the platform where the prefects' desk was, which Henry and Gates stood behind. After Little's expulsion, my interest in Gates had waned almost completely. Not because of anything Gates herself did but, I think, because I associated Gates with Little and with all my discomfort surrounding that situation. Gates soon seemed like someone a friend of mine, rather than I myself, had once been preoccupied by. I still felt a flicker of interest when I saw her, but only a flicker.

"A couple things," Dean Fletcher said. "First off, breakfast ends at exactly five to eight. I've been getting reports of you guys complaining to the dining hall staff 'cause you overslept but you still want your pancakes." People laughed, mostly because everyone liked Dean Fletcher. "When the staff tells you they've stopped serving, it means you better hustle to chapel. Got that? Next thing is, the mail room is a pigsty. Your mothers would be ashamed of you." He reached into a cardboard box set on the prefects' desk; I had not previously noticed it. "Exhibit A," he said, and my heart rate increased, but all he held up was a rumpled *New York Times*. "Papers go in the recycling bins." The next thing he held up was a pair of earmuffs. "Anyone want to claim these? Nope? Then I get to keep 'em for myself." He clamped them on his head, and then I knew for sure. "Or—" he said, and he looked around the big room at all of us waiting. He smiled. "How about this?" All I saw before the room erupted was a flash of hunter green fabric. Everyone around me was screaming. Girls hugged, and boys slapped each other on the back.

I did not scream or hug anyone. In fact, as the noise

gained momentum, I felt its opposite, a draining of excitement. But not a draining of tension—my body was still stiff and alert, and the impulse I had, strangely, was to weep. Not because I was sad but because I was not happy, and yet, like my classmates, I'd experienced an emotional surge, I too felt the need for expression. This phenomenon—being gripped by an overwhelming wave of feeling that was clearly not the feeling of the people around me—had also happened at a pep rally: It made me uncomfortable, because I didn't want anyone to notice that I wasn't jumping up and down or cheering, and it also thrilled me; because it made the world seem full of possibilities that could make my heart pound. I think, looking back, that this was the single best thing about Ault, the sense of possibility. We lived together so closely, but because it was a place of decorum and restraint and because on top of that we were teenagers, we hid so much. And then, in dorms and classes and on teams and at formal dinner and in adviser groups, we got shuffled and thrust together and shuffled again, and there was always the chance that you might find out one of the pieces of hidden information. This was why I felt excited when life was different from normal, when things happened—snow and fire drills and the times we had chapel at night, evensong, when the sky outside the stained glass windows was black. Depending on circumstances, a wild fact could be revealed to you, or you could fall desperately in love. In my whole life, Ault was the place with the greatest density of people to fall in love with.

Gates rang the bell to tell people to settle down. Dean Fletcher stuck two fingers in his mouth and wolf-whistled. "Okay, guys," he said and made a gesture meant to calm us, patting the air with his palms. "Enough. Listen up. We'll be sending a bus to Boston at ten o'clock, and another bus to the Westmoor mall at noon. Sign up in my office if you want to go. I know I don't need to remind anyone that while you're away, all school rules are in effect." This was what teachers always said before you left campus.

When roll call was over, students surged out of the room, toward Dean Fletcher's office or else outside, toward the dorms. I headed to the mail room, which was in the basement, and saw through my mailbox window that nothing was in there. I wasn't sure what to do with myself. My focus up to this point had been avoiding the biology test, and now that I had, I was at a loss. The problem was, I didn't have anyone to go with to Boston or the mall; I still didn't have any friends. Surprisingly, this was not a fact that greatly affected my day-to-day life, at least not logistically. At meals, the sections of the dining hall were unofficially divided by grade, and within your grade—it was strangely democratic—you could sit at any table with an empty seat; formal dinner was even better because then there was assigned seating. In chapel you could also sit anywhere. And the rest of the time, wandering the halls between classes; changing in the locker room for practice, you could inconspicuously be by yourself, walking a few feet behind other people, or standing on the periphery.

It was more when things slowed down, during the parts when you were supposed to have fun, that my lack of friends felt obvious—on Saturday nights, when there were dances I didn't go to, and during visitation, which was the hour each night when boys and girls were allowed in each other's dorm rooms. I spent those times hiding. Most of the other girls propped open their doors for visitation, but we kept ours shut; Sin-Jun didn't seem to care and Dede went down the hall to Aspeth's room.

But on certain occasions, I could not conceal my friendlessness. When we'd taken a field trip to Plimoth Plantation, I'd had to ride on the bus next to Danny Black, a day student whose nose was always running because of allergies; when I asked if I could sit with him, he said in his snot-laden voice, "Fine, but I want the aisle," then stood while I slipped in. There was also the Saturday when the freshman prefects organized an ice-skating party in the hockey rink, and I went because I didn't yet understand that just because it was nighttime, just because this had been billed as a party, it didn't mean I'd find it any easier to talk to people. On the ice, the girls were gliding around in jeans and pink or gray wool sweaters, and the boys were trying to knock each other over. Behind the plastic barrier, those of us who didn't know how to skate or didn't own skates stood by the bleachers. Just standing there in the frosty air, not skating, I felt like my feet were frozen lumps, and you could see people's breath when they spoke. Intermittently, I tried making conversation with Rufina Sanchez, who'd been recruited to Ault from a public school in San Diego and who was so pretty that I'd have been intimidated to talk to her if she were white, but really my attention was on the skaters. Watching them, I felt that familiar combination of misery and exhilaration. After about fifteen minutes, Rufina said to Maria Oldego, who was heavy and from Albuquerque, "This is boring. Let's get out of here." *Boring?* I thought incredulously. When Rufina and Maria left, so did the other kids on our side of the rink, and I was alone; then I had to leave, too.

I might have made my life easier by trying to attach myself to Dede, but pride prevented it. And at times, I did attach myself to Sin-Jun, but afterward I often felt depressed, like I had talked too much and, because of the language barrier, like she hadn't understood me anyway. Besides, Sin-Jun had recently become friends with Clara O'Hallahan, a chubby, annoying girl in our dorm.

As other students filtered into the mail room, I decided I'd stay in the dorm all day. While my classmates spent money on clothing or cassettes, I could study, I thought. Maybe I'd even do well on the biology test. I left the schoolhouse. It had begun to rain outside, and on the circle, a bunch of boys were playing football, slipping and rolling in the grass. Listening to their cries, I felt a familiar jealousy of boys. I didn't want what they had, but I wished that I wanted what they wanted; it seemed like happiness was easier for them.

As I approached the dorms, I could hear music. It was all

the same song, I realized, though it wasn't coming from a single source and it wasn't all synchronized. It was the Madonna song "Holiday," with the lines, "If we took a holiday/ Took some time to celebrate/ Just one day out of life/ It would be/ It would be so nice." When I reached the courtyard, I saw that in dorm windows—but only the windows of girls' dorms, I noticed, not of boys'—stereo speakers faced out, balanced against the screens, sending music into the air. I wondered how so many girls had known to do this. It seemed a kind of animal intuition, like elephants in the savanna who know, from generation to generation, the precise spot to find water.

There were speakers in the windows of our room, Dede's speakers; her parents had sent her a stereo the second week of school. (Dede's mother also sent her care packages with cashmere sweaters and French chocolate that came in a box where each piece, shaped like a shell or a medallion, had its own correspondingly shaped nest; Dede gave the chocolate to Sin-Jun and me because she was always on a diet. As for the care packages from my own mother, I'd learned to wait until I got back to the dorm to open them. Once she had sent three shiny pink cartons of maxi pads, accompanied by a note that said, in its entirety, *Kroger was having a sale. Miss you. Love, Mom.*) When I got inside, Sin-Jun wasn't there, and Dede was in her industrious mode, hurrying between the bathroom and our room—filling her water bottle, stuffing her backpack, yelling to Aspeth. From the threshold of our room, she called down the hall, "Is Cross going?" Aspeth said something I couldn't hear, and Dede sighed and called, "Why not?" Aspeth did not respond. After several seconds, Dede said, "Cross has been so moody lately," and based on the lowered volume of her voice, it seemed she was speaking to me. "Going out with Sophie is bringing him down," she added.

Cross Sugarman was the tallest, coolest guy in our class, a white guy who was an even better basketball player than Darden Pittard. Though Cross was a freshman, he was dating a junior named Sophie, which I knew because I'd read it in Low Notes. Low Notes ran in *The Ault Voice*, the school paper; they were festively mean-spirited comments about new couples, ex-couples, and people who had recently hooked up, all written in a veiled way to escape faculty comprehension. There would be people's initials, and then a pun on their names—for Cross and Sophie, it had been, "S.T. and C.S.: It feels SO good to Cross the grade divide." The fact that Cross had a girlfriend had, apparently, not prevented Dede from developing an enormous crush on him, which struck me as both predictable and pathetic—of course Dede would fixate on the most popular guy in the class. Liking him was like saying the Grateful Dead was your favorite band, or saying chapel was boring, or the dining hall food was gross. But I knew that Dede had no chance with Cross. Yes, she was rich, but she was also Jewish, and, with a big nose and the last name Schwartz, she wasn't the kind of Jewish you could hide. She took care of herself, her legs were always freshly shaven, her hair always smelled good, but she simply wasn't that pretty.

Once in the mail room I'd seen Dede and Cross Sugarman and a few other people standing together. Dede had been shrieking with laughter, looking up at Cross and pulling on his arm with both her hands, and the expression on his face had been one of such mildness, such utter detachment, that I'd actually felt a pang for Dede.

"If Cross thought Sophie was bringing him down, he probably wouldn't be going out with her," I said.

"He's almost broken up with her like five times," Dede said. "The main reason he's dating her is because she's a junior."

I laughed. "That makes Cross sound kind of lame." To utter such a statement felt pleasingly blasphemous.

"You don't know him the way I do."

"I didn't claim to. I've never even talked to him."

"Exactly." Dede was standing before the mirror above her

bureau. She applied lip gloss and rubbed her upper and lower lips together while looking at her reflection with wide, serious eyes. "He's trapped in an unhealthy relationship," she said. "He doesn't like her that much, but he feels obligated to her."

"Maybe you should go for someone without a girlfriend."

"Oh, I don't *like* Cross. We're just good friends." Dede turned from the mirror. "You're not going to Boston, are you?"

"No."

"I am."

"I can tell."

"Aspeth and I are going shopping on Newbury Street. And we're having lunch at this Thai restaurant that's supposed to be super-cool. Don't you love Thai food?"

I had never had Thai food before, which Dede probably could have guessed.

"Like Pad Thai," she said. "Yum, that's my favorite. Have you seen my tortoiseshell headband?"

"No."

"You're not hanging out here all day are you, Lee?" she said. "You should do something fun. Surprise holiday only happens once a year."

"Of course I'm not staying here," I said.

"You're going to the mall?"

Without thinking, I nodded.

"It's kind of a trashy mall," she said. "Remember that time Aspeth and I took a taxi there? It was a waste of time. The shopping is much better in Boston. Oh, but you're probably going to the movies, huh?"

I nodded again.

"What movie are you seeing?"

I hesitated. "Actually," I said. "Actually, the reason I'm going to the mall is that—well, I'm getting my ears pierced." As I said it, I felt blood rush to my face. I had never considered getting my ears pierced; I wasn't even sure my parents would allow it.

"Oh, Lee! That's great. That'll look so good. And you'll wear dangly earrings, right? Not just studs?"

"Yeah, I guess."

"This is going to be such an improvement."

It occurred to me to take offense, but it was clear that Dede was only trying to be supportive. There was something guileless about her—all her unpleasantness was close to the surface, like the earth's crust; once you got below it, she was strangely innocent.

Dede was right; the mall was kind of trashy. The lighting was bright white, and the floor was made of shiny, fake-looking orange bricks. Several of the spaces where stores had once been had chrome grates pulled over them; behind the grates, they were dark, and vacant except for a few boxes or a lone office chair. I walked past a store selling clothes for plus-sized women, a music store, and then a string of restaurants: a sub shop, a pizza place, a diner with lit-up panels of glistening hamburgers. I kept seeing other Ault students in groups of two or three. After the bus had let us off—it hadn't been full, and no one had taken the seat next to mine—I'd hoped that I would be able to blend into a crowd of strangers, but the mall was almost empty. I told myself that the other students were probably going to the movies, which would start in less than an hour, and then I could wander around in peace. First I had to get my ears pierced.

The mall didn't have the kind of girlish store that sells barrettes and cheap jewelry. My only option seemed to be the male counterpart to such a store—a place with a motorcycle in the window that had flames running up the back panels, and lots of leather clothing.

A guy in his late thirtes, with a long ponytail and a denim jacket with the sleeves cut off, stood behind the counter. "Help you, miss?" he said.

"I'm just looking." I needed a couple minutes, I thought. I walked to a rack of leather jackets and touched the shoulders.

The jackets were very soft and had that deep, bitter smell.

"Help you?" the guy said, and I turned. But this time he was talking to Cross Sugarman, who stood in the entrance of the store looking around. As I turned back toward the jackets, I couldn't keep from smirking. Cross's presence didn't matter to me; what was gratifying was that his absence *would* matter to Dede. Then I remembered how warmly Dede had acted when I'd told her I was getting my ears pierced, and I wondered if I should feel guilty for being spiteful.

I approached the counter. "I want to get my ears pierced." I paused. "Please."

"Piercing's free," the man said. "Earrings run from six ninety-nine up."

He unlocked a door to the counter, pulled out a velvet tray of earrings, and slid it toward me. There were moons and crosses and skeleton heads, all in both silver and gold. I felt a twinge of loneliness; getting your ears pierced was an activity to do with another girl, with a friend, so she could help you choose. I pointed to a pair of silver balls, the plainest pair I saw.

"Sit there." The man nodded his chin toward a stool on the outside of the counter. He came around, and I saw the piercing gun, a white plastic square-edged object that was mostly featureless, with a silver rod that would jump forward, through my ear.

"Do you ever miss?" I asked. I laughed, and my laugh came out high and nervous.

"No," the man said.

"Does it hurt?"

"No." He set the gun against my right earlobe.

I thought that if I had a friend, even if it were only Dede, I would squeeze her fingers. I felt a pinching sensation, and then a burn. "Ouch," I said.

The man chuckled.

I wanted to stand and run from him. But if I ran, I'd have only one ear pierced. The idea that I was trapped made it difficult to breathe. I could feel the gun touching my left earlobe, the man's fingers in my hair. He pulled back on the trigger, and I shuddered, my shoulders jerking up.

"What the hell!" The man curled his body around so we could see each other's faces and glared down at me. "You want this done or not?"

"Sorry." As I looked at him, the composition of his face began to dissolve. A glowing, pulsating greenish spot—like when you look at a lightbulb and then look away—covered the tip of his nose and part of one cheek. A wave broke in my stomach. "Oh my God," I said softly.

He moved out of my line of vision and pressed the gun to my earlobe again. The green spot remained in the air where his face had been; it expanded outward, seething. I closed my eyes.

Afterward, I could hear, but I couldn't see anything. I felt as if I were lying beside a railroad track and the wheels of a train were spinning next to my ears. The whole world was skidding past, everything that had ever happened flipping in circles, and I was responsible. "You know her?" said a gravelly voice, and another voice said, "I don't know her name, but she's in my class."

"She on something?" said the gravelly voice. "What's she on? Why aren't you two in school?"

"We have the day off. Do you have a washcloth?"

"Sink's in back."

"If you get it. I'll stay with her."

I felt the wetness against my forehead before I felt my own body. Then I could see them, but I was being pulled between the spinning green world and the static world of their faces in front of me. "She's coming out of it," said the second voice. "Hey. *Hey*. What's your name?"

I blinked. I tried to say *Lee*, but the noise that came out was more of a prolonged croak.

"You fainted." It was Cross Sugarman—he was the person talking to me. "Are you diabetic?"

I couldn't answer.

He turned and said to the ponytailed man, the one with the gravelly voice, "Do you have any candy or soda?"

"This ain't a 7-Eleven."

"Yeah, I realize that." Cross looked back at me. "Are you diabetic?"

I swallowed. "No."

"Do you want us to call an ambulance?"

"No."

"Have you ever fainted before?"

"I don't know." My words emerged slowly. The spinning green world was gone entirely. I felt exhausted.

"What's your name?"

"Lee."

"And you go to Ault, right?"

I nodded.

"Me, too," he said. "My name is Cross."

It struck me, even at that moment, as modest of him to introduce himself. Of course I knew his name.

I tried to sit up—I'd been lying on the floor—and Cross leaned over and stuck his hands beneath my armpits.

"Easy," he said. He turned to the man. "You don't have any soda?"

"Restaurants are that way." The guy jerked his head toward the entrance of the store.

When I was upright, Cross peered at my face. "What day is it?" he said.

"Surprise holiday," I said.

He smiled. "Go like this." He wiped his mouth with the back of his hand. When I mimicked the gesture, a string of saliva clung to my knuckles. "We'll find you something to eat," he said.

We walked slowly toward the entrance of the store.

"Wait," I said. "I didn't pay."

"I wouldn't sweat it."

When we had stepped back into the bright humming light

of the mall, he said, "Man, what a prick." After about a minute, he nudged me. "Here."

We turned into the diner, and a waitress led us to a booth where we sat facing each other. The reality of Cross before me was jarring: his tallness, his pale skin and cropped brown hair, his blue eyes, which seemed to contain both intelligence and boredom. I would not have imagined that Dede and I had similar taste, but Cross Sugarman was the best-looking boy I had ever sat so close to. And this fact was both thrilling and mortifying. It was as if I had, as in a dream, plucked him from his own world, the world of lacrosse games and sailboats and girls with long blond hair wearing sundresses, and pulled him into mine: a grimy restaurant in a depressed mall, on a rainy day. "Sorry," I said. "For—I mean—I don't know—"

"It's no big deal."

"But you're being so nice to me."

He looked away and made a kind of grumbling sigh, and I knew immediately that I had said the wrong thing.

When he looked back, he said, "This has or hasn't happened to you before?"

"Once it did, a few years ago. After a soccer game when I was in sixth grade."

"My sister faints," he said.

The idea of Cross having a sister was intriguing. I wondered if she thought he was cute, or if she felt lucky to live in the same house he did.

"She fainted on a plane coming back from California. The flight attendants asked if she wanted the pilot to land the plane, but she told them no. I thought she should have told them yes."

"Yikes," I said. There was something in the mildness of Cross's tone and expressions that made me unsure how to react to the things he said. Normally, you could tell just by observing people when you were supposed to nod, or laugh, or frown in sympathy. But Cross's expressions were all so muted that I'd have thought he was hardly paying attention

66

to what we were talking about. It was his eyes that made me know this wasn't true—they were watchful, but not the way I imagined my own were; his was a disinterested, unself-conscious watchfulness.

The waitress appeared, and Cross ordered a vanilla milk-shake. I opened the menu, and the quantity of words was overwhelming. I closed it. "I'll have a vanilla milkshake, too," I said. After the waitress left, I said, "I wonder if it's bad for me to have dairy right now."

Cross shrugged. "You'll be okay." There was something in his shrug I envied—an ability to prevent misfortune by choosing not to anticipate it.

I looked down at the table and then back at him. "You don't have to stay here," I said. "You probably were planning to go to a movie, right? And I'll be fine. Not that I don't appreciate—" The only thing I could think of to say was *you taking care of me*, and that seemed even worse than *you're being so nice to me*. Lamely, I said, "But you really can go."

"What about my shake?"

"Oh, I can pay for it. Especially after you helped me."

"What if I want my shake?"

"Well, you can stay if you want to. I'm not telling you to leave. I just thought—"

"Relax," he said. Then he said, "Lee."

In this moment, I understood for the first time in my life what it was to feel attracted to someone. Not to think they were funny or to enjoy their company, or even to find one thing about them cute, like their dimples, or their hands, but to feel that physical pull toward them. I just wanted to close my eyes and have my body against Cross's.

"Are you a freshman?" Cross said.

I nodded.

"Me, too," he said.

He seemed so much older, I thought, as old as a man—eighteen, maybe, or twenty.

67

"I think I've seen you before. Do you live in McCormick's?"

"No, Broussard's." I didn't ask what dorm he lived in because I knew. There were fewer than seventy-five people in our class, and I knew everyone's name; even the people I'd never talked to.

"I have Madame Broussard for French," he said. "She's kind of strict."

"Do you know Amy Dennaker?"

He nodded.

"Well, Amy does these imitations of Madame. She'll be like—" I paused. I had to do the accent; it wouldn't be funny without the accent. "Like, 'There is foie gras on my bidet!' Or, she's invented this poodle that Madame keeps, named Ooh La La. So she'll say, 'Ooh La La, if you do not stop barking, I shall send you to the guillotine!'"

I looked at Cross; he appeared unimpressed.

"I guess you have to be there," I said. But it almost didn't matter that he hadn't laughed, because I had said something entirely unnecessary, I had told a story. For a moment, I had shrugged off my flattened Ault personality. "Where are you from?" I asked.

"The city."

"Boston?"

"New York."

"How did you end up at Ault?" Something was definitely different; apparently, I was to be the one carrying the conversation; and this was not even an unfamiliar dynamic. Back in South Bend, both in class and at home with my family, I had been curious and noisy and opinionated. I had talked like a normal person, more than a normal person.

"It was either here or Overfield," Cross said. "The teachers here seemed more laid-back. It's all old men in bow ties at Overfield."

"So you always knew you would go to boarding school?"

"Pretty much."

"I guess that's how it is for people from the East Coast," I said. "It's different where I'm from."

"Where's that?"

"Indiana."

"Oh, yeah? You're a Hoosier?" He might have been making fun—I wasn't sure. "You like basketball?"

"I don't really follow sports," I said. "No offense."

"What does that mean?"

"Well, since you're a big athlete. Aren't you?" As I said it, I realized I was revealing the lie of our introduction in the store; I had already known who he was.

"I'm into sports," he said slowly.

"That's all I meant."

"You think that makes me a meathead?"

"That's not—"

"It's okay." He held up his hands, palms toward me. They were huge. "I think we understand each other."

"I never said that you're a meathead."

"I do use silverware," he said. "At least in public."

My heart was beating faster. This was a kind of teasing I didn't like, when boys mocked you in a way that assumed you could not, just as easily, mock them back; they took for granted their own wit, and your squeamishness and passivity.

"I'm literate, too," he said. "I read the newspaper."

"Congratulations," I said. "How about the bathroom? Have you gotten the hang of indoor plumbing?"

We regarded each other. My face was hot.

"I know it can be tricky," I continued. "But it makes living in a communal environment a lot nicer for everyone."

Both of us were silent. Then he said, "Well, well, well," and it was in such a strange voice—the voice, perhaps, of a high-spirited Southern grandmother—that I knew if he was making fun of me, he was also making fun of himself. His goofiness made me forgive him; it was un-Aultlike. "Indiana, huh?" he said. "What's Indiana like?"

"There's a lot of land. You don't feel crowded. And people

are friendly. I know that's a stereotype about the Midwest, but it's true."

"So why did you leave?"

I looked at him quickly, but he seemed only curious this time, not sarcastic. "I don't know," I said. Then I said, "I thought my life would be more interesting if I went to Ault."

"Is it?"

"I guess so. It's definitely different." Since arriving at Ault six months before, I hadn't actually considered this question. In fact, my life at Ault *was* more interesting than my life at home had been. I was less happy and my life was more interesting; Perhaps that was not the worst trade-off in the world.

"My life is better here," Cross said. "I went to an all-boys' school in New York, so that completely sucked."

I laughed. "You like going to school with girls?"

"Sure."

Then, because I didn't want him to think I was implying that he liked going to school with *me*, I said. "You go out with Sophie Thruler, don't you?"

"Jesus," he said. "What are you, a spy?"

"But you do, right?"

"Is it the KGB or the FBI that you work for? Just tell me that."

"It's the KGB. They're really, really interested in your love life."

"Sorry, but you'll have to tell your apparatchik that you have no news."

"Why not? I know you're going out with her."

"We hang out sometimes."

"Is it true love? Do you want to marry her?"

He shook his head. "You're crazy," he said, but I could tell that there was something about me he didn't mind.

The waitress set our milkshakes on the table. They came with long spoons, in tall glasses that narrowed at the bottom. Seeing how big they were, I thought that it might take us hours to drink them; perhaps we'd have to stay at the table for the whole afternoon, talking and talking. When I took the first sip, it was frothy and sweet, and I wondered why I never drank milkshakes in my usual life.

"I'm not going to marry Sophie," Cross said. "And I could tell you why, but then I'd have to kill you."

"I don't mean you should get married now," I said. "But in the future. Reverend Orch could do the ceremony."

"Sophie and I are never getting married in a million years," Cross said. He set his spoon on the table, lifted the glass, and tilted it back, and as I watched the milkshake tumble into his mouth, I felt that affection you feel for boys when you see one of the ways they're different from you that's not a bad way. When he set the glass back on the table, less than a third remained—obviously, he did not share my impulse to make our milkshakes last as long as possible—and a white mustache hung over his upper lip. I felt a quick rise of panic; for Cross to look foolish in front of me seemed a reversal of the world's natural order. But then he wiped his mouth. Of course he was not the kind of person who unknowingly sat there with food on his face. "Here's one reason," he said. "Sophie smokes."

What I thought immediately was, *But that's against school rules.* I bit my tongue.

"Also, when it rains, she won't go outside because of her hair. She thinks it gets frizzed or something."

"What if she has class?"

"If she has to, she'll go out. But she doesn't like to." Cross tipped back his glass again and swallowed the rest of his milkshake. "But she can be cool. You know what's cool about her? Actually, never mind."

"Oh, come on."

"You'll probably be offended."

"Now you definitely have to tell me."

"It's something most girls don't like."

"I won't be offended."

71

"She loves giving blow jobs."

I blinked at him.

"I knew I shouldn't have told you," Cross said.

"No." I looked down. "It's okay." In my mind, I had a flash of Sophie kneeling before Cross while he sat on the mattress of a lower bunk, both of them naked. The image seemed so grown-up, and so foreign. Everything I didn't understand and wasn't part of at Ault rose up and loomed over me, like buildings in a city; I felt myself shrink back into a small, hunched figure, walking against the wind. When I looked up again, I knew that my ability to talk to him unguardedly was gone. Who was I to be having a conversation, to be joking, with Cross Sugarman?

"I didn't—" he began, and too loudly, I said, "No, no. It's fine."

We watched each other for several more seconds. "So what about you?" he said. "Do you have a boyfriend?"

I shook my head quickly.

There was more silence. We seemed trapped inside it.

"Listen," he finally said. "I was planning to go to this movie. I'm supposed to meet John and Martin, you know those guys?"

I nodded. They were also freshmen, teammates of Cross's from basketball; John Brindley was in my biology class.

Cross looked at his watch. "I'm kind of late, but—"

"You should go," I said. "You definitely should go." My wish for him to leave felt desperate in its intensity. I did not understand how things had become so abruptly uncomfortable, but I knew it was my fault. And now he would think that I was even weirder than if we'd never spoken, if I'd just been some anonymous girl he passed in the halls of the schoolhouse.

He set a few dollar bills on the table and stood. I looked up at him. *Just be normal for one more minute*, I thought. *Come on, Lee*. I tried to smile, and my face felt like a rotting pumpkin. "I hope it's a good movie," I said.

"I'll see you around." He lifted one hand in the air, as if to wave, but just held it there. Then he was gone.

For the first time, I looked around the restaurant. I saw no other Ault students. Being alone, I felt embarrassed and relieved. When the waitress came back, I thought that I would order more food, a real lunch—ideally, something huge and numbing, like a hamburger that came with a puffy bun and lots of french fries. I pulled a menu from behind the napkin holder and was trying to decide between a cheeseburger and a ham-and-cheese sandwich when Cross reappeared.

"Hey," he said. "Why don't you come?"

"What?" I snapped shut the menu.

"Why don't you come to the movie? You're just hanging out here, right?"

"Oh, that's all right. I mean, thanks, but you don't have to—"

"No, it's not like—"

"It's okay," I said. "I hardly even know John and Martin."

"Lee." He stared at me. "It's just a movie. Come on." I could feel his sense of hurry—the movie was about to start, if it hadn't started already.

"I'm fine." I gestured around the booth. "I don't mind being by myself." I knew right away that this was one protest too many; the amount that I needed him to convince me that it was okay to come, that he *wanted* me to come, exceeded the amount that he cared. "Actually, wait. I will go." All I had in my wallet was two ten-dollar bills; and suddenly the urgency of the movie felt too pressing to allow for getting change. I set a ten on the table next to his one-dollar bills; and though it occurred to me to take those, it also occurred to me that it could seem chintzy, and then we were leaving the diner and I was skipping to keep up with his long strides. We headed out of the mall, into the rain, then jogged across a parking lot— normally, I did not like running in the presence of boys, but I knew he wasn't looking at me—and ended up in front of the glass windows of the theater. Cross held the door for me as

73

we entered, and I wondered briefly if he would pay for my ticket, but when he didn't, it seemed stupid that the thought had crossed my mind. The movie had started; I followed him into the darkened theater, the screen bright and loud above us. As we walked down the aisle, someone hissed, "Yo, Sugarman," and Cross pulled me by the forearm into that row.

After we sat, I was panting slightly, and I could tell he was, too. My clothes were damp from the rain. The image on-screen—two men were standing in a seedy kitchen, one of them holding a gun—seemed incomprehensible and irrelevant. I never arrived at movies after they'd started because it was confusing, plus you missed the previews. But this movie, a movie about mobsters that I wouldn't have gone to on my own, was beside the point.

While looking straight ahead, I noted each time Cross shifted or sighed, each time he laughed, though his laughter also was subdued; on his other side, John and Martin kept guffawing. Cross smelled like soap, and like the rain we'd come in from, the smell of the earth in spring. Our bodies did not touch at all, but sometimes our clothes did—our sleeves, the legs of our pants. I didn't know if this was a thing anyone besides me would notice.

For the whole movie, I had that sense of heightened awareness that is like discomfort but is not discomfort exactly—a tiring, enjoyable vigilance. I did not get a grasp on the movie's plot, or the names of any of the characters. Then it was over, and the lights came on, and I felt self-conscious; in the dark, I could be any girl, crossed legs, shoulder-length hair, but in the light, blushing and fidgety, I was me. Because I was on the outside of the row, I was in front of the boys walking up the aisle to leave. I hadn't stood until they were standing, and as we walked, I was afraid to look back to see if they were still behind me. Maybe this was the place Cross and I would part ways, I thought. And maybe we wouldn't even say good-bye, now that he was with his friends again; maybe I was just supposed to know.

74

In the lobby of the theater, I paused at the water fountain and glanced over my shoulder. They were right behind me after all. They kept walking, then stopped perhaps ten feet beyond the fountain, appearing to wait. I swallowed, stood, and approached them slowly.

Martin was reenacting a part from the movie where one guy had strangled another; he was performing the re-enactment on John, who was sticking his tongue out and making his eyes bulge. "And then he's like, 'Now do you remember? *Now* do you remember?'" Martin said. John gagged noisily, and all three of the guys cracked up. I stood slightly farther away from them than they stood from each other, and tried to seem amused.

"You like that, Lee?" Cross said.

I didn't know if he meant the whole movie, or the strangling in the movie, or Martin's rendition of the strangling. "It was pretty good."

"There were some nasty parts, huh?" John said, and I could tell, by the friendliness of his tone, that my presence was no big deal to him. We had never introduced ourselves, and it was apparent we were not going to now.

"I closed my eyes for the nasty parts," I said. "The part by the dumpster—I think I missed most of it."

"The dumpster scene was awesome," Martin said. "You should go back and see the next showing right now."

"You guys hungry?" Cross said. "I'm hungry."

"I'm starving," Martin said.

And then we were walking back through the parking lot— it had stopped raining, though the sky was still low and gray—to the sub shop, and I was still with them. It seemed fine that I was with them; it didn't seem like they wondered why I didn't leave them alone, or why I wasn't with a group of girls. They all got subs and I got a pack of pretzels. At the table, they kept talking about the movie, repeating lines from it; Martin tried to do the strangling thing on Cross, but Cross laughed and shrugged Martin away. I decided that if Martin wanted to do it on me, I would let him, but he didn't try.

The next place we went was a video arcade. Walking there, I thought that maybe this was where we'd part ways—I hardly knew how to play video games—but then it seemed like it would be weird and formal if I paused to disentangle myself from them. And the arcade had pinball; I knew how to play pinball. We all got quarters, and I stood before the bright, zinging machine, jamming them in whenever I lost a game.

I had just used the flippers to knock the ball all the way back when, beside me, someone said, "Not bad."

I turned—it was Cross—and as I did, I heard the ball roll down the mouth of the machine. "Whoops," I said. We both looked at the place where the ball had disappeared.

As my points audibly added up, he said, "You might be better at this than I am."

"I *might*?"

"That's not an insult."

"I'm *sure* I'm better than you." Impulsively, I said, "I'm a state champion."

He looked at me skeptically.

"I was a prodigy," I said. "I traveled around the country. But then I burned out."

"You're kidding, right?"

"It's how I got into Ault. You know how they love it when you have a special talent?"

"I don't believe you," he said, but I knew he did, a little, or he wouldn't have needed to say so.

"When I was nine, I was crowned Hoosier Pinball Princess," I said. "My parents were so proud." As I looked at him, I felt the comers of my mouth pulling up, and then he knocked my head with the palm of his hand, half tap and half rub, and said, "You're so full of bullshit."

"But you weren't sure," I said.

"I was sure."

"No, you weren't. I can tell. You weren't."

We grinned at each other. He was so handsome, I thought,

and as soon as I thought it, the moment began to crack. Thinking of him as Cross, as part of Ault, was where I ran into problems. It was okay when we were just talking.

I was relieved when Martin came over. "You guys want some pizza?"

"You're hungry?" I said. "Again?"

They got an extra-large, and this time I ate some, even though it had pepperoni on it and I hadn't eaten pepperoni since Dede told me it was smoked with boar semen. Halfway through his fourth slice, Martin set it down on the paper plate and gripped his stomach. "Whose idea was this?" he said.

"It was Lee's," Cross said.

"It was not!" In my own voice, I could hear an insincere insistence, that girlish tone of flirtation.

"It was a bad idea, Lee," Martin said. "A bad fucking idea."

"You want some Tums, Marty?" John said. Then he said, "Does anyone know what time it is?" We all turned to look at the clock on the wall. It was five to six, and the bus back to school had left at five-thirty. "Fuck," John said. "I'm already on Saturday detention for missing chapel twice this week."

"Do we call Fletcher?" Martin asked.

"We can take a taxi," Cross said. "It's not a big deal." The way he said it, how calm he was, made me wonder if he'd realized already that we'd missed the bus—if he'd realized it at the time even, and let it happen.

Cross was the one who called, from a pay phone, while the rest of us stood around. Martin was still moaning about how full he was, and John kept saying. "How the fuck did this happen?" I had less than five dollars left in my pocket, and it was a half-hour ride back to school. But no one else seemed concerned about money, and I said nothing.

"A taxi will meet us outside the movie theater," Cross said after he'd hung up. When we walked back there, it was sprinkling outside and the sky was dark. Waiting just inside the theater, no one spoke much, but it felt less like an awkward silence than a tired silence. Girls would still be talking to each other, I thought.

I had been in a taxi only one other time in my life, right after my mother gave birth to my brother Tim, and my brother Joseph and I rode to the hospital to meet up with our parents and see Tim for the first time. It was a sunny afternoon; I was ten years old, and Joseph was seven. For the whole ride, I imagined that the driver was going to kidnap us, and I pictured myself opening the door while the car was in motion, rolling out, and pulling Joseph with me. But then the driver delivered us to the hospital entrance and my father was waiting there to pay him.

In this taxi, I knew we would not be kidnapped—not just because I was less dumb than I'd been when I was ten but also because there were too many of us to kidnap, and Cross was too tall and strong. It was a maroon taxi. Martin got in the front seat, and John went around to the far side of the back seat, and then Cross opened the door closest to us and climbed in, and I followed him. I was surprised that he sat in the middle; at home, the boys I knew had been calling that the bitch seat since fourth grade.

The seats were blue Naugahyde, and inside the taxi it smelled like stale cigarette smoke and fake-pine air freshener. A cardboard tree hung from the rearview mirror. The radio was on low, set to a big-band station, and there was lots of static. The windshield wipers swished back and forth, and in the intervals between swishes, everything out the window turned blurry.

I had the same consciousness of Cross beside me that I'd had watching the movie, but this time, instead of feeling nervous about how to act when the movie ended, I felt sad because I knew the day was almost over. We would get back to school, and then what? It was hard to imagine that I could go from having no friends to being friends with Cross Sugarman. It was too great a leap. Besides, I had no proof that Cross truly liked me. He had been nice because I'd fainted.

That was all. I didn't want to be like Dede, presuming chumminess, using what someone gave you as an excuse to grasp for even more.

John leaned forward, peering at me from the other side of Cross. "You think biology will be hard?" he asked.

The test—over the course of the day, I had forgotten about it. "Probably," I said. "I've hardly studied."

"I was planning to study last night, but when I heard it would be surprise holiday, I blew it off."

I smiled, "Me, too."

"Surprise holiday is like this illusion." John leaned back, and his voice sounded far away. "It makes you feel like you have all the time in the world, but before you know it, the day is over. They should give us surprise week."

"You'd get so bored," Cross said.

"Nah, I have a million things I could do." John was still talking when Cross lifted his left arm. At first, I thought he was setting it on the seat behind my back, and I felt a bolt of anticipation in my chest; then I realized he was setting it on me. His hand cupped my shoulder, and there was the slightest pull, a pull toward him. I gave into it. My body fell against his: my leg pressed to his leg, my arm filling the hollow between us, the top of my head just below his collarbone. This development struck me as remarkable—there I was, with Cross's arm around me, when Martin or John could have turned at any moment and seen—but it also seemed un-surprising. Sitting in the diner earlier in the day, I had thought how much I wanted to be touching Cross and now I was; I could feel the rise and fall of his chest. And we matched each other well, our bodies fit. I didn't know enough then to realize that doesn't always happen—that sometimes you cannot settle on an angle with the other person, your weight won't balance, your bones poke.

Whenever Cross responded to John, his voice was perfectly placid. Once Cross said, "Okay, but when would spring break be?"—they were still talking about a whole week of surprise holidays—and they could have been at a table in the dining hall, shooting the shit after dinner. I decided that I liked this gulf between the normality of Cross's tone and the abnormality of the situation; it made what was happening between us a secret.

He touched my hair, first so briefly that it felt accidental; then his fingers raked through and started over again, and every so often, he rubbed the back of my neck with his thumb. My whole body was hot liquid; I felt beholden to him, and painfully happy. From the radio came the sound of trumpets. The rain outside made everything soft, the roll of the tires over the road, the fuzzy traffic lights, and on Cross's other side, John was talking and talking, and I wished that we could keep driving all night long and that for the whole ride, everything would stay just as it was in this moment.

It did last, but only for a little bit. Then we were turning in to the gates of Ault. Cross leaned between the two front seats and, just like that, his arm was not around me, his fingers were not in my hair. "Left," he said to the driver. "Past the chapel."

In front of a cluster of dorms—not the cluster I lived in, because Broussard's was on the other side of the circle—the taxi stopped, and the driver turned on the inside light. I blinked as if I'd been awakened. I didn't dare look at Cross, so I turned and peered out the window, but all I could see was darkness. Other people would be able to see in, I thought, if they were passing by, and I found myself hoping they were not. I did not want anyone to wonder what I was doing in a taxi with Cross and John and Martin.

"Okay," Cross said, and I could tell that he was talking to me. I glanced over, and we looked at each other for several seconds. Martin and John were getting out of the car. "Bye, Lee." Cross nodded his head once.

I said, "But what—" and he turned back. I had no idea what to say next, though, and after a few seconds, he turned again. For a long time, I wondered if there were a certain thing I could have uttered to change the outcome of the situation. I imagined what I didn't say as a single perfect sentence, a narrow, discrete rectangle, like a ruler; it was unknowable to me, but somewhere in the world, it existed. When Cross shut the door behind him, the light inside the taxi went off, and I was able to see the three of them walk away. I heard laughter as the taxi pulled forward.

In the rearview mirror, I made eye contact with the driver. I had not really looked at him before—he was middle-aged and heavyset, with gray stubble and a plaid cap. "Now where?" he said. He had a thick Boston accent. "What building?"

I pointed. "That one."

When he stopped the taxi again, I was horrified to see that the meter read 48.80. I said, "I have to run inside and get some money. I promise I'll come back."

He shook his head. "Your boyfriend paid."

"My boyfriend?"

"But you pay again if you want. I won't stop you." He had a rumbling laugh.

"Thanks." I pulled the door handle.

"What college is this?" the driver said.

"It's a high school. It's called Ault."

"All this for a high school?" He gave an impressed whistle.

"I know," I said. "We're lucky."

When I entered the room, Sin-Jun and Dede looked up from their desks. "Lee is back," Sin-Jun said, and Dede said, "We thought you'd died."

"I missed the bus from the mall," I said. "I had to take a taxi."

"Okay, so?" Dede said. "Did you go through with it?"

"Oh," I said. "No, I did." I pulled back my hair and angled my ears toward them, first my right and then my left. They approached me, and I wished that I had chosen

81

more interesting earrings; there really wasn't much to see.

"Ahh," Sin-Jun said. "Very exquisite."

"The left one looks red," Dede said. "But I'm sure if you use hydrogen peroxide, it'll be fine."

"What does hydrogen peroxide do?"

"Didn't they explain this to you when they did the piercing?"

"A man did it," I said. "He was kind of mean."

"You're supposed to clean them every night so they don't get infected. You do it at the same time that you turn the earrings."

"You turn the earrings?"

"God, Lee, they didn't tell you anything. Hold on." Dede walked to her bed, squatted, pulled out a clear plastic box from under it, and returned to Sin-Jun and me with a brown bottle and several cotton balls.

I turned to Sin-Jun. "How was Boston?"

"Boston is good, but it rains all day."

"Yeah," I said. "At the mall, too."

"Here," Dede said. "Sit down."

I sat on her desk chair. Sin-Jun sat on Dede's desk and propped her bare feet on the seat of my chair. Dede stood beside me and tucked a lock of hair behind my left ear. Our positions reminded me of the piercing itself, and I thought of telling them how I had fainted. But I wasn't sure yet if it was a funny story or just a weird story, and besides, if I mentioned fainting, I'd have to mention Cross.

Dede unscrewed the cap of the hydrogen peroxide, pressed a cotton ball to the opening, and tipped the bottle upside down. She set the bottle on the desk and held the cotton ball against my earlobe. Very gently, she rubbed it around the earring.

I couldn't tell them about Cross, I thought. I couldn't tell them because Dede liked him and because she wouldn't believe or understand it, and I couldn't tell them because I myself was unsure what there was to believe or understand. It

82

wasn't like he'd kissed me, or made any declarations. What could I claim? For years and years, I felt this way, not just about Cross but about other guys—if they didn't kiss you, it didn't mean anything. Their interest in you had been so negligible as, perhaps, to have all been in your head.

I thought of how it had felt to sit so close to Cross in the taxi, the weight of his arm across my shoulders, the warmth of his body beneath his clothes. I thought how that was what I wanted, that if I could just have that—just Cross next to me, not flowers, not poems, not the approval of other students, not rich parents or good grades or a prettier face—I would be happy. That was the thing that if it were happening to me, I wouldn't feel distracted or wish to be somewhere else; all by itself, it would be enough. As I thought this, I also thought that I wouldn't get it—surely, I wouldn't—and I felt my eyes fill. When I blinked, tears ran down my face.

"Oh, Lee," Dede said. "Oh, honey." Sin-Jun leaned forward and patted my shoulder, and Dede said, "I'll be done in two seconds." She took the damp cotton ball away from my ear, and I realized that they thought I was crying because it hurt.

3

Assassin

I MET CONCHITA MAXWELL in the spring, on the first day of lacrosse practice. When Ms. Barrett told us to split into pairs and toss a ball, I watched as the girls around me turned to each other, murmuring and nodding. It had become a ritual in sports and in class—the time when everybody divided, and I had no one to divide with. Then the coach or teacher would say, "Is anyone not paired up?" and I and one or two other students would meekly raise our hands.

"Hey," said a voice behind me. I turned and saw Conchita. "Want to be partners?"

I hesitated.

"Take ten minutes," Ms. Barrett called out. "Just get the feel of throwing and catching."

"Let's go over there." Conchita pointed to a corner of the field a few feet from where the woods began. Though I hadn't yet responded to her offer, it was clear to both of us I wasn't going to receive another one. "By the way," she said, "I'm Conchita."

"I'm Lee."

"I've never played lacrosse before," she said cheerfully. I'd never played, either—in fact, I had purchased my stick less than an hour before, in the school store, and it

84

smelled like leather and new metal—but I said nothing.

Though Conchita and I had never spoken, I already knew who she was. In fact, I'm sure everyone at Ault knew who she was, mostly because of how she dressed. She was a skinny girl with a large pile of short black puffy hair and dark skin, and I'd first noticed her in the dining hall several months back, in purple clogs, a pair of tights with horizontal purple and red stripes, purple culottes (they might have been knickers—I wasn't certain), and a red blouse with a huge ruffly collar. The final accessory was a purple beret, which she'd set at a jaunty angle. I had thought at the time that she resembled a member of a theater troupe specializing in elementary school visits. For lacrosse practice, Conchita looked slightly more conservative—she was wearing a chartreuse tank top, white shorts, and chartreuse knee socks, which she'd actually pulled up to her knees. Apparently a hat enthusiast, she sported an Ault baseball cap with a still-stiff brim; the cap made me wonder if, after all, she was trying to fit in rather than to stand out.

As we walked, Conchita sneezed three times in a row. I considered saying *Bless you* to her, then didn't.

She pulled a tissue from the pocket of her shorts and blew her nose loudly. "Allergies," she said. It was early April then, just after spring break, a perfect afternoon of cobalt sky and bright sun. "You name it, I'm allergic to it."

I didn't try to name anything.

"Grass," Conchita said. "Pollen, chlorine, mushrooms."

"Mushrooms?"

"If I eat one, I break out in hives for up to a week."

"That sucks," I said, and I could hear in my own voice not a meanness; exactly, but a lack of deference.

We positioned ourselves ten yards apart. Conchita set the ball, a rubbery white globe like the egg of some exotic creature, in the webbing of her stick and thrust the stick forward. The ball landed in the grass several feet to my left. "Don't say you weren't warned," she said.

I scooped up the ball and propelled it back; it landed even farther from her than her shot had from me.

"I take it you're a Dylan fan," Conchita said.

"Huh?"

"Your shirt."

I looked down. I was wearing an old T-shirt of my father's, pale blue with the words *The Times They Are A-Changin'* across the front in white letters. I had no idea where he'd gotten it, but he'd worn it to jog in, and when I'd left for Ault I'd taken it with me; it was very soft and, for a few weeks, it had smelled like home.

"You realize that's one of his most famous songs, right?" Conchita said.

"Yeah," I said. "Right." At Ault, there was so much I didn't know. Most of it had to do with money (what a debutante was, how you pronounced Greenwich, Connecticut) or with sex (that a pearl necklace wasn't always a piece of jewelry), but sometimes it had to do with more general information about clothing, or food, or geography. Once at breakfast when people were discussing a hotel I'd never heard of, someone said, "It's on the corner of Forty-seventh and Lex," and not only did the names of the streets mean nothing to me, but I wasn't even certain for several minutes what city they were talking about. What I had learned since September was how to downplay my lack of knowledge. If I seemed ignorant, I hoped that I also seemed disinterested.

"I'm sure you've heard the song," Conchita said, and she began to sing. "Come gather round people wherever you roam, and admit that the waters around you have grown and . . . I can't remember the next part . . . something something something . . . if your time to you is worth saving." To my surprise, she had a pretty voice, high and clear and unself-conscious.

"That does sound kind of familiar," I said. It didn't sound familiar at all.

"It's sad to see what's happened to Dylan, because he had

such a powerful message back in the sixties," Conchita said. "It wasn't just music to make out to."

Why, I wondered, would music to make out to be a bad thing?

"I have most of his stuff," Conchita said. "If you want to, you can come by my room and listen."

"Oh," I said. Then, because I didn't want to either accept or decline the invitation, I said, "Here," as I flung the ball. It went far beyond her, and I added, "Sorry."

She scurried after the ball, then sent it back. "We probably won't have to go to the away games. I've heard that when it's a big team, sometimes Ms. Barrett lets the people who aren't that good stay on camptus. No offense, of course."

"I haven't heard that," I said.

"Maybe it's just wishful thinking. But I could really use the time."

To do what? I thought. I knew Conchita didn't have a boyfriend—only about twelve people in our class of seventy-five ever dated, and they always went out with each other—and I didn't think Conchita had many friends, either. The only person I could remember seeing her with was Martha Porter, a red-haired girl from my Latin class on whose last test the teacher had written across the top—I'd seen this because Martha and I sat side by side—*Saluto, Martha! Another marvelous performance!* On the same test, I had received a C minus and a note that read *Lee, I am concerned. Please talk to me after class.*

"Lacrosse was originally played by the Huron Indians," Conchita said. "Did you know that?"

"Yes."

"Really? You knew that already?"

The fib had slipped out spontaneously; when pressed, I found it difficult to lie on purpose. "Actually," I said, "no."

"It dates back to the 1400s. Makes you wonder how it became the favorite game of East Coast prep schools. You're from Indiana, aren't you?"

87

I wasn't sure how she knew where I was from. In fact, I knew that she was from Texas, but knew this only because, in addition to reading old yearbooks, I regularly perused the current school catalog, where everyone's full names and hometowns were printed in the back: *Aspeth Meriweather Montgomery, Greenwich, Connecticut. Cross Algeron Sugarman. New York, New York. Conchita Rosalinda Maxwell, Fort Worth, Texas.* Or, for me, *Lee Fiora, South Bend, Indiana.* I did not have among other things, a middle name.

"I bet people don't play lacrosse in Indiana," Conchita said. "But some of these girls"—she nodded toward our teamnmates—"have been playing since first grade."

"Things are different on the East Coast." I tried to sound noncommittal.

"That's an understatement." Conchita laughed. "When I got here, I thought I'd landed on another planet. One night the dining hall was serving Mexican food, and I was real excited, and then I show up and the salsa is, like, ketchup with onions in it."

I actually remembered this night—not because of how the food had tasted, but because I had spilled that very salsa on my shirt and sat for the rest of dinner with a red stain just below my collarbone.

"My mom is Mexican," Conchita said. "I'm spoiled by her cooking."

This actually did interest me. "Is your dad Mexican, too?" I asked.

"No, he's American. They met through work after my mom immigrated. And I have two half-sisters, but they're way older. They're, like, adults."

For the first time, I caught the ball in my webbing.

"Nice job," Conchita said. "So do you like it here?"

"Yeah, of course!"

"What do you like about it?"

"I think that's a really weird question," I said. "Do you not like it or something?"

Conchita appeared unruffled by my rudeness. "Hmm." She set the tip of her stick against the grass, like a cane. "I can't tell if we've decided to be honest. At first, I thought you and I were going to. I'd gotten the impression you weren't the same as everyone else, but now I'm thinking I might've been wrong." She seemed perhaps a little sad but still not angry, not at all—she was a lot slyer than I'd given her credit for.

"Since we've never met," I said, "I don't know how you could have *any* impression of me."

"Please, Lee. You're not going to act like we don't all have ideas about each other, are you?"

The remark shocked me. Certainly, I had ideas about other people, but Conchita was the first person I'd encountered who seemed to have ideas about me. Besides, in spite of my zest for gathering information about other students, I would never have revealed what I'd learned to the people whom it concerned; I knew enough to know that if, say, over dinner you said to some guy you'd never spoken to before, *Yeah, you have a sister who went to Ault, too, right? Alice? Who graduated in 1983?* it would only creep him out. Not that I personally felt creeped out by Conchita's research; mostly I felt curious. "Fine," I said. "What are your ideas about me?"

She could have gamed me in this moment in the way that I was gaming her, but she didn't. "I have a hard time believing you like it here," she said. "That's the first thing." She hoisted her stick into the air again and shot the ball forward, and it thunked against the ground midway between us. "You're always walking around with your head down. Or at roll call, you just study and don't talk to people."

Abruptly, I felt myself sink into another mood. I didn't retrieve the ball but just stood there, with the base of my stick propped against my right hip—not the right way, not even the right side, to hold it, I later learned—and stared at the manufacturer's logo painted over the aluminum.

"You seem thoughtful," Conchita said. "And I don't see

how any thoughtful person couldn't have some problems with this school."

I have always found the times when another person recognizes you to be strangely sad; I suspect the pathos of these moments is their rareness, the way they contrast with most daily encounters. That reminder that it can be different, that you need not go through your life unknown but that you probably still will—that is the part that's almost unbearable.

"Maybe we're alike," Conchita said.

I looked up. I wasn't sure I wanted to make this leap.

"I've always thought, I bet I could be friends with her," Conchita said. "You know how you just get that feeling? But if I'm wrong, you can tell me."

I thought of the day she'd worn the beret, its bright purple woolly fabric; if I had noticed it, surely other people had. Then I thought of how my life at Ault was a series of inter-actions and avoidance of interactions in which I pretended not to mind that I was almost always by myself. I could not last for long this way, certainly not for the next three years; I'd been at Ault only seven months, and already, my loneliness felt physically exhausting.

But then the whistle blew—Ms. Barrett was summoning us—and in the shifting activity, I managed not to give Conchita an answer.

Gates was running roll call alone the next morning, but near the end, Henry Thorpe came and stood on the platform. Gates moved aside, and Henry stepped in front of the desk, and even though he hadn't said a thing, people started laughing—he seemed to be imitating himself running roll call on another day. A lot of times students performed skits as announcements, and occasionally, if the senior class had a big test, they'd filibuster by performing lots and lots of skits, or making joke announcements; once, nearly twenty members of the senior class came up, one by one, to wish Dean Fletcher a happy birthday.

"So I guess that's it for today," Henry said. "I'll just ring the bell now." With exaggerated gestures, practically in slow motion, he reached to the left side of the desk where the button for the schoolwide bell was, but before he pressed it, a figure stepped forward from the fireplace near the front of the hall. The person was wearing a black robe with a black hood and carrying an oversized water gun, and when he aimed the gun at Henry, an arc of water shot over the heads of all the students sitting at the desks between the fireplace and the platform. The water hit Henry near the heart, soaking his shirt.

"Ach!" he cried. "I'm down! I'm down! They got me." He grabbed his chest and staggered around the platform—I looked at Gates, who was standing behind Henry smiling at him like an indulgent older sister—and then Henry stepped forward and fell face-first onto the desk, his arms hanging limply in front of him.

Students cheered wildly. Not so much around me, because I sat in front with the other freshmen, and most of my class-mates didn't seem to know any better than I did what was going on. But the farther back you got in the room, the more loudly people were yelling and clapping. The person in the cloak pulled back his hood—it was Adam Rabinovitz, a senior—then threw his fists in the air. He said, or this was what I thought he said, though it was hard to hear, "Victory is mine."

I knew three things about Adam Rabinovitz, all of which intrigued me without inspiring any desire ever to speak to him. The first was a bit of lore from two years before I'd gotten to Ault. Often at roll call people made announcements about missing notebooks or lost articles of clothing—*I left a green fleece jacket in the library on Monday afternoon*—and as a sophomore Adam had come up to the platform one morning, said in a completely normal voice, "Last night, Jimmy Galloway lost his virginity in the music wing, so if you find it, please return it to him," and then stepped off the platform, while Mr. Byden glowered and students turned to each other in shock and delight. Jimmy was Adam's roommate, a good-looking blond guy, and I wondered, though this bit of information never got included when the story was told, who the girl had been.

The second thing I knew about Adam also had, in a way, to do with sex. In the fall, a plaster-of-Paris display had gone up in the art wing. a joint project by two senior girls who both wore sheer scarves around their necks and silver hoop earrings and lots of black and who probably smoked, or would start when they got to college. They were *serious* about their art, and that must have been why they were allowed to include in the display a variety of plaster body parts, including a breast and a penis; the breast was never identified, but after great speculation, the dominant theory on campus was that the penis belonged to Adam Rabinovitz. The third thing I knew about him, and this made the other two all the more interesting, was that supposedly he had the highest GPA in his class; at any rate, he was headed to Yale.

On the platform, Henry came back to life, and Adam joined him. "Okay, here's the deal," Adam said. "Assassin is starting again, and this is how we're doing it this year. If you're a student, we're assuming you want to play, so if you don't, cross your name off the class lists in the mail room by noon today. If you're faculty, we're assuming you don't want to play"—here, Dean Fletcher made his own whooping cheer, eliciting laughter—"That means you *do* want to play, right, Fletchy?" Adam said. "Whoever gets Fletchy, remember: He's really psyched for the game."

People laughed more, and Adam continued. "So for you freshmen and freshwomen, I'll give a rundown. The object of the game is, you kill all your classmates." Again, there was laughter, laughter that makes this day and this game seem longer ago than it was; at the time, certain teachers and students expressed disapproval of Assassin, but they were viewed as the humorless minority.

"How you kill them is pretty simple," Adam said. "The game starts at one p.m. tomorrow. Check your mailbox by twelve o'clock, and you'll find a piece of paper with a name on it and a bunch of orange stickers. The name you get is your target, and that person won't know that you have them. You have to kill them by putting a sticker on them without anyone seeing. If there's a witness, you have to wait twenty-four hours before making another attempt. Once your target is dead, you take over their target, and you need to get their stickers. And don't forget that someone else is targeting you. Any questions?"

"How many licks does it take to get to the center of a Tootsie Pop?" a girl yelled.

"It depends on your tongue," Adam said. "Is that the best you can do?"

"What's the meaning of life?" someone else shouted.

Mr. Byden, who was standing next to Gates, tapped Henry on the shoulder, and Henry leaned in and whispered something to Adam.

Adam nodded. "I'm receiving word from on high that we need to wrap up. So, basically, watch your back and trust no one. And if you have any questions, find me, Galloway, or Thorpe." He stepped off the platform, and Henry followed him.

"You should have told them whoever wins gets the title grand master assassin," I heard Henry say as they passed my desk. The next announcement had begun, but I was still watching the two of them.

"Or they get to blow you," Adam said. "Whichever they choose." They both snickered, and I smiled, as if the joke had been meant for me, too.

At that point, listening to them, I wasn't thinking much about Assassin. What the announcement left me with mostly—I couldn't have articulated it then, and I might not have believed it if someone else had suggested it—was the sense that I wanted to *be* Adam Rabinovitz. The interest I felt in certain guys then confused me, because it wasn't romantic, but I wasn't sure what else it might be. But now I know: I wanted to take up people's time making jokes, to tease the dean in front of the entire school, to call him by a nickname. What I wanted was to be a cocky high-school boy, so fucking sure of my place in the world.

I was leaving the gym after practice when I heard Conchita call my name. During the last twenty-four hours, I had recalled with embarrassment my earlier snottiness toward her. I waited for her to catch up with me, and when she did, we began walking up the flagstone path to the circle. "Hard practice," she said.

I had noticed that when the team jogged to the boathouse and back, Conchita was one of the stragglers—as most of us were starting the return route, headed away from the river, she was still heading toward it, walking instead of running and breathing in through an asthma inhaler. For a split second, I'd considered stopping, but already Clara O'Hallahan was walking beside her.

"When I was down at the river, I thought about joining crew," Conchita said. "Have you seen the coxes? They just sit there shouting orders."

"But I heard your teammates throw you in the water when they win a race, and imagine being thrown in the Raymond River. You'd give birth to a two-headed baby."

Conchita laughed. "I'm not giving birth to any baby unless it's through immaculate conception." As if I hadn't understood, she added, "I'm a virgin, of course."

I willed myself not to turn and stare at her. What kind of person *advertised* her virginity?

"Hey, want to come back to my room and listen to Bob Dylan?" she asked. We'd reached the end of the path—her dorm was on the west side of the circle, and mine was on the east.

"Now?" I said. It was one thing to leave the gym with Conchita because we were both headed in the same direction and another thing entirely to accompany her to her dorm, to go somewhere with her.

"It's okay if you can't."

"No, I guess I could," I said. "For a little while."

As we climbed the staircase in Conchita's dorm, I said, "Who are your roommates?"

"I have a single."

"I thought you were a freshman." Singles, in spite of their undesirability, were never assigned to freshmen.

"No, I am," she said. "But I have insomnia, so they made an exception. Some nights I don't sleep at all."

"That's horrible." I'd never met an insomniac my own age.

"I nap when I can."

We entered her room, and my first thought was that it had been furnished by someone who was trying to decorate for a teenage girl without ever having met one. There was something creepily professional about it, like the set of a television show: the ruffly pink curtains (typically, shades hung at the windows of dorm rooms), the pale blue throw rug spread over the standard tan carpet, the framed poster of the Eiffel Tower, the heart-shaped mirror encased in a heart-shaped frame of white wicker. There was a low white plastic table with a large dish of candy, a vase of fake pink and blue flowers, and white beanbags on either side. (All the whiteness did vaguely impress me because at home, my mother never bought anything white, not furniture or sheets or clothing. Every year until I was twelve, I'd asked for white patent leather shoes for Easter, and every year my mother had refused, saying, "They'd get dirty so fast it would make your head spin.") Over Conchita's bed, her name was spelled out in pink cursive neon; something about the neon being lit in the daytime, in an empty room, struck me as deeply depressing. On the bureau rested a stereo that was, improbably enough, also pink, but what was truly remarkable about the room, even more than the décor, was the size. It definitely wasn't a single. It was a double with one bed in it.

"Sit anywhere," she said, and I sat on one of the beanbags. "Are you hungry? I have some food."

"I'm okay."

Ignoring me, she perched on her tiptoes and reached for something on her closet shelf. When she pulled it down, I saw that it was a large basket containing—in unopened packaging—potato chips, sunflower seeds, macadamia nuts, chocolate chip cookies, animal crackers, and several pouches of cocoa powder. Even the arrangement of the food in the basket looked professional, and I felt, suddenly, like I was attending a slumber party to which everyone else who'd been invited had chosen not to come.

"I'll just have some candy," I said, gesturing toward the table. "But thanks for pulling that down." As she hoisted it back up, I leaned forward and reached for a caramel. All the candy wrappers, I saw, were coated with a thin layer of dust.

"There's something I have to do," Conchita said. "Can you keep a secret?"

I perked up. "Of course."

She lifted the dust ruffle from her bed and pulled out a telephone.

"I didn't even know there were jacks in the rooms," I said, though as secrets went, this wasn't great. The kind I preferred were about specific people.

"We had it installed. Dean Fletcher and Mrs. Pamasset okayed it, but I'm not supposed to tell other students. My mom convinced them I needed it in case I have an asthma attack in the middle of the night!"

"But if you were having an asthma attack, you wouldn't be able to use the phone."

"I could dial 911." Conchita paused. "The truth is that my mom is kind of overprotective. When I first got here she would try calling me on the pay phone and either it would be busy, or no one would answer and she couldn't leave a message. Anyway, I'll put on the music in a second. I just have to call her really fast."

She dialed, and after a moment, she said, "Hola, Mama." Although I was taking Spanish, I didn't understand anything after that except possibly—it was hard to know for sure—my own name. I thought about how much money it must have cost to furnish this room, and then I thought about how maybe it was a cultural thing, how even though her family didn't have a lot, they were willing to pour what they did have into objects that were tangible and conspicuous. I had recently read an article about *quinceañeras*, and I thought that Conchita would probably have one when she turned fifteen. And maybe I'd even be invited and—because it would be fascinating and because it would happen far from Ault—I'd go. I could ask my parents for the plane ticket as a combination birthday and Christmas present.

When Conchita hung up, I said. "Do you talk to your mom every day?"

"Yeah, at least once. It's really hard for her with me gone."

I spoke to my own mother on Sundays, when the rates were lower, and we never spoke for long because I always seemed to call when she was starting dinner or putting my brothers to bed. Sometimes after I hung up the phone—even when other girls were waiting to use it, which was usually—I sat in the booth for a moment doing nothing. I thought about how my parents had not wanted me to go to boarding school, how my brothers had cried the day I left, and how quickly they appeared to have adjusted to my absence. I knew they missed me, but by now they seemed to find the fact that I didn't live at home a lot less surprising than I did.

Conchita walked to the stereo. "As promised," she said. "Ladies and gentlemen, I present to you Mr. Bob Dylan." As the sound of a guitar became audible, Conchita turned the volume knob clockwise. I heard a deep soft voice crooning the song "Lay, Lady, Lay." It wasn't what I'd expected—it was softer, and twangier. Most surprising of all, it *did* sound like make-out music, or maybe sex music: Dylan was singing about a man with dirty clothes but clean hands, and about how a woman on a bed was the best thing the man had ever seen.

"I like it," I said.

Conchita turned the volume down. "What?"

"I like it."

"Oh. Me, too." She turned it up again.

Why wait any longer for the world to begin? Dylan sang. *Why wait any longer for the one you love, when he's standing in front of you?*

Out the window, the light was turning from the bright yellow of afternoon to the more muted shade of dusk. This was always the time of day I felt the saddest, when I most believed my life should be something other than what it was, and the music compounded the feeling—I found myself wishing I could exist inside the song, lying on white sheets while a shy man in dirty clothes approached me. I could love such a man, I thought; he'd be wearing a flannel shirt, and I would pull him to me, my arms tight around his back, the warmth of his skin coming through the fabric.

Then the song ended. I didn't want to look up, to make eye contact with Conchita; I didn't particularly want to be in the same room with her.

"Here's another good one," she said. "It's called 'Subterranean Homesick Blues.' "

The word *homesick* gave me hope, but the song was just clever chanting. It sounded political, and I wanted another song of longing. Conchita played a few more songs, switching CDs, sometimes cutting off the songs midway. By the end, the one I still liked the best was "Lay, Lady, Lay." As I was leaving, Conchita said, "You can borrow the album."

"That's okay."

"You're welcome to."

"I don't have a CD player," I said.

"Do your roommates? You room with Dede and Sin-Jun, right?"

She really had done her research.

"Dede has a stereo," I said. "But we're not good friends."

I had my hand on the doorknob when she said, "Want to get dinner in town? The dining hall is having halibut, so I just thought if you're not busy."

If there was no formal dinner, you were allowed to leave campus, but I never did. The only time I went into town was on the weekend, when I borrowed Sin-Jun's bike and rode to the grocery store to buy toothpaste or saltines.

"We could get pizza or go to that Chinese place," Conchita said.

I'd never set foot in either restaurant. Somehow, the more time that passed without my going, the more I felt like going required an invitation; these places seemed to belong to other people, to juniors and seniors, or to rich students, or to students with friends. But here, in this moment, I'd received an invitation. Conchita liked me, I thought. She was kind. If I accepted her offer, I could do the things that other people did. "Let's get pizza," I said. "I'll go get a bike and meet you back here."

"Wait."

I turned.

"I don't have a bike," she said.

"I don't either. I'm borrowing Sin-Jun's."

She hesitated. "I mean I don't know how to ride a bike."

I blinked at her.

"I've walked before," she said. "It doesn't take that long."

Outside her dorm, we headed out the campus gates and turned onto the two-lane road. "So you just never learned?" I said, and I hoped that she couldn't tell how astonished I was. I had never heard of anyone over the age of five who didn't know how to ride a bike.

"There wasn't any special reason if that's what you're asking."

"But when you were little, didn't the kids in your neighborhood ride bikes?"

"I didn't know the other kids that well."

I thought of my own neighborhood, how gangs of children between the ages of eight and twelve would ride around, how I had done so myself. We'd go down to the park and back, and just before darkness, as the streetlights were flickering on and the hum of the cicadas was thickening, we'd pedal home, sweaty, with streaks of dirt on our faces.

"Do you wish you knew how?" I asked.

"I haven't thought about it much."

We both were quiet. Then I said, "I could teach you. At least I could try."

She did not respond immediately, but I could feel a kind of happy nervousness come over her, a tentative excitement. I couldn't see her face because we were side by side, but I sensed that she was smiling. "You don't think it's too late for me?" she asked.

"Definitely not. It's one of those things where once you know how, you can't believe you ever didn't know. It would probably only take a few days." I thought about how Conchita wouldn't want other students to see. "We could use the road behind the infirmary," I said. "We could do it in the morning, maybe, before chapel."

My first target in Assassin was Devin Billinger, a boy in my class who had, at that time, no particular significance to me. In my mailbox, I found the slip of paper with my name and his name typed on it and, attached by a paper clip, the sheet of round orange stickers. All around me, other students were finding their assignments, talking noisily. It was the beginning of sixth period, and I left the mail room to walk to the dining hall for lunch. I was just outside the stairwell leading from the basement to the first floor when, amazingly, I came face-to-face with Devin himself. Like me, he was alone. We made eye contact and did not say hi, and he turned into the stairwell.

I was still holding the assignment sheet and the stickers. I peeled off a sticker with my index finger and thumb; keeping it affixed to my fingertip. Immediately, both my hands began to shake. I entered the stairwell. "Devin," I said.

He stopped a few steps up and looked back. "Huh?"

Without saying anything. I closed the space between us. When we were standing on the same step, I reached out and placed the sticker on the upper part of his left arm.

100

"You're dead," I said, and I bit my lip, trying not to smile.

He looked at his arm as if I'd spit on it. "What the fuck is that?"

"It's for Assassin," I said. "You're my target."

"It hasn't started yet."

"Yes, it has." I held out my wrist to him, so he could read my watch: It was ten after one.

"This is bullshit." His voice was more than irritated; possibly, though I didn't know him well enough to be certain, he was furious. He glared at me and turned, as if to continue up the steps.

"Wait," I said. "You have to give me your target."

"I don't have to do anything."

We looked at each other, and I actually laughed. In theory, pissing off Devin Billinger should have unnerved me. He was one of a group of six or seven guys in our class known as bank boys—most of them were from New York and most of their dads had jobs having to do with investments and brokerage and other money-related matters I had no grasp of. (Technically, a bank boy didn't have to be from New York or have a banking father—he just had to seem as if he could.) But the reality of Devin's anger was more ridiculous than scary; he reminded me of a pouting six-year-old. "Are you planning to cheat?" I asked.

"Why are you so righteous? It's a game."

"And I'm just playing by the rules."

Devin glared at me, then shook his head. He reached into his pocket, withdrew some small crumpled bits of paper, and thrust them toward me. "Here. Are you happy?"

"Yeah, I am." I said. "Thank you."

The next morning, when we were supposed to meet for Conchita's first bike lesson, gray clouds hung overhead and thunder rumbled in the distance. I wondered whether Conchita would show up; she seemed like someone who might change her plans due to the mere intimation of bad weather.

101

But when I got to the road behind the infirmary, she was waiting, wearing a hot pink transparent rain slicker and a matching hat—a sou'wester, like what fishermen wear, except that I had difficulty imagining any fisherman in transparent pink.

I had ridden over on Sin-Jun's bike, and I slowed down, came to a stop next to Conchita, and climbed off. "Start by getting on the bike," I said.

She slung one leg over so she was straddling the crossbar, her feet planted on the ground.

"Now sit down," I said.

She eased backward.

"Put your feet on the pedals."

"Are you holding on?"

"Yeah, of course." I'd been gripping the carrier, and I moved one hand to the crossbar and one to the back of the seat. "Does that feel steadier?"

She lifted her right foot and set it on the pedal, then lifted her left foot. But the pedals had toe clips, and Conchita missed the opening and kicked the pedal so it spun several times. "Sorry," she said.

"Just try again."

The second time, she successfully inserted her foot.

"Okay," I said. "Now kind of push down. You use—I guess you use your thigh muscles."

She pushed. The right pedal went down, and the left pedal came up, and then nothing else happened.

"You keep doing it," I said. "That's what makes the bike go forward." She began pumping again. Her motions were still jerky, but they were continuous, and she was moving. I jogged along.

"I feel like I'm tilting to one side," she said.

"You sort of are. The faster you go, the smoother the ride will be."

"This is Sin-Jun's bike, right?" she said. "You must get along with her better than Dede because you didn't want to borrow Dede's stereo."

"Sin-Jun is more laid-back," I said. "Dede's okay, but she's not laid-back."

"Dede's problem is that she wants to be Aspeth Montgomery."

This observation was accurate. But it was also odd— Conchita's tone made her seem familiar with Dede, when I suspected they'd never had a conversation.

"Do you think Dede and Aspeth will room together next year?" Conchita asked. Though request forms weren't due until late May, rooming had, since spring break, become a common topic of conversation.

"I doubt it." Dede would like nothing better, I knew, but in the final hour, I didn't believe that Aspeth would agree to it.

"Imagine wanting to room with Aspeth," Conchita said. "She's so mean."

"Do you know her?"

"Oh, I've known her forever."

This didn't seem possible. Aspeth lived in my dorm, not Conchita's, and even if the two of them had been on sports teams or in classes together, Aspeth was always surrounded, literally buffered from the rest of Ault, by a group of girls like Dede. I thought of Aspeth's long pale hair, the clothes she wore—now that it was spring, pastel button-down shirts and khaki skirts and white or navy espadrilles—and her tan, shapely legs and the light sprinkling of freckles across her nose, which always made her look as if she had spent the afternoon playing tennis in the sun. Then I glanced at Conchita on the bike beside me, her glowing pink rain slicker and hat, her dark puffy hair. "I didn't realize you guys were friends," I said.

"I've known Aspeth my whole life. Our dads used to work together. I've been in her class since kindergarten."

"I thought Aspeth was from Connecticut."

"Her family only moved there a few years ago. Before that, they lived in Texas."

"So do you guys hang out much?"

Conchita turned to look at me, an expression of faint amusement on her face. "Yeah, constantly. Haven't you seen us?" Then she said, "Lee, when will you quit playing dumb with me? Aspeth and I were friends when we were little, but she stopped talking to me in fifth grade because she became too cool." Conchita sounded matter-of-fact, not resentful. I think that she accepted her status as an outsider, that perhaps she had done so even before she came to Ault, while I remained perpetually hopeful that circumstances would conspire to make me beloved.

"So what about Sin-Jun?" Conchita said. "Do you think you two will room together?"

"Maybe." I was pretty sure Sin-Jun was planning to room with plump, yappy Clara O'Hallahan. I imagined they'd let me get a triple with them, which would be better than a single, but not by much. Just as rooming with Aspeth would secure Dede's status as a bona fide popular person, rooming with Sin-Jun and Clara would signify, if only to me, that I really was one of the mild, boring, peripheral girls.

We were well past the infirmary. "Let's turn around," I said. "We can just keep going up and back."

On Wednesday, after killing Devin, I'd killed Sage Christensen (she was a sophomore on the lacrosse team), and at dinner I'd killed Allie Wray, a senior. Both exclaimed in surprise when I tagged them. but neither seemed to care particularly. "I'm so bad at these games," Allie said agreeably as she passed over her stickers and her target.

Yet I, apparently, had an aptitude for Assassin, and I found myself wondering—it was impossible not to wonder—if I had any shot at winning the whole game. What if I surprised everyone? What if all the boys (boys, definitely, were more into it) got so preoccupied killing each other that they forgot about me and I just stuck around, beneath the radar? Because, undeniably, the qualities that I usually lamented in myself— my invisibility, my watchfulness of others—now served me well. Maybe at the end there would come the unlikely inevitability of victory, like when I played hearts with my family and, every so often, shot the moon.

And even if I didn't win Assassin, I still liked the extra pulse it created in the dining hall and the schoolhouse. Some people would tell you who they had, and some people were secretive—it was like grades—and supposedly a bunch of sophomores had drawn up an enormous chart, like a family tree that circled in on itself, connecting all the players. But of course, such a chart wouldn't remain current for long, because people's status changed hourly. I also heard that Mrs. Velle, the registrar, had given out other students' class schedules to Mundy Keffler and Albert Shuman, who were seniors, but that after more people came by her office asking for schedules, she refused. Waiting in line for breakfast, I was told by Richie Secrest, another freshman, that at least half the student body had been killed in the first twenty-four hours. I wasn't surprised—both Dede and Sin-Jun had been dead by the previous evening. I was toasting my bagel when I heard Aspeth say to Cross Sugarman, "If I hear another word about that goddamn game, I'll scream."

"Yeah, because you're out already," Cross said. "Don't be a bad sport." (In such proximity to Cross, I stared at the floor, feeling clammy and unattractive from having been outside with Conchita.)

"No," Aspeth said. "Try because it's lame. And because there are enough basket cases at this school as it is."

"Sure," Cross said. "I completely believe you."

They were standing about three feet from me, and then their bagels fell down the slide to the front of the toaster, and they were gone. So Cross was still in, I thought, and that was when I had the idea: If I stayed alive, eventually the game would lead me to him. Or it would lead him to me, which would be even better. For Cross to be in possession of a piece of paper with my name on it, for him to travel around campus in search of me, to reach out and place a sticker on

105

my body—the possibility made me almost sad, almost terrified, with hope. For the first time since we'd ridden in the taxi together more than a month before, we'd be forced to talk; he'd have to acknowledge me.

Life is clearest when guided by ulterior motives; walking to chapel, I felt a sense of true purpose. I was on my way to kill McGrath Mills, a junior from Dallas whom I'd inherited from Allie Wray. I'd heard McGrath was good at lacrosse, and I thought that an athlete would probably be harder to kill—there was more of a chance he'd be into the game.

I'd decided the night before that my best bet was in the rush after morning chapel. Therefore, I'd left breakfast early, without Conchita, and I found a seat in chapel near the back. Usually I sat near the front, but I knew the back was the province of drowsy junior and senior boys and of students using chapel time to finish their homework. As the seats around me filled, I kept an eye out for McGrath. At seven fifty-eight, he took a seat two rows in front of me. While Mr. Coker, a chemistry teacher, gave a talk about how he'd developed patience by observing his grandfather during boyhood fishing trips to Wisconsin, I intently watched the back of McGrath's head.

Though you were free to leave chapel after the hymn, I usually waited until the recessional was over. On this morning, however, before the last notes of "Jerusalem" rang out, I followed McGrath toward the exit. A bottleneck had formed at the doors—this was why normally I waited—and people were pushing each other and joking around. Parker Farrell, a senior, said, "Hey, Dooley, watch your back!" and then another guy shouted, "Quit grabbing my assassin!"

Two people stood between McGrath and me, and I wormed past one, then the other. With my right hand in my pocket, I'd transferred an orange sticker from the sheet to my finger. On the threshold of the chapel, McGrath was only a few inches from me; seeing the weave of his red polo shirt up close was like seeing the pores on another person's face.

I withdrew my hand from my pocket and placed the sticker on his lower back, and I had not taken my hand away when Max Cobey, a junior standing to my left, said, "I saw that, whatever-your-name-is freshman girl, and you're so busted. Hey, Mills, look at your back."

McGrath turned toward Max, and Max pointed at me.

"She just tried to kill you," Max said.

McGrath turned around. I was looking down, blushing furiously; without raising my chin, I glanced up, and I saw that McGrath was grinning. "You?" he said.

The swarm was moving forward, and the three of us found ourselves outside, in front of the chapel.

"You're totally busted," Max said again, quite loudly, and he pointed down at me; he was several inches taller than I was. But he didn't seem hostile, as Devin had; rather, he was simply enthusiastic. A few other junior guys, friends of either Max's or McGrath's, gathered around us.

"What's your name?" McGrath said. He had a Southern accent, a slight twang, and he'd stuck the orange sticker from his shirt onto the pad of his middle finger.

"My name's Lee."

"Did you try to kill me back there, Lee?"

I darted glances at the faces of the other boys, then looked back at McGrath. "Kind of," I said, and they laughed.

"Here's what I'm gonna tell you," McGrath said. "It's okay to *try*. But it would be wrong to succeed. You got that?"

"Tell her," one of the other guys said.

"Let's recap." McGrath held up his right hand, the hand with the sticker. "Try, all right," he said. He held up his left hand. "Succeed, wrong." He shook his head. "Very, very wrong."

"I'll see if I can remember."

"Ooh," Max said. "She's feisty."

Already, I felt like I had crushes on both him and McGrath.

"All right now, Lee," McGrath said as he turned away. "I'll be watchin' you."

"Me, too," one of the other boys said, and he mimed like he was holding binoculars in front of his eyes. Then he smiled at me, before catching up with his friends. (*Simon Thomworth Allard, Hanover, New Hampshire*—that afternoon in the dorm, I studied the school catalog until I'd figured out his identity.)

I was leaving the dining hall after dinner that night, wheeling Sin-Jun's bike beside me for Conchita's next lesson, when I glanced over my shoulder and saw Edmundo Saldana, a quiet-seeming sophomore I'd never talked to. Though several students had left the dining hall just before I had, Edmundo and I were alone; I was about ten feet in front of him.

"Are you trying to kill me?" I asked.

He scowled noncommittally.

My heartbeat picked up. "If you try to, I'll yell," I said. "And they'll turn around." I gestured ahead. I was half-bluffing—probably I wouldn't yell because it would be melodramatic. But I also might, because of how much I wanted to stay in the game.

"It's all kind of stupid," Edmundo said. He mumbled his words, but I was listening intently. "I'm not that into it, you know?"

"So you *are* trying to kill me?" I couldn't believe that I'd been right—as soon as I'd asked him, I'd realized he could easily have been headed to the library.

"I don't really care," Edmundo mumbled. "You want to live, I won't kill you. I don't know why they play this." He was barely making eye contact with me, and I wondered if it was all a setup—he'd pretend not to care while inching closer, and then he'd pounce. But when I thought back to other times I'd noticed him around—Edmundo was from Phoenix, he was (I was nearly sure) on scholarship, and he and his roommate, a rich zitty white kid from Boston named Philip Ivers, supposedly did nothing but play backgammon in their room—it seemed like maybe Edmundo was always this shy and evasive. Certainly, he was an even more uncomfortable person than I was.

"If you don't care, then will you let me live?" I said. "Will you turn around? Or you just stay here, and I'll keep walking."

"It doesn't matter," Edmundo said. "You keep walking, fine."

When I told Conchita what had just happened, she said, "Edmundo has you? Edmundo Saldana?"

"Yeah, why?"

She had climbed onto the bike and was pedaling while I held on—she had definitely made progress, even in just the first lesson. "No reason, really," she said. "I'm in MSA with him." MSA stood for Minority Student Alliance, and I knew practically nothing about the group, except that it met on Sunday nights.

"You don't have a crush on him, do you?" I asked.

"On Edmundo? Are you for real?"

"You just got kind of excited when I mentioned him."

"I don't believe in crushes," Conchita said. "What's the point?"

The question was unanswerable. What was the point of being a person, what was the point of breathing air?

"Don't tell me you have a crush on someone," she said. She glanced at me, inadvertently turning her arms as she twisted her neck. The bike swerved to the left, and she quickly faced straight ahead again. "Who?" she said. "I won't tell. I promise."

"I'm not telling someone who thinks all crushes are pointless." In fact, I had never talked about Cross with anyone. I had not even said his name aloud since surprise holiday. But I had thought of him so often that sometimes when I saw him, it was weird—real Cross, moving-around Cross, Cross talking to his friends. *He* was the person I always thought of?

Part of the reason I hadn't talked about him was that it preserved his specialness, but another part was that I'd never

109

before had an eager ear. "You really can't tell anyone," I said. "I'm serious."

"I would think you'd know you can trust me," Conchita said, and she sounded hurt.

"It's Cross," I said. "On surprise holiday—"

"Cross? You like *Cross*?"

"Conchita, do you want me to tell you this or not?"

"Sorry."

"So it was surprise holiday," I continued, "and we ended up in a—what's so wrong with liking Cross? Do you even know him?" I was strongly reminding myself of someone, but it took a few seconds to figure out that the someone was Dede.

"He's in my math class," Conchita said. "He seems okay, but I'd imagine you liking someone more like—maybe like Ian Schulman."

"I don't even know who that is."

"He's a sophomore who's really good at art. He draws comic strips and stuff. And he wears black Converse sneakers."

"Are you sure that you don't like him?"

"I don't have time to," Conchita said. "Seeing as Edmundo and I are passionately in love."

In spite of myself, I laughed.

"So go on," she said. "It was surprise holiday and then what?"

After I'd told her—the mall, the taxi, Cross stroking my hair—she said, "Did he kiss you?"

"John and Martin totally would have seen that," I said, and as I felt myself implying that circumstances had prevented our kissing, I thought maybe this was why you told stories to other people—for how their possibilities enlarged in the retelling.

"Wait a second," Conchita said. "Cross has a girlfriend."

"He wasn't cheating," I said, and we were turning around—already, I had lost count of how many times

110

Conchita had ridden up and down the road—so it was possible for her to fix her gaze on me without fear of tilting. "He really wasn't," I said. "Kissing is cheating. Sitting next to someone in a taxi isn't."

"Would you feel that way if you were Sophie Thruler?"

She had turned the bike around completely and was facing north again. "Go," I said. "Start pedaling." The truth was that I rarely thought of Sophie. She was beautiful, she was a junior, and Cross may have been her boyfriend, but he could not possibly matter to her as he mattered to me. If they broke up, I suspected she'd be dating some other guy within a week. But I didn't even want them to break up—if Cross wasn't going out with anyone, there'd be danger present in the glance of every other girl, in their proximity to him in chapel, their laughter during conversations. As long as he was off-limits to me, he was off-limits to the rest of the female population, too. "Never mind about Sophie," I told Conchita. "The point is that now I'm hoping I'll get Cross or he'll get me for Assassin."

"I thought you can't control who you get."

"True, but the game is getting exponentially smaller." I had the fleeting thought that I might be using the word *exponentially* wrong and also that, in front of Conchita, it was okay; she was not judgmental. "The more people I kill, the better my chances of getting to him."

"You're assuming he won't get killed by someone else."

"I think he's watching out. Anyway, aren't you impressed by how I'm using Assassin as a means to an end? I'm being Machiavellian." In the fall, all freshmen had read *The Prince*.

"Mr. Brewster would be proud," Conchita said. "And just think if you marry Cross—maybe he'll give you extra credit."

I looked at her, and she was smiling. And we both were sweating from the activity of the bike. and I could feel then how I had capitulated to Conchita. We were friends. She must have felt the same thing. because she said, "There's something I want to ask you."

I knew what she would say. But I feigned oblivion. "What?"

"I was thinking maybe we could room together next year."

I could picture it easily. In fact, I already had: Our room would have ruffly pink curtains, and I would eat all her food, and we'd listen to Bob Dylan while we studied. It wasn't the worst scenario imaginable, but it made me uneasy. There was what we already had in common—our dorkiness, our scholarships—and also what we might grow to have in common. (I feared my own malleability.) I saw us staying in the dorm on Saturday nights, donning our pajamas early, ordering Chinese food, throwing water balloons at each other—spazzing out. And I wasn't sure I wanted to spazz out. I wanted to have boyfriends, I wanted my life to be sorrowful and complicated and unwholesome, at least a little unwholesome. "Wow," I said. "I hadn't thought about it. I'd have to check on some stuff before I could say for sure."

"Stuff with Sin-Jun?"

I nodded. "What about Martha Porter?" I said. "Aren't you guys pretty good friends?"

"Martha is great. But her roommate, Elizabeth, was bulimic, and she didn't come back after Christmas. Martha said she's gotten so used to having a single she'll probably request one again for next year."

So other people shared my ambivalence about rooming with Conchita; I wasn't surprised.

"Just let me know," Conchita said. "The forms still aren't due for a while. And in the meantime, my mom is coming to Boston this weekend, and I wanted to invite you to lunch with us on Saturday. I invited Martha, too."

Oddly enough, given that it was less than an hour away, I had never actually been to Boston—I'd only passed through the city on the way to and from the airport, riding on an Ault bus. But now, when people back home asked how I liked it, I'd be able to give a real answer.

"I've told my mom all about you," Conchita said, and I

112

couldn't help wondering why Conchita was such a fan of mine, especially when no one else was. How had I charmed her so effortlessly, or less than effortlessly—unwillingly even? Had it been my lack of interest, was the explanation really that simple and obvious?

"I'll try to live up to her expectations," I said.

Killing time in the room before curfew—Sin-Jun wasn't there, and Dede was napping, which probably meant she was planning to stay up late studying for a test—I caught sight of my reflection in the mirror over Dede's bureau, and it struck me suddenly that I didn't look like someone who could win a schoolwide game. I wasn't sure what such a person looked like—just not like me. I had wavy brown hair and thin lips and thick eyebrows (not man-thick but thick for a girl) and I knew I had an overly intense stare. "What are you looking at me for?" my mother would say when she was driving, or, at the kitchen table, "What? Is something in my teeth?" Sometimes I could even feel myself doing it, inspecting another person's face when we were close together, but it was hard to stop—where else was I supposed to set my eyes? It was even weirder if you never looked at the other person at all.

I stepped closer to Dede's mirror and peered at my skin, inspecting it for potential breakouts. I had turned my head and was scrutinizing the left side of my jaw when Dede said, in a muffled voice, "What are you doing?"

"Nothing."

"If I don't finish Latin," she said, "it'll be all watery."

"You're asleep, Dede," I said. "Go back to sleep."

At curfew, Sin-Jun and I stood in front of the kitchenette eating raw cookie dough. By the time everyone had checked in and announcements were finished, we were two thirds through the package, and I was beginning to feel sick. Amy Dennaker approached the refrigerator, took out a Diet Coke, and, while not looking at me, said, "McGrath thought it was

113

really funny how you tried to kill him in chapel today. He's so cocky."

There was something uncharacteristically conversational, almost friendly, in Amy's tone. "Did you know his room is right below Alexis and Heidi's?" she added, and I could tell because of how her voice had a bubble of happiness in it: Amy had a crush on McGrath.

I passed the cookie dough back to Sin-Jun, and she hesitated. "Maybe I'm not eating no more."

Amy was watching us.

"Did you want some?" I asked and, even though it was Sin-Jun's, I held out the package.

Amy dug out some dough with her middle finger and forefinger, and it struck me—I had never considered it one way or the other—that she was probably a person who did not wash her hands after going to the bathroom. "I'm on your side," Amy said. "I say bring McGrath down."

So then she'd have something to tease him about, I thought. I wasn't unsympathetic—I understood machinations, the need for an excuse.

"The problem is that his friends will be like bodyguards now," I said.

"True." Amy nodded.

"Maybe you crawling through his window while he sleeps," Sin-Jun said. "At night he has no bodyguard."

I laughed, and then my eyes met Amy's. "I'd be breaking visitation," I said. "I'd have to go before the disciplinary committee."

"You shouldn't go *in* there—" she began, and then I knew, I said, "Oh, like send down a threat? Or dangle something?"

"Yeah, just make him nervous."

"I know what," Sin-Jun said brightly. "We use fishing pole!"

"Where the hell would we find a fishing pole?" Though Amy sounded scornful, I reminded myself that she was talking to us of her own volition.

"There is some in basement," Sin-Jun said. "I have seen in storage."

"I know what you're talking about," I said. "Back by that metal locker." The basement ran beneath several dorms, creating a through-way rumored to be used by students who made illicit night visits to members of the opposite sex. "But we can't go down there after curfew," I said.

"We ask Madame," Sin-Jun suggested.

"Ask her?" Amy said.

"It can't hurt to try," I said.

When we knocked on the door to Madame Broussard's apartment, she answered quickly. Neither Amy nor Sin-Jun said anything, and I realized I was the leader by default. "Hi," I said. "We have a question. This is kind of weird, but you know Assassin? And you know McGrath Mills? He's my target, and we want to make him feel scared. Just as a joke. So I know it's after ten, but we're hoping—"

"We need to go down to the basement and get a fishing pole," Amy said. "For two minutes. Can we?"

"For what reason do you need a fishing pole?" Madame asked. Overall, she seemed far less surprised by our appearance at her door than I'd have anticipated.

"We want to send something down to McGrath's room, like a note," I said. "He lives underneath Heidi and Alexis. But we'll be quiet, and we won't take very long."

"But if you do such a thing"—Madame began, and I thought she was going to say, *you will violate curfew*. What she said instead was—"McGrath will know he is your target."

"No, he knows already," I said. "I tried to kill him when we were leaving chapel, and a bunch of his friends saw me."

"These were other junior boys?" It was astonishing—Madame seemed genuinely interested.

"Yeah," I said. "Mostly guys from his lacrosse team."

"Well." Madame nodded her head once, decisively. "I think we teach these boys a lesson."

And then all three of us, Amy, Sin-Jun, and I, were following her out of the common room and down the basement steps, and it turned out the fishing poles weren't where we remembered, and we paused, momentarily stumped, and then I said, "We don't *need* a fishing pole. We could just use a broom or something," and we were climbing the stairs and crowding around the common room closet, then hurrying down the hall to Heidi's and Alexis's room and as we explained the idea again, this time with Madame joining in, their expressions shifted from confusion to amusement to enthusiasm, enthusiasm that seemed as abrupt and as weirdly sincere as our own.

"You know what you should use is a pillowcase," Heidi said. "Then you can write really big." She rummaged in her laundry bag, and this seems distinctly Aultish to me now, the casual sacrifice of a pillowcase in the service of a joke. There was so little attention paid to the fact that pillowcases, like everything else, cost money. Heidi tossed it to me, and Alexis passed over a black marker.

With the cap off, I paused. "What am I writing?"

All of us were silent, a loaded, electric silence. "I know where you live," Alexis suggested.

"I see you when you're sleeping," Heidi said.

"I smell your blood," Amy said. "And it smells"—she glanced at Madame—"*très délicieuse*."

"We will not bring the French into this," Madame said.

"So far, I like 'I see you when you're sleeping' the best." I said. "But does that sound too Santa Clausy?"

"I am always watching," Sin-Jun said.

We looked at one another, the six of us—it felt, with this number of people, not unlike a meeting convened to make a serious decision—and as Heidi and Amy nodded, I said, "That's good. It's simple but creepy."

Amy moved several books off a desk so we could spread the pillowcase flat. Then I wrote, in capital letters, *I'M ALWAYS WATCHING*.

"Draw an eyeball," Heidi said.

I made the almond shape, the iris and the pupil, the lashes on both the bottom and the top.

"You must sign it as well," Madame said.

I hesitated. "With my name? Or no, what about—" I wrote, *Love, your assassin*, and Sin-Jun clapped. "It is perfect."

When we taped the pillowcase to the broomstick, it was obvious that it would work better with two poles; Alexis ran off and returned with a mop. Heidi lifted the screen and Amy and I—I knew she wanted to be directly involved in the dangling, I could feel how focused she was on McGrath—stuck our upper bodies out into the night. I was holding the broom upside down, clutching the neck of it near the bristles, and she was holding the mop. Light emanated from the window below us, which meant their shades weren't down. Leaning over, Amy knocked the mop handle against the brick exterior of the building. "Yoo-hoo," she called. "Special delivery, boys."

Ten seconds passed. I felt a rising worry that neither McGrath nor his roommate, Spencer, would notice, and my apprehension was not even really for them but for us in the room, how our plan would have come to nothing. And then I heard shuffling down below, a few male voices. "Hey, Mills," someone called, and a few seconds later, unmistakably, there was the sound of McGrath's laughter. He poked his head out a window one over and twisted around, looking up at us.

"Hey, baby," Amy called. (I would never, ever have said *Hey, baby* to Cross Sugarman.)

"Hi, McGrath," I said.

"What the hell is going on out here?" McGrath said. "Y'all are crazy."

Another guy stuck his head out and said—not to us but to someone back in the room—"This is hard-core." Behind me, Alexis and Heidi and Sin-Jun and Madame crowded close. Heidi opened the other window, and after a moment she also was hanging outside the building.

Then a third person—there seemed to be a group in the

guys' room, too, at least three or four of them—reached out and grabbed the pillowcase.

"Hey!" Amy said. "No touching!"

"That's not what you tell most guys, Dennaker," said the guy grabbing the pillowcase; it was Max Cobey.

"Bite me," Amy replied.

"Who else is down there?" Heidi asked.

"Who else is up there?" Max said. "It sounds like a herd of elephants."

"As a matter of fact, it's a bunch of incredibly hot women wearing nothing but G-strings and lipstick," Amy said. "And for only ninety-nine cents a minute, you can call up and talk to anyone of us. Operators are standing—"

"That is enough for now, Amy," I heard Madame say, and I was half-relieved and half-disappointed. "We will leave the boys alone."

"We gotta go," Amy called down. "Farewell, so long, auf Wiedersehen, good-bye."

We began pulling up the mop and broomstick, and McGrath, who had disappeared into the room, stuck his head back out. "I don't get to keep it?" he said. "After all that harassment?"

"You can keep it," I said, as if it were my pillowcase to give away. "But only if you promise to use it tonight."

"I'm gonna use it *every* night," McGrath said, and that was the last I heard before I was back in the room and the night was outside again.

On Friday morning after Latin class, as we were collecting our books, I said to Martha, "You're going tomorrow, right? With Conchita?" Martha and I had hardly spoken before, and initiating conversation made my heart pound. But it would be weird to ride into Boston together, never really having talked, when we'd spent the last seven months sitting side by side in Latin. Especially when I had the feeling that the reason we'd scarcely talked was because of me—on the very first day

118

of class, when I was so terrified to be at Ault that I could barely make eye contact with people, Martha had said, "I've never taken Latin. Have you?" and I had said, "No," looked away, and folded my arms. A few months later, Tab Kinkead had farted while standing at the chalkboard translating the sentence *Sextus is a neighbor of Claudia*; most people hadn't heard, but when I'd seen Martha try without success to stifle her laughter, I'd known for sure that I'd made a mistake—she was someone I could have been friends with.

In the hallway, Martha was saying, "Conchita's mom is super-nice."

"Do you know where we're eating?" I asked. Logistical questions were, in my opinion, the best questions of all; they were the most innocuous.

"We're meeting at Mrs. Maxwell's hotel, so we'll probably go somewhere around there," Martha said. "You're on the lacrosse team with Conchita, aren't you? She really likes you."

I could feel what I was supposed to say in response— *Conchita's great*, or *I really like her, too*—but I just couldn't form the words. Martha's remark made her seem, not in a bad way, like a camp counselor: generous and encouraging, happy to see people getting along.

"What sport are you doing?" I asked.

"Crew, and actually I'm pretty sure this'll be my only free Saturday for the whole spring, so I'm glad to be going somewhere."

"Is crew as intense as everyone says?"

"It's beautiful to watch, but when you're in the boat, you're basically grunting and sweating the whole time."

"Whenever I see people rowing, I always think of Jonas Ault in, like, 1880," I said. "I can picture him wearing one of those unitard things and sporting a handlebar mustache."

Martha laughed. Later, one of our jokes was that she was an easy laugh, a laugh slut. But something I always appreciated about her was how she made you feel witty. "Oh, yes," she said, adopting an affected tone. "Crew is very civilized."

119

"A sport for gentlemen," I said, and I wondered why I'd never spoken to Martha before.

I knew from the list posted outside Dean Fletcher's office that McGrath was a server at Ms. Prosek's table this week, and it was this knowledge that had helped me, as I'd lain awake around four o'clock in the morning, formulate a plan to kill him. Like all servers, McGrath would arrive to set the table twenty minutes before formal dinner started. When he did, I decided (and it was a decision so thrilling, an idea so perfect, that after it came to me, I did not fall asleep again before my alarm clock beeped at six-thirty), I'd be waiting beneath that table to place the sticker on his leg.

After lacrosse practice, I rushed to the dining hall and arrived by five-thirty, ten minutes before McGrath was due. Only five or six students were in the dining hall, including that night's dining hall prefect, a senior named Oli Kehlmeier. (Being one of the three dining hall prefects was actually desirable—they oversaw the waiters at formal dinner, which meant they could boss around the younger boys and flirt with the girls.) Oli was busy spreading white cloths on the tables—it surprised me to see a dining hall prefect in fact working—and I decided to take a cloth myself from the stack near the doors to the kitchen.

I smoothed the cloth over Ms. Prosek's table, then scanned the dining hall. No one was paying attention to me. I moved a chair out of the way, crouched, crawled under the table, and pulled the chair in. I was sitting with my heels pressed to my rear end, my knees forward, but that quickly became uncomfortable, and I switched to sitting Indian-style. There wasn't much room to maneuver. My elbow knocked a chair, and I froze, but I heard nothing from the outside—no proclamation of poltergeist, no face appearing at the level of my own to ask what the hell I was doing—and I relaxed again. A few old-looking globs of gum were stuck to the unfinished underside of the table, I noticed, and I could smell both the table and the floor, though neither of them smelled particularly like wood; they smelled more like shoes, like not-so-dirty running shoes, or a child's flip-flops.

At twenty of six, I tensed, anticipating McGrath. As more and more servers arrived, I felt certain that every set of approaching footsteps was his. All the tables around Ms. Prosek's appeared occupied, and surely, I thought, they would see me, surely they'd notice the pale blue fabric of my skirt (was it gross that I was sitting on the floor in my skirt?), or see my sandaled foot. But no one approached. At the table to the right of mine, the server, I could tell by her voice, was Clara O'Hallahan, and she was singing to herself; she was singing the Jim Croce song "I Got a Name." A little later, I heard a boy say. "Reed was in a bad mood today, huh?" and a girl said, "No worse than usual." I waited to hear someone mention Assassin, but no one did. Eventually, the voices all became a blended, increasingly noisy hum, punctuated by the clinking of silverware and glasses. It was ten of six. McGrath wouldn't dare miss formal dinner when he was serving. I thought, or would he? Just for skipping, you got table wipes, but if you were the server, I was pretty sure you got detention.

He arrived at four of six; well before he'd gotten to the table, I heard his cheerful drawl. Someone must have remarked on his lateness because he was saying, as he came closer, "It's the two-minute method. Watch and learn." Above my head, he set down what sounded like plates, then silverware. Before I could stick him, he'd left again, and he returned with a tray of glasses. His calves were mere inches from me— he was wearing khaki shorts, his leg hair was blond and thick—and he was whistling.

There were two entirely discrete feelings I had at this moment. The first was a disbelieving glee that I was really about to kill McGrath Mills. When you are accustomed to denial and failure, as maybe I was or maybe I only believed myself to be, success can feel disorienting, it can give you pause. Sometimes I found myself narrating such succcess, at

121

least in my own head, in order to convince myself of its reality. And not just with major triumphs (of course whether I'd ever experienced a major triumph, apart from getting into Ault in the first place, was debatable) but with tiny ones, with anything I'd been waiting for and anticipating: *I am now eating pizza, I am now getting out of the car.* (And later: *I am kissing this boy, he is lying on top of me.*) I did this because it struck me as so hard to believe I was really getting what I wanted; it was always easier to feel the lack of the thing than the thing itself.

The second feeling I had at this moment was a sad feeling, an abrupt slackness. I think it was McGrath's leg hair. Also, his whistling. McGrath was a person. He didn't want to be killed, he didn't know I was waiting underneath the table. And it seemed so unfair to catch him by surprise. I didn't want to win the whole game, I knew suddenly. I wanted admiration, of course, schoolwide recognition, but I couldn't possibly get through all the little moments it would require, just me and the person I was supposed to kill. With Devin, it had been okay because he'd been such a jerk, and with Sage and Allie, because it hadn't mattered to them if they remained in the game or not. But McGrath was nice, and he seemed to care at least a little about staying alive, and yet it would have been ridiculous for me not to take him out, with the opportunity quite literally in front of me. And it wasn't even that I entirely *didn't* want to. It was just that it seemed complicated. From now on, I thought, I'd do whatever was necessary to get to Cross. But I wouldn't be zealous, I wouldn't think the game itself actually mattered. This was the decision I was making as I extended my arm and placed the sticker on McGrath's calf—I placed it just to the side of his tibia bone, almost exactly halfway between his ankle and knee. Then I pushed out the chair in front of me and emerged from beneath the table on my hands and knees. Looking up at McGrath from that position, I couldn't help feeling a little like a dog.

His expression, as I'd feared, was one of naked surprise. I

am not even sure he recognized me immediately. I stood, and said, uncertainly, "I just killed you,' and though McGrath broke out laughing, I think it was only because he was a good sport.

"Oh, boy,' he said in his Southern accent. "You nailed me. Man, did you get me good. How long were you under there?"

I shrugged.

"That's a well-deserved win. Hey, Coles, look who was under my table. I know, she was stakin' me out!" McGrath turned back to me.

"Sorry," I said.

"Don't be sorry. What are you sorry for? You got me fair and square. I gotta give you my stickers, right? But you know what?" He felt in the back pocket of his shorts, and in the pockets on both sides of his blazer. "I left 'em in my room," he said. "Can I give 'em to you later? I'll come up to your dorm and do a hand-delivery."

"That's fine," I said. "Anything's fine." (Of course he didn't have his stickers. The game didn't *really* matter to him.)

I knew right away that I had ruined it. Whatever jokiness had existed between us—I had killed the substance of it. McGrath would be friendly to me from now on (and I was right in thinking that, he always was friendly, for the year-plus that remained before he graduated from Ault) but the friendliness would be hollow. In killing him, I had ended the only overlap between our lives. "Assassinate anyone lately?" he would ask, months later, when we passed each other, just the two of us in a corridor of the third floor between fifth and sixth periods. Or, "How are your pillowcases holdin' up?" I might laugh, or say, "They're okay"—something short. McGrath didn't want to talk, of course, it wasn't as if we had anything to say to each other. I knew all this, I understood the rules, but still, nothing broke my heart like the slow death of a shared joke that had once seemed genuinely funny.

* * *

123

On Saturday morning, I waited outside the dorm courtyard; Conchita had said her mother would send a car to pick us up at eleven. It was seventy degrees, sunny and breezy, and I thought of how Martha had said she was glad to be going somewhere; I was glad, too. I could see a black limousine across the circle, and on the circle itself, two boys tossed a softball. I tilted my face toward the sky and closed my eyes. When I opened them again, perhaps a minute later, the limousine was in front of me, and Conchita's head was poking through an open window in the back. "Hey, Lee," she called. "Climb aboard."

As I approached the car, I tried to arrange my face in an unsurprised expression. I had never ridden in a limousine. Inside, seats of gray leather lined the sides and rear of the car; a darkened window divided the back from where the driver sat in front. Conchita, I saw, was wearing a purple T-shirt, a denim jumper with oversized orange buttons, white tights, and high-heeled, open-toed straw sandals; she looked less like a member of a theater troupe than like a four-year-old permitted for the first time to dress herself. Martha was dressed normally and wasn't, to my relief, wearing a skirt.

"We're trying to decide what music to listen to," Conchita said. "The only stations that come in very well are reggae and—what did you call it, Martha?"

"Gentle jazz," Martha said.

"I vote for reggae," I said.

"We thought that's what you'd say, but we wanted to make sure." Conchita pushed a button, and the window between us and the driver came down a few inches. "Will you set it to the first station?" she said. "Thanks." Without waiting for a response, she pressed the button, and the window rose. Then I knew, I finally understood, that Conchita was rich. And understanding this confused everything else I knew about her. Why did she need to act weird? Why did she mention her Mexicanness so often, why did she talk about feeling like an outsider? If she was rich, she belonged at Ault. The equation

124

was that simple. Being rich, in the end, counted for the most—for more, even, than being pretty. And yet, as I thought about it, it wasn't that Conchita had ever hidden anything from me. Her elaborately decorated room, even her wardrobe, which was peculiar but not cheap-looking—these had been signs to which I'd turned a blind eye. My assumption that she was a scholarship student was, I realized, offensive; it was embarrassing. (It was embarrassing and yet—and yet now, knowing I'd been wrong, I was free to room with her. I could give in, it would be okay. Thinking this felt the way peeing in your pants does when you're five or six: a complicated relief, one best ignored in the present moment.)

"Okay, listen to this," she was saying. "I've been waiting to tell you guys until I was with both of you at the same time—I heard that Mr. Byden used to date Madame Broussard."

"No way," Martha said.

"Mr. Byden the headmaster?" I said. "But he's married."

"It was a long time ago," Conchita said, "but what if he still carries a torch for Madame?"

"How do you know this?" I asked.

"Aspeth told me. Her dad and Mr. Byden went to Harvard together in the sixties, and I guess Madame was living in Boston then."

"Imagine kissing Mr. Byden," I said. "He'd make you keep three feet on the floor." This was the rule for visitation; also, the couple was supposed to leave the door open. "And what's really gross," I added, "is think about Mr. Byden having a boner."

"*Lee*," Conchita said, and it occurred to me that I might have genuinely offended her.

"An erection," I said. "Whatever."

"*Stop* it." She covered her ears with her hands.

"They probably had pet names for each other," Martha said.

"Shnookums," I suggested.

"Apple dumpling," Martha replied.

"Cheese pie," I said, and for no real reason, both of us convulsed with laughter.

"What?" Conchita said. It wasn't that she hadn't heard— by then she'd uncovered her ears.

"It's not—" I began, and then I made eye contact with Martha and started laughing again.

"What?" Conchita was looking between us. "What does cheese pie mean?"

Martha wiped a tear from her eye. "It doesn't mean anything," she said. "Lee just made it up."

"Then why is it so funny?"

"Well—" Martha struggled to remain composed. "It's just like, *cheese pie*?"

"Apple dumpling," I repeated, and both of us began snorting.

"Martha let a boy touch her boobs," Conchita said.

"Thanks, Conchita." Martha appeared unperturbed.

"I would never do that," Conchita said. "At least not before I'm married and then I'm only having sex in the dark."

"Yeah, right," Martha said, and her tone was affectionate.

"Have *you* had sex?" I asked her, and as soon as I'd said it, I felt myself clutch. Really, I hardly knew her; I had forgotten how little I knew her.

"God, no," Martha said. "My mom would kill me." She didn't seem to have found the question intrusive. "Conchita, when a guy goes up your shirt, it's just skin," Martha said. "It feels kind of good."

"Would you let a guy touch your boobs, Lee?" Conchita asked.

"It would depend on the guy." I thought of the song "Lay, Lady, Lay," the man in dirty clothes.

"I'm really surprised," Conchita said. "I didn't realize that you were promiscuous, too."

For the third time. Martha and I burst out laughing.

"I wish I was promiscuous," I said.

"Don't say that." Conchita looked stricken.

"I'm kidding," I said, and she looked relieved, and then I couldn't resist saying, "Sort of," and she looked stricken again. "Oh, Conchita," I said, and I moved over to her seat and put one arm around her shoulders and rocked her back and forth a little. She seemed young to me in this moment, and very charming. We'd gotten onto Route 128 by then, and there was something about the speed of the car, something about the car being a limousine, something about the sunshine and the conversation—I was happy for real. The sense I always had at Ault that what I had to offer was inadequate, that I needed to be on guard, was drifting away, rushing out the open sunroof.

The hotel was near the Boston Common; it was the fanciest hotel I'd ever been inside, but by then, this fact did not surprise me. Corinthian columns flanked the lobby, and green marble lined the floor and ceilings. Conchita approached the concierge's desk to ask where the restaurant was, and Martha and I followed her, all of us still giddy from the ride, and I could feel that the hotel staff and other guests in the lobby were looking at us and that we were three girls to them, we were ordinary, and in this moment, our ordinariness was not a bad thing. On the contrary—in being underdressed and a little loud, in traveling in a pack, we were fulfilling their idea of teenagers, and I felt proud of us.

In the dining room, Conchita cried out, "Mama!" and hurled herself into the arms of a woman who was both very pretty and very fat. Mrs. Maxwell kissed Conchita all over her cheeks and chin, and then they both were crying and speaking to each other in Spanish and turning to us to apologize for crying. Mrs. Maxwell was seated and did not rise to greet us, though she did extend her arm. It was tan, and many gold bracelets hung from her wrist. "I am delighted to meet my daughter's friends," she said. When Conchita introduced me, Mrs. Maxwell said, "Ah, the Bob Dylan fan." She wore loose pale green silk pants and a shirt of the same fabric, with a plain neck and wide sleeves; even from several feet away, I could smell her perfume. Her skin was smooth and brown, darker than Conchita's, and her dark hair was pulled into a loose bun.

"Thank you for having us to lunch," Martha said, and I said, "Yeah, it's really nice of you."

In the whole dining room, only a few tables besides ours were occupied; near us, a beefy man sat by himself. A waiter brought us menus, tall leather rectangles with the descriptions of the food written in calligraphy. Only one of the entrees was under twenty dollars and it was grilled vegetables. It was oddly liberating to realize I had only fifteen dollars in my pocket—I wouldn't be paying, I wouldn't even try, because I couldn't. The bottom of the menu featured the date, and when I realized they must have printed a new menu daily, the idea seemed remarkable. I had suspected before, and the whole day only reinforced the suspicion, that money could make your life nice, that you could want it not for reasons of greed but for reasons of comfort, because it allowed you to send for your daughter and her friends in a limousine, to eat food that tasted good in a pretty setting, to be heavy and still wear nice clothes. One of my mother's friends was about as fat as Mrs. Maxwell, but she wore sweat-pants and flowered smocks.

Mrs. Maxwell said, "I would like each of you to tell me your life story. Lee, you will go first."

I laughed. But then I did it—I started with my mother going into labor in a swimming pool, told about how in kindergarten I'd insisted on wearing the same pair of brown rubber cowboy boots for the entire year, how I'd had an imaginary friend named Pig, what ages I'd been when my brothers were born. I got all the way up to Ault. They asked questions, but not cornering questions, and then our appetizers came—we'd all ordered appetizers, it had seemed to be expected—and then Martha told her story: how she'd thought she was dying when she lost her first tooth, how she'd won the spelling bee in second grade, all the snow

128

days she'd had growing up in Vermont. The main courses arrived, and mine was roast chicken with mashed potatoes and cranberry relish; it felt like Thanksgiving.

We had dessert, too, all of us ordering different tortes and mousses and sticking our forks and spoons into each other's food. Conchita's mother was talking about things at home, people they knew, a wedding she and Conchita's father had attended the previous weekend. "And here is a funny story for you, *mi hija*," she said. "'We have hired a new worker to help Miguel in the garden, and his name is Burro."

"That's his nickname or his real name?" Conchita said, and I caught Martha's eye. *A new worker to help Miguel in the garden?* we repeated to each other.

We all had coffee, even me, though I never drank coffee at school, and then we kept talking, and another hour had passed, and it was the time we'd arranged for the limo driver to retrieve Martha and me; Conchita would stay overnight at the hotel with her mother. We stood and hugged Mrs. Maxwell before we left. Smashed against her enormous breasts, inhaling her perfume, I felt a kind of love for her; how lucky I was to have stumbled into this world.

In the limousine, as soon as the driver shut our door, Martha and I turned to each other. "Isn't Mrs. Maxwell cool?" Martha said.

"It's like she actually really wanted to know about our lives."

"I'm so full right now. The lime mousse was incredible."

"And that chocolate thing—if I'd eaten another bite; I'd have had to unbutton my pants."

"How about the bodyguard?" Martha said. "That was wild."

"What do you mean?"

"That guy at the next table. With the earpiece."

I hadn't noticed an earpiece, but it was true that the man

had stayed as long as we had; I'd imagined that he'd stayed because he was entertained by our conversation. "Why does Conchita's mom need a bodyguard?" I asked.

"I don't know if she *needs* a bodyguard, but she definitely has one. Do you not know who the Maxwells are?"

I shook my head.

"Conchita's dad is the CEO of Tanico."

There was a Tanico station three blocks from my parents' house in South Bend—long before we'd met, apparently, a piece of Conchita's life had touched a piece of mine.

"There's tons of stories about the Maxwells," Martha said. "Starting with, I guess her parents' marriage was a big scandal. Her mom had been the cleaning lady in her dad's office. That's how they met."

"No way."

"Yep. He was married at the time to another woman. Conchita's mom was, like, nineteen, and she'd just emigrated from Mexico and hardly spoke English. This was big news back in the early seventies—when I mentioned Conchita to my parents the first time, they were like, 'Not the daughter of Ernie Maxwell?' "

"Why? What's her dad like?"

"There was a profile of him recently in *Fortune*. It used to be in the library until someone took it. But, apparently, his nickname is the Oil King. He comes from this family that's been in the business for a while and they'd already made a lot of money, but he's supposed to be ruthless and really successful. He's really old, too. In the pictures in the magazine, he looks at least seventy, and he's short and bald. He and Conchita actually look alike. Plus, he was wearing orange leg warmers."

"Really?"

Martha laughed. "No, Lee. He was wearing a suit."

"I've never heard Conchita talk about any of this."

"She says stuff sometimes, but she plays it down. I think

that's why she came to Ault, to try to fit in. But it hasn't been exactly like she imagined."

Again, I felt the impatience with Conchita I'd felt when I'd seen the limosine. She could fit in if she wanted to.

"She misses her mom a lot," Martha was saying. "No one here coddles her, which is probably the reason for all her hypochondria."

"She's a hypochondriac?"

"Well, she definitely doesn't have insomnia—my room is right next to hers, and she snores like a trucker. I'm not saying she lies, though. Her reality is different from other people's, but that's why I get a kick out of her."

"If she doesn't have health problems. how come they let her have the phone and the big room and all that stuff?"

"Lee," Martha said. "Come on." She held out one hand and rubbed her thumb up and down against the other fingers. "Ault is probably salivating at the thought of all the science wings and art studios the Maxwells can build."

At the time, it surprised me how openly Martha referred to the Maxwells' money. and later, when I went to Martha's family's house in Vermont the first time, I could see that they, too, clearly were wealthy. But there were different kinds of rich, I eventually realized. There was normal rich, dignified rich, which you didn't talk about, and then there was extreme, comical, unsubtle rich—like having your dorm room professionally decorated, or riding a limousine into Boston to meet your mother—and that was permissible to discuss.

"Would you ever room with Conchita?" I asked.

Martha made a grimace—not a disgusted grimace, but a guilty one. "She's mentioned it to me, but it's kind of hard to imagine."

I glanced out the window; there was a taxi in the lane beside us. When I looked back at Martha, I said, "This might sound really weird, but can you imagine us rooming together?"

"Oh my God! I've been thinking that the whole day."

131

Martha was grinning, and so was I, and it was only partly because I wouldn't have to room with Conchita after all. It was also because I knew right away, there in the limo that the Maxwells were paying for: From then on, as long as I was at Ault, I would never be alone. Martha and I would get along, our friendship would last. I felt certainty and relief. Years later, I heard a minister at a wedding describe marriage as cutting sorrow in half and doubling joy, and what I thought of was not the guy I was seeing then, nor even of some perfect, imaginary husband I might meet later; I thought immediately of Martha.

That night, back on campus, I passed Edmundo in the courtyard outside our dorms with his roommate Philip. "Hi, Edmundo," I said. "Hi, Philip." I tried to sound confident and in control—I didn't want them pulling some trick like Matt Relman and his roommate Jasdip Choudhury had, where Jasdip had shut his eyes while Matt killed Laura Bice.

"Hi," Edmundo said, once again barely making eye contact.

His shyness emboldened me. "It's a nice night, isn't it?" I said.

"I don't have you anymore," he said. "I got killed a few days ago."

"By who?" My pulse was racing. I'd been walking around obliviously, when I could have been eliminated—when my chances of getting to Cross could have been eliminated—at any moment by a person who wasn't Edmundo.

"I can't tell you," Edmundo said, and if he had smiled at all, I'd have believed I could charm it out of him (weren't shy, awkward boys just waiting to be cajoled by high-spirited girls?), but his tone and expression were serious. In fact, it didn't seem like he particularly wanted to be talking to me at all. And I could feel from Philip a similar lack of interest, an impatience even. Was my status so low that even true and official nerds eschewed my company?

"Why can't you tell me?" I said.

"Because." Edmundo shrugged.

The three of us stood there, me looking between them, neither of them looking at me. Philip's skin was truly horrible, covered, especially on his chin, by both scabs and white-capped pustules. If my skin were like that, I thought, I would be afraid to leave the dorm. I felt myself soften toward him, even though he didn't like me, and toward Edmundo, for being something good in Philip's life of hideous acne.

"Fine," I said. "Never mind."

I had already opened the door to Broussard's when Edmundo called back to me, blurring his words so that I couldn't understand them until the whole sentence was finished. What he said was, "You worry too much."

Conchita and I met for a bike lesson on Sunday evening, after she got back from Boston. When the lesson was over, I walked with her toward her dorm, wheeling Sin-Jun's bike beside me. Martha had said she thought it was okay to wait awhile, at least until Conchita brought up the subject herself, to reveal our decision, but hiding the news made me anxious. We were passing the library when I said, "I want to tell you something. It's not that big a deal, but Martha and I are rooming together next year."

Conchita stopped walking, and I saw that she had burst into tears. I touched her shoulder. "Don't cry."

She raised both her elbows to the level of her face, as if to create a barrier between us. A few guys were approaching from the opposite direction. "Let's go over there." I pointed to a circular marble bench just beyond the library—the bench had been given by the class of 1956, contained a statue of a cherub in its center, and was never, to my knowledge, used by anyone.

"Come here." I patted the marble next to me. "I'm sorry, Conchita," I said. "I really am. But you need to calm down."

"What about us rooming together?" Her face was a slimy red raisin.

"Us meaning you and Martha or you and me?"

"You and me."

"I consider you a really good friend. I just think it's hard to share a small space."

"You and Martha will share a small space."

"Yeah, but—you have so much stuff."

"That's because of my mom's decorator. I don't even like most of it."

"Also, Martha and I have a lot in common. We get along."

"You had never even talked to Martha before I introduced, you."

"We talked sometimes. In Latin," I should have ceded the point, but I felt filled with the righteousness of what was, technically, the truth.

"When did you guys decide this?"

"Yesterday. Plus, Conchita, you have insomnia."

"You decided it on the ride back to school? Did you ask her or did she ask you?"

"It was mutual. We came to a decision."

Conchita had been sounding firmer. But when she spoke again, her voice trembled—I think it trembled with hope. "It could be all three of us," she said. "We could get a triple."

I could have said yes. Martha, I knew, preferred a double, but I was pretty sure I could talk her into a triple. "That wouldn't work," I said. "Groups of three always fight."

"We didn't fight in Boston."

"That was just one day. But, Conchita, this doesn't change anything. I still want us to hang out. We became friends this year without living in the same dorm."

"We're not friends." With a lavender tissue she'd pulled from a pocket she wiped her nose but did not blow it. Snot remained behind, smeared around her nostrils.

"Of course we're friends," I had never imagined we'd arrive at this moment, with me trying to convince her. "You're overreacting. By tomorrow, you won't even care about this. Let me walk you back to your dorm." I stood and looked

134

down at her scrawny heaving shoulders; in the fading evening light, I noticed for the first time that the laces of her running shoes were yellow-and-orange striped. "Conchita, I don't know what you want me to do."

"Leave me alone."

The chapel bells rang once; it was eight-thirty. People who say leave me alone never mean it, and this was something that I knew. "Fine," I said. "If that's what you want."

When I'd killed McGrath, he'd told me his target was Alexander Héverd, a sophomore. Alexander was from Paris, he was (I'd heard) a druggie, and he was handsome in a grace-ful but not feminine way. He was medium height and quite thin, with narrow hips, and when he wore jeans—on the nights when we didn't have formal dinner—instead of wear-ing running shoes, as most Ault boys did, he wore tan leather shoes that you might have thought were dorky, or even orthopedic (they had a thick rubber sole), except that the fact that Alexander Héverd was wearing them meant they had to be, in some way, whether or not it was visible to you, deeply cool. I had never spoken to him, but I'd once been behind him going through the food line in the kitchen, and his voice, which was only faintly accented, had seemed utterly assured and possibly condescending. But maybe I'd only thought that because he was French.

The problem was that even though McGrath had told me I was inheriting Alexander as a target, McGrath hadn't given me the piece of paper verifying this, nor had he given me the stickers. I still had stickers—in fact, I had several sheets of them—but it felt important to have the paper with Alexander's name on it. Though no one, including Devin, had made me prove I had them, I wanted proof for myself. Because what if McGrath had gotten mixed up and really I was supposed to kill Alex Ellison, who was a senior?

By Monday, McGrath still hadn't dropped off the piece of paper. True, I'd been away from campus most of Saturday, but

all day Sunday, at chapel and then at lunch afterward—
Sunday lunch was supposed to be the nicest and was
therefore usually the worst, often including bloody lamb—
and then in the dorm, he could have found me. Finally, on
Monday evening at formal dinner, I approached him again, at
the site of our last terrible interaction, and he smacked his
head and told me he'd leave it off later that night, definitely,
he wouldn't forget. Which, actually, he didn't. I killed
Alexander the next day by following him out of roll call. His
target was Riley Haddix, also a sophomore. Standing there
while Alexander tried to find his stickers (within a matter of
seconds, it seemed too late to tell him I didn't need them, it
seemed like he might think I'd already wasted his time) made
me feel chunky and American and overheated.

But I had to keep playing, because how else would I get to
Cross? And it was, with every passing day, less clear to me
how many people were left, how close I was, and how much
time remained for either of us. As far as I could tell, no one
had made an attempt on my life since Edmundo had told me
he'd been killed. But even if the person who had killed him
wasn't trying to kill me, that assassin's assassin would, or that
assassin's assassin's assassin. Especially because the remaining pool of players—maybe there were fifteen of us left, or
maybe fifty—had to be mostly self-selecting. So I looked over
my shoulder when I was walking, I tried never to be out in the
open by myself. But what I felt more strongly than the possibility of my own death was the possibility of Cross's. Maybe
he'd decide the game was no longer cool. He'd get tired of it.
Normally, when I saw him around campus, I liked to watch
him but keep my distance. But now I edged closer, sitting at
the table next to his at breakfast and again at lunch, waiting
to overhear a scrap of conversation about the game. I even left
lunch just behind him (if he were paying attention, he might
well have thought he was my target already), and finally I got
what I'd been waiting for. He was fifteen feet in front of me,
talking to John Brindley and Devin Billinger, and he said

something that I missed the beginning of but caught at the end: "—unless it's someone who tries to get me in the shower." All three boys laughed. "If he comes for me in the shower," Cross said, "then it's like, okay, man, if it's worth that much to you."

Bingo, I thought. Cross was still alive.

In Latin class, Martha told me Conchita had gone to the infirmary before breakfast. She was not at lacrosse practice, and then she wasn't there again the next day, either. During this time, Martha and I consulted each other frequently, or at least I consulted Martha. The first thing I'd done after leaving Conchita sitting outside on Sunday evening was call Martha from the pay phone in Broussard's. (If I went to their dorm, of course, I risked running into Conchita.) It had been strange—the truth was, it had been exciting—to need to talk on the phone to someone who was also on campus.

"She's definitely angry," Martha told me on Monday, and when I said, "At both of us or at me?" Martha replied, "Mostly at you. She's being irrational because she feels hurt, but she'll get over it." As usual, because she was Martha, this did not sound callous.

After Conchita missed a second practice, I went to the infirmary to find her, and the nurse said she'd returned to her dorm. Standing outside her door, I could hear music that I thought might be Dylan. I knocked, and Conchita called, "Come in."

Clearly, she'd expected someone else—when she saw that it was me, she drew her lips together and furrowed her eyebrows, like a child making a mad face.

I gestured toward the stereo. "Good song."

"What do you want?"

"I was worried about you."

"Before or after you stole my best friend? But the real question is if you were using me to get to Martha all along or if you just took an opportunity when you saw it."

137

"Conchita." I didn't mean to, but I actually smiled.

She glared at me.

"We're not on a soap opera," I said. "Stealing friends isn't something that happens in real life."

"How would you know? You didn't have any friends before me."

"That's not true." I thought of Sin-Jun. Then I thought of Heidi and Alexis, whom I hadn't spoken to since the night of the dangling pillowcase; I was pretty sure they didn't count.

"I overestimated you," Conchita said. "I thought you were smart and neat. But really you're shallow and conformist. You don't have an identity, so you define yourself by who you spend time with, and you get nervous that you're spending time with the wrong people. I feel sorry for Martha because I bet she has no idea what you're like. If Aspeth Montgomery told you she wanted to be your roommate next year, you would drop Martha in a minute."

Again, listening to Conchita's analysis, I felt the sting of truth, and that old relief, a relief bordering on gratitude, that someone recognized me. Flawed as I was, someone recognized me.

"Why don't you try to be a bigger person?" she said. More softly, she added, "We could still room together. I would forgive you."

"Are you not going to accept my apology if I won't room with you?"

"If all you want is for me to accept your apology, I will. There. I accepted it."

"Will you come back to lacrosse?"

"Missing lacrosse has nothing to do with you. The pollen count has been really high." She looked away from me. "I need to take a shower."

I was out in the hall when I heard her door open again, and when I felt her hand against my back, simultaneously, I thought she was trying to hug me from behind—I even thought maybe she was embracing me sexually, maybe

138

Conchita was in love with me—and I knew, I knew in the smallest and most certain part of my mind, that she was killing me.

I turned around.

"You're dead." Her voice was flat, not satisfied in any way. Looking back, I think she killed me not because doing so brought her pleasure but because not doing so—granting me an exemption when I had treated her as I had—would have pained her. Later, I tried to piece it together, but since I couldn't talk to her, my sense of the situation was incomplete. What I came up with was that she had had Edmundo, and that when she'd learned he was my assassin, she'd killed him to protect me—she'd killed him before the weekend, when she would be away from campus and couldn't be killed herself. She was colluding in my attempt to win, and then she stopped colluding. Or maybe it was more complicated than that, maybe she killed even more people to get to me and offer protection, At the time, it seemed important to figure out the links between us, the chronology of events, but it quickly stopped seeming important at all. I never got into Assassin again after freshman year, though people kept playing the whole time I was at Ault. I'm not sure when it was abolished, or maybe it's still played under a different name: Sticker Tag. Or, Elimination. This is the kind of thing you stop knowing when you're gone from a place, but even before I was gone, I lost interest; I became one of the people who found the game ridiculous and annoying.

But then, at the time, in the hallway: I looked at Conchita's face, scanning for evidence that she was joking, or would rescind my death. The possibility had to exist because it was so wrong, in my opinion, for her to have killed me. Assassin had nothing to do with the two of us. It had to do with Cross, and what kind of heart did Conchita have if she could remorselessly block the crush of another girl? Only if she liked the boy herself could there be justification; otherwise blocking someone else's crush was always and absolutely wrong.

And I did see signs—in her eyes I saw them, and around her mouth—that she would reverse her decision, but only for one reason, only if I'd be her roommate, and in a way, Conchita was blameless because I don't think she knew she would make this reversal, or if she did know, she knew I wouldn't go along with it. That is to say, she wasn't black-mailing me. Our friendship was over. Maybe it could have recovered if only she had had a reason to resent me without my having a reason to resent her back. I can imagine that such asymmetry might have created a fragile balance, requiring for-giveness from only one of us. But instead our resentment was mutually supportive, like a wall held up with equal force from opposite sides.

It seems to me now that I was greatly indebted to Conchita; though it wasn't voluntary on her part, she gave me Martha. She literally created the circumstances that allowed me to get to know Martha, but Conchita also did something bigger and harder to quantify: She reminded me that I knew how to make friends. For this, I owed her a lot, but at the time, I believed that in killing me, she'd gotten her revenge; I believed I owed her nothing at all.

And there was something else that happened that strange week. It happened on Sunday night, before I told Conchita I was rooming with Martha, before she killed me and we said bad and unretractable things to each other: Conchita learned to ride a bike.

That evening, when I showed up behind the infirmary, Conchita was sitting cross-legged in the grass. I got off the bike, and she threw one leg over it. I gripped the carrier. "Okay," I said. "Ready." I began to jog as we moved forward.

She glanced over her shoulder. "Now my dad wants to meet you, too," she said.

I pictured short, bald Ernie Maxwell—I still hadn't seen a photo of him—and thought how strange it was to say *my dad* and to be referring to someone other people had heard of.

"I'll look forward to it," I said. A lock of hair fell into my eyes and I lifted my hand and tucked it behind my ear. Conchita was suddenly farther away from me than she'd been before, and I realized with a jolt that I wasn't holding on. She was riding the bike by herself, gliding forward with perfect balance. I continued to jog, trying to close the space between us, but without me weighing her down, she had picked up speed.

"Hey, Conchita," I said. "Don't freak out, but I'm not touching the bike. You're riding it without my help."

Immediately, she pulled the brakes and set her feet on the road.

"You were doing so well," I said. "You should have kept going. I'll start you over." It occurred to me that it might not happen again, at least not right away. But that was okay. She'd made progress. Having ridden once, she would know what she was capable of.

"You're holding on, right?" she said.

"Yeah, I'm holding on. Now pedal."

I *was* holding on, but very loosely, and I lifted my hand as soon as she gained momentum. She kept going, and I stopped, and she rode away from me. "Lee!" she called. "You let go! I can tell!"

"I know, but you're okay. Look at you."

"I'm stopping. Okay? I'm stopping." She stopped and turned around as she always did, sliding off the seat and dragging the bike sideways.

"Now come back to me," I called. She was about twenty yards away, and I thought that people might hear us yelling. Then I thought, *Oh, who cares?*

"I just start?"

"Yeah," I said. "Exactly like when I'm there."

Even from that distance, I could see her inhale and exhale several times, then square her shoulders.

"You can do it," I shouted.

And then she was riding toward me; she was beaming. The

141

wind pushed back her dark hair, and her knuckles, I observed as she came closer, were white. I began to clap. "Hooray," I cried. "You're doing it! You're on fire!"

She sailed right past me.

"Look at her go!" I called. "Who can catch Conchita Maxwell?"

She lifted her right hand, to wave at me perhaps, and the bike wobbled, and she quickly set her hand back down. I held my breath, but she regained her balance. She was fine, better than fine, she was great. As I watched her hunched back grow smaller and smaller, I felt as happy for myself as I did for her. I had taught Conchita to ride a bike—it was incredible. And this was a feeling, perhaps the only one from our brief friendship, that never went sour.

4

Cipher

IN IDLE MOMENTS during sophomore English, I used to look at Ms. Moray's pin and speculate about how she'd acquired it. It was silver, shaped to resemble an open hardcover book, the pages stacked fatly like wavy hair falling on either side of a part. She wore the pin three or four days a week, and I wondered if there was any logic to when she did. I could imagine the pin having been a gift from her parents—from a mother, especially—or perhaps from a professor or high school teacher who wanted to wish her luck as she entered this tough, worthy profession. Or maybe it was from an old neighbor, or a relative. It wasn't from a friend or a boyfriend, I was nearly sure—when she came for a year to teach at Ault as an intern, Ms. Moray was twenty-two, which didn't seem all that young to me because I was fifteen, but it definitely seemed too young to be receiving a frumpy accessory from a peer. Pins were okay for women in their forties, maybe for women in their thirties, but before that it seemed they ought to stick to earrings and necklaces.

When I entered Ms. Moray's classroom in September, the first thing I noticed was that Cross Sugarman, whom over the summer I'd spent hours and hours thinking about, wasn't there. Because I had English during the last period of the day and because Cross hadn't been in any of my other classes so far, his absence exacerbated my fear that I'd never see him this year, that we'd probably never talk, and that he definitely wouldn't fall in love with me. The second thing I noticed after entering the classroom was that printed in chalk across the blackboard, it said, *"Literature is an ax for the frozen sea within us."—Franz Kafka.* The third thing I noticed was that some sort of chaos was occurring in the back of the classroom, near one of the open, screenless Palladian windows. Darden Pittard was holding aloft a running shoe, and several other students seated at the long rectangular table were loudly offering advice.

"Just whack it," Aspeth Montgomery said, and my freshman roommate Dede said, "But you'll make it mad," and Aspeth said, "Who cares? It'll be dead."

Norie Cleehan, who was a pale skinny girl from Colorado with long limp brown hair and a soft voice, said, "Leave it alone, Darden. It's not bothering anyone." I took the empty seat next to Norie. It was a bee, I saw—that was the source of all the chaos.

Across the table, Dede, who had twisted around in her chair to watch Darden, glanced over her shoulder, and our eyes met. "Hi, Lee," she said. "How was your summer?"

I hesitated, searching the question for sarcasm or hostility. "It was good," I said slowly. "How was yours?"

"Awesome. I was—eek! Get it away! Get it away!" The bee had just whizzed by Dede's right ear, and she was pawing the air around her head. The bee flew behind her, and she shouted, "Where is it? Where'd it go?"

Beside her, Aspeth laughed hysterically.

"I got it," Darden said, but as he stepped forward, the bee shot away from him and toward me. It was a blur zooming at my face. Without thinking, I clapped my hands together in front of my nose, and when I felt a sting and then a stickiness, I knew I'd gotten it. What I wasn't sure of was whether I'd meant to. The room was silent.

After several seconds, Darden said, "Holy shit, Fiora. Not bad," and at the same time, the teacher walked through the doorway.

"I'll pretend I didn't hear that," she said, and then she grinned, and you could feel the impression she was making sink over the room, all of us seeing her in the same way: *She's cool*, we thought. *We got the cool intern for English!* She wasn't exactly pretty—she had an upturned, vaguely piggish nose, and brown eyebrows that looked even thicker and darker than they were because her chin-length hair was blond—but she was pulled together, kind of sporty. She wore a short-sleeved oxford shirt, a wraparound denim skirt, no stockings, and clogs. Her calves were tan and muscular, the legs of someone who'd played field hockey at Dartmouth. Every fall, Ault had three or four new interns, recent college graduates who came for a year to teach and coach.

She approached the head of the table and pulled a folder from a pale blue suede satchel. "I'm Ms. Moray," she said. "And don't even think of calling me Mrs. Moray because that's my mother."

People laughed.

"I'm here to teach sophomore English," she continued. "So if you're not here to *take* sophomore English, then I recommend that you use this opportunity to make a quick getaway."

Darden stood, and there was more laughter, and then he sat down again.

Ms. Moray cocked her head. "Okay, wise guy. You're the first person whose name I want to know."

"My name's Darden Pittard."

She scanned the class list. "Gotcha. That's a very assonant name. Who knows what assonance is?"

Dede raised her hand. "Is it like *the red robin*, or *the big balloon*?"

"Close. But that's alliteration, which is consonants. Assonance is the repetition of vowel sounds, like D*a*rden

Pittard. In short, Mr. Pittard, you bring poetry wherever you go."

"I've got an assonant name," Darden said. "I like that, man."

I wondered if establishing a rapport with Darden was a strategic move on Ms. Moray's part—Darden was one of the most popular guys in the sophomore class. People genuinely liked him, and on top of that they liked the fact that they genuinely liked a big black guy from the Bronx.

"Okay," Ms. Moray said. "Now as for the rest of you—"

I couldn't bear it any longer. I half-stood, my hands still clamped together, and said, "Sorry, but may I go to the bathroom?"

"Why didn't you go before?"

"I just want to wash my hands," I said, and the class started laughing. I didn't think they were laughing at me, not exactly, and I wasn't actively embarrassed but I could feel embarrassment hovering in the air. Killing a bee with your bare hands could be considered, by my classmates, gross or weird—like spreading cream cheese on your pancakes in the dining hall, or carrying around your used maxi pads in the schoolhouse during the day and then throwing them away at night in your own dorm room, both of which were things a girl named Audrey Flaherty, a junior who played the cello, was rumored to do. I didn't want to become my class's version of Audrey.

As my classmates tittered, Ms. Moray's gaze darted around the room. She seemed, for a few seconds, confused, and then abruptly resolute. "You can wait until after I take attendance." She looked back down at the sheet of paper. "Okay, so Oliver—"

"I'm sorry, but I'll be really fast, and the bell hasn't rung yet." I stood all the way up. My desire to wash my hands, to do away with the evidence, felt like a physical craving.

Our eyes met again—I could see in Ms. Moray's face that she was deciding I was a much different person than I was, a

146

class cutup or a troublemaker—and as we regarded each
other, the bell rang. "Yes, it has," Ms. Moray said. "Take a seat.
And the rest of you remember to empty your bladders before
class."

My classmates chuckled—a teacher had used the word
bladder—and I felt a surge of anger.

"All right," Ms. Moray was saying. "Oliver Amunsen—
where are you?"

Oliver raised his hand.

"Did I pronounce that right?"

Oliver nodded.

"Norie Cleehan?"

"Present," Norie said in her soft voice.

When Ms. Moray called my name, I said, "Here." We made
eye contact, and she nodded once, as if filing away information: *The name of the obnoxious girl is Lee Fiora.*

Aspeth said under her breath, "Raise your hand, Lee."

I ignored her; my hands, which felt warm and itchy, were
still joined, resting on my lap beneath the table.

"Come on," Aspeth said. "Give us a peek."

"Is there a problem?" Ms. Moray was looking between
Aspeth and me, and she settled on me.

"No," I said.

"Is there something you want to share with the rest of us?"

No one spoke, and I realized they were all waiting for me. I
said, "Well, there's this." I lifted my arms and opened my hands
to reveal a mishmash of dark congealing liquid and flakes of
wings and tiny tufts of black and yellow fur; there was a swollen
red lump on my left palm where I'd been stung. Ordinarily, of
course, I thought it best to remain inconspicuous, but the
gesture had a certain irresistible theatricality, and an inevitability. Sometimes you can feel the pull of what other
people want from you, and you sacrifice yourself, you risk seeming odd or unsavory, to keep them entertained.

Like the audience of a sitcom, the class gasped and
giggled.

147

"What is that?" Ms. Moray asked.

"I killed a bee."

She made a noise that it look me a few seconds to recognize as an irritated sigh. "Fine," she said. "Go wash your hands and then come back." Her irritation surprised me; I'd expected it all to be okay between us once she knew what the problem was.

Standing in front of the mirror above the bathroom sink, I felt, underneath my sense of agitation over having made a teacher mad on the first day of class, a vague and surprising happiness, and I tried to think of why. I ran backward through the sequence of events that had just occurred, and then I remembered—after I'd killed the bee, Darden Pittard had called me by my last name. He had said, "Not bad, Fiora." And it had seemed like no big deal, like I was the same as any other girl, someone a guy could be casually friendly with. These were the types of almost-compliments that I hoarded.

When I returned to the classroom, Dede was saying, "—and my favorite book is *Marjorie Morningstar* because it's just something you can really relate to. Oh, and I'm from Westchester County." While Aspeth announced what her favorite book was and where she was from, I tried to think of what I'd say when it was my turn. *Jane Eyre*, maybe—over the summer, back in South Bend, I'd read it in a single twenty-four-hour period, although that had had as much to do with the fact that I'd been bored as that I'd liked the book. But it appeared Aspeth was the last to go. Either Ms. Moray had forgotten about me, or she just didn't feel like letting me speak.

"All right," she said. "Now if I can turn your attention to—"

"Ms. Moray?" Aspeth said. "Excuse me, but before we go on, will you tell us where you're from and what your favorite book is?"

"Why do you want to know?" Ms. Moray's tone was, if this was possible, flirtatious—pleased but reticent.

"We told you," Aspeth said.

"Aha," Ms. Moray said. "Payback."

"We want insight into your character," Darden said.

"I grew up in Dubuque, Iowa, which is up north, and I went to the U of I for undergrad—go, Hawkeyes." She lifted one arm, and a couple guys laughed. So she hadn't played field hockey for Dartmouth, I thought, and then, knowing she was from Iowa, I recognized a certain Midwesternness in her. It was in her clothes, especially the denim skirt, and also in her gestures. She was not entirely at ease, I realized, and as soon as I thought it, I thought, *Of course she's not.* Not only was it her first day teaching at Ault, it was her first day teaching, period. This was the moment when I noticed her pin; she wore it on the right side of her shirt, just below her collarbone. "I was a lit major," she continued. "Phi Beta Kappa—you know, just to toot my own horn." She laughed, and no one laughed along with her. At Ault, you didn't toot your own horn; also, you didn't imagine that acknowledging that that's what you were doing would make it okay. "It's tough to pick one book as my favorite," Ms. Moray continued, "but I'd probably say *My Ántonia.*"

I saw Dede write *My Ántonia* in her notebook. "Who's that by?" she asked.

"Who wants to tell"—Ms. Moray glanced at the attendance sheet—"Dede who wrote *My Ántonia*?"

No one said anything.

"You guys know, right?"

Again, there was silence.

"Don't tell me that the students at an elite institution like Ault don't know who Willa Cather is. I thought you guys were supposed to be the best and the brightest." Ms. Moray laughed again, and even though I didn't like her much, I felt mortified on her behalf. This was another misstep, talking about Ault the way a magazine article might, or the way someone in town—someone who worked at the grocery store, or the barber shop—would.

149

"Did Willa Cather write *O Pioneers!*?" Jenny Carter finally said. "I think my sister had to read that for a class at Princeton."

"You mean your sister *got* to," Ms. Moray said. "Cather is one of the foremost writers of this century. You should all make a point of reading at least one book by her." She gestured toward the chalkboard behind my side of the table, where the line from Kafka was printed. It occurred to me then that she must have entered the room before class, written it there, then left again. "How many of you noticed this on your way in?" she asked.

A few people, not including me, raised their hands.

"Who wants to read it aloud?"

Dede kept her hand raised. After she'd read it, Ms. Moray said, "Who agrees with Kafka?" and I spaced out. I had never participated much in class discussions at Ault—someone else always expressed my ideas, usually in a smarter way than I could have, and as time went on, the less I spoke the less it seemed I had to say. Near the end of class, Ms. Moray gave us our homework, which was to read the first thirty pages of *Walden*, and, by the following Monday, to write two hundred words about a place where we went to reflect on our lives. "Be as creative as—" she said, and, as she was speaking, the bell rang. "Yikes," she said. "Do they think we have a hearing problem? As I was saying, be totally creative with this assignment. If there's not a place you go, make up one. You guys *comprende*?"

A few people nodded.

"Then you're released until tomorrow."

We all stood and gathered our backpacks and I looked at the floor around my chair to make sure I hadn't dropped anything. I was terrified of unwittingly leaving behind a scrap of paper on which were written all my private desires and humiliations. The fact that no such scrap of paper existed, that I did not even keep a diary or write letters except bland, earnest, falsely cheerful ones to my family (*We lost to St.*

Francis in soccer, but I think we'll win our game this Saturday; we are working on self-portraits in art class, and the hardest part for me is the nose) never decreased my fear.

I was one of the last to leave the classroom and when I got into the hall, Darden and Aspeth and Dede were walking a few feet in front of me. I slowed down, letting the space between us widen. They all laughed as they disappeared into the stairwell, and I waited for the door to shut all the way behind them before I opened it again.

I was standing in front of the stove in my pajamas, heating up chicken noodle soup, when Tullis Haskell appeared in the common room. It was a little after nine on Saturday night, and everyone else in the dorm—just about everyone else on campus, in fact—was at the first dance of the school year. While Martha had been getting dressed; fastening her bracelet, applying lip gloss, I'd sat at my desk talking to her. The fact that she hadn't tried to convince me to go had made me feel a tiny drop of disappointment but mostly a great flood of relief, a sense that finally at Ault I'd made a friend who understood me. After Martha had left, I'd listened as the sounds of the dorm—running water and radios and other girls' voices—became quieter, then stopped entirely. Then I'd changed into the bottoms of my pale blue cotton pajamas and an old T-shirt, gone downstairs to the common room, flicked on the TV, and dumped the contents of the soup can into a pan. It wasn't bad to spend a Saturday night by myself. Really, it was all a matter of expectations, and in my second year at Ault, I knew not to expect much. As a freshman, I had at times believed that if my sadness were intense enough, it would magnetically draw a handsome boy to my room, to comfort me, and that had served as an incentive, when alone, to lie around and weep. But nothing had ever come of my exertions, and I'd finally realized that time passed faster if you were doing something, like watching TV or reading a magazine. Besides, my nebulous wish for a boy had narrowed to a specific wish for Cross Sugarman, and he would be at the dance, and if I writhed and wailed and chanted his name, he'd still be at the dance.

I was stirring the broth when I heard a male voice say, "Hey there," and when I turned, Tullis was standing in the entrance to the common room.

"Hi," I said. Tullis was a senior who, at the talent show the previous winter, had played "Fire and Rain" on the guitar. Sitting in the audience (I had attended the talent show because I could observe it passively, watching other people act enthusiastic without having, as at a dance or a pep rally, to muster any enthusiasm of my own), I had experienced an evolution of powerful feelings toward this boy—Tullis— whom I had never previously noticed. First, he set a stool onstage, disappeared, and reemerged carrying his guitar, which hung from a blue and yellow strap. As he crossed the stage, a guy called out, "Serenade me, Haskell," and Tullis didn't react at all. (His face was serious and slightly vulner- able, as if he had recently awakened from a nap; he had thoughtful features and a ponytail, unusual for an Ault boy, that was about six inches long.) Watching him onstage, I wondered if he was liked or disliked by his classmates, and, as I wondered, I felt the affinity for him that I felt for all un- deserving outcasts—not for the flat-out definitively awkward or ugly kids (of whom, at Ault, there were few) but for the people who, it seemed to me, could have been either popular or unpopular and who ended up—by choice? Could choice have played a role?—on the periphery. Tullis sat down and strummed the guitar a few times and, without saying any- thing, began to play. I recognized the song before he started singing, and the feeling of affinity I'd had swelled into some- thing else, something further from sympathy and closer to affection. He understood sadness, clearly, because who could choose to perform "Fire and Rain" without understanding sadness? I tried to decide if he was cute, and as he kept playing, I thought, *Maybe he is*, and a little later, I thought, *He definitely is.* By the second verse, I was picturing how something might happen between us, how someday soon we'd pass in the mail room and I'd shyly compliment him on his performance (a performance that was, as I imagined this scenario, less than half-finished), and he'd shyly thank me, and we'd start to talk and soon, inevitably, we'd be a couple. It would just happen, and then we'd always have each other and the rest of Ault would seem distant: We'd sit together in chapel and make out in the music wing at night and I'd go to his family's house for Thanksgiving—I had a dim idea that he was from Maine—and following the late afternoon meal, we'd go for a walk on a rocky beach overlooking the water, I'd be wearing his dead grandfather's hunting jacket, and we'd hold hands as he told me for the first time that he loved me. Onstage, Tullis kept his eyes downcast, and when he got to the line, "Sweet dreams and flying machines in pieces on the ground," he looked up solemnly, I could feel a shift in the audience. I glanced first to one side and then to the other, and I saw that all the girls in my row, and in the other rows that I could see, were rapt. I began to panic. If we were both loners, that was one thing, but if there was a whole herd of girls vying for his attention, it was hopeless. What overture could I make that would distinguish me without seeming freakish? I couldn't; it was impossible. The song ended, and when the auditorium erupted, the pitch of the eruption was distinctly feminine. Tullis stood and bowed his head once, and then, as the cheering continued, waved and walked offstage. In front of me, Evie Landers turned to Katherine Pound and said, "I never realized that Tullis is hot." *No!* I thought. *No!* Then, abruptly, I thought, *Fine. Fine, Tullis. Go out with another girl instead of with me. I could take care of you, I could make you happy, but if you don't believe that, then I can't convince you.* At curfew that night, people were still talking about him, and someone said, "Isabel is so lucky," and I remembered suddenly, just as I'd remembered that Tullis was from Maine, that Tullis was going out with a short, pretty girl named Isabel

Burten. By then, though only a few hours had passed, my own welling of emotions seemed ridiculous. It was as if I'd seen a stranger in an airport and embraced him, mistaking him for a relative—Tullis was no one I ever could have loved or been loved back by; for God's sake, we'd never even talked! And oddly enough, early the next week, I did pass him in the mail room, at a time when it was quiet, when I could have said something about his performance without feeling self-conscious, but instead I said, and I felt, nothing at all.

Seeing him in the common room seven months later, I also felt nothing, or almost nothing—I did wish that I were wearing a bra. And I was glad that I was making chicken noodle soup, which was innocuous. I had the idea that the more meaty or spicy a food was, the more incriminating to a girl—a steak-and-cheese hoagie with onions, for instance, which I could but never would have purchased from Raymond's House of Pizza on Sunday afternoon when someone in the dorm organized an order, would be downright mortifying.

"Do you know how to cut hair?" Tullis asked.

"What?"

"Hair," Tullis said. He held his index and middle fingers sideways and moved them in front of his body, making them open and close.

I stared at him. I had imagined that he would ask me to try to find someone upstairs and, though I was pretty sure the dorm was empty, I'd been prepared to go and check, just to be polite. "Your hair?" I asked. "Or someone else's?"

"Mine. I'm just kind of"—he shrugged, then reached back and pulled once on his ponytail—"sick of it."

I considered my experience: In kindergarten, I had cut a doll's hair and found it deeply satisfying to do so, even though the doll had looked terrible and my mother had been displeased. Also, at the age of nine, when my mother had refused to let the woman at Easy Cuts give me layers on the grounds that they were too grown-up, I had, upon arriving

154

home, snuck into the bathroom and given them to myself. This also had not looked particularly attractive. But to cut Tullis's hair—the weirdness of the situation appealed to me. "Sure," I said. "I'll cut your hair."

"Awesome." He smiled, and I thought that if I'd known that smile was coming, I'd have told him yes before he'd finished his first question.

"Do you want to do it here?" I gestured around the common room, which contained a fireplace, a television, two pilly orange couches, five or six pilly blue chairs, a few bookshelves built into the wall, and, next to the kitchenette, a round table with several wooden chairs.

"Here's fine," Tullis said. "Do you have scissors?"

"Yeah. They're not, like, special haircutting scissors, though."

"That's cool. And we should probably get a towel. You want me to go get a towel? I'm just in Walley's." So that was why he'd shambled into this common room—because ours was the girls' dorm closest to his own. It occurred to me that maybe cutting hair was one of the things, like baking chocolate chip cookies or holding a baby, that all boys thought all girls knew how to do. If he did think that, it was sweet—I didn't want to be the one to reveal that he was wrong.

"I can get a towel upstairs." I said. I had only my own towels, which I washed in the machines in the basement, but Martha, like most students, got the laundry service. Every Tuesday morning before chapel, you left your used towels, along with your other dirty laundry, in a yellow drawstring bag with your last name printed on it, on the steps of your dorm. When you got out of chapel, there was a new bag waiting with fresh towels and last week's clothes, now clean. This magical transformation occurred for the fee of three thousand dollars a year. When my father had seen the price in one of the many mailings Ault had sent me the summer before I enrolled, he said that for half that much per student, using only a washboard and a bar of soap, he'd abandon my

155

mother and brothers and move to Massachusetts with me to do the laundry of every kid at Ault.

I turned off the soup on the stove and hurried upstairs. From our room, I took a towel still in its plastic casing (Martha wouldn't mind my borrowing, and she didn't go through all her towels in a week anyway), and I pulled the scissors from my desk drawer and my brush from the top of my dresser. Also, while I was up there, I put on a bra. I considered changing my shirt, but I thought Tullis might notice and think I was trying to impress him; he might think I was dumb enough to imagine all it would take was a different outfit. Heading back to the common room, I took the stairs two at a time.

"Why don't you sit here?" I pulled one of the wooden kitchenette chairs in front of the TV so he could watch a show while I cut. He sat down, and, from behind, I set the towel over his shoulders, walked around so we were facing each other, and pulled two corners until they overlapped with no space between the towel and his neck. "Take your ponytail out," I said, and he did. I scrutinized him. Our faces were perhaps two feet apart, mine a little higher than his, and normally it made me squirm to be this close to a boy—I imagined that my pores appeared enormous, my skin blotchy—but this situation wasn't about me; standing before Tullis, I felt dispassionate, practically professional. "Do you want to keep the same shape but you want it to be shorter, or do you want it to be more of a typical guy's haircut where it's close to your head all the way around?"

"What would you do?"

"I don't think you want it super-short." *Because*, I thought but did not say, *I wouldn't know how to do that.* "But it can be kind of shaped to your head." I walked around behind him again and began to brush his hair. It was pale brown with lighter streaks, not as soft as a girl's but still nice. I reached my arm over his right shoulder and tapped my fingertips just under his chin. "Keep your head straight." Immediately, he

156

lifted his head and pulled back his shoulders. I held the scissors up and snipped a lock of hair. There was a certain physical pleasure in the act, hair against metal, the sound and feel of the slice. I realized that I didn't know what to do with what I'd cut. "Hold on a sec," I said, and I took some newspapers out of the trash can and spread them by the chair. I let the lock drop soundlessly and reached for another.

"You don't think my hair needs to be wet, do you?" he said.

This hadn't occurred to me—why hadn't it occurred to me? But it seemed that if I told him to wet his hair at this point, I'd undermine my credibility. "No, you're fine," I said. "I can do it this way."

After a moment, he said, "I always wondered why they make you get it wet at the barber. Like, what does that do?"

Behind him, I tried to keep the smile out of my voice. "It's just a preference people have," I said. "Some people think it makes it easier. But, actually," I added, growing bolder, "it can be confusing because your hair looks longer when it's wet, so you might cut more than you mean to." The statement was, in fact, true, but I had no idea where I'd gotten it—a magazine probably.

We didn't speak for several minutes. At first, I was cutting no more than half an inch at a time, going across the back so it was even, then cutting half an inch more. But he wanted it all off, he'd said, and it *was* awfully long, and my current method wasn't particularly efficient. In a single snip, I took four inches, and as I did, I felt the glee of the irreversible. I sensed that Tullis was absorbed in the television program, which was about the search for the lost island of Atlantis. A few more minutes passed. He had a fraction of the hair he'd awakened with in the morning. It occurred to me that given how drastic it was, other students would remark on his haircut, and that he might mention that I had done it. *Lee Fiora?* they would say. *How did that happen?* Or maybe just, *Who's she?* It was possible that news of the event might even reach Cross Sugarman.

"Why didn't you wait until Monday and go into town for this?" I asked.

"You know how you get an idea in your head and you're like, 'Why wait?' It was time. That's how I felt."

I hesitated, then said, "Why aren't you at the dance?"

"The dance?"

"The one in the student center."

He laughed. "I know where the dances are. That's not really my thing, you know?"

"Yeah." After a pause, I added, "Me neither."

"I went the first few years here, but it's pretty much the same week after week."

"Yeah, I guess." Never having attended a single dance, I wasn't in a position to know, but it seemed I might as well agree. "Okay," I said. "It's pretty short."

He reached back and made a loop with his thumb and index finger, as if to catch his ponytail, but all his fingers circled was air. "Holy shit."

"Is that okay?"

"No, yeah, it's great." He rubbed his fingertips a few times against the place where his hairline and his neck met. "It's totally what I wanted. It's just different."

"I still need to clean it up. Put your shoulders back again."

He did as I'd instructed, and I resumed trimming. The part I was least sure of was the hair that grew from the crown of his head—how long was I supposed to leave it? I walked in front of him again, my body between him and the TV, and I pushed back the hair that fell on either side of his temples. "Do you want bangs? You do, right?"

"Do I?"

"I think it would look kind of weird if you didn't have them."

"Sure, then. That's cool."

"Close your eyes."

He did, and for several seconds, I looked at his face. There were freckles across his nose and cheeks that you couldn't see

158

from farther away, and, on the right side of his chin, a mostly healed zit that he'd popped, from the looks of it, three or four days ago. Also on his chin, there was a little golden stubble around the tip, and there was some above his mouth, too. I felt a tenderness, almost a protectiveness, toward him that surprised me. It was strange to remember that I'd thought I had a crush on him, though I also knew that such a crush, a false crush if crushes were not all by definition false, could rise again with enough distance. But here, with the two of us positioned so close together, he reminded me of myself; he was far too much like me for me to love.

I continued cutting, and every time I stepped away from him to examine my progress, I thought, *Not bad*. Maybe I actually could cut hair.

At last, I said, "Open your eyes. I think you're done."

"Is there a mirror around here?"

"In the bathroom." I pointed to the door next to the phone booth, and when he walked over, I followed him and stood behind him.

"Whoa," he said, and my heart seized, but then he grinned. He ran one hand back through it. "Hey, nice job," he said. "Thanks a lot."

I grinned back at him. "My pleasure."

"I should pay you or something."

"Oh, God." I shook my head. "Of course not." The thought was mortifying, uncomfortably close to being paid to, say, vacuum a dormmate's room.

"Hey, you know what?" Tullis said. "Would you mind shaving the back of my neck? Would that be totally gross?"

In fact, the request flattered me.

"I can get my razor," he added.

"I'll just use one of mine. It's no big deal." The razor I retrieved from my toiletry bucket upstairs was pink plastic. I filled a mug with water from the kitchen sink and set the mug and a bar of soap on top of the television. Tullis sat in the chair again, turning around so he was straddling it, his back to the TV. I dipped my fingers in the water, rubbed them against the soap, then rubbed my fingers against his neck. As soon as I was touching his skin, with him facing away from me, it became possible again to imagine having a crush on him. We didn't speak at all as I spread the lather, set the razor against his neck, pulled on it, dipped it in the cup of water, set it back against his neck. "Arguments that Atlantis was the island of Thera," said the television narrator, "are bolstered by evidence of a volcanic eruption on Thera in 1500 B.C., which caused the majority of the island to sink into the sea." What was Tullis thinking? I wondered. What did my fingers feel like to him? But I doubted I was a girl guys saw in that way. Only in the taxi with Cross had I gotten any evidence that someone might.

When I was pretty sure I'd shaved all the hair from his neck, I ran my fingers over his skin, and it was very smooth. "Okay," I said, and my voice sounded ordinary. "All finished."

He reached back and rubbed his neck. "Thanks," he said. "I could have tried to do that, but I'd probably have cut myself, like, ten times." He stood and carried the chair back to the table, and while he did, I bundled up the hair-strewn newspaper and smashed it down in the trash. I could feel that he was going to leave in the next minute or so. Up until this point, I'd hoped no one would return to the dorm because I didn't want to have to explain what was going on; if it all got called into question, Tullis might change his mind in the middle. Plus, I'd felt that Tullis and I were developing a sort of rapport (it was low-key, I knew that, it wasn't like we were now going to be friends) and I hadn't wanted it interrupted. I could imagine one of the other girls in the dorm approaching, standing in my way probably, shrieking, "Tullis, I can't *believe* you're letting her cut so much! Tullis, you are *crazy*!" But now that the haircut was complete and he was about to take off, I felt a twinge of disappointment that no one had seen it happen. I had liked this incarnation of myself, I realized, and I wouldn't have minded an audience for it. It was like when Tim, the younger of my two brothers, was born, and my mother would let me take him outside and push him in a stroller as long as I stayed on our street and I always thought—I was eleven—that if only the boys from my class, a few of whom did live nearby, could see me, surely they'd all develop crushes on me immediately because I was so cool like this, so grown-up. I mean, taking care of my baby brother? Out all by myself?

I poured the soapy water down the drain and set the mug in the sink. I was still holding the razor. I could imagine saving it, not to use, not to do anything with, just setting it in the cardboard box under my bed where I kept old notebooks and term papers and the programs from school performances. But Tullis might notice if I didn't throw away the razor, and it might seem weird, it might seem Audrey Flahertyish. I tossed it in the trash.

"Thanks again," Tullis said.

"No problem."

He had approached the sink, and we stood facing each other. He stuck out his hand, and we shook. "I see a big future for you," he said. "Salons all across the country. Celebrity clients."

I rolled my eyes. "That would be a really good use of my Ault education."

"You could do worse. All right. I'll see you around." He was a few feet from the door when he turned back. "I'm really sorry. This is terrible. But your name—is your name—"

"Lee," I said. "Lee Fiora."

"Right, right." He nodded. "It's like, Ault's so small, but by the time you're a senior—"

"It's okay," I said.

"All right. Well, thanks, Lee." He grinned, and I thought again that he really did have the best smile in the world. Also, I thought, I had given him a first-rate haircut. How this had happened was beyond me.

He was turning again when I blurted out, "Actually—" and he said, "Oh, sorry, I'm Tullis—"

"No, I know who you are. I just wanted to tell you, I know this was a long time ago, but I wanted to tell you that I thought when you played guitar in the talent show last year, that was really good."

He was still smiling. I loved boys, I thought. All of them.

When he left, he waved the way he had before he'd exited the stage after singing "Fire and Rain."

The place where Dede went to reflect on life, according to her essay for English class, was a window seat on the landing between the first and second floors of her family's house in Scarsdale. Darden said he reflected while riding the 2/3 subway, and Aspeth said she reflected during the summer, whenever she took her grandfather's yawl out on Long Island Sound. (I believed that Aspeth spent the summer on Long Island, and that her grandfather had a boat and even that she went out in it, but not that she went out by herself—it was my observation that beautiful and popular people rarely spent time alone.) Martin Weiher read about how he reflected while on the toilet, and that got a laugh, and then Jeff Oltiss read the same thing, and people didn't laugh as much for him, because he wasn't as cool as Martin and because he'd gone second.

No one had volunteered when Ms. Moray had asked if anyone wanted to read their paper aloud, so she'd called on Dede, and then Darden, who was next to Dede, had said he'd go, and the line had continued around the table. After Jeff, it seemed to be my turn. As the progression of readers had approached me, my heart had beat increasingly quickly, and heat had spread over my face. I felt some anxiety about my essay—I doubted that it was particularly well written, and it definitely wasn't funny—but, more than that, I felt the unhappy anticipation of people watching and listening to me. And now that I was supposed to read, I found that I could not. I just couldn't. I knew that my voice would come out quivery and breathless and that my consciousness of this fact would only exacerbate it until, ultimately, my own agitation would make it seem physically impossible to endure another second. It would seem as if the moment would simply fold in on itself, though what a moment folding in on itself entailed I wasn't sure—spontaneous combustion perhaps, or perhaps the floors would buckle and we'd be rolled in on ourselves like ingredients in a gyro.

"I pass," I said. "We can do that, right?"

"Why do you want to?" Ms. Moray asked.

"I just would rather."

Ms. Moray sighed, as if I were trying to eat up class time by dithering—as if she herself hadn't made it seem like reading aloud was optional. "Everyone else has gone," she said. "If you don't go, it's not fair."

I was not sure that I'd ever heard an adult attempt to support an argument by claiming unfairness. But if I challenged Ms. Moray again, I could tell that this, whatever it was, would become solid and tangible; it would be a situation, something people would talk about after class was over.

I looked down at my essay, which I'd typed the night before on Martha's computer. "Reflecting on one's life is an important part of reaching decisions and understanding one's ethics and values," I began, and I could tell that my voice was barely audible. "Many people, like Henry David Thoreau, have a special place they go where it is quiet and peaceful. For me, this place is at my father's—" Here I trailed off completely. Abruptly, I understood why I had felt so hesitant before. "I can't read this."

"You were doing fine," Ms. Moray said.

I did not look at her or my classmates, though I felt them watching me. "You can start over again if you want," Ms. Moray said, and her voice contained a kindness it hadn't before.

"No," I said.

"Lee, no one is judging you. You need to get comfortable reading your work aloud because you'll be doing it a lot this year."

I said nothing.

"Can you tell me why you don't want to read?"

I could feel then not that I *would* cry but that I might; the possibility had sprung into existence. It would be best to speak as little as possible.

Ms. Moray sighed again, but it was a new sigh, not the impatient one from before. "You don't have to go today," she said. "But in the future, be prepared to read whatever you've written, and that goes for all of you. No exceptions. Norie, you're up."

At the end of class, Ms. Moray said, "Lee, talk to me before you leave."

I finished putting away my books and then remained in my chair, my backpack zipped on the table before me. I held my essay on my lap, prepared to give it to her. After all, it didn't matter that much what *she* thought—I believed that teachers were like doctors, detached in their judgments.

When the room had cleared out, Ms. Moray sat down across from me. She was wearing a lavender mock turtleneck and a black blazer—it had gotten cool already—and the book pin was affixed to the left collar of her blazer. Below her left breast was a short horizontal line, perhaps three inches long, of white chalk, which I was pretty sure she was unaware of; also, her skin was a little greasy, especially at the corners of her nose.

"I want you to read your piece aloud," she said. "Now. To me. I understand being reluctant to speak in class, but it's something you need to get over."

I said nothing.

"I'll read it anyway," she said. "Unless you choose not to hand it in and take a zero on the assignment." The way she said this, it was obvious she didn't consider it remotely likely.

But it wasn't a bad idea. Generally, my fear relied on the hypothetical, and an actual specific consequence, any consequence at all, nearly always seemed less severe than whatever amorphous series of events I'd felt the need to guard against. A zero on an essay that probably counted for five percent of my total grade for the semester wasn't a big deal at all.

"I could take a zero," I said. It was definitely the best option—at this point, I'd drawn too much attention to the essay, and she might ask questions, she might not be detached. My essay could have seemed neutral, but I'd made a fuss.

She squinted at me. "But you did the assignment."

"Yeah, but then I changed my mind."

Ms. Moray opened her mouth as if to speak, then closed it, then opened it again. "I want you to read your piece to me," she said. "I'm not giving you another option."

I never argued against absolutes. "Okay," I said, and I saw that she was surprised. "I should just start right now?"

"Right now. Go for it!' Her voice thickened with enthusiasm. *No, no*, I thought. *We're still in the same moment we were in before.*

I moved the paper from my lap to the table. "Reflecting on one's life is an important part of reaching decisions and understanding one's ethics and values. Many people, like Henry David Thoreau, have a special place they go where it is quiet and peaceful. For me, this place is at my father's store. My father's store is called Mattress Headquarters. It is located in South Bend, Indiana. When I used to live at home, I did not go to the store on weekdays because I had school. Instead, I went on the weekends. In the back of the store, there is an office and behind the office, there is a storage room with many mattresses. This is the room where I reflect because it is quiet and comfortable, and I could lie on all the mattresses, which some of the piles reached almost to the ceiling. The best part of this room is that I can hear other people talking, especially my father because he has a loud voice. I can listen to my father and other people such as customers and sales staff and know I am not alone, yet I do not have to join in the conversation. In this place, I think about many issues, such as what profession I would like to go into, college, and politics. I believe that reflecting is very important in developing as a person and realizing one's priorities."

I looked up. "That's it."

"I have to say, I have no idea what you were so bashful about. That's exactly what I'm looking for. And reading to me wasn't that bad, was it?"

I shrugged.

"I especially liked the part about being able to hear your father's voice." The fact that Ms. Moray was being so nice— pityingly nice—indicated that, despite her earlier misimpression, she had figured out what kind of person I was: not a smart-ass, not at all.

"I just don't understand why you didn't want to read it before," she said.

That, actually, had been my main concern—that she'd know immediately. That she didn't know both relieved me and made me think less of her.

"You might feel like you've gotten off to a bumpy start in this class," she said. "But I want you to know I'm totally open-minded. Anyone in my classroom who shows a willingness to work will do just fine. Besides," she added, and, to my horror, she actually winked. We were the only ones in the room! What was I supposed to do back? Didn't she realize that this wasn't a movie about boarding school, where the student and the teacher could have a little burst of chumminess and then it would cut to another scene, like the student at soccer practice or the teacher riding her bike back to her cottage on the edge of campus? No, we were still in the same room, both of us having to breathe and speak in the aftermath of her wink. "I'll admit to a soft spot for a fellow Midwesterner," she continued. "It seems like there aren't a whole lot of us at Ault."

I tried to smile.

166

"You did say you're from Indiana, didn't you?"

"Yeah," I said. "From South Bend."

"You know, I dated a guy who grew up there," she said. "Evan Anderson. You don't know him, do you?" She gave a self-deprecating laugh, as if to show that she knew how unlikely this was.

"I don't think so." I pushed my essay across the table, stood, and picked up my backpack.

As I was leaving, she said, "Hey, Lee?"

From the doorway, I turned around.

She was standing, too, and she pulled her shoulders back, bent both arms, balled her hands into fists, and thrust her fists forward. "Confidence!" she said.

Again, when I tried to smile, I couldn't tell how convincing it was. Walking through the empty schoolhouse and back to my dorm, I thought how exhausting Ault was, all the chatter and the expressions you had to make: Attentive! Inquisitive! I let my face sag, but then I saw someone ten yards in front of me, emerging from the courtyard. It was Charlie Soco, a senior, another person I'd never spoken to. I glanced at his eyes and saw that he wasn't looking at me, and then I looked down and then as we came closer to each other, I slid my backpack off one shoulder so it was in front of me and unzipped one of the outer pockets and pretended to rummage in it. In this way, when Charlie and I passed, I avoided saying hello.

Quite a few people made comments to me about Tullis's haircut, and at lunch one day, Aspeth and Dede were discussing it when I sat down. I waited for them to acknowledge my role in it, but neither of them did.

"He looks ten times better," Aspeth was saying.

"Lee," said Emily Phillips, who was sitting next to me, "aren't you the one who cut it?"

When I nodded, Dede said, "You?"

I nodded again.

"But you don't even know Tullis."

It was true that since the start of this school year, whenever we were in English class, Dede had been perfectly civil, even, at times, friendly. Still, I couldn't help but enjoy watching her work herself up. "He asked me to," I said.

Dede narrowed her eyes. "Do you *know* how to cut hair?" If I had concealed this ability from her during the year we'd lived together, I could see her thinking, what else might I be hiding? *I'm a trapeze artist,* I wanted to say. *I speak Swahili.*

"Of course I do," I said.

"Could you cut mine?" asked Nick Chafee, who was sitting at the head of the table.

"Sure."

Dede's mouth was hanging open, as it did whenever she was confused or outraged. Nick Chafee wasn't cute, but he was known to be especially rich, and, clearly, Dede doubted my ability to interact with him unsupervised.

"Can you do it tonight after dinner?" Nick said. "I'll come to your dorm."

"Or I'll come to yours." I had never set foot in the common room of a boys' dorm. But I could hear how I sounded casual, and it was because Dede was watching, because defying her expectations was irresistible. If I made eye contact with her, surely I would laugh and give proof that I was faking it. I concentrated very hard on biting into my tuna melt.

Emily Phillips said, "Could you cut my hair, too?"

Before I could respond, Dede said, "Are you crazy? Guys' hair and girls' hair is completely different!"

"I just want to get rid of the split ends," Emily said.

"That's no problem," I said. In fact, it would be a lot easier than what I'd done for Tullis, "I can do yours tonight, too."

"Actually, I have a French test tomorrow, but what about Wednesday night?"

As it happened, I had a Spanish test Thursday. Not that it

really mattered—I never did that well on anything, so it was a better use of my time to cut hair than to study.

"I can't believe this," Dede said.

"Want me to cut yours?"

"No!" she said, and everyone at the table laughed.

Over the next several weeks, I cut the hair of more and more people, perhaps twenty-five of them by late October. Certain things I'd done with Tullis became habits—that I never had them wet their hair first, that I always made them close their eyes when I was standing in front of them, that, of course, I didn't charge. Around campus, people suddenly talked to me more, especially teachers and boys. Tullis himself always greeted me warmly and by name; once, when I was hurrying through the gym to get to the soccer field, Reynolds Coffey, the male senior prefect, yelled, "Yo, Lee, where are your scissors?"; and another time, as I was leaving the dining hall after formal dinner, Reverend Orch, the chaplain, who was completely bald, set his hand on my forearm and said, "From all that I hear, Miss Fiora, it is my great loss that I cannot employ your services."

In such situations, I was always demure, I'd hardly even reply. But when it came to actual haircutting. I felt a confidence that I had not experienced in any other situation since arriving at Ault. Sometimes I didn't even give the haircut that had been requested, I gave the one I thought would look good—lopping off an extra few inches, say—and the individual might seem puzzled (not angry, never angry, just puzzled), but everyone else always loved it. I learned to use an electric razor, which numbers corresponded to which lengths, and even though that was something a guy could have done on his own, some wanted me to do it for them. Oliver Amunsen said, "I trust you more than I trust myself."

In my hands, beneath my fingers, people's heads felt warm and vulnerable, and I had the sense that I could have cut their hair with my eyes closed, by touch alone. I was never nervous;

in fact, I'd experience a suspension of any conscious feeling at all. I almost always chatted with them a little, rarely for the whole time, and I never worried either that I was talking too much or that the silences between us were awkward. Afterward, when the person had left and I was alone, vacuuming or sweeping up the hair, I felt a sense of achievement. I was proud of my ability. Though normally I thought pride of any sort was distasteful, this was okay because cutting hair was a neutral act, nothing to brag about. It was like being good at untying knots, or good at reading maps.

We had finished *Uncle Tom's Cabin* shortly before the day of our group presentations. The assignment had been to choose an important scene from anywhere in the book, say why it mattered, and act it out. My partners were Norie Cleehan and Jenny Carter, and we did the part where Cassy and Emmeline hide in the attic and pretend to be ghosts to scare Simon Legree; I was Legree.

After we went, the only group left was Darden, Aspeth, and Dede. "We have to go put on our costumes," Dede announced.

"Great," Ms. Moray said. No one else had bothered with costumes.

They left the room, and while we waited, a generous, giddy energy hung in the classroom—we'd been getting up from our seats and talking in bad Southern accents and clapping for one another at the end of each performance. During one burst of applause, I had thought that we were probably making as much noise as one of those classes you hear down the hall—usually while you're taking a math test—that's shouting and laughing like they're at a party. "I must say, I had no idea there was so much acting talent in this class," Ms. Moray said.

Aspeth stuck her head into the room. "One thing we have to tell you," she said. "This is a modern interpretation. That's okay, right?"

Ms. Moray nodded. "Absolutely."

"It's the part where the Shelby slaves get together in Uncle Tom and Aunt Chloe's cabin." Aspeth was still visible only from the neck up. "It's while Mr. Shelby is in the big house signing over Uncle Tom and Harry to Haley."

"And why is this important?" Ms. Moray asked.

"We're showing the sense of community the slaves have and how Uncle Tom is their leader and they rally around him when they know he's leaving."

"Terrific. Go to it."

"Just one more sec."

Aspeth disappeared, and the door clicked shut. A minute later, Darden flung it open and strode through, Aspeth behind him gripping his waist like in a conga line, and Dede behind Aspeth. Darden wore a fedora set at an angle, a pair of oversized sunglasses, several gold and silver and pearl necklaces, and a long shiny red raincoat, tight across his shoulders, which I recognized as belonging to Dede. In his right hand, he carried a cane. Dede herself had on a cream-colored knee-length silk slip, and Aspeth was wearing a striped bikini top (the stripes were pink, mint green, and pale blue) and a tennis skirt; on their feet, both girls wore high heels.

"Choo-choo!" Darden cried. He thrust his fist into the air and rolled it forward a few times, then tipped his head back toward Aspeth and Dedee. "Ain't that the finest-looking ho train you folks ever seen?" From various parts of the table, I heard snorts of laughter, and someone—it might have been Oliver—called out, "Uh-huh, brother!" As if in response, Aspeth and Dede held their chins in the air, moved their heads all around, batted their eyelashes.

The three of them slithered and wiggled the length of the chalkboard, until they were between the far end of the table and the windows. Darden leaned over and stuck his cheek down toward Jenny Carter. "You give Big Daddy Tom some love, sugar."

171

Jenny had a look on her face that was both startled and amused. Her gaze jumped to Ms. Moray, and when I looked, too, Ms. Moray was squinting as if confused. This was a confusion I shared. I literally did not understand what Darden and Aspeth and Dede were doing, what the unifying principle was behind their weird clothes, their gestures, Darden's lingo. I sensed that most of my classmates did understand. Jenny puckered her lips and kissed Darden.

"Thanks, baby," Darden said. He took a step back, and Aspeth and Dede rearranged themselves so they were on either side of him, their arms linked through his, gazing up at him, stroking his shoulder or his forehead. "My ho's, you know why we're here tonight." Darden said. "And Daddy might go away, but you know he always gonna be looking out for you. It ain't easy when Master Shelby—"

"Stop it," Ms. Moray said, and her voice was loud and sharp. It was strange to hear a normal voice. "That's enough. All three of you, sit down. But first change out of those clothes."

Darden and Aspeth and Dede regarded her silently. Their posture was already different—Aspeth's arms were folded, she wasn't touching Darden at all—and none of them were smiling.

"We were just—" Dede began.

"Right now," Ms. Moray said. "Hurry."

They walked quickly past us, back into the hall. In their absence, the rest of us looked at one another, looked away, looked back; Chris Graves put his head down on the table. When Darden, Aspeth, and Dede returned, they sat without speaking.

"Would someone like to explain what that was about?" Ms. Moray said.

No one said anything. I couldn't tell if she was asking all of us or just them, and I also couldn't tell if she was really asking for an explanation—if, like me, she hadn't understood—or if she was asking for more of a justification.

172

"Really," Ms. Moray said. "I'm curious—curious about what could *possibly* make the three of you think it's either relevant or appropriate to portray Uncle Tom as a pimp and the other slaves as prostitutes."

Of course. I was an idiot.

"Uncle Tom is a *Christ* figure," Ms. Moray said. "He's a hero."

Darden was looking down, and Aspeth was looking across the room, her face blank, her arms crossed again. To watch Aspeth be scolded was odd and not, as I might have imagined, enjoyable. I would have felt sorry for her, actually, except that she seemed unaffected by Ms. Moray's comments; she seemed mostly bored. Of the three of them, only Dede was looking at Ms. Moray. "We were being creative," Dede said.

Ms. Moray smiled unpleasantly. "Creative how?"

"By, like, we were—well, with a modern-day parallel—we just thought it would be fun."

"I'll tell you something," Ms. Moray said. "And this is a lesson that could serve all of you well on that day not so far in the future when you find yourselves out in the real world. The next time you're being *creative*, the next time you're having *fun*, you might want to stop and think about how your behavior looks to other people. Because I'll tell you, what this seems like to me is nothing but racism."

Everyone looked at her then, even Darden and Aspeth. Racism didn't exist at Ault. Or it did, of course it did, but not like that. Kids came from all sorts of cultural backgrounds, with parents who had emigrated from Pakistan, Thailand, Colombia, and some kids had families that still lived far away—in my dorm alone, there were girls from Zimbabwe and Latvia. And no one ever made slurs, it wasn't like you got ostracized if you weren't white. Racism seemed to me like a holdover from my parents' generation, something that was not entirely gone but had fallen out of favor—like girdles, say, or meatloaf.

"We weren't being racist," Aspeth said. Her voice contained none of Dede's anxious eagerness, Dede's earnest wish to set things straight. Aspeth knew she was right, and the only question was whether it was worth demonstrating this to an inferior mind like Ms. Moray's. "How could we be?" Aspeth said. "Darden is black."

This was a bold and possibly inappropriate thing to say—Darden's blackness, in our post-racist environment, was not a thing you remarked on.

"That's your defense?" Ms. Moray said. "That Darden is—?" Even she seemed unable to say that he was black, which affirmed Aspeth's power. But then Ms. Moray appeared to regain control. "Listen," she said. "Internalized racism is still racism. Self-hatred is *not* an excuse."

I glanced at Darden, who was looking down again. He inhaled, puffed out his cheeks, exhaled, and shook his head. I didn't think he was self-hating, and I certainly didn't want him to be—*I* was self-hating, and wasn't that enough? Did there need to be so many of us?

"There's also the issue—" Ms. Moray said, but Darden interrupted her. "We made a mistake," he said. "How about we leave it at that?" He was looking up at Ms. Moray, his mouth set in a firm line. He seemed to me in this moment like an adult—his deep voice and his physical size and his reasonableness, how it appeared he wanted the situation resolved more than he wanted himself exonerated. I wished that I were friends with him so that I could tell him after class I'd been impressed by his behavior and it wouldn't just seem like I was trying to get on his good side.

Ms. Moray hesitated. It had seemed before that she was just warming up, but this was a relatively easy way out. "Fine," she said at last. "But I'll make one more point. And that's that this wasn't only offensive in terms of the racial stereotypes you guys were playing off. I'm also deeply, deeply troubled by the sexism here. And, no, the fact that you're women doesn't make it okay for you to objectify yourselves. Our culture

174

teaches women that our primary worth is our appearance, but we don't have to accept that idea. We can flaunt our bodies, or we can choose to have integrity and self-respect." Ms. Moray's voice had turned high, she sounded a little too impassioned, and I saw Aspeth roll her eyes at Dede. She shouldn't have been using the word *women*, I thought. All of us in the room, except for Ms. Moray herself, were girls.

Later that day—news of what had happened in class spread quickly, and even Martha pressed me for details—I was in the locker room when I heard Aspeth talking about it yet again. "Rah, rah, rah," she said. "Let's go burn our bras."

The next day, while we waited before class for the bell to ring, Ms. Moray said, "Who's psyched to learn?" Then she pretended to be a cheerleader, waving her hands in the air, shouting, "E-N-G-L-I-S-H—what's that spell? English!" We didn't have cheerleaders at Ault, and she was making the joke to show that she forgave us; she didn't seem to realize that she herself had not been forgiven.

One Saturday afternoon in early November, Martha and I were reading in our room. She was at her desk, and I was lying on my back in bed, on the lower bunk, holding up my Western European history textbook until my hands fell asleep, then shutting my eyes and setting the open textbook over my face, the pages pressed to my cheeks, while I waited for the pins-and-needles feeling to pass. As the afternoon wore on, the intervals during which I was reading shrank and the intervals when my eyes were closed stretched. It was during one of the latter periods that I heard Martha stand and, it sounded like, pull on a jacket. I lifted the book.

"I'm going to town," she said. "You want anything?"

I sat up. "Maybe I'll come."

"I'm just running some errands."

Although it seemed like she didn't want me to go, I couldn't imagine this was the case. The feeling Martha gave me, a feeling I got from no one else except, at times, my parents, was that I was excellent company, that almost no situation existed that would not be improved by the addition of my incisive observations and side-splitting wit. "Martha, don't you know that buying hemorrhoid cream is nothing to be ashamed of?" I said.

She smiled. "I promise that if I get hemorrhoids, you'll be the first to know." She zipped her backpack.

"Martha, why are you—" I began, and at the same time, she said, "I'm getting a haircut." Then she said, "What were you going to ask?"

"Nothing," I said. "You're getting a haircut?"

"Don't be offended. I think you're a really good haircutter. I honestly do."

"I'm not offended." In fact, I wasn't yet sure if this was true. "But why are you acting so weird?"

She sighed and, still wearing her backpack, sat down at her desk. In a regretful voice, she asked; "Am I?"

"Yes."

"I just feel funny about it," she said. "I mean, why do you cut people's hair?"

"Why do I cut people's hair? I don't know. Why are you asking me?"

We weren't having a fight. Really, it was difficult to imagine fighting with Martha because she was the most un-angry person I knew. Even in this moment, she seemed, if anything, sad. Still, I felt an unfamiliar tension between us.

"I'm asking because—oh, I don't know."

"Say it," I said. "Whatever you were going to say, just say it."

She paused. "I think you cut people's hair, especially boys, as this way of having contact with them without having to really get close."

"You mean physical contact or just social contact?"

"Well." She considered the question. "I guess both."

"So I'm a pervert?"

"No! Oh, no, Lee, that's not what I meant at all. It's totally

176

normal to want to be close to people." Martha's goal was to be a classics professor, but there were times when I could more easily picture her as a therapist, or possibly an elementary school principal. "But it's like you're doing people a favor, and what do you get from it? No one ever helps you clean up. It's not an equal trade. And I just think you deserve better."

I looked down at my thighs against the mattress.

"You can be friends with, like, Nick Chafee," Martha said. "If you want to, that is. Personally, I don't think Nick is any great shakes. But it's not like the best you can do is to cut his hair."

I believed that Martha believed this. Whether Nick Chafee believed it was a different story.

"Maybe I'm making too big a deal of this," Martha said.

"No, I appreciate you saying something." I swallowed. "I do."

Martha stood again. "I just feel like it's better for me to get a haircut in town. You don't have to do anything for me."

"But I would be happy to cut your hair," I said.

"I know." She was next to the door, gripping her bike key in one hand. "Thank you."

"Martha," I said as she stepped into the hallway. She turned around.

"Does everyone think that about me? That I cut hair so that—" I wanted to say, *so that I can talk to boys even though I'm a loser*, but Martha hated it when I insulted myself.

"Of course not." She grinned. "People are too busy thinking about themselves." (No one was ever better at reassuring me than Martha—before tests, she reassured me that I could pass, and before formal dinner, she reassured me that my clothes looked okay, and before I went home for Christmas or the summer, she reassured me that my plane wouldn't crash. She reassured me that no one had noticed when I'd tripped walking out of chapel, that I would be happy in college, that it didn't matter if I'd spilled root beer on her futon cover, and

177

that I didn't have bad breath; if I doubted her, she would lean her face in and say, "Okay, breathe on me. Go ahead, I don't care." Sometimes still I think, *What did I ever give back to you?*) "I'll be gone a couple hours," Martha said. "Don't go to dinner without me, okay?"

I nodded. "I would have been able to tell you'd gotten a haircut. Even if you'd snuck out, I'd know when you got back."

"Yeah, well." She grinned. "Remind me never to go into espionage."

As I watched her leave, my mind shot ahead to a time in the future when we would not share a room, when our daily lives would not overlap. The idea made me feel as if I were being held underwater. Then I thought, *You're being ridiculous; you have almost three more years together*, and I could breathe again. But I knew, I always knew—and as unhappy as I often was, the knowledge never made me feel better; instead it seemed the worst part of all—that our lives at Ault were only temporary.

Ms. Moray was at the board, showing us how to divide a line in a poem into stressed and unstressed syllables, when I felt Dede nudge my thigh. I turned, but she was looking straight ahead.

A few seconds later, I felt more of a pinch. I looked down and saw that she was trying to pass me a piece of paper. At the top, in handwriting I recognized as Aspeth's, it said, *RATE-O-RAMA for 11/8*. Beneath this was a grid, with *Dress*, then *Shoes*. then *Makeup* along one side; along another, it said *Aspeth*, then *Dede*, then *Lee*.

In the boxes adjacent to her name, Aspeth had written, for *Dress*, "3.4." For *Shoes*, she had written, "6.0." And for *Makeup*, she had written, "0.8," and she had added, the words cramped into the box, "*Can someone please tell this woman the heyday of aqua eyeliner is LONG past?!?*" Dede, meanwhile, had given *Dress* a 2.8, *Shoes* a 6.2, and *Makeup* a 1. Under Aspeth's comment, she'd written, "*Agree!*" which was the most apt and succinct summary of their relationship I could imagine.

Ms. Moray returned to the table, and I let the piece of paper sit untouched on my lap, like a napkin. But the truth was, I felt cornered by it. Yes, there were things I didn't like about Ms. Moray, but they had little to do with her clothes. And besides, didn't Aspeth and Dede understand that written words trapped you? A piece of paper could slip from a notebook, flutter out a window, be lifted from the trash and uncrumpled, whereas an incriminating remark made in conversation was weightless and invisible, deniable in a later moment.

Yet how could I not participate? They had extended an invitation, and if I refused, surely another one would never be offered. At the same time that Jeff Oltiss began reading aloud the Emily Dickinson poem that started "The most triumphant Bird I ever knew or met/Embarked upon a twig today," I set my pen against the piece of paper and, over the three empty boxes that awaited my ratings. Wrote, "All overshadowed by the pin—a real dazzler!" Before I could think more about it, I passed the paper back to Dede.

After class, I dawdled as I always did. In the stairwell, Aspeth glanced back—she and Dede were about twelve feet ahead of me—and our eyes met. "Such a good call on the pin, Lee," she said. She'd stopped walking, so Dede had stopped, too, and I caught up to them. "It's like, whose grandma did she steal that from?" Aspeth continued. "From now on, accessories get a category, too."

"Definitely," Dede said.

"So, Lee," Aspeth said, "I have something to ask you."

Dread reared up in me. Maybe she'd say, *Have you ever kissed a boy?* Or: *What kind of cars do your parents drive?*

"Can you cut my hair?" she asked.

"Oh," I said. "Sure." So great was my relief at the mildness of the question that it was only after I'd agreed to it that I remembered my conversation with Martha. Not that it had been conclusive, but it had given me pause.

179

"Since there's no formal dinner tonight, let's do it at six," Aspeth said. "Then there'll still be time to get to dinner before it closes."

On nights when there wasn't formal dinner, Martha and I went to the dining hall at six, the minute the doors opened, and usually I'd been ravenous since quarter after five; There was a group of people we sat with, the other sophomores who showed up early. They were mostly kind of dorky guys, and I was beginning to sometimes actively participate in the conversation instead of simply waiting until someone said something that required a response. But still—this was Aspeth.

"Six is fine," I said.

I knocked on her door three minutes after six, having arrived at five of, waited until six exactly, decided six exactly was probably worse than being a little early, and waited a few more minutes. From outside the door, I could hear pounding music, and I had to knock repeatedly before Aspeth answered. She was wearing a T-shirt, a red cardigan sweater with tiny, pearly star-shaped buttons, underwear, and no pants. Her long blond hair was wet, with grooves running along her scalp where she'd combed it back. She made a face at me, a kind of joking-apologetic face, then darted to the corner to turn down the stereo, leaving me an unobstructed view of her golden haunches: thin, smooth thighs, and the twin scoops of her ass encased in—fleetingly, this surprised me, and then it made complete sense, how the choice was both classic and sexy—white cotton underpants. The music on the stereo was the Rolling Stones, and it occurred to me that Aspeth was the kind of girl about whom rock songs were written. How could Dede bear to be around her? Even though it was just the two of us, I felt like her chaperone.

When she'd adjusted the stereo, Aspeth said, "Give me two secs. I was hoping my jeans would be dry, but I don't think they are"—here, she gripped in several places a pair of jeans hanging over a desk chair—"so I have to wear my other ones." She lifted a second pair of jeans from the top of a laundry basket, stepped into them, and pulled them up, buttoning them over her flat stomach. As she did, I felt my own insignificance—how I was someone in front of whom she could prance around in her underwear and yank on conspicuously dirty clothes, and how it wasn't because we were close, it was because she didn't care what I thought. Whereas I kept trying out in my mind things to say—*Can you believe how cold it's gotten?*—before rejecting them as stilted or boring or the kind of thing a boy who had a crush on her would say while trying to make conversation.

I looked around. Though Aspeth and I had been in the same dorm the year before, I'd never entered her room. Aspeth's roommate this year was a girl from Biloxi named Horton Kinnelly—Dede had longed to become Aspeth's roommate for sophomore year and had even believed she would, but I don't think anyone else had shared this belief—and on the two unmade beds were duvets with floral covers. (As always, the floral duvets made me think of Little Washington.) White Christmas lights, currently turned on, were taped high up along all the walls, and on the north wall they'd hung an enormous orange and green tapestry. Above one desk were lots of postcards and a map of Tibet, and above the other was a blue felt banner that said Ole Miss in white letters. On the third and fourth walls were several huge black-and-white posters—one of John Coltrane, another of a thin, shirtless, staring Jim Morrison (most girls had posters of still lifes from the MFA in Boston)—as well as the photo collages that were a staple of all Ault girls' rooms: pictures of you and your friends in fleece hats, skiing, or in bathing suits, at the beach; of you and your friends in formal dresses, before a dance; of you and your friends in Ault sports uniforms, your arms slung around one another's necks after a winning game. There were computers on both desks, and two stereos, and on all the surfaces there were notebooks and textbooks and

181

catalogs and a combination of cheap and expensive toiletries: a tall white plastic container of hand lotion, some talcum powder, several gold tubes of lipstick, mouthwash, a bottle of Chanel (I had never seen Chanel in real life), a carton of generic band-aids, and on the floor in front of the door there was a gray peacoat with satin lining, which Aspeth stepped on —stepped on, with her shoe—as we exited the room. Also, she left on the lights, Christmas and otherwise, as well as the music. Following her down the hall—before the haircut, we were picking up someone else, but either I hadn't caught who it was or she hadn't said—I felt overstimulated and vaguely irritated. The room I shared with Martha seemed so quiet and plain, our lives seemed so quiet and plain. Had Aspeth been born cool, I wondered, or had someone taught her, like an older sister or a cousin?

"So who are we meeting?" I asked. Aspeth was walking quickly, and I was a couple steps behind her.

She spoke, but I thought I must have heard her wrong, so I said, "Who?"

She turned. "What? You don't like him or something?"

"No," I said. "I just didn't—did you say Cross? Like, Cross Sugarman?"

She smirked. "Like, *the* Cross Sugarman? The *famous* Cross Sugarman? Why, do you have a crush on him?"

"No," I said, but I remembered that the more vehement I was, the more obvious it would be that I was lying. "I hardly know him," I added.

"I told him I was getting my hair cut and he was like, 'I've gotta see this.' So I said we'd swing by his dorm and get him."

In the last couple months, I had been in the common rooms of nearly all the boys' dorms. Most of them smelled weird and were littered with pizza boxes, and the more guys present, the more unwelcoming they were, slouching with their hands in their pants, talking and laughing about a topic that was probably but not definitely sex, glancing at me in the hopes that I either had or hadn't understood their coded remarks and had or hadn't been offended. Or else they'd be playing some game, throwing around a basketball so that it flew toward my head and I had to stumble away, mid-clip, from the person whose hair I was cutting, or maybe the game was even more made-up, maybe they were kicking a pizza box and trying not to let it touch the ground as it became increasingly punctured. The TV was always turned on and set to something jarringly loud or really boring or, as in the case of the Sunday when I'd cut Martin Weiher's hair while he watched a monster truck show, both. Always before showing up at a boys' dorm, I'd have made sure I looked nice, maybe borrowed Martha's perfume, but once there, I'd feel utterly irrelevant, or even worse, like an intruder. Girls always liked when boys were around, but it often seemed to me that boys preferred to be by themselves, talking about girls in the hungry way that, I suspected, they found more gratifying than the presence of an actual girl. Yet strangely, in the loud sour inhospitable lairs of my male classmates, as out of place as I felt, I never really wanted to leave; sometimes I'd prolong a haircut by cutting individual strands, pretending to even things up. (Once I finished a haircut, it was unthinkable that I'd stay, that I'd just *hang out*. This might have been fine for other girls, but I needed a reason.) I wanted to stay, I think, because the way these boys were, their bluntness, their pleasure in physical acts like wrestling and burping, the way everything was too noisy and disorderly to ever feel awkward—this all seemed perhaps preferable to, truer and more lively than, the way that girls were. At least it seemed preferable to the way I was, trying to look pretty, trying to seem smart, when wasn't I just as full of disgusting urges as any boy?

Inside the common room of Cross's dorm, a bunch of guys were sitting on the couches, eating hamburgers and french fries and drinking out of huge wax cups—someone must have persuaded a teacher to drive him to McDonald's and put in an order for the whole dorm. Usually when I entered a boys' common room, I stood in the doorway, waiting for someone to notice me and offer assistance. When I entered with Aspeth, Mike Duane, a senior and a big football player, immediately stood and walked toward us. "What's the word?" he asked and pulled Aspeth toward him in a bear hug. I had never, literally never, been hugged by an Ault boy.

"Tell Sug to get his ass out here," Aspeth said.

"I'll find him," said another guy and scrambled off down the hall.

"Man, Aspeth, why're you always coming around looking for Sug?" Mike said. "Why don't you look for me?"

Aspeth laughed. "Are you lonely?"

"I'm lonely for a hot girl is what I'm lonely for." He still had his arm around Aspeth's shoulder, and he began to rub her back. I would not have wanted Mike Duane to touch me like that. In his hulking strength and his red skin and heavy stubble, there was something potentially scary. "You should have been here—" Mike began, and then I heard Cross say, "Hey, Aspeth." He nodded once at me. "Lee." My heart was beating furiously.

"Let's get this over with," Aspeth said. "I'm starving." So, in fact, was I—the smell of food filled the common room, and what I'd much rather have done than cut Aspeth's hair was grab a pack of french fries, sprint away, and eat them somewhere by myself. Except that Cross had just appeared, and I'd rather have been in Cross's presence than anything. "Lee, where should we go?" Aspeth asked.

"I guess wherever." This was not the haircutting me but the normal—the shaky and uncertain—me. "We could just stay here."

"It reeks here," Cross said. "Let's go to the basement."

Mike Duane extracted another hug from Aspeth and then we both followed Cross out of the common room. In the basement, we entered a large room with a concrete floor, fluorescent lights, and narrow horizontal windows close to the ceiling; the room was empty except for a

184

humming soda machine, two laundry machines, and two dryers.

"I just realized," Cross said. "You probably need a chair, don't you?" He turned and disappeared back up the stairs.

We also needed a towel to put around Aspeth's shoulders, and newspaper to spread on the floor, but he was gone.

Aspeth yawned. "I'm so fucking tired. I was up until like three in the morning last night."

"Wow," I said. But Cross was requiring so much of my attention and anxiety that I no longer had any left for Aspeth. This piece of time was about his absence, before he returned with the chair.

"And the night before that I was up until two."

I was wondering how far back we'd go in her sleep schedule when Cross reappeared. He was carrying a wooden desk chair with metal legs, holding it by the back so the legs stuck into the air and the seat rested on his shoulder. It seemed an especially boyish, cute way to carry a chair. He set it in front of the soda machine, and Aspeth sat down.

"You'll get hair on you," I said. "You might want to take off your sweater."

She did as I said—so even with Aspeth, I had that peculiar authority—and passed it to Cross. "How pretty," he said in a high, feminine voice, and he tied the arms of the sweater over his shoulders. The gesture horrified me.

"Red's definitely your color," Aspeth said.

"Thanks, doll," he said in the same voice as before.

I felt an urgent wish for him to take off the sweater, and to stop talking that way. His behavior wasn't funny, and the kind of funny it was trying to be was so ordinary, so lame even. Plus, I knew Cross wouldn't act this way in front of only me, that his performance was for Aspeth's benefit. Previously, I'd felt a secret hope that he was observing the haircut not because of her but because of me. It was less difficult than it probably should have been to believe that Cross felt exactly the way about me that I felt about him. I didn't always believe this, but there were times—between classes, say, when we almost collided in the stairwell, and then we just stood there for a few seconds on the landing, face-to-face, not moving, before we continued in opposite directions. If things were normal, wouldn't he have said something, like *hi*, and couldn't it perhaps be a promising sign that instead he'd said nothing?

"I want to keep it all the same length but shorter," Aspeth said.

Cross laughed—a normal, masculine laugh, thank God. "How can it be shorter if it's all the same length?"

"Therein lies the paradox," Aspeth said. This was something people at Ault said a lot, a kind of catchphrase they'd been using since I'd arrived the year before. The first time I heard one of my own classmates, Tom Lawsey, use it, there was something embarrassing about the self-consciousness of it, the fabricated newness, as if he'd gotten a nose job and then pretended otherwise. But the expression was so common that I pretty much stopped noticing, and once—not at Ault but at home over the summer, when my mother asked me how I planned to finish making the chocolate chip cookie dough when it turned out we were out of eggs—I even heard myself say it. (Of course, that really hadn't been much of a paradox at all; I'd solved it by walking two houses down to borrow from the Orshmidts.) Another thing that had been popular to say for a while, among my classmates more than the rest of the school, was the word *patina*. It had gained popularity in my Ancient History class, where it went from being a term for the green film that formed on bronze or copper to meaning something vaguely dirty—while wiggling their eyebrows or licking their lips guys would say (not to me, of course, but to other girls), "You have a nice patina." But *patina* ultimately hadn't had the staying power of, *Therein lies the paradox*.

I said to Cross, "Aspeth means she wants all the strands of hair to be the same length as each other but for all of them to be shorter."

Cross looked at me blankly. He'd probably understood all along.

"Exactly," Aspeth said. "See, Sug, Lee gets it."

From the plastic bag I'd been carrying since I'd left my room almost half an hour before, I pulled out scissors and a hairbrush (not my own—soon after cutting Tullis's hair, I'd bought one for general use, which I never cleaned and no one ever asked if I cleaned). I stood behind Aspeth and brushed her still-damp hair. Her shampoo smelled both nutty and floral, and I could see again why boys loved girls like her. "How many inches?" I said.

"I'm thinking four or five."

"Are you sure?" Normally, I liked to cut as much as possible, I liked drasticness. But Aspeth had such outstanding hair that it seemed like I might be doing a disservice to the entire Ault community. "Let's start with three inches and see how you like it."

"But when it's long, it tangles more. Maybe you should just shave my head."

"You'd look good with a shaved head," Cross said.

This was more the way I remembered him, how he could flirt by talking in an utterly ordinary way—how, in fact, the flirtatiousness lay in the discrepancy between his calm, sincere tone and the improbable nature of what he was saying.

"Fine," Aspeth said. "Take it all off. Make me bald."

I lifted a lock and snipped, then scanned the room and saw, as I had expected, no trash can. I let the hair drop onto the bare floor.

Cross came around and stood next to me. "Holy shit!" he said. "Oh my God! You *are* going to be bald, Aspeth." What I had cut was even less than three inches, but Cross felt like teasing her; he had no crush on me whatsoever.

"Shut up," Aspeth said. Probably she liked him back. The official word, as transmitted to me by Dede the year before, was that Cross and Aspeth were "good friends," and in fact, as freshmen, they'd both been going out with other people, but both of those relationships were over; Cross and Sophie Thruler had broken up back in October. If Cross and Aspeth liked each other, I thought, they really ought to just go out. It would be a stunningly unsurprising development.

"I don't know about this," Cross said. "You're putting an awful lot of trust in Lee, and, Lee, what are your credentials?"

I was bent over, and I turned my head to look up at him. The expression on his face was lighthearted. For several seconds, I said nothing, and I felt him meet and absorb my own expression, his smile straightening, and I felt that an understanding passed between us—*I am not no one, I am not nothing, I do not exist as a backboard for you to bounce your jokes off of*—but how can you ever be certain? Maybe he just thought I couldn't think of anything to say.

"Lee has cut a ton of people's hair," Aspeth said. "She was the one who cut Tullis's."

"No shit." Cross had moved around so he was standing in front of Aspeth again.

Aspeth lifted her head, probably subconsciously, to make eye contact with him. I could have pressed her head back down, but I didn't. I was ceding to her; in fact, I felt a perverse desire to aid their union. I almost didn't mind the way Aspeth was pretending she and I were aligned, us against Cross, girls against boy. "And Tullis's haircut was awesome," she was saying. "So there."

"So there? Geez, Aspeth, you should really consider becoming a lawyer. Is nanny-nanny-boo-boo next?"

There was something repellant about watching Cross flirt; it felt overly personal, like seeing him pick food from his teeth.

"Stick your head in doo-doo," Aspeth said, and they both laughed, and then she said, "Isn't that how it goes? Nanny-nanny-boo-boo, stick your head in doo-doo." This time, they said it in unison—things said in unison, like winks, made my skin crawl—and I had to fight the urge to bolt from the basement. They were losers! They were bigger dorks than I was! The trick, of course, would be to remember this at roll call when I saw them from far away, seeming coolly impenetrable.

"Aspeth," I said. They were still laughing, and I tried to come up with a different topic. "Do you think Ms. Moray will wear those boots tomorrow?"

"You have Ms. Marinade, too?" Cross said.

"Lee and Ms. Moray hate each other," Aspeth said. "They've had major battles."

Was this true?

"Were you part of the pimp thing?" Cross asked.

"No, but they've clashed other times," Aspeth said.

"Lee, I didn't know you were so"—Cross paused, and we made eye contact, and I thought that depending on what he said next, this might be a flash of the other Cross, the one I'd thought I liked—"angry," he said. It hadn't been a flash.

"I'm not." I probably sounded angry in this moment, but I didn't care.

"Marinade was never a first-draft pick, though, right?" Cross said.

"Shut up," Aspeth said.

"I thought everyone knew."

"Will you seriously shut up?" Then Aspeth seemed to reconsider something—apparently, me—because she said, "Okay, Lee, you can't tell this to anyone, but Ms. Moray was a last-minute addition to the faculty. I guess they'd hired this other woman to be the English intern, and she was super-smart, she went to Yale, she was black and everything so they were psyched for that, and then at the last minute, in August, her fiancé, who lives in London, got testicular cancer and she went to be with him. They were totally scrambling to find a replacement, and here's Ms. Moray, who, big coincidence, wants to teach but has no job lined up for the fall. So they hire her and, like, two days later she drives out from South Dakota."

189

None of us spoke—I had even stopped cutting Aspeth's hair—and then Cross said, "Cancer o' the balls. Ouch."

"How do you know?" I asked Aspeth.

"Renny told me." Renny Osgood was the woodworking teacher, a guy in his early thirties who'd graduated from Ault and then, alone among Ault faculty, not gone on to get a college degree. His handsomeness was commented on with regularity in the student paper, and he was rumored to have had an affair with a senior girl a few years back, though no one ever knew the girl's name; in any case, he did have "friendships" with certain current students, and Aspeth was one of them. "She's out of her league here," Aspeth said. "Not only as a teacher, but with coaching, too—you can tell she's a decent athlete, but she has no experience with field hockey. She doesn't even know the names for plays."

Of course Ms. Moray had no experience with field hockey—barely anyone played it in the Midwest. I had a sudden vision of her, back in September, finding out she'd been hired at Ault and packing up all her belongings in a hurry and heading East. I pictured her driving alone, changing radio stations when they turned staticky, staying at night in a motel where she could stand in the door of her room and see an endless field of soybeans interrupted only by a pro-life billboard or a water tower. From Iowa (not South Dakota) she'd probably taken I-80 to Cleveland, then picked up 90—that was the route my father and I had gone when he drove me to Ault to start my freshman year.

"She got lucky," Aspeth said. "She's a shitty teacher, but Ault was in a bind."

But she hadn't been a shitty teacher when she'd been hired. She'd never taught before. And who was Aspeth to decide she was shitty now? She was still inexperienced. Rarely did I wish I were not party to a piece of gossip, but it struck me that I really hadn't needed to know that Ms. Moray had been Ault's second choice.

"Okay," I said to Aspeth. "You're all finished."

Aspeth stood and ran her fingers back through her hair, one hand on each side of her head. I was slightly disappointed to realize how tidy I'd been—though the floor beneath the chair was littered with hair, virtually none of it had been scattered on Aspeth's shirt. She turned to Cross. "How do I look?"

"Ugly," he said.

Aspeth stuck out her tongue at him, yet even then she was not remotely ugly. She looked at her watch. "Fuck," she said. "Dinner is only open for fifteen minutes."

She walked toward the stairwell, and Cross followed her. I couldn't tell if I was also supposed to follow. Plus, there was the matter of cleaning up.

"Hey, Aspeth," I called.

She said "What?" without turning around.

"There's a lot of hair still on the floor."

She glanced over one shoulder. "There's not that much."

There was so much you could have made a wig from it. "Do you guys at least want to put the chair back?" I said.

"Oh, yeah." Cross walked back and hoisted the chair onto his shoulder again, and this time, the motion seemed charmless.

"Thanks a zillion, Lee," Aspeth said, and they both disappeared.

I looked from the hair on the floor to the stairs. It may have been Aspeth's hair, but it was still pretty gross just to leave it there. In the end, I went back up to the common room, borrowed a broom and dustpan, swept it up, dumped it in the trash—as I did so, I had a fantasy of transporting it across campus and dumping it instead in Aspeth's bed, but this probably was a disciplinary offense and even if it wasn't, it was highly Audrey Flahertyish—and then returned the broom to the dorm closet. The common room had emptied out, and there were a few french fries stuck forlornly to the table in front of the couches. I considered eating them—after all, I had missed dinner—but that would be pretty Audrey

Flahertyish, too. Martha had been right, I thought as I walked back to my dorm. And this was it, the last time: I was retiring from cutting hair.

The assignment for *Song of Myself* was to write about something that mattered to us, to take a stand, and in the days before the assignment was due, I couldn't think of anything. "The death penalty," Martha suggested on the way to formal dinner.

"Would I be for or against it?"

"Lee!"

"I'm assuming against."

"You'd be against it because it discriminates against minorities and poor people. The overwhelming majority of people who get the death penalty are uneducated black men. Plus, a lot of people sent to death row have turned out to be innocent." Martha knew this sort of thing both because her father was a lawyer and because she was a generally more serious and better-informed person than I was. The information floating around in my own brain concerned, for instance, the name of a famous actor's pet Shih Tzu (Petunia), or why a model had recently been shipped to rehab (for anorexia, with additional rumors that she'd been snorting coke).

"The death penalty's a good topic," I said. "But maybe not for me."

"You could do welfare or abortion."

"Dede will do abortion."

"Okay, fine, toenail polish—pro or con?"

"Perfect." I said. "You're a genius." We were quiet as we passed the chapel. I was so much less lonely, things were so much better for me, now that I was rooming with Martha. "Hey," I said. "What if I do something on prayer in school? I could compare public and private schools and say something like it's fine at a place like this because everyone who's here made a choice to come. But it's not really fair in public school because what if you're Jewish or Buddhist?"

"That sounds okay," Martha said. "It's not great because it's not something you're passionate about, but it sounds good enough."

When we turned in the papers, to my relief, Ms. Moray didn't make anyone read aloud. They were to have been a minimum of 800 words, and counting my name, the date, the words "Sophomore English, Ms. Moray," and the title, mine had been 802. I imagined that she hadn't had us read them in class because they were too long, but when she handed them back the next week, it turned out she did want us to read. "I like for you guys to know what's on each other's minds," she said. "Norie, why don't you start?"

She seemed to have forgotten to return my paper, and I raised my hand, but she didn't call on me, so I put it down. I wasn't going to interrupt; it would be better to wait until it was my turn. Chris's paper was about the importance of sports in school; Aspeth's was about how travel expands your horizons; Dede's was about how she'd become pro-choice. (Since the day Dede had passed me the ratings sheet, I purposely hadn't sat next to her, but I had watched to see if she and Aspeth had done it again, and they had; they'd done it daily. I was too far away to read what they wrote, but on the day Ms. Moray wore a kilt, complete with an oversized safely pin, I knew they'd trash her—a kilt was another idea of boarding school that only an outsider would have.) Jenny's essay was about how her best friend in second grade had died of leukemia, which didn't exactly seem like a strong belief she had, but it was so sad that I thought she deserved an A anyway.

I was beside Jenny, and when she had finished reading, Ms. Moray said, "Jeff, you can go ahead."

"Ms. Moray?" I said.

"You're not going," she said. "And you know exactly why." Her face was flushed. I could feel the other students watching me, and I turned to Jeff, as if to give him my blessings to go

193

ahead, as if I had any idea what was happening. The only thing I could imagine was that this was somehow related to my refusal to read back in the second week of school.

When the bell rang, Ms. Moray said, 'We'll pick up here tomorrow. Darden and Martin, remember to bring your papers back to class. Lee, stay here, and the rest of you are dismissed.'

After everyone had gone, she took something—my paper—from under her grade book and shoved it down the table toward me. It slid about halfway and stopped, still out of my reach. I glanced at Ms. Moray before leaning in to take it, and something in her expression made me freeze.

"I could flunk you for the term if I wanted to," she said. "Your lack of respect for me as a teacher and your lack of respect for this classroom—I'm dumbfounded, Lee. I don't know if this is something we can work through."

I waited to see if there was more, and when it seemed almost definite that there wasn't, I said very quickly, "I'm sorry, but I'm not sure what you're talking about."

She raised her eyebrows disbelievingly, but I held her gaze. The longer I held it, I imagined, the more likely that I might persuade her of my ignorance. She was the one to look away, and when she did, I reached for the paper. The title I had chosen, which now had a red F circled above it was "Prayer Is Not A Good Idea In Public Schools." Next to the title I'd put an asterisk, and beside the asterisk on the bottom of the first page I'd written, "This is not an issue I truly care about, but I believe it fulfills the assignment." This remark was surrounded by a jungle of red writing, which I scanned, though not all the words were legible: *Then why did you bother to write it?! Do you not understand . . . your glibness and utter lack of regard for . . . because this assignment, the entire purpose of which . . .*

I looked up. "I didn't mean that I don't care like I don't care at all, I just meant I don't *care* about it."

"That makes no sense."

"I was just telling the truth."

"Then why didn't you pick another topic?"

"I couldn't think of one."

"There's nothing you feel strongly about? Here you are, you're going to this incredible school, being given every advantage, and you can't think of anything that matters to you. What do you plan to do with yourself?" She waited, and I realized it was a question I was supposed to answer.

"You mean for a job? Maybe—" It had occurred to me that I might like to be a teacher, but surely this would seem suspect. "Maybe a lawyer," I said.

She made a scoffing noise. "Lawyers stand for something. They believe in something. At least the good ones do." She refolded her arms. "I don't know what to do with you, Lee. I don't understand you. You're a cipher. Do you get anything at all out of coming to this class?"

"Of course."

"What?"

"I'm not sure what you're asking specifically."

"I'm asking if you get anything out of coming to this class. It's a pretty simple question."

Neither of us spoke, and as the silence stretched, I felt further and further from the last thing she'd said. Perhaps I could change the subject entirely, reply to a different topic— I could say, *And that's why parrots make really good pets*. Or, *It's because I've always wanted to visit New Mexico*. When I thought about it, it seemed a little ridiculous, a little arbitrary, that this was the conversation we were having; fighting with Ms. Moray felt inorganic.

But I couldn't say those things. It would be bizarre. She would think there was something wrong with me, something more wrong than what she already thought.

"I like the reading," I said. "I think it's interesting."

"What book has been your favorite?" I could hardly finish speaking before she was barking another question.

"I like, um, *Song of Myself*."

"What do you like about it?"

"I don't—" I made a kind of involuntary gulping sound. I was not about to cry, but it sounded like I was, and immediately, Ms. Moray's expression softened. "I don't know," I said. "The words."

"I like Whitman, too," she said. "That's why I assigned him."

She was staring at me—with less hostility than before but still staring—and I looked away, at the chalkboard, at the window, down at the table. When I looked back at her, her stare had not wavered.

"You can go through life disengaged," she said. "You can be a person who always says no, who's not interested, not enthusiastic, who's too cool to be part of things. Or, at some point, you can say yes. You can develop interests, take a stand, reach out to people. I see the way you don't talk to your classmates before or after class. People want to be friends with you. Dede and Aspeth want to be friends with you, and at some point, I hope you'll give them the chance."

I felt the corners of my lips twitch. To smile at this moment would be the worst thing I could do; it would enrage her. But she was so *wrong*. She was wrong about everything, and her wrongness was, if absurd, also flattering. I was not disengaged, I was not disinterested, Aspeth certainly did not want to be my friend, and I was one of the least cool people I knew—all I ever did was watch other students and feel curious about them and feel dazzled by their breeziness and wracked by the impossible gaping space between us, my horrible lack of ease, my inability to be casual. And not feel strongly about things? I felt strongly about everything—not just my interactions with people, their posture or their inflections, but also the physical world, the smell of the wind, the overhead lights in the math wing, the precise volume of the radio in the bathroom if it was playing while I brushed my teeth. Everything in the world I liked or disliked, wanted more or less of, wanted to end or to continue. The fact that I had no opinion on, for instance, relations between the U.S. and China did not mean I didn't feel things. As for whether I was a cipher, that was more difficult to say because I didn't know what the word meant. But I would definitely look it up in the dictionary when I got back to the dorm.

"Are you hearing me?" Ms. Moray asked.

"Yes."

"I mean, do you *get* what I'm saying?"

"I know. I—I get it." She wanted more from me. She wanted me to talk as much as she was, to confide. But I had nothing to say. I was not what she believed me to be except at this moment, with her, because she'd invented me. "Do you want me to rewrite the paper?" I asked.

"This isn't about the paper. Yes, the paper pissed me off a whole lot, but this is, and I know this sounds dramatic but the stakes are high here, this is about your life. About you making something of your life. I want you to remember this conversation."

Why had she picked me? I wondered. What in my demeanor provoked her?

"I want today to be the day you decided to say yes." She slapped her palm against the table. It was a slap of excitement—her fury was gone—and it made me think of Aspeth; if Aspeth had witnessed this scene, this would be a gesture she'd imitate later, the fervor of it. Even if I didn't know the reason, I was glad that Ms. Moray had chosen me to freak out on because I would only tell Martha about it, I wouldn't spread it all around the school. "Will today be the day?" she asked.

I swallowed. "Okay."

"You don't sound certain."

I was supposed to say *Yes!*—to really shout it—but I didn't. It wasn't that I was unwilling to humor her, more that I was unwilling to lie. Did she actually think, if I cried out enthusiastically, that it would mean anything? Wasn't she a little old to believe that a person could transform her outlook in

197

the span of ten minutes? Before, her comments had seemed like a misunderstanding of me, but they'd had a relationship, even in their inaccuracy, to my life. This part of her presentation had nothing to do with me at all; she was acting like a football coach, or a motivational speaker. I'd had this thought before but never explicitly and never with sadness rather than disdain. As I looked at her agitated, hopeful face, I thought, *You're not that smart.*

She came to my dorm that night, knocking on the door around nine o'clock. Martha was at the library, and I was eating graham crackers and reading *Glamour*. She didn't wait for me to open the door but turned the knob herself and stepped inside. Seeing her in the threshold was both surprising and perfectly natural—since I'd left her classroom, my head had been pretty much continuously buzzing with pieces of our conversation, and her presence felt merely like the physical manifestation of what I'd already been imagining.

"I'm not interrupting, am I?" she said.

I stopped chewing. "No."

"Here's what I want." I could feel the energy coming off her body—she'd had an idea, she'd decided something, she'd walked briskly through the cold air across campus—and how it contrasted with my own inertia, my bad posture, the crumbs dusting the front of my shirt. I sat up straighter.

"I want you to cut my hair," she said. "I'll give you a grade for it. And that's how you can make up the paper. Whatever grade I give you for the haircut replaces the F."

I looked at her and felt suddenly, extremely tired. "How's that for a deal?" she said.

"Um, okay." Of course I was going back on my vow to stop cutting hair. She was my teacher, and I had no choice, but even if it had been someone else, another student, I still wouldn't have said no, and I didn't over the next few months. For a while, I kept saying yes and then I'd say, *What about in a few days?* and I wouldn't follow up, and sometimes I'd say, *You know, your hair looks kind of complicated and I wouldn't want to mess it up.* Still, the last haircut I gave wasn't until well into my junior year.

Ms. Moray grinned. "You'll see that this is no favor on my part. My hair desperately needs to be cut."

I hesitated. "You want me to do it now?"

"That'd be great. I brought the tools." She reached into her bag, took out a brush and a pair of scissors—of all the people whose hair I cut, she was the only one who ever provided her own—and held them up. "I imagine these'll do the trick. Should we adjourn to the bathroom?"

It wouldn't have occurred to me, but I was relieved by the suggestion; having her in my room made me uneasy.

I carried a chair into the bathroom and set it on the tile floor between the stalls and the row of sinks. Ms. Moray sat. I stood behind her, holding one of Martha's towels. It would be weird to put it on her, to pat her shoulders or touch her throat. I walked in front of her and handed her the towel. "Here," I said. "So the hair doesn't get all over you."

"Ah," she said. "Very thoughtful. Excellent customer service, Ms. Fiora. Should I be getting my hair wet?"

"You don't need to." Standing behind her, I told myself that hair was just hair. I could pretend she was someone else.

She bent her neck forward. I saw that she had a mole, a tiny tan bubble just below her hairline, and I felt a wave of repulsion. I could smell her hair, a distinct human smell, not the perfume of Aspeth's shampoo. At the crown of Ms. Moray's head, the hair was clumped together in darker, moist-looking bunches. Either she hadn't washed it lately, or it got greasy fast—probably, to be fair, it got greasy fast, because her face was greasy, too. I began to brush. Ms. Moray's hair was thick, thicker than it looked, which meant it would take longer to cut. But I would be careful, I wouldn't rush it. The situation called for thoroughness—the fact that I was capable of doing this well made doing it well an obligation.

We didn't speak. I think she'd have liked to, but I gave her

199

no encouragement, and as the minutes passed, I could feel her becoming calmer, settling into the lull of her own stillness. I did the back, the right side, the left, then came to the front and made sure it looked even. I brushed it all once more, to see if there were any stray long pieces. It was 9:45. then 9:50, and I could hear people returning to the dorm for curfew at ten. What was Ms. Moray thinking as I cut her hair? She was twenty-two years old then—I found this out later in the year because in March, she brought us cupcakes for her twenty-third birthday—and her mind was a city I couldn't yet imagine.

But later I could imagine it; I could see her as having been in a clearly recognizable stage of her life. She was a young woman who had moved alone to a different part of the country, and she must have been acutely conscious of all these factors—that she was young, that she was a woman, that she was alone; her happiness, if she was happy (I have no idea if Ms. Moray was happy), must have felt so tenuous. This is why, looking back, I am almost sure that she bought the silver book pin for herself. To have done so would have been the act of someone trying very hard. On the afternoons when I used to gaze at it, fastened to her button-down shirts or turtleneck sweaters, while she sat at the head of the table or stood at the chalkboard, when I thought of all the ways she might have obtained the pin, that's the one possibility that didn't occur to me. To think it would have seemed unbearably depressing, it would have seemed pathetic (it is, of course, a mark of my own youth at the time that to try too hard struck me as so sad, as if the world were not full of many greater sorrows), and it might have elicited from me true and continuous sympathy instead of mere intermittent pangs.

When the haircut was finished, Ms. Moray turned from side to side in front of the mirror. She said, "This is great, Lee. I see what all the fuss is about." Before she left, we stood facing each other in the hall outside the bathroom, and she said, "Really, I can't thank you enough." I could tell that she was considering hugging me, and I willed her not to.

I would not want to see her now, I would not want to apologize to or thank her, I do not believe she influenced my life in any lasting way, as the best teachers are supposed to do. But something about her is haunting to me: perhaps her blend of bravado and sincerity, perhaps the mystery of what happened to her next (as far as I know, no one from Ault was ever in touch with her after she left), perhaps only her mistakes because she made so many.

For the haircut, as I had known she would, she gave me an A.

5

Parents' Weekend

WHEN I ENTERED the dining hall, I saw that it was as quiet and empty as on a Sunday morning, though actually it was just after six on Friday night. In the section where juniors sat, only one table was occupied, and even that was only half full. I set down my tray between Sin-Jun and Nick Chafee, the blond, not especially handsome guy whose grandparents had started the Chafee Museums in Philadelphia and San Francisco. Across the table sat Rufina Sanchez and Maria Oldega, who were the only Latina girls in our class besides Conchita and were roommates and best friends. Rufina had long wild black hair and swollen lips and dark, thin, arched eyebrows over big eyes, and she wore tight jeans and tight shirts. Maria wasn't nearly as pretty, and she was heavier, though she, too, wore tight clothes. Also, she wasn't deferential toward Rufina, she didn't talk less in groups, and that was something about her that had always impressed me.

When I'd sat, I turned to Sin-Jun. "Your parents aren't here this year?"

She shook her head. "Too far."

"I guess especially if they've been before," I said. When they'd come from Seoul our freshman year, Sin-Jun's parents had taken me out for dinner at the Red Barn Inn, which was, apparently, the only restaurant between the Ault campus and Boston that most parents could abide. The dining room had been filled with Ault families, and many of the parents seemed to know one another independently of their children; they lingered by each other's tables, called out to one another in joking tones. When Mr. or Mrs. Kim spoke to me, I had a hard time concentrating on what they were saying over the background din, and when I responded to their questions about where I was from and whether I liked Ault, I didn't know if my answers made sense. Mrs. Kim had a dead front tooth and bright, shiny red lipstick, and she ate approximately a tenth of the food on her plate and didn't ask for a doggie bag; Mr. Kim was balding and smelled of cologne and cigarettes. They both spoke fluent, heavily accented English and were both short. Like most Ault parents, they were rich—Sin-Jun's dad owned a bunch of running-shoe factories—but they were Korean rich, foreign rich, and that was not at all the same as New England, or New York, rich. Most of the other parents resembled one another: The fathers were tall and thin and had gray hair and rueful smiles, and they wore suits. The mothers' hair was ash-blond and they wore headbands and pearl earrings and gold bracelets and black cardigan sweaters with gold buttons over long plaid skirts, or else—the skinny ones wore this—pantsuits in beige or charcoal, with silk scarves around their necks. (Also, the mothers had names that made it hard to imagine they'd ever held real jobs: Fifi and Tinkle and Yum.) In addition to dining at the same restaurant, they all stayed at the same hotel, a swanky Sheraton on I-90; they rented separate rooms for their children, and according to rumor, all the kids staying there, which was most of the kids in the school, got trashed and ended up skinny-dipping in the indoor pool, or making out in the hall by the ice machine. The Kims had not invited me back to the Sheraton, but, honestly, I wouldn't have wanted to go—Sin-Jun and I probably would have gotten in our beds and just lain there in the dark, listening through the walls to

203

the thumping and shouting of other people's good time. Sophomore year, Martha invited me to go to the Red Barn for dinner with her parents, and I went, but when she'd invited me this year, I'd declined and only in the moment of declining had I realized how much I'd hated it all along.

"My father think of coming, but my mother say plane ride make her so tired," Sin-Jun said.

"When you're flying from Asia, it's worse coming west to east," Nick said. "When I got back from Hong Kong, I slept for like a week."

I didn't respond to Nick's remark, and neither did anyone else. I finished cutting my spaghetti, set down my knife, and wound noodles around my fork.

"Lee," Maria said, and I looked up from my plate. "Your parents aren't here, either?"

"They're coming tomorrow." Immediately, I felt a welling anxiety that someone would ask why they were arriving late— after all, the headmaster's welcoming tea had occurred that afternoon—and I would not want to admit that they were driving, not flying, from South Bend. ("All the way?" someone might ask. "What is that, twelve hours?" and I would have to reveal that in fact it was eighteen.)

"Just make sure they come after our game is finished," Rufina said. "That's something no parent should see." Though we were juniors, Rufina, Maria, and I all still played on JV soccer.

"It is the first time for your parents to visit, yes?" Sin-Jun said.

"Besides when I started here," I said, though only my father had dropped me off.

"Dude," Nick said. "I'm so happy my parents aren't coming. My brother goes to Overfield, and it's parents' weekend there, too."

"What, they like your brother better?" Rufina asked.

"The official reason is that he's a freshman so it's his first

204

parents' weekend. Not that I'm complaining." Nick grinned. "Really."

Everyone laughed, including me—over time at Ault, I'd realized that it was an act of aggression not to react to a situation as everyone else was reacting, a request for attention—but I felt surprised. Didn't Nick feel guilty, wasn't it a betrayal to insult people you were close to in front of people to whom you weren't close? On sitcoms and in movies, a casual antipathy for your parents was the norm—men dreaded going home for Christmas, women wrangled with their mothers over wedding plans—but such scenarios bore no relation to my own experience. I knew my parents so well, they were so real to me: the sound of their car pulling into the driveway, the smell of my mother's mouthwash, my mother's red bathrobe and the brand of her cottage cheese, and the way my father could burp the alphabet and carry both my brothers, one under each arm, up the stairs at the same time. How could I speak of my parents casually, ever, at all, unless I was not really thinking of them but thinking only of the words *my mom* and *my dad*?

"You know why I like parents' weekend?" Maria said. "Because the food is so much better. Not this"—she gestured toward the few limp noodles resting in watery marinara sauce on her plate—"but like tomorrow, the lunch is going to be so good."

Rufina snorted. "And then all the parents can say, *Ault takes such great care of its students. I am so glad we decided to send little Teddy here.*" Rufina was speaking in a snooty accent on top of her normal accent; the overall effect made her seem cheerfully goofy, not bitter as I suspected I would have if I mocked Ault. She turned to Maria and said in her normal voice, "You think they'll have those brownies again? Those were *good.*"

"We went to the tea at Mr. Byden's," Maria explained.

"Until we got kicked out for wearing jeans," Rufina added, and they looked at each other and laughed.

205

I, of course, had not attended the tea; it was meant to welcome parents and I hadn't yet had any parents on the premises. I was not real friends with either Rufina or Maria, but I'd always felt a mystified admiration for the way they seemed not to care what people thought of them. They didn't seem to feel either beholden to Ault for its gifts—they were both on scholarships, and wasn't a scholarship, in essence, a gift?—or worshipful of its conventions. But there were two of them and only one of me and you could not act irreverent alone, not really. Plus, while I could pass, their ethnicity made their status as outsiders definitive.

"Hey," Nick said. "My brother just sent me this Pink Floyd CD. You guys want to go to the activities center and listen?"

"Maybe," Maria said.

"What about you?" Nick looked at Rufina, and I wondered for the first time if he was interested in her. Surely he didn't want to be her boyfriend—Ault guys almost never went out with minority girls, and if they did, it was some geeky guy and some Asian or Indian girl, never a black or Latina girl from a city and definitely never with one of the bank boys. But maybe Nick thought Rufina was pretty, maybe that explained his presence here. Because it was, in fact, kind of odd that Nick Chafee was hanging out with a group of girls like us. Even if his own parents weren't visiting, it seemed he ought to be at the Red Barn Inn with the parents of a friend.

"You want to, *chica*?" Maria said, and she poked Rufina's upper arm.

"Ouch," Rufina said. Maria poked Rufina again, and Rufina said, "Quit it or I'm reporting you for roommate abuse." Then she laughed loudly, with her mouth open. The intensity of the laugh so exceeded the exchange that had prompted it that I realized that Rufina must be happy. I had never thought of her as happy before, and I wasn't sure when it had happened, whether her mood was temporary or permanent. I wondered, did she like Ault? Her complaints aside, did she feel as if the school belonged to her? I had a

206

sudden memory from our freshman year of sitting next to her on a bus returning from an away game. It was early November, a bleak day of gray skies, and because the score had been close—from the second half on, Ault had been losing by only one goal—the coach had kept us both on the bench for the whole game. At first we had talked a little, and cheered for our teammates, and sometimes stood and walked around or stretched, to stay limber in case we got subbed, but it was so cold that after a while we simply sat there—Maria had been on the bench, too, and a couple other girls—and huddled together wordlessly. When the game ended, I didn't care that we'd lost. Back on the bus, still in my uniform, I took a seat next to Rufina, and my body seemed to thaw and expand. Riding down the highway, the trees on either side brown and bare, the grass dead, the sky nearly white, I was able to submit to the moment, this interval of time. Back on campus, I'd have to navigate the chaos of the locker room (because I hadn't played in the game, it would seem un-necessary to shower, but I wouldn't want to be observed not showering) and then the separate chaos of dinner, and then there would be the empty time to fill in the dorm before bed. That wouldn't be a lull when I could space out because I was where I was supposed to be, because something, if only our return to campus, was being achieved and all I had to do was wait; in my room, I was responsible for myself, the choices were mine. I leaned my head against the back of the seat and listened to the sounds of the bus, the intermittent crackle of the driver's CB, the voices of the few girls not either sleeping or reading, the shadow of music that was someone else's Walkman playing an unrecognizable song. The bus seemed the best place for me to be in this moment—not a great place, I wasn't *enjoying* myself, but I'd have had a hard time naming anywhere better. And then beside me, I felt a shaking, and when I turned, I saw that Rufina was crying very quietly. She was looking out the window, and I could see only part of the left side of her face, which was flushed and streaked with makeup; back then, when she'd first arrived at Ault, Rufina had worn a lot of makeup, even during games—mascara, and black or purple eyeliner. Her right fist was clenched and held in front of her mouth, and she was heaving slightly. How long had she been crying? And was I supposed to say something or pretend I didn't notice?

I craned my neck in the other direction, peering up and down the aisle. No one else had any idea. I heard Rufina sniffle, and before I had made a conscious decision to do so, I'd set my fingertips on her forearm. "Do you want me to get Ms. Barrett?"

She shook her head.

"Do you want a tissue?" It was a napkin, actually, which I pulled from the backpack at my feet; I'd used it while eating a turkey sandwich on the ride to the game, and it was spotted by some mashed crumbs and a splotch of mustard.

She removed her fist from in front of her mouth, swallowed, turned to me, and extended her hand, palm up. When our eyes met, her expression was so plaintive that I wished the napkin were clean. She bent her head, blew her nose, then looked out the window again. We were passing a cluster of evergreens, shadowy in the approaching dusk, when she said, "I just want to know if it'll always be like this."

This was not what I'd expected. First, I had not expected that her voice would be as controlled as it was, and I also had expected her to be more specific about what was bothering her: *I miss my boyfriend* (I'd heard that Rufina went out with someone from back home in San Diego, an older guy who was in the Army) or *I can't believe Ms. Barrett didn't let us play*. What could I say to what she'd said? Either I had no idea what she was talking about or else I understood exactly, and given these two options, I wanted the latter to be true, but if I asked another question, then it wouldn't be; if I made her explain even a little, it would mean I didn't understand at all.

I took a breath. "No," I said. "I don't think so."

I waited to see if either of us would say anything else. She was still looking out the window, and I looked, too, and saw that it had started to snow.

And now two years had passed, Rufina wore hardly any makeup, she wore her hair not slicked back in a long ponytail as she once had but loose, she talked often and unself-consciously, even in front of guys like Nick. I wondered if I also had changed since our freshman year. Certainly not as successfully—I was less naïve, a little less anxious, but I was fatter, too, I'd gained ten pounds in the last two years, and also my identity felt sealed. Early on, I had imagined I might seem strange and dreamy, as if I spent time alone by choice, but now I was just another ordinary-looking girl who hung out most of the time with her roommate (similarly ordinary looking), who did not date boys, did not excel in either sports or academics, did not participate in forbidden activities like smoking or sneaking out of the dorm at night. Now I was average and Rufina was happy. And she was sexy, too—either she had not always been this curvy and golden-skinned or else I hadn't noticed. I wondered if she felt like she was wasting her time at Ault, being trapped in Massachusetts during the years she was beautiful.

"You should come listen," Nick was saying to Rufina, and then he said to Sin-Jun and me, "You guys should, too."

"You know we have nothing better to do," Maria said to Rufina.

"I got work," Rufina said, which was truly remarkable—that Nick seemed to be pursuing Rufina and that she was rebuffing him. Not that he was *really* pursuing her, I knew.

"I do, too,' I said and stood. Nick was being surprisingly nice, but I couldn't imagine he truly wanted me to come to the activities center. "Have fun," I said in what I hoped was a warm way.

Of course, now I wonder where I had gotten the idea that for you to participate in a gathering, the other people had to really, really want you to be there and that anything short of rabid enthusiasm on their part meant you'd be a nuisance.

Where had I gotten the idea that being a nuisance was that big a deal? Sometimes now I think of all the opportunities I didn't take—to get a manicure in town, to watch television in another dorm, to go outside for a snowball fight—and of how refusal became a habit for me, and then I felt it would be conspicuous if I ever did join in. Once when I was a sophomore, I was at a lunch table when Dede was organizing a group of people to go to a restaurant before the spring formal. She went around the table, pointing at each of us and counting, and when she got to me, she said, "Okay, not you because you never go to the dances." And that was true, but I'd have gone to a restaurant, I'd have put on a dress and ridden the charter bus and sat with my classmates at a big round table in a big room with an oversized red cloth napkin on my lap, I'd have drunk Sprite through a straw, have eaten warm rolls and roast beef and dessert; all of that would have been manageable. But in the moment of Dede bypassing me, how could I have explained this?

And there was something else, another reason I didn't want to go to the activities center with Nick. I believed then that if you had a good encounter with a person, it was best not to see them again for as long as possible lest you taint the previous interaction. Say it was Wednesday and there was an after-dinner lecture and you and your roommate struck up some unexpectedly fun conversation with the boys sitting next to you. Say the lecture turned out to be boring and so throughout it you whispered and made faces at one another, and then it ended and you all left the schoolhouse. And then forty minutes later, you, alone now, without the buffer of a roommate, were by the card catalog in the library and passed one of these boys, also without his friend—then what were you to do? To simply acknowledge each other by nodding would be, probably, unfriendly, it would be confirmation of the anomaly of your having shared something during the lecture, and already you'd be receding into your usual roles. But it would probably be worse to stop and talk. You'd be compelled to try prolonging the earlier jollity, yet now there would be no lecturer to make fun of, it would just be the two of you, overly smiley, both wanting to provide the quip on which the conversation could satisfactorily conclude. And then what if, in the stacks, you ran into each other again? It would be awful!

This anxiety meant that I spent a lot of time hiding, usually in my room, after any pleasant exchange with another person. And there were rules to the anxiety, practically mathematical in their consistency: The less well you knew the person, the greater the pressure the second time around to be special or charming, if that's what you thought you'd been the first time; mostly it was about reinforcement. Also: The shorter the time that elapsed from your first encounter to your second, the greater the pressure; hence the lecture-to-library agony. And finally: The better the original interaction, the greater the pressure. Often, my anxiety would set in prior to the end of the interaction—I'd just want it to be over while we all still liked each other, before things turned.

As I left the table, Rufina called, "You have fun with your parents."

My parents—I had forgotten about them. I walked toward the kitchen to put away my plate and silverware, and I felt a knotting in my stomach. Since they'd decided to come, I'd imagined their visit often, the things on campus I'd want to show them, but now that they were almost here, their impending presence seemed an interruption, an in-convenience even. Not that I didn't enjoy spending time with my parents, but wasn't I finally becoming comfortable at Ault, weren't dinners like this evidence of my increasing sense that I belonged? I had entered the dining hall alone, and then, even though Nick had been there, I'd participated in the conversation, eaten spaghetti—my entire first year at Ault, I hadn't dared eat noodles in public—and weren't those signs of progress? It struck me suddenly that my parents might be bewildered by me, the Ault version of me for whom it was a daring act to eat spaghetti. In sixth grade, in South Bend, I'd won first place in a pie-eating contest at my elementary school carnival. I'd scarfed down the pie using no hands, collected a gold plastic trophy shaped like a vase with handles, thrown up in a trash can, and proceeded directly to the U-Turn, a ride on which my friend Kelli Robard and I sat in a caged compartment that spun and flipped. But I had changed since then. I was different. And no matter what my parents might think, this—my Ault self—was now my real self.

Outside, it was dark and cool. The stars were bright white, and the almost-full moon was gleaming. The next two days were supposed to be perfect late-October weather, sunny but not hot, and all over campus, the leaves had turned gold and red. For the last two years, the weather had been similarly ideal for parents' weekend, which was unsurprising; Ault often seemed to me like a person who always got what he wanted.

And I didn't resent this institutional good fortune—on the contrary, I felt grateful to be a citizen of it. Though I personally did not always get what I wanted, I still was part of Ault's universe of privilege; I spoke its language now, I knew its secret handshake. My sense of belonging had perhaps never been as acute as on this evening, and I don't know if I recognized it then—later, it was obvious—but surely the timing was no coincidence. It was because my parents were coming and because I knew they would not belong. I think it often comes down to nothing but contrast—the way that it's only when you're sick that you wonder why, during the months and months of being up and about, you never appreciated your health.

First I was sitting outside the schoolhouse, on the limestone steps leading to the entrance on the building's north side, because my parents would be driving in the gate fifty yards away. They'd said they would arrive around nine. At six that

212

morning, while I'd still been in bed, the pay phone in the common room had rung and I'd bolted down the steps to answer it, knowing no one else's parents would call so early. They were just past Pittsfield, New York, my mother said, my father was getting coffee, and they couldn't wait to see me.

I was wearing a tan cotton knee-length pleated skirt. through which I could feel the coldness of the steps, and a navy wool sweater and bluchers with no tights, and I was reading my physics textbook, or at least holding it on my lap. Saturday classes had been canceled and virtually no one was up. It was a cool, sunny morning, and the mist was burning off the huge grass circle and, beyond the buildings, off the athletic fields. I thought of the things I could spend the day doing if my parents weren't coming—going running, or making a picnic. (Of course, these ideas were disingenuous. I didn't much like running. and I'd never make a picnic—what would I do, dash into town and buy a baguette?)

I tried to think what my parents wanted from the weekend. I was planning to give them a tour of the campus, and I knew my mother would like to meet Martha. My father was trickier. It seemed so much easier to enter his world—to hang out at his store, to help him rake the yard in the evening, to bring him a beer from the refrigerator while he watched the game (for years, my brother Joseph and I had fought over who got to open the bottle)—than to expect him to enter mine. When I was at school, we weren't in close contact by either phone or mail. He'd written me just once during my time at Ault, three times if you counted the Easter cards that they all signed, while my mother wrote me letters every two weeks or so. Her letters were both newsy and dull—*Ran into Mrs. Nielsen and Bree at the mall last weekend, they asked all about you. Bree said she has a teacher named Pertoski (sp?) for math and he's real tough, I said I didn't think you ever had him*—and usually after finding an envelope from her in my mailbox, I did not open it immediately; sometimes I even unearthed one in my backpack that I'd been carrying around for three or four days. But when I did open them, I read every word and I kept them all; it seemed mean, it made me feel sad, to put a piece of paper with my mother's handwriting on it in the trash.

As for my own letters to my parents, and many of the comments I made over the phone—they were lies. Afer all, Ault had been my idea. I'd filled out the applications on my mother's old typewriter, and the only parts my parents had helped with were the financial aid forms. Then, when I not only got into several schools but got offered scholarships as well, the biggest scholarship from Ault, I had no choice but to go. Why would I have gone to the trouble of applying if I hadn't wanted to go? But it was clear my parents always saw boarding school more as an "opportunity" than as a definitively good plan. And thus I could never express my unhappiness to them—not early on, when it was most intense, or later, in its more watered-down daily form. Even believing I liked Ault, my father would say from time to time, "Why don't you come back home and go to Marvin Thompson?" Or, after I told him about the nickname, "Aren't you sick of those Massholes yet?" And maybe I wasn't that unhappy anyway, if I was so set on staying.

At ten of nine, it occurred to me that my parents might miss this gate and go to the other one, and then they'd be wandering around campus looking for me. In my head, they were like Hansel and Gretel heading into the forest, and it seemed necessary that I act as their guardian. I jogged down the steps and hurried around the driveway toward the other gate. This time, I stood just outside it, where surely I wouldn't miss them. Unless, of course, they'd driven by already, gotten confused, and were at this very moment knocking on the door to a boys' dorm.

For several minutes, I leaned against a brick column with a concrete ball at the top. My mind had skittered off to something other than their arrival when I heard a honk. They were twenty feet away, ten feet, then right beside me in their—

214

our—dusty Datsun. My mother rolled down the passenger's-side window, and from the driver's side my father called, "Heigh-ho, heigh-ho," and my mother smiled gigantically and stuck her head and arms out and I stepped forward and stooped, and as we embraced I felt a flicker of awkwardness, our faces crushed together, my cheek shoving her big plastic glasses, before I remembered that it was my family and all the usual rules of awkwardness did not apply. "Lee, you look wonderful,' my mother said, and my father grinned and said, "She doesn't look that good to me," and my mother said, "Oh, Terry."

A silver Saab pulled in behind my parents' car and idled there, not honking. "You guys should move," I said. "Here, let me get in." I opened the back door, and when I climbed inside, it smelled like car trip, stuffy and sour. An empty Burger King bag rested on the seat, and several soda cans rolled on the floor. I could not suppress a comparison between this and the kind of food Martha's parents brought on their drives down from Vermont: vegetable soup in thermoses and cracked wheat bread and cut-up fruit that they ate with their real silverware from home. Stowed behind the back seat were my parents' suitcases, two large, light blue, fake leather squares. When Joseph and I had been younger, we'd made nests out of these suitcases, I remembered suddenly, padding their interiors with blankets, then climbing in and pulling the flaps over us like roofs that we propped up with our heads. The memory filled me with an odd, preemptive exhaustion—everything about my parents, even their luggage, reminded me of something, or made me feel a certain way.

My father accelerated and we rode through the gates of Ault. It had been more than two years since my father had driven me there to start my freshman year. He began to turn left as he'd done that other time, and I said, "Go right, Dad. There's a parking lot behind the dining hall." In fact, there was another parking lot to the left, behind the schoolhouse. But that one got more pedestrian traffic, more students who might catch sight of my parents' shitty car. My self-consciousness about the Datsun was something I'd anticipated, something I had to live with but could not acknowledge—a bride descending the aisle with an itchy nose.

"Honey, which one is your dorm?" my mother asked.

"You can't see it from here. It's through that arch."

"This is all just beautiful." She looked back and smiled, and I could tell she intended the remark as a compliment to me, as if I deserved credit for Ault's appearance.

"Now go right again," I said.

This early in the day, a lot of parking spaces were still open. My father pulled into one and turned off the ignition. He looked at my mother, then at me. "Should we just stay in the car and see if our asses get permanently attached to the seat?"

Normally, I'd have laughed—in general, my father made me laugh a lot—but instead I hastily said, "Thank you guys for coming. For driving so far."

"Honey, we wanted to," my mother said as we all climbed out. "Ignore Dad. Now what I need first is a bathroom and then we want you to show us everything."

We entered the dining hall through the back, and I led them toward the bathrooms. Just outside the women's room, I again had that sense of unease about leaving either of them alone, even briefly. It was probably smarter to stay with my father in the hall because he was the one who could get into more trouble—he could provoke it somehow, whereas my mother would only bumble into it—but I had to go to the bathroom myself. And, really, wasn't I being ridiculous? I followed my mother, and pushed into the stall next to hers. As I was setting toilet paper on the seat, she released a long, sighing fart and began to pee. "Lee, do we get to meet Martha?" she asked from her stall.

"I was thinking I could give you a tour of the campus, and then we can swing by the dorm. And then at noon, there's the lunch, and my soccer game is at two."

216

"Tell me again who you're playing."

"Gardiner."

"*Gardener*, did you say? Like flower garden?"

"It's pronounced the same, but it's spelled differently."

"Now why is it called that?"

"Mom, I have no idea. It's just a school in New Hampshire." She did not respond and, feeling mean, I added, "It was probably someone's last name."

She flushed the toilet—conversing with her required so much attention that I had not yet started to pee—and then I went myself. I heard her wash her hands, and then she called, "Honey, I'm going to find Dad." Maybe she, too, felt concerned about him being on his own.

When I emerged from the bathroom, they were looking at the framed pastel drawings on the wall. "Are any of these by you?" my mother asked. "Did you wash your hands, honey?"

"Of course."

"Your mother's afraid you'll get WASP germs," my father said.

This was a familiar joke—at home, after we returned from church and my mother told my brothers and me to wash our hands, my father would say, "Your mother's afraid you'll get Catholic germs"—but this version of it surprised me; it surprised me that my father knew what a WASP was.

"Oh, stop it, Terry," my mother said.

I wondered if she knew, too.

"None of the drawings are mine," I said. "I'm not taking art this semester." (My parents were not the kind—like Conchita Maxwell's mother—who knew every class I took, every way I spent my time.)

"You can see where we eat," I said. "It's this way." They followed me into the dining hall proper. The windows there reached almost to the ceiling—nearly fifty feet—and sunlight was streaming through all the panes on the east side of the room. On the south side, two steps led to a dais on which was set an extra-long table—this was where the headmaster sat during formal dinners and where seniors sat the rest of the time—and behind the table hung a school crest the size of a rowboat. Covering most of the rest of the wall were white marble panels with the names of all the senior prefects from 1882 on. In the main hall of the schoolhouse were wooden panels with the names of everyone from every class, but these were more special; there were fewer names, and they'd been engraved and then painted gold. All the tables in the room had already been set in preparation for lunch, and the kitchen staff was setting out napkins hunched up to resemble fans. I turned around. "I'll show you the chapel."

Neither of my parents moved. "It's like on our glasses." My mother was pointing to the wall behind the headmaster's table.

"Yeah, the school crest." The first Christmas after I'd started at Ault. I'd given my parents a set of four highball glasses from the school store. My mother put them out for dinner when I was home—because there were five of us, one person always got a different glass—but I doubted they used them when I wasn't there.

"And what are the other things on the wall?"

"They're lists of who the"—my mother wouldn't know what a prefect was—"kind of like class presidents," I said. "All the people who were class presidents their senior year here."

"Can we look at them?"

I squinted at her: "You won't know any of the names,"

"So?" my father said.

He and I eyed each other. "I'm not saying you can't," I said. "I just don't understand why you want to." My father continued to watch me. "Fine," I said. I crossed the dining room, and I heard them following me.

But—of course this was true and of course I'd forgotten it—they did recognize some of the names. They recognized three of them: a graduate from the thirties who'd gone on to be a U.S. vice president, one from the fifties who'd become head of the CIA, and, from the late seventies, a movie actor. I had told them before about these alumni, and about other alumni, not necessarily senior prefects, who'd gone on to acclaim; to people outside the school, it was the existence of famous graduates—and not, say, current students' median SAT scores—that seemed to most validate Ault. At home, if my parents' friends knew one thing about the place I went to school, it wasn't where it was or even what it was called; it was the names of the celebrities who'd graduated before me.

The three of us stood by the headmaster's table, our necks craned. "There's a girl here now whose dad is a senator," I said. I wasn't sure why I was revealing this—maybe because they'd be interested and because I knew that I hadn't been acting very pleasant.

"What's the name?" my father asked.

"Tunniff. She's from Oregon."

"I wouldn't mind meeting a senator this weekend."

I turned my head sharply to look at him, but he was still gazing up at the wall. Though he could probably feel my stare, his expression remained placid. It was impossible to tell if he was kidding—whether he was saying this because he knew it would bother me or because he had no idea. "Let's keep going if you want to see the whole campus," I said.

We walked to the chapel, which was empty except for someone practicing the organ. In the nave, we stood looking at the vaulted ceiling a hundred feet above us—a hundred and three, actually—and my father said, "I'll be damned." As they peered up, it struck me that my parents were less like characters from a fairy tale than like tourists in Europe. (Not that I had ever been to Europe myself, but Ault made you familiar with the cheesiness surrounding certain phenomena, even if you weren't familiar with the phenomena themselves—European tourists and a cappella singing groups and middle-aged Jewish women with hoarse voices and shiny sweatsuits and long painted fingernails.)

My father said, "This is where you pray for your sins. Flea?"

"Where I pray for yours," I said. "I don't sin."

He grinned, and I felt a smile come onto my own face.

"What about Mom's?" he asked.

At the same time, I said, "She doesn't sin, either," and my mother said, "I don't sin."

"See?" I said, "If we both think so, it must be true."

"Au contraire," my father said. "If what happened this morning between your mother and Burger King wasn't gluttony, then I'm a monkey's uncle."

"Terry, I didn't even eat the last hotcake," my mother said.

"Guess what, Dad?" I said. "It looks like you're a monkey's uncle."

"What do you think that makes you?"

"I'm fully human." Dropping my voice, I added, "Because we all know my real father is Mr. Tonelli."

"Oh!" my mother said. "The two of you are disgusting." Mr. Tonelli, who was in his early eighties, lived in the house behind my parents'; his wife had died a few years before, but even when she was living, we had all been convinced that he was in love with my mother.

"Have you heard the latest?" my father said.

I shook my head.

"They went on a date."

"That's nonsense." My mother had walked several feet away from us, picked up a hymnal, and begun leafing through it.

"Where?"

"Ask her."

"Where, Mom?"

"Mr. Tonelli isn't driving these days because of his glaucoma, and he asked if I could take him to get some dinner from Szechwan Garden. That's all."

"That is most definitely not all." My father was still grinning.

"There was some miscommunication," my mother said. "I thought he wanted to pick up the food, but it turned out he wanted to stay there. And, really, I had no choice but to join him, and then he insisted I order—"

"He *insisted*," my father repeated. "Here, her husband and sons are at home holding dinner for her, but when Mr. Tonelli *insists*—"

"Lee, I had a shrimp and black bean dish that was fabulous," my mother said. "You know I'm not a big fan of seafood, but Mr. Tonelli suggested it, and it was just delicious."

"Look at her trying to change the subject," my father said.

"Did he kiss you good night?" I asked.

"Oh, you're revolting," my mother said. "You're worse than Dad." My father and I smirked at each other. These were the best times with my family, when we were teasing one another or being gross. We talked about diarrhea at the dinner table; after we ate a meal with garlic, my brothers would bring their faces near mine and try to breathe into my mouth; and when Joseph got kicked off the bus once for singing a song about the scrotum, my father was so tickled he made Joseph write down the lyrics. (It was sung to the tune of the "Colonel Bogey March"—*Scrotum: It's just a sac of skin/ Scrotum: It holds your testes in . . .*) And then at Ault I never mentioned such things, certainly not to anyone other than Martha. And Martha's own family, apparently, never mentioned such things to one another. She once told me she had never even heard her mother burp. The way my family behaved felt both truthful and indecorous—another version of my real self, perhaps the realest of all, but one I took pains to conceal. Just a few months before, when Martha and I had eaten lunch at a table of boys, they'd been speculating about why a classmate always missed breakfast, and one of them formed a circle with his thumb and other fingers and jiggled his hand back and forth. Another of them, a guy named Elliot, turned to me and said in a not-unfriendly way, "You know what that means, Lee?" Did I know what that meant? Was he serious? I had been raised in a house where my father shouted up the stairs to my six- and thirteen-year-old brothers. "Quit whacking off and come down for dinner!" But when Elliot asked me, I actually blushed, as if even my physiology were conspiring in the lie of my seemliness.

My father snapped his fingers. "What say we blow this pop stand?"

My mother replaced the hymnal in the little space on the back of the seat, and we went out the front door, and as we did so, we collided with Nancy Daley, a willowy senior, captain of the squash and tennis teams, who had her parents in tow. The six of us stood in a kind of benign face-off, and then I said, "Hi. These are my parents." I glanced back at them, "Mom and Dad, this is Nancy Daley."

My mother extended her hand. "Nice to meet you, Nancy." My father shook her hand, too.

My heart was pounding—the thing was, I had never talked to Nancy before. Literally. And I had introduced her only because I hadn't known what else to do, because suddenly, with parents present, the protocol of Ault seemed absurd: that you could live for years in the same small community with people, that you could know their names and their secrets (as a sophomore, Nancy had hooked up in the music wing with Henry Thorpe, then a senior, and while they were hooking up, Henry had opened the classroom window, reached out. gathered snow in his hands, brought it back inside, and smeared it on her breasts), and that even with such knowledge, you could when passing on campus—you were supposed to, if you'd never really met—not speak or smile; possibly you would not even make eye contact. Surely neither Nancy nor I would have uttered a word had our parents not been there. And it wasn't that this absurdity offended me philosophically—it was just that I knew it would strike my parents as strange, and knowing that had made me panic. (But really, who cared what my parents thought was strange? What did I need to convince them of? It was Ault people I wanted to convince.)

My mother was shaking Nancy's parents' hands—"I'm Linda Fiora," I heard her say, and Nancy's mother said, "I'm Birdie Daley"—and my father was following suit. "Where are you folks from?" my father asked.

"Princeton," said Nancy's mother. She was wearing a silky maroon skirt with a swirling paisley pattern and a maroon sweater set, and Mr. Daley was wearing a suit. My own parents were dressed more nicely than they usually were on a Saturday, my father in khaki pants and a khaki blazer (surely, since they were not part of the same suit, that was some sort of faux pas) and my mother in a red turtleneck and a gray corduroy jumper. Over the phone, I had haltingly explained to my mother that most parents dressed up; I had felt unable to request that they should, but she had understood,

"We're from South Bend, Indiana," my father said. "Just got in about an hour ago, and we're damn glad to be here."

The Daleys laughed, or at least Nancy's parents did; Nancy herself gave a watered-down smile.

"Are you a junior, too?" my mother asked Nancy.

Nancy shook her head. "A senior."

"Oh, gosh," my mother said, as if a senior were as rare as a black pearl or an endangered tree frog.

"We better go," I said loudly. "See you later." I did not look at Nancy, and I hoped that she would know by my not looking that I recognized this exchange as merely random and would never try to talk to her again—that I might even, to make up for my transgression, go out of my way *not* to talk to her.

"Enjoy the weekend," Mr. Daley called after us. Once outside, I realized I was actually holding on to the sleeve of my mother's turtleneck, tugging her along. I dropped my hand and surveyed the circle and the other buildings—many more people were wandering around—and felt a sense of dread at the thought of completing this tour, let alone of enduring the rest of the weekend. They'd leave after brunch the next morning, which was only twenty-two hours away, and for roughly

223

ten of those hours, they'd be at their motel. So twelve hours. But twelve hours was infinite! If we left campus, it would be different. If we went into Boston, say—in Boston, we'd get along, we could visit the aquarium or walk the Freedom Trail or sit in a restaurant, eating clam chowder; I would even let my mother take my picture inside, right there at the table.

But we were at Ault; it was best just to move forward into the next moment. As we walked toward my dorm, my mother said, "And Martha will be there now?"

"She should be."

"Will her parents be there?"

"They got in yesterday, so they're probably just at their hotel now."

"Where are they staying?"

I hesitated. "I don't know."

"And Martha's dad is a doctor, right?"

"No, he's a lawyer."

"Why did I think he was a doctor?"

"I don't know." This, too, was a lie. She thought so because Dede's father was a doctor.

"Be sure to introduce us to Martha's mom and dad at the lunch. I want to tell them thank you for how nice they've been to you."

I did not respond. Her questions, her little efforts—didn't she know that Easterners didn't really care? Niceness for its own sake wasn't a virtue to them. I could remember talking about this once with her, in a conversation during my Christmas vacation the year before. I'd been sitting at the kitchen table reading the newspaper and she'd been standing at the sink with her yellow rubber gloves on, washing pans. She had wanted to know, was it true that people in Massachusetts weren't friendly like at home? I said that it was a stereotype, but that, like most stereotypes, it contained some truth (this statement was, verbatim, one I'd recently heard a senior, a guy who was head of the debate team, make at a formal dinner when we'd been assigned to the same

224

table). Then I said that it didn't bother me that much, the unfriendliness, that you got used to it. At the time, the topic had made me feel smart and grown-up, to be talking with my mother not about how the Martzers had finally painted their house, or how it looked like Bree Nielsen had gained weight, especially in the face—no, not chitchat, but an idea, a *concept*. Heading toward the dorm, I wondered if my mother had any memory of our conversation.

I knocked on the door to the room Martha and I shared, in case she was changing clothes. "Come in," she called, but before I could reach for the knob, my mother had stepped forward, pulled her glasses down to the tip of her nose, and was peering over the top of them at the photographs taped to our door. She pointed, her finger touching the photo, at one of Martha and me side by side in a swimming pool, gripping the side so only our arms and shoulders and wet heads were visible. "Now where was this taken?"

"At Martha's house."

"When were you there that it was warm enough to swim?"

"Right before school started this year."

"That's not your striped bathing suit, is it?"

"I was borrowing one of Martha's suits."

"I didn't think it looked like the striped one, but—"

"You can come in," Martha called again from the other side of the door, and I called back, "Two seconds." I looked at my mother. "Any other questions?" I wasn't even being sarcastic, not completely; but when her eyes widened, I could tell I'd injured her.

"Must be nice having a pool," my father said. He said it the same way he'd said he wouldn't mind meeting a senator, and I felt my irritation with him blossom into genuine anger.

I opened the door. Martha was sitting on the futon, folding laundry and setting it on the trunk we used as a table; and, as we entered the room, she stood. With my parents still behind me, I flared my nostrils and rolled my eyes. Martha smiled at my expression, but then she turned it into a smile for my parents' benefit, walking toward us with her arm extended. "It's great to finally meet you," she said. She shook their hands and asked them about the drive and what they thought of Ault so far.

"It's just so pretty," my mother said.

Martha nodded. "Sometimes when I'm walking around I want to pinch myself because I can't believe I get to live in such a beautiful place." Was this true? I felt that way myself, but Martha was more accustomed to fancy things than I was. Maybe she was being polite—truly polite, not bare-minimum-polite like Nancy Daley.

"Martha, Lee told us about you being elected to the discipline committee," my mother said. "What a big honor."

"Thanks," Martha said, and I said, "She wasn't elected. She was chosen by the headmaster."

"That's what I meant," my mother said. "I think it's terrific. Your dad must be real proud."

For several seconds, no one spoke.

"Didn't he go to Ault, too?" my mother said, but her voice was thinning with doubt. "I thought—"

"No, he did," Martha said. How had my mother known that part, when had I told her? And why had she felt the need to bring up any of it? So this was where I got my tendency to hoard information about other people, though at least I knew better than to mention the information in front of them. "But it's funny, actually," Martha was saying, "because my dad didn't have the greatest time here. It was when it was still all-boys, and I guess there was a lot of hazing. When it came time for me to apply to boarding school, he was like, you can go anywhere except Ault. And of course Ault is the place I ended up liking the best."

"I'm glad to know Flea isn't the only one who disobeys her parents," my father said.

Martha laughed. "Flea?" she repeated. "You never told me that one." To my father, she said, "I can't imagine Lee being disobedient."

226

"Then you have a very weak imagination, Martha."

At this, she really laughed. It would almost be worse for Martha to like my parents than not to like them. If she did, then for the rest of the weekend, every time all of us were together I'd be waiting for her positive impression to crack. Not that it *should* crack, not that I thought badly of my parents, but if one of my classmates liked them, even Martha, it would probably be—I could see it now, watching her talk to them—because they seemed "refreshing," or perhaps "authentic." Precisely *because* they were disheveled, because my father used colorful expressions, because they'd driven from Indiana. But anyone who saw my parents as cute would surely be disappointed. My father in particular had his own ideas and appetites, and he was not like a lamb in a petting zoo who would not bite back.

"Martha, you don't play soccer, do you?" my mother said.

Martha shook her head. "Field hockey."

"That's what I thought. Do you have a game this afternoon, too?"

"Everyone has games today," I said.

"Will Martha's game be at the same time as yours, Lee? Because, Martha, we'd love to get to see you"—my mother made little quote marks with her fingers— "'in action.'"

"That's so nice of you," Martha said. It was difficult to imagine her parents suggesting they attend one of my games, and impossible to imagine them having done so within the first ten minutes of meeting me. "My game's at two-thirty, and, Lee, when is yours?"

"Around then. And they're at opposite ends of campus. Sorry, Mom, but don't think you're going to see Martha unless you want to go to her game instead of mine."

"There's an idea," my father said.

"Mr. Fiora," Martha said. "Be nice." So she had indeed decided she liked him—we needed to get out of the room as quickly as possible.

My father perched on the edge of my desk and picked up

a women's magazine. "Glad to see you're hitting the books, Lee. Ah, what have we here—" He flipped the magazine around and held it up so we could see it. Across both pages, in huge red letters, the headline read, "Oh, *Yeah!* How to Have the Best Orgasm Ever."

"That's gross, Dad," I said. "Put it down."

"Gross? Whose magazine is it?" He was grinning and I thought that maybe this was the part where things turned— this was when my father revealed himself to Martha to be a pervert. (Not that he was one; just that this was when it would seem like it.)

"Let's go to the schoolhouse," I said. "Come on."

" 'Ho-hum sex?' " my father read. "'We've all been there. Sure, the first few months of a relationship are blissful, but pretty soon —' "

"Dad," I said. "Stop it."

"'—Pretty soon you're wearing sweatpants to bed, and he's trimming his nose hair in front of you. Face it—' "

"I'm leaving," I said. I yanked open the door—I couldn't even look at Martha—and I heard my mother say, "Terry, she wants to show us the rest of the school. Martha, you'll have to forgive—" The door shut. I leaned against the wall, my arms crossed, and waited for them. When they emerged, my father's expression was one of boyish guilt, as if he'd done something inappropriate but charming. I turned and began walking.

"What?" he said, and then, to my mother, "What's the big deal? It was her magazine."

I remained a few paces in front of them as we headed down the steps, crossed the common room, and went back outside. I could feel my mother straining to catch up with me. Still behind, she said, "Lee, Martha is just a delight. Now, I'm sure you've told me before, but does she have brothers or sisters?"

"She has a brother."

"And is he older or younger?"

"Mom, who cares?"

"Well, Lee, I care," my mother said softly, and then—not softly at all—my father said, "Watch how you talk to your mother."

I glanced over my shoulder. "Watch how you talk to me."

"I beg your pardon?"

Forty yards away, the terrace in front of the schoolhouse was crowded: men in blue blazers, a woman in a pink plaid wool suit, a woman in a green straw hat with an oversized brim. It was almost ten, and the sky was cloudless and cerulean. The other parents' voices sounded from this distance like the hum of a cocktail party.

"Lee?" my father said. His tone was one of cool anger, but underneath the coolness—I knew my father far too well— there was a catch of excitement. This was the thing about my father, that he didn't defer to place or situation. Have it out with me here? In front of all these people? Sure. No problem.

"Nothing," I said.

He was silent for a few seconds, then said, more quietly than before, "Nothing. Yeah, I'll bet nothing."

On the terrace, my father picked up name tags for both of them while my mother and I stood by the refreshments table; she had taken a Danish and some orange juice. "You really don't want any?" She held the plastic cup toward me for the third time. "It's fresh-squeezed."

"I told you I just brushed my teeth," I said.

None of us spoke much as we made our way through the schoolhouse—the main hall with the rows and rows of desks, a few of the classrooms, the auditorium where guest lecturers spoke (Martin Luther King, Jr., had spoken at Ault once, which was something that tour guides were supposed to tell prospective applicants; what they were not supposed to say was that at the time King had visited, there hadn't been a single black student enrolled in the school). My mother asked questions, and I answered them neither curtly nor at length. I found myself drifting from the present moment, thinking first

229

about the soccer game, how I'd definitely be put in because Ms. Barrett played everyone on parents' weekend, and then thinking of Cross Sugarman. My crush on him had not, of course, ended the evening I'd cut Aspeth's hair. For twenty-four hours, I'd thought I didn't like him at all, and then we'd passed in the dining hall and abruptly I'd liked him again exactly the same amount. The afternoon before, I'd seen Cross and his parents. He had been wearing a jacket and tie, and when our eyes had met, he'd lifted his chin slightly in acknowledgment, which was not something he usually did. And I'd thought that it was because of his parents, how in some way their presence made us closer, or highlighted what we had in common—that we were both Ault students and that all these tall, well-dressed grown-ups milling around campus were not.

In the mail room, my father said, "So this is where my letters come?" and I knew that he'd forgiven me, or at least that he was willing to pretend he had.

"I hardly have room for all of them," I said. "They might have to give me a second mailbox."

"Just as long as they don't charge you extra," my father said.

And then it was time for lunch. We were hurrying back to the dining hall, but this time it was packed. Mr. Byden made some remarks and the parents laughed and then Reverend Orch said grace and we sat down. There was roast chicken, and pasta salad with black olives and red peppers, and rolls. On either side of me, my parents tore into it.

"Aren't you hungry?" my mother said.

"No, I am." I took a bite of the pasta, which was soft and oily.

When we'd been looking for a place to sit, we hadn't seen Martha or her parents, which was a relief, and I'd spotted some empty chairs at a table where two freshmen, skinny boys in glasses, were sitting with their parents. Then we were joined by Mrs. Hopewell, one of the art teachers, who had thin messy hair and watery eyes and usually wore a paint-covered smock over her clothes—for lunch, she had on a batik print dress—and who was rumored to smoke pot with her husband, a carpenter who didn't teach at Ault and wasn't at lunch. Mrs. Hopewell was manageable, the whole table was manageable—being surrounded by people whose opinions didn't really matter to me, I'd gotten lucky.

As my parents spoke to the boys' parents—the boys' names were Cordy and Hans, and one of them, though I couldn't remember which, was a math prodigy—I scanned the dining hall until I located Cross. He and his parents were at a table with his roommate, Devin, Devin's parents, Reverend Orch, and Dr. Stanchak, who was head of the classics department.

"Psst." My father was cupping his fingers sideways in front of his mouth. "Is that the senator? Two o'clock." My father nodded toward a table to our right. "The guy with the alcoholic's nose."

"Jesus, Dad."

He wasn't whispering, or even talking that quietly.

My father laughed. "Am I right? Looks like a real glad-hander to me."

"I have no idea who that is," I said. "But Robin Tunniff isn't sitting at that table, so I really doubt that's her dad."

"Well, where is she?"

I glanced at the tables in front of us—the Sugarmans and Reverend Orch were sharing a hearty laugh—then turned around and looked across to the other side of the dining hall. "I don't know," I said.

"You swear?!'

I looked him in the eye, because this time I could. "Of course I swear."

But then, when we went up to get dessert from the long table where the salad bar usually was, stocked now with cookies and brownies and a coffee urn on either end, I saw Robin and, next to her, an otherwise nondescript man wearing a tie dotted with little American flags. It was just my father and me—my mother, after eating the pasta off my plate, had declared herself stuffed—and it seemed actively unkind to deny him the sighting. This would be my concession to him for the weekend, the gesture that proved I was not a rotten daughter after all.

"Dad," I murmured, and I nudged him.

He'd been pouring cream into his coffee, and some of it dripped over the lip of the cup onto the saucer. "Hey, there," he said.

"No," I said. "Quick. The thing we were talking about—alcoholic nose. But this time the real thing." I looked back at Robin Tunniff's father, and I sensed my father following my gaze. "The tie," I said.

"Gotcha."

We stood quietly in the hubbub, staring at Senator Tunniff, and I could feel my love for my father. This was one of the best things about family, how you knew each other's shorthand.

And then he'd set down his cup and saucer and was striding around the end of the table. He was quickly beyond the point where I could have grabbed his blazer, though I probably wouldn't have anyway. "Oh God," I said, and a mother standing next to me looked over, and our eyes met, but she did not say anything. I started walking, then stopped again a few feet behind him.

". . . a great admirer of yours," I heard him saying, and they were shaking hands, the senator and my father.

My father's back was to me. I could see only the senator's face, and Robin looking blankly between them. The senator appeared utterly genial. They spoke for perhaps thirty seconds, then they were shaking hands again, and my father set his left palm against the senator's upper arm. The senator laughed, and I wished that I had never come to Ault, or that I'd been born a different person, or that at the very least I could lose consciousness immediately but not in a way that would be disruptive, not, say, by fainting and collapsing to the ground—more like by simply vanishing.

When he turned away from the senator, my father almost bumped into me. His expression was one of distracted exuberance, and I wondered if it had actually meant something to him to meet this man, if he had not simply been trying to anger or embarrass me. He gestured over his shoulder with his thumb. "Good guy."

I was speechless. Or at least in this context I was. It was better to suspend my fury until we were out of the crowd.

"I'm going back to the table," I said.

"Let me grab my coffee. And pick up a brownie for your mom, will you?"

"She doesn't want anything."

"Trust me, she'll want a brownie." He chuckled, and I thought maybe my father did not understand me at all, that if he did he'd be contrite. He'd done it on purpose, but he'd still be contrite.

Back at our table, Cordy's parents were standing to leave, and Mrs. Hopewell and Hans's parents were already gone. I couldn't tell if Cordy's parents had been waiting for my father and me to return or if they'd have taken off then anyway, leaving my mother at the table by herself, peering around with her wide eyes. I hated them all at this moment, the indifferent students and faculty and the inconsiderate parents and my own family, for being somehow reliant on kindness that wasn't extended.

While we ate dessert, the dining hall cleared out. My father broke a sugar cookie in two and dipped half into his coffee. "Tell your mother about my new friend."

"Tell her yourself."

"Who?" my mother said. "What are you two talking about?"

"Dad just accosted Robin's father."

My mother looked confused.

"You know how there's a girl here whose dad is a senator?"

I said. "Well, Dad just went up and started talking to him."

"You were the one who pointed him out to me," my father said. His tone was still merry.

"I wouldn't have if I'd known you were going to bother him."

"Bother him? Lee, for Christ's sake, he's a public figure. He likes meeting people."

"You have no idea what he likes!" I cried. "You've never seen him before. You've never even heard of him. And here he is, trying to have a normal weekend with his family, and you go up and pretend to—"

"You need to relax." My father's tone was no longer cheerful. He turned to my mother and said, as if I wasn't there, "He was a real stand-up guy. Not a phony."

My mother nodded, and I watched them both, my entire body tensed. "You're insane." I made sure to say it calmly.

My father looked at me. "Beg your pardon?"

"You're totally insane. You talk to this guy for two seconds, then you act like you're old friends. Why do you even care? Do you think it proves something that you talked to him?"

"I'm not sure what you're getting at," my father said. He dipped the other half of the cookie into his coffee cup.

I had already taken a breath before continuing to speak, but as I watched him, I felt a sudden draining of momentum, a pull from this instant that we were hovering in. He was looking at me expectantly, holding his cookie a few inches above the cup, and the bottom third of the cookie, which was stained a darker tan from the coffee, was beginning to decompose, threatening to fall off into the liquid below. It seemed heartbreaking, it seemed unbearable, that I was aware of this and he was not. It seemed heartbreaking that he liked the taste of a sugar cookie dipped in coffee, that it was a treat to him. The small rewards we give ourselves—I think maybe there is nothing sadder.

And it wasn't as if I actually thought he was insane. But as long as I felt the impulse to convince him that he was acting

234

like it, weren't our roles reassuringly entrenched? The worst thing would be to recognize him as a thirty-nine-year-old man possessing certain virtues and certain foibles, making his way as he knew how.

"I just think—" But what was it that I just thought? "It's like asking for someone's autograph," I said, and I knew the indignance was gone from my voice. "Just like, what's the point? I don't understand why people do it."

"Maybe not," my father said. "But you have to admit that a lot of folks disagree with you."

"The Orschmidts' son has a whole big collection of autographs," my mother said. "Sharon was telling me that last summer when they went out to Los Angeles he got one from, Lee, you would know who this is, he's a real big star. Oh, I'm terrible with names, but Sharon said the actor was just like talking to you or me."

The three of us were quiet.

"So," I finally said, "does Mr. Orschmidt still wear a wig?" There. I had given in.

"Lee, I don't think that's nice to say," my mother said. "Mr. Orschmidt is such a pleasant man."

"The fact that he wears a wig doesn't mean he's not pleasant," I said.

"Honey, on a man, it's called a toupee, but I really don't think he'd appreciate that kind of talk. In our day, people didn't used to discuss private business."

"Back when your mother was a girl and dinosaurs roamed the earth," my father said. "Right, Linda?" It was always like this: We rode over the moment, like a roiling river, on my mother's back.

"Oh, stop it," my mother said. But we were fine, we were fine, we'd made it to the other side.

Four minutes before the end of the first half, Ms. Barrett put me in for Norie Cleehan—I was a fullback—and then took me out again four minutes after the start of the second half. During my time in, Gardiner had scored two goals.

I took a seat next to Maria on the bench. "Where's your parents?" she said.

I pointed across the field. A few parents had brought blankets or folding canvas chairs, but mine were just sitting on the ground. My father, probably, was ripping out blades of grass and blowing on them to make a whistling sound. It was another of his tricks that had once deeply impressed me.

"Aww," Maria said. "Mama and Papa Fiora. I bet they're happy right now.

"Maybe."

"They're *so* happy. They're like, 'Honey, did you see Lee get up in number twenty's face? I'm *proud* of Lee.' " Coming from someone else, the remark might have seemed mocking, but Maria was worse at soccer than I was. She also was a fullback, and on the field, she moved in a leisurely way; sometimes, when the forward from the other team got too far past her, she'd stop altogether and just watch the forward close in on the goal, as if she, Maria, were not a participant but a spectator. This tendency made Ms. Barrett apoplectic. "Are your parents taking you out for dinner tonight?" Maria asked.

I nodded. When my mother had said, "Daddy and I want you to pick somewhere nice," I'd mentioned a Chinese restaurant because I knew that by *nice* she did not mean, for example, the Red Barn Inn.

"That'll be good," Maria said. "Get off campus."

"Do you want to come?" I asked. I blurted it out before I'd really thought about it, because it seemed like maybe it was what Maria was hinting at. Also because—surely this was offensive, but it was true—a Chinese restaurant would probably seem nice to her as well.

"Sure," she said. "And Rufina, too?" Rufina was playing halfback then, her long ponytail bouncing behind her as she jogged up the field.

"Yeah, of course," I said.

236

"Hey, look," Maria said. "'They're waving at you."

It was true—both my parents were. They would like Maria and Rufina, I thought, and they would like that I'd invited along friends, and it would make my father feel generous to take us all out; at home, my parents had always encouraged me to have other kids over to our house. I lifted my hand and waved back.

In the afternoon, I rode with my parents to the motel. We had lost the game seven to two, and it had occurred to me by the end that the Gardiner coach had told her team to stop scoring. That would have been decorous and boarding-school-like, given that all the parents were watching.

My mother and I sat in the car while my father checked in. They were staying at the Raymond TraveLodge, which I had found for them by looking in the yellow pages several weeks before; the room, which the motel could not guarantee as nonsmoking, would cost thirty-nine dollars. "You played wonderfully," my mother said.

From the back seat, I laughed. I was still wearing my uniform, my hair still pulled back.

"What?" my mother said. "You did." Then she laughed, too. "You did!"

"Which goal that Gardiner scored while I was in did you like better? The first or the second?"

"Those were big girls on the other team," my mother said. "What was my dainty Lee supposed to do?"

We were both quiet, and it was a calm, unawkward silence; with lunch and the game behind us, it felt like things might be okay.

"Oh, look." My mother knocked on her window, which was rolled up. "Aren't they pretty?" Twenty feet away, on top of a shed, two robins were perching and turning. "It looks like they're having a party and waiting for everyone to arrive."

"But they're worried that nobody is going to come," I said.

"Oh, but now—" A sparrow alighted on the roof. "The

237

first guest," my mother said. Something about animals always pleased my mother—whenever we were on the highway and passed cows or horses, she'd tap my brothers or me and say, "Look." She did the same when we were passing bodies of water, or driving over bridges, especially if I was reading as we did so.

"Lee, Daddy and I are so excited to see Ault," she said.

At this moment, my father emerged from the entrance. From the way his lips were set, it looked like he was whistling.

"Me too," I said.

Maria and Rufina, when I knocked on the door of their dorm room, were both dressed up. Rufina had on a skirt and sweater, and Maria was wearing black pants and a button-down shirt. A few minutes before, without showering, I had finally changed out of my soccer uniform into jeans. In my room, I'd found a note from Martha: *My parents want to meet yours! Where are you? Call me at Sheraton tonight!!* My parents were waiting in the car, and I crumpled the note and threw it away.

"You guys look nice," I said to Maria and Rufina. "But, I mean, we're not going—" Maybe they'd imagined I was inviting them to the Red Barn Inn. "We're just going to the Golden Wok," I said. "Is that okay?"

They looked at each other, then back at me. "Sure," Maria said. "That sounds great." They definitely had thought we were going to the Red Barn Inn.

In the car, my mother asked where they were from and whether they liked Ault. Rufina said, "Not really," and laughed.

"Why not?" my mother asked.

"It's just snobby," Rufina said. "A lot of snobs."

How could she get away with making the most predictable complaint, and how could she do so having become beautiful? (And she'd go on to Dartmouth, and Maria to Brown. I didn't know this at the time, of course, but if I had it would

238

only have increased my bewilderment. If you were beautiful and went to an Ivy League college, then really, who cared about everything else?)

"I have to agree," my father said. "One fellow I saw today, I thought, poor guy, he has a neck injury. Then I realized, nope, he's just got his nose in the air."

"No joke," Rufina said. "And the kids are worse than the parents."

"Nothing like inheriting a whole lot of money to make you think you must really deserve it," said my father.

I stiffened. The actual word *money* made my skin crawl. Besides which, my father's remark was probably something the priest at their church had said in a sermon, or something my father had picked up from *Reader's Digest*.

But Rufina just said, "You got it."

"And, Maria, what about you?" my mother said. "Have you liked Ault?"

"Some good, some bad," Maria said. "Depends what day you ask me."

"Were you girls at the lunch?" my father asked. "What a ratfuck, huh?"

They roared with laughter, and I looked out the window. Why did he have to try so hard? No one expected that much from parents.

"What's a ratfuck?" Maria said.

"Tell her, Flea." In the rearview mirror, I could see my father grinning.

"It's just a big crowded event," I said.

"That's hilarious," Rufina said. "I gotta remember that one."

At dinner, Rufina ordered shrimp in lobster sauce and to compensate, though I doubted my father would know I was compensating, I ordered mixed vegetables. Rufina and Maria both ordered soda, which was not something we did in our family—at restaurants we always had water—but it probably wasn't fair to hold that against them; most people in the world ordered soda at restaurants. When our fortune cookies came, we went around the table reading them: *You love sports, horses and gambling but not to excess; Your winsome smile will be your sure protection; You will be the best!* The dinner hadn't been a disaster, really, everyone had liked one another, but it still had been a mistake to invite them. I'd had to remain on high alert, waiting.

Back on campus, when we were letting them off before I got out myself, Maria stepped out of the car but Rufina remained in the seat. "That was a good dinner," she said, and she patted her flat belly.

"We really enjoyed meeting you," my mother said.

Rufina looked at me, then my father, my mother, me again. "Are you—you guys are staying at the Sheraton, right?"

"The what?" my father said.

"I thought—" Rufina paused. "See, I told Nick I'd meet him there."

Nick? I thought. *Nick Chafee?* Then, because it has always been in moments of genuine surprise that I try hardest to act at ease, I said, "We can take you there. It's not where my parents are staying, but it's no problem."

"Does someone want to clue me in to what's going on here?" my father said.

"Rufina needs a ride to a hotel," I said. I turned back to her, "It's fine. We can take you."

"Hold on just a second," my father said. "What hotel are we talking about and just who is this Nick fellow?"

Rufina started to speak, but I interrupted her. "She needs to go to the Sheraton, which is where a lot of the parents stay. And Nick is in our class, and it's not like you're staying in a room with him, right, Rufina?"

Rufina nodded. Of course she was staying in a room with Nick.

Both my parents were twisted around to look at us, my father's right elbow hanging over the seat. Maria had disappeared into the darkness.

240

"And I'm supposed to believe that?" my father said. He seemed not angry but slightly amused.

"It's true," Rufina said. "I'm staying with a bunch of me and Lee's girlfriends."

"Don't you need permission to be away from campus?"

"I filled out a form in the dean's office this morning."

"Dad," I said. "You're not her father. Just drive her there. It's none of your business."

"None of my business?"

This is the point where, if I had been Rufina, I'd have gotten out of the car. Ride or no, I would not have wanted this proximity to another family's fighting. But I wasn't Rufina— Rufina was going to the Sheraton now, to get extremely drunk, probably, and to fool around with Nick Chafee. And with fooling around as the reward, our squabbling was only a distraction to be endured. I myself had never fooled around, drunk or otherwise, but even I knew how when you really liked a boy, all the little daily incidents shrank and slipped away. You carried around your anticipation of seeing him again and retrieved it when you felt bored or anxious, like a memory of something good.

"I'm not sure when it became your responsibility to decide what's my business," my father said.

Not now, I thought—couldn't he see that the situation was not about us? We were only vessels, meant to carry Rufina through the night and into the arms of the boy who was waiting for her.

"Terry." My mother shook her head slightly. Then she mouthed something to him—I think she mouthed. *Later*. She recognized our role here.

"I'll say what I want to in my own car," my father said, but even as he said this, he shifted from park to drive and we glided forward. I still don't know if he was acquiescing to me, or to Rufina, or maybe to my mother.

When we were back on the main road, I said, "It's on 90. Do you know how to get on 90?"

My father said nothing, and my mother said, "Daddy knows because that's how we came in."

It could have been worse, I thought—if we'd had to stop at a gas station and get directions.

For the rest of the ride, which was almost twenty minutes, no one spoke. In the dark car, on the dark highway, we weren't necessarily in Massachusetts—we could have been anywhere. My father and my mother and me and this strange, pretty girl sitting across the seat—for a minute, I could not remember her name. What was she doing with us? It made sense that the rest of us were in the car together, but her presence felt curious and perplexing.

Then the disoriented feeling passed. (*Rufina*—of course.) So she and Nick were involved; now it seemed ludicrous that I had not realized this earlier. Beauty trumped race, apparently. Or was it possible that my belief about race and dating at Ault had simply been wrong? Or was I mostly right, but wrong to think that any pattern existed as a rule? There could always, of course, be exceptions. Sometimes—more often than not, though it was not until I was older that this fact stopped surprising me—things really were as they appeared to be. A boy and girl flirting, and then it turned out they were together—only I could be startled by such news.

When we dropped off Rufina, she walked through large automatic glass doors beyond which were a rose-colored carpet, a table with a huge vase containing dozens of flowers, a chandelier above the flowers. We pulled away, and none of us spoke on the ride back, either.

In the campus driveway, my father turned off the car but left the headlights on. It was nearly eleven o'clock, the time for Saturday curfew, though only a fraction of the students would be sleeping in the dorms tonight.

My father set his hands on top of the steering wheel. "I won't be—" he started, and his voice came out squeaky from not talking for so long. He cleared his throat. "I won't be attending chapel or brunch tomorrow," he said. "I'll see you at Christmas, Lee."

"Are you joking?" I said, and my mother said, "Terry!"

"I'm not joking at all." He didn't look at either of us.

"Honey, why—" my mother began, and he cut her off. "I don't need to be subjected to this kind of treatment. Not from anyone, and especially not from my sixteen-year-old daughter."

"It wasn't—" I said, but he cut me off, too. Probably during the drive he had been planning what he'd say. His voice was steady, simultaneously angry and calm.

"I don't know what's happened to you, Lee, but I can tell you this much. You're a disappointment. You're selfish and you're shallow and you have no respect for your mother and I, and I'm ashamed of you." *Your mother and me*, I thought—even at that moment, that was what I thought. "When you started at Ault," my father continued, "I said to myself, I'll bet there are a lot of kids who'd think real highly of themselves going to a place like that. And I thought, but I'm glad Lee has a good head on her shoulders. Well, I was wrong. I'll say that now. We made a mistake to let you go. Your mother might feel different, but this is not what I drove eighteen hours for."

No one said anything, and my mother pulled out a tissue and blew her nose. Sometimes when my mother cried, I caught her tears, and I very much did not want to catch them now.

I swallowed. There were many things I could have said in this moment, and the one I chose was, "I didn't ask you to come."

"Lee!" My mother's voice was anguished.

Abruptly, my father was unfastening his seat belt, opening his door, stepping outside, pulling my door open as well. "Get out," he barked. "Right now."

"No."

"I said get out of my car."

"It's Mom's car, too."

My father glared down at me, shaking his head; apparently, there were no words left to express my repugnance.

"Fine," I said. I stepped out, folded my arms, and stood facing him. "You can tell me how terrible I am. But maybe you should think about how you act. You think it's so funny to embarrass me and say weird things in front of my friends, and when I get upset, you pretend like you didn't do anything."

"Embarrass you? Is that what taking those girls out for dinner is called?"

"Oh, right. Like we go out for one meal and then I'll just ignore how you act the rest of the time."

"I didn't know I'd asked you to ignore anything. I'm thirty-nine years old, and I'm pretty comfortable with myself, Lee. And that's a hell of a lot more than I can say for you. I'll tell you one thing I don't feel the need to do and that's make excuses."

"Good for you," I said. "Congratulations."

And then—I don't remember any anticipation or fore-knowledge of this, only a stunned awareness that it had already happened—he raised his right hand and slapped me across the face. His hand was hot, and then my face was hot, and tears were splashing onto my cheeks, but I think they were only because of how much it hurt. And the thing I did, before I met my father's eyes, before I said a word or lifted my own hand to feel my jaw and cheek, was look around. We were near the chapel, and about thirty feet away, illuminated as he passed under a lamppost, was a classmate of mine named Jeff Oltiss. Our eyes met. His expression, especially from that distance, was unreadable but, I thought, not unsympathetic. Jeff was not someone I knew well—we'd been in Ms. Moray's English class together our sophomore year, but that was it—and we never spoke after this, and for the rest of my time at Ault, I thought of him only as the person who had seen my father slap me. If I ran into him today on the street in San Francisco or New York—he could be married, have children, be an astrophysicist or an accountant—that is all he would be to me: the person who saw me get slapped by my father. When we were still at Ault and passed in the dining hall or gym, we did not talk or greet each other, but I felt that a recognition flickered between us. He knew.

I turned away from him, back to my father. "You're an asshole," I said, and I was sobbing by then.

"And you're an ungrateful little bitch." He kicked shut the back door, slid into the front—before his own door closed, I heard my mother's voice but could not make out what she said—and revved the engine. Then they were gone. To get back to my dorm, I'd need to follow Jeff through the arch that led to the courtyard. But instead I walked in the opposite direction, out onto the circle. Standing there in the vast expanse of grass, treeless except at the edges, I looked around at all the big partly lit buildings and then at the glowing stars overhead. Out there on the circle, it was not so bad. Inside, in the light, surrounded by furniture and magazines and throw pillows and picture frames—then it would be bad.

When the phone rang early in the morning, it was as if I had been waiting for the call. I jumped out of bed, hurried down the steps to the common room, and yanked open the door of the phone booth. "Lee," my mother said, but she couldn't speak because she was crying so hard.

"Mom," I said. "Mom, I'm sorry. I want you guys to come back—"

"Daddy's checking out now," she said. She breathed deeply several times. "He wants to get an early start. But, Lee, I hope you know that he loves you so much and he's so proud of you. I hope you know that."

"Mom—" My chin was starting to shake, my lips were curling out.

"And we really looked forward to this weekend, and I'm sorry it had to turn out like this."

"Mom, it's not your fault. Mommy, please. Please don't cry." But I was crying, too. Over the noise of her own tears, I don't know if she noticed. "Why don't you come back?" I said. "Even if Dad doesn't. You'll like the chapel service."

"Lee, I can't. He wants to get on the road. What I want you to do is I want you to call him in a few days and just say you're sorry. And I know he was wrong, too, and he shouldn't have hit you and it makes me very sad—" She was gasping again.

"It's okay," I said. "It didn't hurt. Really, Mom, it didn't hurt."

"I have to go, Lee. I love you. Okay? I love you." Then she'd hung up, and I was holding the phone, listening to nothing. When I got back to the room, I saw on Martha's alarm clock that it was not yet six-thirty.

Later, when we referred to it—there was nothing that ever happened to my family that did not become a joke or anecdote—it became the weekend from hell, when it was unclear whether my father or I had behaved more atrociously. In my mother's version, everything could be traced back to the fact that Lee was looking at one of those trashy magazines she loves and Dad started teasing her and then you know how two people with tempers can get into it. Also, my mother always asked after Rufina and Maria, both in her letters and in conversation when she'd call them "the Spanish girls," or else "the girl with the boyfriend and the other girl."

It was the last time my father ever hit me—he'd done it when I was growing up, spanking more than slapping, and really only when my brothers and I were being either completely wild or willfully disobedient—and it also marked the beginning of a long period during which I did not cry in front of either of my parents.

When I was in college, I always had a phone in my room, and my father called often—I think the pay phone system at Ault had simply struck him as a pain in the ass—and

246

sometimes he didn't even leave a real message but uttered a single absurd sentence into the answering machine, or recited jokes. (*How do you make a Kleenex dance?* Or, on Halloween, *Lee, why can't witches have babies?*) My roommates, of course, thought he was very funny. Later, after I graduated from college, he bought a cell phone, and then he called me daily. I always talked to him, even at work, even when I was busy, and I always let him be the one to end the conversation. It was not that I really thought I could redeem myself for that weekend, or for going to Ault to begin with. (How was I supposed to understand, when I applied at the age of thirteen, that you have your whole life to leave your family? Or maybe it was going to Ault that turned me into the kind of person who would always, for reasons of schooling, then work, stay away.) No, it wasn't that I thought I *could* redeem myself, more that I thought I owed it to him to show I was trying. As for my mother: She never punished me, she never even scolded me. And because of this, because unlike my father she never asked me to pay her back, it made what I owed her unpayable. It was an ocean, or a whole cold planet.

Once when I was visiting my parents' house, nosing around in my brother Tim's room, I paused before his bulletin board and noticed a nametag pinned up there, a stiff cream-colored rectangle with a thick red ribbon affixed to the top and an image of the Ault crest in the left corner. *Timothy John Fiora*, it said, and below that, *brother of Lee*, and after my name, the year I'd graduated. At the time it had been written, that date had been nearly two years in the future; at the point when I stood in my brother's room examining it, it was more than ten years past, and Tim himself had finished high school and started at the community college. What surprised me was that my brother's name was not in my mother's handwriting but in my father's. Had he grabbed the extra tag when he'd taken them for my mother and himself, I wondered, written Tim's name (probably he'd made one for Joseph, too), and passed it off to my mother to transport back to Indiana? Or all that Saturday at Ault, had he carried it himself, tucked in the pocket of his khaki blazer, taking care when he sat not to let it bend? And then in the car driving back, had he set it somewhere safe, on the dashboard maybe, or on the seat next to him? They drove straight through, I found out later, and my father drove the whole way. They'd planned to stop around Erie, but my mother fell asleep, and my father decided to keep going. A little after midnight, my mother woke, startled. The engine was off and my father was sitting beside her, cracking his knuckles, gazing out the windshield. "Where are we?'" my mother asked.

'We're home," my father told her.

6
Townie

JUNIOR WINTER

An ambulance took Sin-Jun to the ER in the early evening, right around when formal dinner started. In fact, when Tig Oltman and Daphne Cook found her—Tig and Daphne were sophomores who lived in Sin-Jun's dorm—they were on their way to the dining hall. They opened the door of their room in time to see Sin-Jun appear on the threshold opposite theirs and crumple to the floor, mumbling unintelligibly, one arm pressed to her abdomen as if she'd folded up her shirt to carry a bunch of pebbles, or maybe corn kernels, and she was trying to prevent them from spilling.

It was a Wednesday, and after formal dinner there was an all-school lecture—it was by a black woman who was the choreographer of a dance troupe—and Martha and I were about to enter the auditorium when Mrs. Morino, Sin-Jun's dorm head, stopped us. When I think of the whole incident, the whole rest of the winter even—it was late February then— this is the moment I remember. Martha and I were cheerfully talking about nothing and I was keeping track of Cross Sugarman, who was several feet ahead of us, watching to see where he and his friends sat so Martha and I could sit close by, but not so close that it would occur to him our proximity was intentional. And then Mrs. Morino was approaching us, and I thought maybe she was waving hello—why would she have been waving hello when we were just a few feet apart, when neither Martha nor I had ever had her as a teacher or coach and we therefore hardly knew her?—and I was startled when she stopped in front of us and reached out to take my hands.

"I have some difficult news," she said.

Dread surged through me. Already I was scrolling back in my mind to identify any recent wrongdoing, and so I felt relief—relief that would soon seem shameful and cold-hearted—when Mrs. Morino said, "Sin-Jun is in the hospital. She took some pills. The doctors had to pump her stomach. And she's stable now—I've just come from seeing her—but she's still very fragile."

"Is she sick? I glanced through the double doorway. Cross had disappeared into the auditorium, nearly everyone was seated, and the lights were dimming, I looked back at Mrs. Morino, surprised she was making us late for the lecture; I didn't yet understand that I wouldn't be attending the lecture.

"She took *pills*," Mrs. Morino said, and still I didn't get it—I think this had more to do with my specific idea of Sin-Jun than with my general naïvety, though maybe it was a little of both—and then Martha, who could tell I didn't get it, said, "On purpose, Lee."

"I want to drive you over to the hospital," Mrs. Morino said. "She's a little woozy, but it would be good for her to see another familiar face."

Sin-Jun had taken pills *on purpose*? She had tried to kill herself? More than it seemed shocking, the idea seemed impossible. Sin-Jun wasn't even unhappy; certainly she wasn't suicidal.

I swallowed. "And Martha is coming, too?"

"Let's hold off for tonight." Mrs. Morino said. "I don't want to overwhelm Sin-Jun. You understand, don't you, Martha? You can go on in." Mrs. Morino tilted her head toward the auditorium. "And, Lee, we'll go this way. My car is right out front." She started down the hall, and I followed her. As I walked away, I glanced behind me. Martha was still standing outside the auditorium, an expression of bewilderment twisting her features. When our eyes met, she lifted her hand in farewell, and I felt like a mirror of her—waving back, also bewildered.

Over the next decade, the speaker that night, the choreographer, received more and more national attention— the dance troupe focused a lot on political, especially racial, issues—and I regularly came across articles about her in magazines. I never saw her name without feeling slightly sick in just the way I'd felt after I learned Sin-Jun had taken the pills: that distinct brand of disoriented apprehension when you know something bad has happened but you still don't know all the particulars.

Mrs. Morino drove a navy blue station wagon. Scratch-and-sniff stickers were affixed to the dashboard and dog hair covered the seat. Mrs. Morino taught geometry and Mr. Morino taught American history—I'd never had him as a teacher, either—and they had three children whose names I didn't know, the oldest of whom looked about six; you'd sometimes see the kids in the dining hall, crying or clutching Cheerios or crawling around on the floor. The radio in Mrs. Morino's car was tuned to a classical station and the volume was low, audible only when we weren't speaking. Because it was dark out, I could sense more than see the passing fields and woods.

"Let me ask you," Mrs. Morino said. "Was Sin-Jun ever depressed when you were roommates?"

"I don't think so."

"Did she talk about hurting herself?"

"No."

"Did she get upset about things?"

I tried to remember if I had seen her cry, and a time came back to me, over a grade on an English test. I'd stood by her

251

desk and patted her back, and as I had, I'd caught sight of the grade itself, written in blue at the top of the first page—it was a B minus, which was no worse than most of my grades in English or any other subject. I'd always known, though I'm pretty sure Sin-Jun hadn't been the one who told me, that the year before she got to Ault she came in first in a national math and science competition in Korea, and that she was the first girl who had ever won.

"She worried about her grades," I said to Mrs. Morino. "But besides that, no."

It was true that even when we'd shared a room, Sin-Jun and I had never confided in each other. But when you lived together, you couldn't not know a person: When Sin-Jun awakened in the morning, her black hair stuck up in the back, her face was pale, she couldn't carry on a conversation for a good fifteen minutes; her favorite snack was those crunchy, spicy dried peas that come in foil packs, and also, anything caramel; she most feared snakes, even pictures of them; and the person she loved best was her sister Eunjee, four years younger, still living with their parents in Seoul. But, I thought, maybe this was only information, not true knowledge. And, of course, in the two years since we'd been roommates, our lives had overlapped less and less. Sophomore year, Sin-Jun had started rooming with Clara O'Hallahan, and I'd started rooming with Martha, and we hadn't been in the same dorm anymore.

"Have there been any recent changes in Sin-Jun's life?" Mrs. Morino asked. "Either with her family or here?"

"I don't think so."

"Problem with teachers or other students?"

"Wouldn't Clara know better than I would?" (Was I indicating that I was a bad friend? *Was* I a bad friend?)

"In theory, yes," Mrs. Morino said. "But Clara's pretty distraught. She went over in the ambulance, and she's with Sin-Jun now."

There didn't appear to be much else to say. It wasn't as if

we were going to make small talk, and it was clear that I couldn't answer her questions. As we drove, my mind alternated between consciousness of the foreign experience of riding in Mrs. Morino's car and speculation about Sin-Jun, especially about Mrs. Morino's seeming certainty that Sin-Jun had taken too many aspirin (aspirin, apparently, was what she'd taken) on purpose; as far as I could tell, Mrs. Morino had entertained no other possibility. And then, considering this, I'd be distracted by the physical fact of sitting beside Mrs. Morino. Where had she grown up, I wondered, and how old had she been when she'd married Mr. Morino? Based on her appearance and on the ages of her children, I guessed she was in her late thirties. As I calculated, my mind jerked back to Sin-Jun. Had she said or done anything, ever, to indicate the capacity for suicide? Did she just want attention? She had not seemed to, particularly, in the past.

I tried to recall when I'd last seen her, and it was as mundanely foggy as remembering which clothes I'd worn the day before, or what I'd eaten for dinner. At the hospital, we walked into the main entrance, automatic glass doors beneath a brightly lit porte cochere. It was a small hospital, only three stories, and this seemed comforting—surely if Sin-Jun were in serious danger, they'd have whisked her to Boston in a helicopter.

Inside, the light was bright white, reflecting off the white linoleum floor. We signed in at a desk on the first floor and took an elevator to the third floor, then walked through double doors and past a nurses' station. As soon as we'd opened the doors, a moaning wail had become audible, a kind of crazy wail, and I wondered if we were in the psych ward. And then I thought, so everything Mrs. Morino had said was true. Sin-Jun had attempted suicide, and now she was in the hospital. It wasn't that I'd suspected Mrs. Morino of lying, more that it seemed so hard to believe anything ever happened, or was happening. The big occurrences in life, the serious ones, have for me always been nearly impossible to recognize because they never *feel* big or serious. In the moment, you have to pee, or your arm itches, or what people are saying strikes you as melodramatic or sentimental, and it's hard not to smirk. You have a sense of what this type of situation should be like—for one thing, all-consuming—and this isn't it. But then you look back, and it *was* that; it did happen.

Most of the doors were open, and as we passed the rooms, I could hear the canned laughter and loud voices of television. Suddenly, I remembered: the Friday before. That was when I'd last spoken to Sin-Jun. We had walked to lunch together after chemistry, and we'd talked about spring break, which would be in March. She had said she was going to stay with an aunt in San Diego. Nothing stood out from the conversation, not even a glance or an inflection. I wondered if she'd been planning it then, or if taking the pills had been an impulsive decision. And again, I thought, but why? Didn't she have a perfectly good life? She was not popular, but she had friends—certainly, it was impossible to imagine anyone disliking her. And on top of that, she did well in school. Her English, still, was surprisingly broken, but it was clear she understood other people. And her parents, whom I'd met when we were freshmen, had seemed fine, and even if they weren't fine, they were so far away. Could that have been it, the distance? Or that she missed her sister? But that didn't entirely make sense, either; you didn't take pills because you were homesick.

When we entered the room, Sin-Jun was in bed, and the mattress was raised so she was half-sitting. She was staring ahead with no particular expression on her face, wearing a pale blue hospital gown, and the skin around her mouth was, as Mrs. Morino had warned me, smudged a powdery black from the charcoal the doctors had used to pump her stomach.

But she was not the one commanding attention—that was Clara, the source of the wailing I'd heard before. Clara was bawling as openly and recklessly as an infant: Her face was a splotchy pink, and tears were streaming down her face; her nose was dripping; her mouth was open, with strings of spit running between her upper and lower lips; and from her mouth issued a wordless cry, sometimes sustained, sometimes broken into gasping chunks, that was both grotesque and spellbinding. She was seated in a chair on the right side of Sin-Jun's bed, leaning forward with both her hands pressed against the edge of the mattress, and because the mattress was at least a foot higher than the chair, Clara's posture resembled that of a supplicant. Sin-Jun appeared to be ignoring her completely.

Over the considerable noise, Mrs. Morino yelled, "Look who I brought!" She set an arm around my shoulders and smiled widely.

"Hi!" I shouted.

Sin-Jun did not look at either of us.

It seemed like maybe I ought to hug her, or maybe not. I stepped forward and set my hand against the mattress by her feet, and at last she looked up. "Hi, Lee." She sounded tired but not at all emotional—not embarrassed or regretful or apologetic.

"I'm glad to see you," I called. Sin-Jun hadn't raised her voice, and I'd been able to hear her fine, but I could not check my own impulse to yell.

Apparently, Mrs. Morino felt the same way. "I'm running back to campus," she hollered. She was now rubbing Clara's back. "I need to put the kids to bed. But, Lee and Clara, when Mr. Morino brings me here to stay overnight with Sin-Jun, he'll take you two home. Okay? Does that sound good?'

No one said anything.

"We'll get you back to the dorm in time for curfew," Mrs. Morino said. "And, Sin-Jun, we want you to feel much better. Can you do that for us?"

After Mrs. Morino had left, Clara actually stopped crying and heaved a little, as if catching her breath. I felt the same relief I felt around a shrieking baby who quieted, and also the same unpleasant hunch that this was not the conclusion of the outburst but only a hiatus from it.

"How long have you guys been in this room?" I asked.

"I don't know," Clara said, and each word was shaky and elongated.

I wanted to ask, *How long have you been crying?* To be this dramatically upset seemed physically draining, and Clara was a heavy girl—surely she could not sustain such exertion indefinitely.

I glanced back at Sin-Jun. When our eyes met, I almost started. The way she looked at me was so hopeless, so exhausted, that it seemed scornful. I had an inkling then that perhaps I'd underestimated her. Perhaps in the past I hadn't given her credit for having opinions or experiencing discontent—for being like me. Of course there was nothing I could do for her. I still did not believe she had meant to die, but, yes, she had taken the pills on purpose; she did, after all, possess the requisite will.

"I'm spending the night," Clara announced. "You can't stop me."

Sin-Jun turned her head and addressed Clara for the first time since I'd arrived. "You are not staying in hospital."

"You have to let me. I'm not leaving."

"Mr. Morino is coming to get us for curfew," I said.

"For *curfew*?" Clara glared at me. "Sin-Jun almost *died* tonight and all you care about is curfew?"

Even the explicit reference to death—astonishingly inappropriate, in my opinion—elicited no reaction from Sin-Jun.

"Sin-Jun, do you want us to stay?" I asked.

"I want to sleep," Sin-Jun said. She glanced toward Clara. "Go back to school."

"No! No. I'm not going. I'm calling the Morinos right now and telling them I'm staying. I'll get a cot, just like Mrs. Morino. I'm staying. Do you hear me?" She'd stood and was edging toward the door but doing so tentatively, as if Sin-Jun

256

might spring from the bed and tackle her. I was at the foot of the bed, still barely inside the room, and when Clara got close to me, I stepped back. I did not, as she lurched and burbled, want to make physical contact with her.

When she was gone, the room seemed peaceful. I was both relieved and afraid to be alone with Sin-Jun. I took Clara's seat—I'd get up when she came back—and Sin-Jun and I didn't talk. Finally, I said, "Sin-Jun, do you wish you didn't go to Ault?"

She shrugged.

"You don't have to, right? If you told your parents you don't want to be here, they wouldn't make you stay."

"I not need to tell parents anything. Mrs. Morino is already call them, and my father, he comes tomorrow."

Though I hadn't thought about it before, it made sense that there would be parental intervention. In fact, it surprised me a little that Mrs. Morino had left us alone, without adults, even this briefly. How were we supposed to know how to act by ourselves?

"Clara is really upset, huh?" I said, then quickly added, "We all really care about you, Sin-Jun." It sounded, I thought, like I was reading aloud from a get-well card. But I saw that tears were welling in Sin-Jun's eyes. She blinked and they slid over her eyelids.

"Yikes," I said. "I'm sorry."

She shook her head.

"Sin-Jun?"

She opened her mouth but did not immediately speak, and I felt, simultaneously, the impulse to coax the words from her and the impulse to suppress them. I always thought I wanted to know a secret, or I wanted an event to unfold—I wanted my life to start—but in those rare moments when it seemed like something might actually change, panic shot through me.

"You don't have to say anything," I said. "But let me at least let me get you some water."

She wiped her eyes with the heels of her hands.

"You're probably thirsty," I said and bolted from the room. By the time I found a plastic cup—someone down at the nurses' station gave it to me—then filled it at a drinking fountain, Clara had returned to the room. I set the cup on the table next to Sin-Jun's bed and saw that a cup of water already rested there, half-full, with a straw sticking out.

"Did Mr. Morino say it's okay if you stay?" I asked Clara.

"Why wouldn't it be?" Clara seemed slightly more composed than she had before. At least her face was no longer actively leaking fluid, and Sin-Jun also was not crying.

I looked at my watch. It was eight-thirty, and curfew was at ten; the Morinos probably weren't coming for at least an hour. "I should go downstairs," I said. "I don't want to keep them waiting."

Neither Clara nor Sin-Jun appeared to be paying attention. "I'm not leaving you alone," Clara was saying, and I could see that it was only a matter of time before the floodgates reopened.

"Sin-Jun, I hope you feel better," I said. "'Okay? Here, I'll—" I stepped forward and leaned in to hug her. She did not reciprocate the hug at all, and in my arms she felt brittle and weightless. "Bye," I said. "Okay? Bye,"

"Bye, Lee," she finally said.

I had not told Clara good-bye; and as I left, Clara did not say good-bye to me.

I was so desperate to be gone from the hospital that back on the first floor, despite the wait in front of me, I walked outside and stood beneath the porte cochere with my arms folded, peering across the parking lot. Campus was about five miles away, but if it hadn't been dark out, I'd have started off on foot.

It *was* dark, though, and it was cold, too. I lasted roughly a minute before I went back inside and sat by a soda machine in the waiting area. I wanted very badly to be in the dorm, wearing my nightgown beneath my own clean sheet and blankets.

I had no wallet with me, no money at all. If I did have money, I'd get a root beer, I thought, and then I thought, but if Sin-Jun hadn't wanted to die, was it plausible to believe she'd wanted to end up here? The pills had to have been an impulsive decision, a matter of *not this; anything except this moment.*

So Sin-Jun, too—I had never suspected. Not, probably, that it would have changed the outcome of events if I had. After all, these were not topics you could discuss with someone else; what was there to say to another person about how it felt? You could concoct things you wanted but in certain moments the light shifted or time slowed—on Sundays in particular, time slowed, and occasionally on Saturday afternoons, if you didn't have a game—and you saw that it was all really nothing. It was just endlessness and what you got or didn't get would hardly make a difference, and then what was there? The loathsomely familiar room where you lived, your horrible face and body, and the rebuke of other people, how they were unbothered, how you would seem; if you tried to explain, kind of weird and kind of boring and not even original. Why did their lives proceed so easily? Why was it that you needed to convince them and they needed to be convinced and not the other way around? Not, of course, that you would actually succeed if you tried.

And then at dinner, we talked about what? Teachers or movies or spring vacation. It was just what you did; you socialized, you *interacted*. And the things you said, the walk from chapel to the schoolhouse, your backpack, tests, these were a bridge running above the rushing water of what you actually felt. The goal was: learn to ignore what's down below. Fine if you met someone else who was the same as you, but you had to realize that nothing another person could do would make you feel better about any of it. In an odd way, suicide attempts seemed to me—I wouldn't have thought this as a freshman, but I thought it now, two years later—naïve. They didn't achieve anything, the drama they set in motion couldn't possibly be sustained. In the end, there was always your regular life, and no one could deal with it but you.

Someone approached the soda machine, and immediately I was waiting for him to leave. When he turned around, he said, "Hey there," and I nodded without smiling.

"You okay?" he said. He was a young man, and he was carrying a little girl.

"I'm fine."

"It looked like maybe something was upsetting you."

I didn't say anything.

"I don't mean to invade," the man said quickly. Then he said, "You don't recognize me, do you? Sorry, I should have—here you go." He was wearing a long-sleeved flannel button-down over a white V-neck T-shirt, and from between the two shirts he extracted a lanyard on which hung a plastic badge. With the lanyard still around his neck, he held the badge out to me; in his other arm, he held both the little girl, who was observing us impassively, and his unopened can of Pepsi.

The man was six or seven feet away, and I had to stand and lean in to read the badge. Briefly, I considered not standing, but stood anyway, more out of curiosity than politeness, and then I was glad I had. *Ault School*, the badge said across the top. The Ault crest was superimposed over the whole badge, and in one corner was a head shot of the guy in which he was grinning and sticking out his chin, as if he'd been joking with the photographer; below the photo, it said, *David Bardo, Food Services*.

"Sorry," I said. "You look familiar, but I just didn't—" I trailed off.

"Kitchen staff."

"That's right, of course." And he actually did look familiar, in that vague way of someone you've never noticed before. I wondered just how cold I had been acting, and I was

260

mortified. Because yes, I was someone who would be rude to a stranger, especially a male stranger who approached me in a public place; but I would never be rude to a member of the Ault staff. People unfamiliar with boarding schools probably imagined the opposite, that the students were haughty toward the janitors or the secretaries, but this was not the case at all—twice in the last five years, the senior class had dedicated the yearbook to Will Koomber, who was head of the grounds crew and had a kind of cult following. Will was a black man in his sixties, originally from Alabama, and rumored to be stoned most of the time, which contributed to his popularity. Guys particularly liked him—you'd see them outside during the day, standing just beyond the mulch while Will squatted and shoveled, and you'd hear them say things like "How's your old lady, Will?" or, "You always gotta watch those Feds, huh?" The truth was that overhearing these exchanges made me nervous—the pleasantries seemed so precarious, it seemed so easy for a student to say something offensive and for Will to either react or not be able to react—but I also believed that Will and the Ault boys genuinely liked one another. I was the one overthinking the relationship, not them. Whenever I myself passed Will, especially if I was alone, he'd deliver some brief bit of third-person narration— "She's in an awful big hurry," or, "That's a nice skirt she's wearing today"—and I would duck my head and smile, wanting to express my gratitude to him for talking to me, too, and not just to the athletic guys and the pretty girls.

But the kitchen staff was a little different. Most students didn't seem to know them, or at any rate, I didn't. Whenever I was in the dining hall, I was consumed by thoughts of what food to select, of where to sit, and I didn't pay attention to much beyond my own circumstances. As I stood in front of David Bardo trying to remember the other people who worked in the kitchen, I could come up mostly with rough demographic categories: the women in their twenties, the women in their fifties (in my mind, all the women in both groups had blue eyes and fair hair that they wore in nets or white caps, and all of them were overweight, with pale, chubby forearms). In a humid room adjacent to the kitchen, teenage boys did the dishwashing after dinner. They were often blasting heavy metal, and whenever I set my dirty dishes in the carousel at the front of the room, it surprised me that they were allowed to play that music, and at that volume. Most of these boys were skinny and had bad skin and crew cuts, and one was very fat, the skin on the tops of his cheeks pushing up to give him squinty eyes. The head chef—you knew because he wore one of those tall pouffy hats—looked to be in his forties, with a blond beard; sometimes he stood at the end of the cafeteria line, just past the steaming entrées behind the glass barrier, and made remarks whose content seemed like the hints of a helpful waiter at a nice restaurant but whose tone was always tinged with hostility: "You really should try the sole tonight," or, "If you don't take any egg-plant timbale, you're seriously missing out." (Of course no one *wanted* sole or eggplant timbale—we wanted hot dogs and grilled cheese.)

And then, apparently, there was David Bardo. He was probably in his twenties, and he wasn't tall—he might have been five nine—but he was big, barrel-chested, and broad-shouldered. He had dark cropped hair and a ruddy face with dark stubble. He looked like someone who might play ice hockey outside, on a frozen pond, or who would own a truck and know how to fix it if it broke down.

"Yeah, I recognized you right away," he was saying. "I was like, I know her, she goes to the school. You're, what, a sophomore?"

"A junior."

"Okay, 'cause you've definitely been there the whole time I have, and I started in January of last year. Where're you from?"

"Indiana."

"That's pretty far. But some of the kids are from California, right?"

262

"I guess so."

"I wouldn't mind checking out California. I've got a buddy living out in Santa Cruz now says he's never coming back. You ever been there?"

"No." For some reason, I wished that I had, I wished I could fulfill what I imagined this guy's idea of an Ault student to be: for one thing, well traveled.

"I'm thinking of heading out this summer, maybe July or August. Take a road trip, spend a few weeks there."

Though I had nothing in particular to say to this, I tried to seem pleasantly interested.

"You ever driven cross-country?"

I shook my head.

"I do," the little girl said suddenly, and David Bardo and I both laughed. The girl appeared to be about two, with fuzzy blond hair and heart-shaped earrings. "Do you like road trips?" I asked her. "Are you going to California with your dad?"

"No, no," David Bardo said. "Kaley's not my daughter. You're not my daughter, are you, Kaley girl?" He was looking down at her, rubbing her check with his thumb, and then he turned back to me. "She's my niece. Her mom's having some asthma problems."

A strange expression must have crossed my face.

"No, she's fine," he said. "They just gave her a breathing treatment and now she's resting. Right, Kaley? Mom's resting? This happens two, three times a year."

But it had not been the news about the asthma I'd reacted to; it had been the news that the girl was not his child, the sudden suspicion that this guy was closer to my age than I'd originally thought. I wondered if I'd seemed like I'd been flirting with him, and an agitated feeling came over me; the conversation needed to end.

"Why are you at the hospital tonight?" he said. "If I can ask."

I thought of Sin-Jun, two floors above us, propped against the mattress in her blue gown.

"You don't have to say if you don't want to," he added.

"I came here to see a friend who's sick."

"That's tough." David Bardo smiled with his lips closed, a sad smile, and the corners of his eyes crinkled. "Hospitals suck, don't they? Hey, you need a ride back to school or anything?"

"The Morinos are—some teachers are coming to get me. But thanks."

I peered out the window—I could see little beyond the brightly lit entrance—and as I did, I could feel that David Bardo was watching me. I looked back at him, and for several seconds, neither of us spoke. Then, maybe only to end the silence, I said, "I should, um—" I gestured toward where I'd been sitting—an empty chair surrounded by other empty chairs—as if something there demanded my attention.

"Sure," he said. "Well, real nice to meet you. Except we didn't officially meet, did we? I'm Dave." He extended his hand.

By ten-twenty—that is, twenty minutes after curfew—the Morinos still hadn't shown up. I went to find a pay phone but remembered, when I was standing in front of it, that I had no money. And I had no calling card, either—when I called home from the dorm, I either called collect or jammed in quarters while we spoke—and I certainly wasn't going back upstairs to try to borrow change from Clara or Sin-Jun. I approached the sign-in desk and when I asked if I could use the phone, a woman with a frosted blond French braid said the pay phone was down the hall.

"I know," I said. "But I don't have any money. And I promise I won't take long."

She shook her head. "No outgoing calls."

The woman looked down to write something, and although I felt utterly uncertain what to do next, her lack of cooperation was oddly satisfying. When a situation swung out of my control, when I'd exhausted all the possibilities, I became blameless.

1 returned to the waiting area and had not yet reached the chairs when I saw David Bardo—Dave—and his niece and a woman I took to be his sister. The sister was thin, with long brown hair, and she was wearing jeans and a flannel shirt similar to Dave's. It looked like the little girl had fallen asleep in Dave's arms, her head hanging to one side.

As we approached each other, Dave smiled. "Still here?"

I nodded.

He had stopped, and so had I, but his sister was still walking.

"Everything okay?" he said.

Really, what was I going to do—spend the night at the hospital? I might be blameless, but that wouldn't mitigate the misery of sleeping in the waiting area. "You know how you offered me a ride before?" I said. "Well, if it's okay, I mean if it wouldn't be too much trouble—"

He was watching me with a vaguely amused look, and I felt the same self-consciousness I'd experienced during our first conversation, a combination of discomfort—was he looking at something in particular, did I have some pen mark on my cheek or was someone standing behind me making faces?—and also flattery. The sense of flattery came from the fact that he was paying attention to me: I could tell that I existed as a distinct person standing in front of him, not a generic girl.

"If you need a lift, that's no problem," he said. "Hey, Lynn."

The sister turned; she'd been walking slowly, so she was only about ten feet past us.

"Hold up," he said. "We've got another passenger. This is Lee. Lee, this is my sister, Lynn."

"Hi." I hesitated, unsure whether we would shake hands, and as I was hesitating, she turned again and continued walking.

In the parking lot, Dave set the little girl in a car seat, and when he did, she awakened, whimpering even before she opened her eyes, "Hey there, Kaley," Dave crooned. "It's okay, Kaley girl. Everything's fine."

Kaley's lower lip had been quivering, but it stilled; she shut her eyes again, then brought her thumb to her mouth. Dave glanced over his shoulder—he was standing beside the open back door, and I was standing behind him—and when we made eye contact, he winked and held up his own thumb. "Better than a lollipop." He turned around again, fastening the seat belt over Kaley's car seat, and, with his back to me, I felt myself on the verge of a smirk. But whom would I be smirking for, here in the dark hospital parking lot? To what audience was I trying to express my understanding that a wink, no matter the context, was always cheesy?

When I looked at Dave's sister, who was standing a few feet from the car, I saw, to my astonishment, that she was smoking. Our eyes met. She took a long drag, flicked the cigarette onto the pavement, and stepped on it with her shoe. Then she approached the car and opened the back door on the far side.

"Wait," I said. "I'll sit in back, and you can have the front."

"Doesn't matter," she said, and she climbed in.

Dave shut the back door on Kaley's side—the car was a pale brown Chevy Nova with a dark brown vinyl top and rust eating away the back wheel wells—then opened the front passenger door. Because of the car parked beside us, there wasn't enough room for me to get in with him in front of me. We stood looking at each other.

"Should I move?" I asked.

"Seems like a good idea."

"This way?" I pointed behind me.

"Here." He set both his hands on both my shoulders and pushed me not hard, and only with his hands—against the other car. Then he slid by, and after he had, he stopped and glanced back. "Okay?"

All I needed to say was *okay*, or *yes*. But I was silent. I felt stunned. I wanted the instant to exist again when his hands were on my shoulders and we were standing close together. I wanted it to be just us, not his sister or niece, and maybe when we were standing there he would lean forward, he'd tilt his head toward mine or just press his whole body against me. He would feel solid and strong and warm, and when I gripped his upper arms, my fingers would look small and thin, like the fingers of a girl who'd have a boyfriend.

I swallowed. "Yeah," I said. "Okay."

In the car, he fiddled with the heater as he drove, and from the back, his sister said, "I told you it doesn't work."

"I'm just seeing."

"Lenny's gonna fix it this weekend, but you keep screwing with it now, you'll make it worse."

As she spoke, a blast of air came out of the vents in the front. "Ha!" Dave cried. "It's a miracle!"

"A miracle that you never listen."

"I got it to work, didn't I?" He looked at her in the rearview mirror, and he seemed not defensive but chipper. He turned to me. "Your teacher stood you up, huh? That's no good."

"She has a bunch of kids. Maybe things got confused at home."

"So you like going to that school?"

This was possibly the most complicated question I could imagine; I felt that I couldn't answer it without explaining my entire life. "Sure," I said.

"The people are cool."

It was hard to tell if he was asking or commenting.

"Some of them," I said.

He laughed. "There's this one girl," he said, and I felt my heart pinch; he was going to confide a crush. "She has blond hair, kind of curly. And she just—" He shook his head. "Nobody can stand her. She stands there and says how disgusting the food is. It's like, hello, we can hear you. We ain't deaf."

I laughed, to cover my discomfort over the *ain't*. Probably it had been on purpose, but it was hard to tell.

"Most of you guys, though, you're not too bad," Dave continued. "Lynn used to work at the school, too."

"Really?" I said. "When did you—?" I'd turned around to look at her, and I saw that she, like Kaley, was asleep.

Dave glanced back, too. "She's worn out," he said. "It's hard for her with Kaley. But, yeah, Lynn's the one who got me the job. Put in a good word for me. I'll probably work there another year or two, at least till I graduate."

"Wait, are you in high school or college?"

"Oh, man, that's insulting. That's brutal."

"Does that mean college?"

"I look like I'm fifteen, huh?"

"No." It required effort to say what I said next, because it was acknowledging something I was uncomfortable acknowledging (*I have been looking at you, I have been paying attention, you also are a specific person to me*); it made me complicit. "You don't look fifteen," I said softly.

"How old do I look?"

I hesitated. "Twenty?"

"Twenty-one. But yeah, I'm at East Rock State, over in Rivertown."

I nodded as if I'd heard of it.

"I'm thinking of doing a business major so I can keep my options open. And then probably College of Fairfield. That's what I'm thinking."

"For graduate school?"

"For my B.A. I get my associate's at East Rock, then I transfer the credits."

"Okay, of course." It was not that I was unfamiliar with community college—that's what my cousins attended—more that I wasn't accustomed to it in the context or Ault.

"Where are you gonna go?" he said. "Harvard?"

"Yeah, right."

"I bet you're smart. Get all As."

"I'll probably go somewhere like—" I stopped. When Martha or I thought we'd done badly on a test, we'd say, *I might as well just apply right now to UMass,* but invoking UMass as a last resort would, clearly, be a bad idea. "—to dog school," I said brightly.

"What?" Dave looked across the seat at me.

"Like obedience school," I said.

"You have a dog?"

"No, no, *I'm* the dog."

He looked at me again, and it was a look I always remembered, long after that night and after I'd left Ault. He was confused and was registering a new piece of information and this was what it was: that I was a girl who would, even in jest, utter the sentence, *I'm the dog.* It was a good lesson for me. It was a while before I stopped insulting myself so promiscuously, and I never stopped completely, but still—it was a good lesson.

In that moment, all he said was, "You're the dog, huh?"

And then, because I knew I'd made a mistake and wanted us to leave the place where I'd made it, I said, "I wouldn't say this if your sister was awake, but I don't think it's hot air coming out of the vents."

He stuck one palm up. "That's not hot?"

"Feel one of these."

With his left hand still on the steering wheel, he leaned over; when he held his hand in front of the vent in my corner, his arm crossed over my lap, and his head was only a few inches from mine. I easily could have touched his hair.

He said, "Shit," and sat upright again. (I had not worried, as he'd leaned over, that the car would swerve: he seemed utterly competent, not high-strung enough to have an accident. Or if he did, he'd be calm afterward, he wouldn't be either angry or panicked.) As he twisted the knobs, he said, "At least I know whose side you're on. Protecting me from Lynn, huh?"

"I guess so."

269

"You're probably real cold. Are you cold?"

"I'm okay."

"You want to—" He hesitated for a fraction of a second, then nodded his head toward the seat between us. "You can wear my gloves there."

"Oh—" My impulse, as always, was to politely decline, but he picked one up and passed it to me. It was huge and puffy and made of nylon, a glove to chop wood in during a snowstorm. I put it on.

"See," Dave said. "It's warm, right?"

But the weird intimacy of wearing his glove was constricting me. I could barely talk, certainly I couldn't talk *about* the fact that I was wearing his glove, and I couldn't bring myself to put on the other one.

"They're waterproof." he said, and, in my desperation to change the subject, I blurted out, "Do you think it's strange for people to go to boarding school?"

"I guess it depends,' he said. "Leaving home when you're that young—I could barely dress myself when I started high school.'

"Some of the guys in my class can still barely dress themselves," I said, but when Dave laughed—he laughed hard—I thought of my classmates, most of whom dressed themselves just fine, most of whose wardrobes, in fact, I had memorized for no other reason than that I saw all of them all the time. At Ault, I always felt like I didn't really know the boys in my class, but thinking of them from inside Dave Bardo's car, they seemed as familiar as my brothers.

We'd passed through town and were descending the hill just before campus; through the windshield, I saw the dark outline of the chapel's bell tower. It seemed like we ought to discuss which entrance he'd use and where he'd let me off, but I felt reluctant to raise the subject, just as I'd been reluctant to talk about wearing his glove; it would call too much attention to exactly what was going on.

He turned in to the south gate and made a right into the

dining hall parking lot. He even pulled into a parking space before saying, "Oh, wait, where's the dorm? I'll take you to the dorm."

"This is fine," I said. "Thanks so much." I was already holding the door handle.

"You sure?"

"I'm positive. Thanks." I got out of the car. "Bye. Thank you."

He smiled. "You're very polite."

It would be disingenuous to pretend that it was only as I walked across campus, only after it was too late to turn back, that I realized I was still wearing his glove.

Mrs. Morino approached me as roll call was ending and said, "I'm so sorry about the other night." I already knew from Mrs. Elwyn, my own dorm head, that they hadn't forgotten me—Mrs. Morino had gotten the impression from Clara that I, too, wanted to stay overnight, so she hadn't returned to the hospital until after eleven.

"It's all right," I said. "How's Sin-Jun?"

"Much more like her old self. I'm actually hoping you'll go this afternoon and help her dad bring her back to the infirmary."

Who would watch her to make sure she didn't try again? I wondered. A nurse?

"We don't know if she'll stay at Ault," Mrs. Morino said. "Mr. Byden and her parents and I are talking with her, but in the meantime, it would be great if you could swing by her room and pack a bag for her so she has some things."

'Wouldn't Clara know what stuff she'd want?"

Mrs. Morino sighed "I take it that you don't know Clara and Sin-Jun aren't getting along."

This did not particularly surprise me. Freshman year, when Clara also had lived in Broussard's, I'd tried to steer clear of her from the beginning. And it hadn't been because she was someone who obviously would never be popular, or at least it hadn't been only because of that; it also had been because she irritated me. She was pale, with dark blond chin-length hair, a middle part, and heavy bangs. She was big, especially in the breasts and thighs, and she favored tapered, bleached jeans and long dumpy skirts. In her demeanor, there was something spacey and innocent, something slow and not discontented, and it was these qualities that I found so irritating. But I doubted most people agreed; she was the type about whom most people would say. *She wouldn't hurt a fly.* My real frustration with Clara, I think, was that it seemed like she should be insecure but wasn't.

At curfew, if you ended up sitting next to her, she'd start talking as if you'd been carrying on a conversation before and had been interrupted or as if you'd just asked her a question. She'd do this with anyone—me, Aspeth, Amy Dennaker, even Madame Broussard. The defining aspect of Clara's stories was that she did not provide context and that you did not, for fear of encouraging her, ask for it. She might, for instance, recount some incident from class: "I didn't even know the quiz was today. I said to Shelly, 'Did he tell us there would be a quiz?' and she said no. And in the beginning of the year, I clearly remember him saying, 'I don't give pop quizzes . . .'" As she continued, I'd be thinking, *Shelly? Who's Shelly? Does anyone named Shelly go to Ault?*

Clara also both hummed and sang to herself audibly and unselfconsciously; you'd hear her while you were washing your faces at adjacent sinks in the bathroom before bed. I had never been able to shake the sense that she was, in these situations, trying to elicit some sort of reaction—a compliment on her voice, maybe, or an inquiry into what song she was humming. Or maybe she wanted you to see her as care-free and whimsical. Yet at the same time, coexisting with my feeling that her singing was somehow aggressive, I also saw her as genuinely clueless. It was conceivable that she was singing just because she wanted to sing, because she was care-free and whimsical. And that possibility made me dislike her most of all.

That afternoon, I came face-to-face with Clara outside her and Sin-Jun's room; she was carrying a cup of tea.

"I'm here to get the bag of stuff," I said.

"What for? Is Sin-Jun going home?" Her voice was frantic, and I had a vision of her bursting into tears right there.

"She's going to the infirmary. Has Mrs. Morino not talked to you?"

"I guess she hasn't." Clara's snappishness was preferable to wailing, but only by a little.

"I'm supposed to get her some clothes," I said. "Can I go in?"

Clara didn't reply, but stepped in front of me and pushed open the door. I followed her. They didn't have bunk beds, like Martha and I did, but twin beds with a little table between them. Clara's comforter had large roses in red and peach and orange, and Sin-Jun's was the same one from our freshman year, navy with green piping. It occurred to me that the last time she'd been in the room had been the evening she'd taken the pills.

"Where's her duffel bag?" I asked.

Clara pointed under the bed but let me get on my knees to retrieve the bag myself. So this was to be a solo project, I thought, and when I was standing again, I pulled open the top drawer of the bureau I could tell was Sin-Jun's because I recognized the toiletries lined up across the top—the Korean hand lotion with a graphic of a sleeping baby on the bottle, the perfume that I'd always thought smelled like grapefruit. I could sense, as I lifted Sin-Jun's underwear and undershirts (I'd forgotten that she didn't wear bras) and dropped them in the duffel, that Clara was watching me intently. When I shut the top drawer, Clara said, "You forgot her pajamas."

"Where are they?"

Clara reopened the drawer, pulled out a gray tank top and a pair of boxer shorts and passed them to me. Then she stepped back again and folded her arms.

I went drawer by drawer, and we didn't talk. I set several toiletries in the duffel.

"The shampoo will spill on her clothes," Clara said. "You should always carry stuff like that inside a plastic bag."

'We're not going that far," I said. I surveyed the room, wondering what else Sin-Jun might want and realized I should have bought her a present. "I guess this is it." I said. "Unless you can think of anything."

Clara was watching me suspiciously. "You haven't been in our room once this whole year."

"So?"

"So I don't know why you're acting like you and Sin-Jun are really close."

"I'm not."

"She's changed since you guys were roommates. I bet there are a lot of things you don't know about her."

"Clara, Mrs. Morino *asked* me to come over here. Was I supposed to say no?"

"I just think you're acting kind of fake."

"Well, I'm sorry you feel that way." This was an Aultish thing to say, ostensibly diplomatic yet totally distant. But I actually did feel a twinge of sympathy for Clara. How would I react if, say, Dede were to suddenly usurp my role in Martha's life? Not that that's what I was trying to do with Sin-Jun; it was just sort of happening.

"Wait." Clara said. "Give her this." She tossed a small white stuffed rabbit toward me. I didn't catch it, but I picked it up off the floor. "And tell her not to eat too many peach daiquiris. She'll know what that means." In a strange way, I identified more with Clara in this moment than I ever had before. Her face was pink and strained, focusing on me. The way she usually seemed—obliviously satisfied—she didn't seem at all.

By the time I got to the schoolhouse, where Mrs. Morino had told me to meet Mr. Kim, a cream-colored sedan was waiting out front. Mr. Kim emerged from the car, finished a call on his cell phone—it was the first cell phone I'd ever seen—and soberly shook my hand. I had met him twice before: the first time during parents' weekend when Sin-Jun and I were freshmen, and the second time, later that same year, when Mr. Kim was in Boston for a business trip and came to campus. Both times I'd gone out to dinner with the Kims and both times Mr. Kim had encouraged me to order steak and, unable to think of a reason not to, I'd complied. Mr. Kim was an inch or two shorter than I was, trim, and dressed in a gray suit, a white shirt with no tie, and a beige raincoat that seemed like it couldn't possibly be keeping him warm; his skin was tan and his hair was thinning, especially in the front, where there were just a few groups of strands, which looked and smelled like they'd been combed back with pomade.

Inside the sedan, the seats were pale leather, and the car was already warm; I always forgot how nice things that cost a lot could be. After we drove away from campus, several minutes passed during which neither of us spoke. Sentences floated in my mind—*How was your flight? When did you arrive?*—but it seemed like asking them would be avoiding the real subject. Yet raising the real subject surely was not for me to do.

Out the window, the trees were bare and scrawny-looking, and the road was lined with dirty snow from the week before. I actually liked the desolation of winter; it was the season when it was okay to be unhappy. If I were ever to kill myself, I thought, it would be in the summer.

"If you did not like Ault School," Mr. Kim began (so he was thinking, more or less, about the same thing), "you would tell your father and mother."

"Not necessarily. I wouldn't want my parents to worry because they can't do much."

Neither of us spoke for almost a minute, and then Mr. Kim said, "You would tell teacher or headmaster."

"I would probably tell my roommate." Admitting this felt, somehow, like a betrayal of Sin-Jun.

275

Mr. Kim did not reply, and the silence from before descended again.

After he had turned in to the hospital parking lot and parked, I said brightly, "Are the hospitals different in Korea than here?"

"In big cities, they are the same. In villages, they are not so modern."

"It's winter there, too, right? The seasons are the same as here?"

"Yes," he said. "The seasons are the same."

Inside, we signed in and boarded the elevator. "What's your favorite season?" I asked.

He was quiet, then finally said, "When Sin-Jun was small girl, we took her one night to a party. Our friends' house had many window. While we ate dinner, my friend's wife said to me, 'Look.' Sin-Jun stood before window. Because the night was dark, Sin-Jun saw her reflection in glass. But she did not understand it was her reflection. She thought it was another small girl. When she waved, the other girl waved. When she smiled, the other girl smiled. She begins to dance, and the other girl dances. Sin-Jun is so happy." Mr. Kim sounded neither pleased nor saddened; he sounded simply confused. "She is filled," he said, "with so much delight."

The elevator had arrived on the third floor; pausing, then dropping a little, and I could feel that the doors were about to open. We were both facing straight ahead. Grown men, other people's fathers, were so strange—often I didn't completely understand what it was they did at their jobs during the day, and certainly I didn't understand what occupied their minds. They might tease you or ask you questions, they might even, in elementary school, be your soccer coach, but their attention always felt momentary, before they turned back to the real business at hand. And you *wanted* their attention to be momentary—the ones whose wasn't seemed creepy. Now, however, the situation felt backwards, it felt as if maybe Mr. Kim was asking for something from me. But if he was,

276

what did I have to give? Another person's father could grill your hamburger, could pump air into your bike tire, could carry your suitcase out to the car, but what could you possibly do for him? Wasn't it presumptuous—presuming, specifically, his need and vulnerability—to offer comfort?

As the elevator doors opened I said, "I really think she'll be okay."

In fact, Sin-Jun did not seem particularly okay at all. Leaving the hospital, her father passed her his coat—I hadn't thought to bring one from her room—and Sin-Jun responded irritably, in Korean (it was the most animated I'd seen her since before she'd taken the aspirin). She wouldn't put the coat on, or even hold it, so Mr. Kim draped it over her shoulders. He turned to me and said in English, "You will stay here with Sin-Jun while I retrieve car." After he had walked beyond the porte cochere, Sin-Jun went outside as well. I followed her.

"I think your dad wants us to wait inside."

She gave me an unfriendly look. "I need air."

It was hard to know how to treat her. My impulse was to act as if she were physically ill—at some level, it had surprised me to see her dressed and waiting for us by the nurses' station, and then it had surprised me that she simply stood and walked out rather than being pushed in a wheelchair— yet another part of me saw her as not sick at all; I wanted to grab her by the shoulders and tell her to snap out of it. Her lack of affect seemed ridiculous, a parody of a moody teenager. Not, of course, that I *would* grab her by the shoulders, but the reason I wouldn't was not so much that it would be inappropriate as that, in her new incarnation, I found Sin-Jun intimidating. I could imagine her having disparaging thoughts about me. She had done something fearless and dramatic, something people at school were talking about. The school psychologist was making her way around to all the dorms, starting with girls', talking to students at curfew—Sin-Jun had set these meetings in motion, quiet and easygoing Sin-Jun—and other students who were aware that I had once roomed with her had been asking about the details of what had happened. The girls at least feigned concern (*Is she okay?* Or, *How awful!*) while the guys' remarks were more distant: *That's fucked. What'd she do that for? Was she always psycho?* But this was the thing: Neither the girls nor the guys seemed entirely unimpressed. The fact that Sin-Jun had taken pills made her interesting. It was becoming—I could feel it happening—a phenomenon, another story. It was no longer an act of desperation, or at least not messy, slobbery desperation. And now that Sin-Jun was, by the larger Ault community, being reconsidered (surely, though she hadn't yet gotten back to campus, she could sense this reconsideration; surely, when you were cool, you were always at least slightly aware of your own coolness), I feared her; perhaps she found me dorky.

"Do you want to play gin rummy tonight?" I said.

Sin-Jun shook her head.

"Or tomorrow," I added. (I *was* dorky—she'd be entirely justified in thinking so.)

She was standing a little in front of me, scanning the parking lot, and I couldn't read her face.

"Are you glad you're leaving the hospital?" I asked.

She shrugged.

"You know how you felt bad before? Do you still feel that bad? Or do you feel better?" It was because she was all but ignoring me that I could ask this; I was comfortable in the world with only one person emoting at a time, and if she'd been weeping and confiding, I'd have been distantly attentive, blandly soothing.

"I am fine," she said.

"There have been times when I've felt depressed."

Sin-Jun looked at me squarely. "You are depressed?"

"Sure," I said, and it felt like I was lying. My depression, if that's what it was, was always so ephemeral; it was possible to

278

be distracted from it by hanging out with Martha, or by listening to a chapel talk, or even—this had to mean it wasn't serious—by watching television. "There are things that get me down," I said.

"Which are things?"

"Ault is stressful," I said. "There's a lot of pressure." These were the kinds of complaints students made, but they were asinine. Not once in three years had I thought, *I'm under a lot of pressure*.

"Grades," Sin-Jun said. "They are why you worry?"

"Not as much as I probably should."

She looked at me blankly, and I didn't know if she couldn't tell I was making a joke or if she just didn't find the joke funny. Abruptly, I remembered our first week at Ault. living together in Broussard's. One evening we both had been ready for formal dinner well before we needed to be—when you're new to a place, there's always too much time to fill— so we sat on our beds, just waiting. That early on, I was shy even around Sin-Jun; I hadn't yet determined the hierarchies in a way that classified her as unthreatening,

I'm not sure where Dede was—in the shower maybe—but the room was quiet except for a window fan and the sounds from outside the screens. I didn't even play my music then, fearful that my taste in tapes might reveal something humili- ating. I decided that I wanted to say to Sin-Jun, *I like your skirt*. But sometimes speaking is so hard! It's like standing still, then sprinting. I kept rehearsing the sentence in my head, examining it for flaws.

Finally, I said. "Your skirt is pretty. I like the polka dots."

She smiled, and the blandness of her smile made me almost certain she had no idea what I'd said.

"Do you know what polka dots are?" I asked. "They're the round spots. Like—well, here." I got up and pointed at her skirt.

"Ahh," she said. "Polka dot."

"I have polka-dotted socks," I said. I retrieved them

from the top drawer of my bureau and held them up. "See?"

"Very exquisite," she said. "I also like."

I sat back on my bed, emboldened, and said, "You have nice clothes." I had noticed, actually, that Sin-Jun had a pair of Levi's, and I'd speculated about whether she'd owned them in Seoul or bought them in anticipation of enrolling at Ault.

"You can ask me other words if you want to," I added. And she sometimes did after that—usually words she'd heard but couldn't figure out how to spell, and therefore how to look up herself in her Korean-English dictionary: *centipede*; or *procrastinate*. But more often, I was surprised by what she did know the meaning of: *pineapple, sarcasm, honeymoon*. I'd wonder, was Ault much harder for Sin-Jun than it was for me because it was literally foreign and not just unfamiliar? Or was it easier because its currencies were not her own? Perhaps that made it possible to view its dramas more distantly, even to disregard them.

Except that, as we stood in the hospital parking lot, it seemed apparent that she took her life at Ault quite seriously, that she viewed it not as her American life or her school life but as her actual life.

"Sin-Jun," I said.

She turned.

"I'm supposed to tell you something. It's a message from Clara. She said don't eat too many peach daiquiris."

Sin-Jun regarded me shrewdly, searching my face.

"You know what it means, right?" I said.

"Yes."

"I don't mean to be nosy, but what's going on with you and Clara?"

"Nothing is going on."

"I'm not saying she's a bad person," I said. "Just that I bet she's kind of hard to live with."

Sin-Jun reached out and squeezed my hand. Mr. Kim had parked the car in front of us and was climbing from the front seat "We stop talk about it," Sin-Jun said.

280

After we'd dropped off Sin-Jun's things at the infirmary, Mr. Kim announced that he was taking us to the Red Barn Inn for dinner. It was four-thirty in the afternoon. As we drove, he lit a cigarette—at Ault you never saw an adult smoke—and when we got to the restaurant, we ordered steak, all three of us. Mr. Kim ate half of his and Sin-Jun ate almost none and I finished mine, every bite until all that was left was fat and bone.

The next night, after the dining hall had mostly cleared out, I reentered the kitchen. Dave Bardo's glove was a wad in the front right pocket of my jeans.

"Excuse me," I said to a young woman pulling cellophane over a silver tray of pear halves. "Dave Bardo's not here, is he?"

"He just went to put out the trash. You know where the dumpster is?" When I started retracing my steps out of the kitchen, she said; 'There's stairs right there." She pointed to a pale pink door I had never noticed. It had a round window near the top and a grid of thin lines crisscrossing the pane. When I opened the door, I found myself in a stairwell lined with shiny tan bricks; there was something gymnasiumish about the stairwell, and the smell in it wasn't that different from a gym, either. I had the strange sense that I was not at Ault; no other part of campus, including the actual gym, looked quite like this.

At the base of the stairs was another door, and after I pushed on this one, I was outside in the winter night, standing at the top of a shorter set of concrete steps, and Dave was at the bottom in a T-shirt and apron. I could see the curved muscles of his upper arms, the hair on his forearms—it was dark brown, like a grown man's, but it was not disgusting to me at all.

"Hi," I said.

"Hey there."

When we spoke, our breath was visible.

"I was looking for you," I said.

"Was I hard to find?" He smiled, and it was that leisurely, half-expectant smile—seeing it was like knowing I had remembered something exactly the way it was.

Not, of course, that this affirmation made me any less flustered. "Here." I pulled the glove from my pocket and held it out to him.

He squinted. There was a spotlight on the corner of the dining hall roof, and another one above the door I'd just emerged from, but the darkness still made dark objects shadowy.

"It's your glove," I said. "I accidentally took it when you gave me a ride from the hospital."

"No big deal. I had a feeling you'd bring it back. How you been?"

"Fine."

"Just fine?"

I didn't know how to answer. I said, "You know what, the mashed potatoes tonight were really good."

He laughed. "Thanks."

"Is your sister better?"

"Yeah, she's good again. I've been telling her to take it easy, but you know how it is for single moms."

"My friend is better, too," I said. "I ended up going back to the hospital yesterday to help her dad bring—actually, I don't know. It's kind of a long story. Aren't you cold with no coat on?"

"I'm okay," he said. "You don't have a coat on either."

"But I have a sweater." I held out one arm, my fingers clutching the cuff, as if to offer proof.

"That's a nice sweater," he said. "Is that *cashmere*?" He pronounced it right, but he said it jokily, as if he'd never used the word before. And in fact, the sweater was acrylic. But he assumed—I'd sensed this before and now I was sure—that I was rich, that I was one of the true Ault students. Perhaps that explained his attention to me.

"I'm not sure what material it is," I said.

"It looks soft."

"I guess so." I was still holding out my arm, and I realized just seconds before it happened that he was going to touch either me or my sweater, and realizing this made me feel as if the sun was rising inside me and because this was, without a doubt, a good feeling, it is hard to explain why I snatched my arm away. Very briefly, his hand hovered where my arm had been, and my face burned; I couldn't look at him. When I finally did, he was regarding me curiously.

"I heard it might snow," I said loudly. "Have you heard that? That's what they're saying for later tonight."

He continued to look at me.

"So it's good you have your glove again," I said. "In case you need to shovel your driveway." I wanted to say, *I'm sorry*. But it's hard to rectify an unspoken mistake by speaking; almost always, it only makes things worse. "I should let you get back inside," I said, and neither of us moved.

"I'll tell you what," he finally said. "Those mashed potatoes were no good. What you had for dinner—they were crap mashed potatoes."

"I didn't think they were bad at all."

"You want to taste real mashed potatoes?"

Was I supposed to answer?

"You ever been to Chauncey's?" he asked.

I actually had, my sophomore year. It was, as far as I could remember, indistinct—nicer than a diner but not fancy. But I said, "I don't think I've been there."

"We should go."

"Now?"

"I can't now. I'm working."

"Right. Of course."

"What about tomorrow? Tomorrow's Saturday, isn't it?"

"I'm pretty sure I have some school stuff." Already, I was thinking too much. I was thinking that Saturday was loaded in a way Friday wasn't—we had Saturday classes, so Friday

283

was still a school night, but Saturday was pure weekend. If I went out with Dave on a Saturday night, I was pretty sure we'd be going on a date.

"How's Sunday?" he said. "Sunday I'm off."

What I needed to do was just be calm. I needed to come up with the next words to say, to concentrate only on the immediate task in front of me and not give in to the sense that this moment was a monstrous pulsating flower, a purple and green geometrical blossom like you might see in a kaleidoscope. "Sunday is okay," I said. "I'll meet you here."

"In the parking lot?"

"It's kind of hard to find my dorm," I said. "And they're weird about letting guys inside."

"Gotcha. What about seven o'clock. Is seven good?"

I nodded.

"These are gonna be the best mashed potatoes of your life. Poems have been written about these mashed potatoes."

By you? I wanted to teasingly ask him. But I couldn't because my anxiety was exploding, the flower was swirling outward infinitely. "I have to go study," I said. As I walked down the steps, I could have brushed against him. But there were so many tricks I didn't know then, so many gestures that I'd have thought would lock you in and represent promises. I turned sideways so we didn't touch at all.

When I was on his other side, he turned and patted my shoulder. "You be good, Lee."

This is what I want to tell my sixteen-year-old self. Say, *I'll try.* Say, *I won't do anything you wouldn't.* You're not promising him anything! What I said was, "Now you have your glove back."

When I told Martha what had happened, she cried, "You have a date!" and leaped out of her chair to hug me.

"But it's on Sunday."

"So what?" She pointed at me and said in a singsong, "You have a date with Dave Bardo, you have a date with Dave Bardo."

284

I wanted her to stop. And it wasn't because I was afraid that if we presumed too much, we'd jinx it. It was more that it just sounded weird, it sounded hard to understand.

"I barely know him," I said.

"That's the point. You go out for dinner, and you *get* to know him."

"Why would he have asked me out?"

"Lee, I can't read his mind. Maybe he just thinks you're pretty."

I winced. This possibility was not flattering to me; it was terrifying. There were other things a guy could think I was, and he wouldn't be entirely wrong—nice, or loyal, or maybe interesting. Not that I was always any of those things, but in certain situations, it was conceivable. But to be seen as pretty was to be fundamentally misunderstood. First of all, I wasn't pretty, and on top of that I didn't take care of myself like a pretty girl did; I wasn't even one of the unpretty girls who passes as pretty through effort and association. If a guy believed my value to lie in my looks, it meant either that he'd somehow been misled and would eventually be disappointed, or that he had very low standards. What I wanted to know about Dave was, had he noticed me before that time in the hospital, or had I piqued his interest during that conversation? But why would he have noticed me before, or why would I have piqued his interest then? Was I the best that he could do?

"I don't know about this," I said. I pictured sitting across the table from Dave at Chauncey's, and then, as I reached for the bread, knocking over my water glass. The worst would be when he reassured me that it was no big deal. And it would be no better if he knocked over a glass. It would not comfort me if he, or any guy, said softly, with a smile meant just for me (in fact, softly and with a smile meant just for me would be the deadliest parts), *You know, I'm nervous, too. Or, I don't know what I'm doing, either.* He should just be competent and shut up—that would be ideal.

"What exactly are you afraid of?" Martha said.

"I know. I'm being weird."

"No, really. Answer the question. What are you afraid of?"

I was afraid that Dave had chosen Chauncey's because he thought it was nice, when it wasn't that nice. I was afraid he'd tell some jokey story, ostensibly to the waitress but really for my benefit, and I'd be worrying the whole time about whether it was actually going to be funny, and if it wasn't funny, would I be able to muster up appropriate laughter? And to compensate, not wanting to miss the punch line, I'd begin tittering halfway through. I was afraid of how even though I would put on lotion before I left the dorm, I'd feel like the skin around my mouth was peeling, and this suspicion would be another conversation under the one we were having, a continuous murmur that would rise in volume as we sat there. It would be demanding more of my attention, most of my attention, then almost all of it, and just before I went to the bathroom to check for sure (as if, thirty seconds after I came out of the bathroom, I wouldn't start wondering about the peeling all over again), I'd be tilting my head and shifting my chin to prevent him from looking at me straight on. It was so hard to feel comfortable with another person was the problem, and what guarantee was there that it would be worth it?

"First dates are supposed to be awkward." Martha said. "And then after you've been going out for six months, you look back, and you think about how funny it was when you didn't know each other."

"So I should go?"

"You definitely should go. And you should wear your turtleneck sweater because it makes your boobs look big."

"Yuck," I said.

"If my boobs looked as big as yours in that sweater, I'd steal it from you." Martha wiggled her eyebrows lasciviously, and I thought how liking a boy was just the same as believing you wanted to know a secret—everything was better when you were denied and could feel tormented by curiosity or loneliness. But the moment of something happening was treacherous. It was just so *tiring* to have to worry about whether your face was peeling, or to have to laugh at stories that weren't funny. All I really wanted was this, I thought—to sit around in the dorm, goofing off with Martha.

Martha had gone to the library, and I was sitting at my desk, working on algebra—or, more precisely, gazing at the pages of the textbook in front of me without actually absorbing anything—when Adele Sheppard, a senior, stuck her head in the room. "Phone call," she said, then ducked back around and let the door shut.

I felt myself tense. Friday was not a night my family would call. So what if it was Dave, just wanting to chat? (Could he have gotten the number for Elwyn's? That seemed unlikely.) Or, far worse, what if it was Mrs. Morino or a nurse from the infirmary calling about Sin-Jun? They'd been wrong to let her come back to campus, and she'd found a razor, or tied a sheet to a pipe near the ceiling. But when I picked up the phone, it was Sin-Jun herself who said, "Lee, I have favor to ask. I leaving on Sunday with Father."

"For good?"

"Maybe yes."

"Wow, I'm sorry. Or is that—are you glad?"

"Maybe it's better to be home. The favor I ask is for you to get passport. It's in middle drawer of my desk. You can do this?"

"Yeah, that's no problem. Do you need it tonight?"

"Tomorrow is fine. Lee, I have very fat stomach now. Do you know why?"

"You don't have a fat stomach."

"It is so full with caramel. I eat a whole bag."

"That sounds delicious," I said, and I suddenly felt how I'd missed Sin-Jun, how I still missed her in this moment.

* * *

287

Because of the rush on Saturdays between the end of morning classes and the start of athletic games in the afternoon, the dining hall didn't make a real lunch but simply set out sandwich fixings and fruit and cookies on a long table, and you could eat the food there or stuff it in a brown bag and take it with you on the bus. I had a home game, so I didn't need to hurry. I made a turkey sandwich and went to sit at a table with Dede, also on my basketball team, and Aspeth, who played squash, and a couple guys. Sitting there, I could feel the relief of the weekend come over me. I even felt okay about our game—we were playing against Gordon, whom we'd beaten back in December by more than twenty points.

I had just bitten into a potato chip when I felt a hand on my back, and I turned—calmly, I turned, assuming at a level below consciousness that it was Martha or someone else unremarkable—and when I saw that it was Dave Bardo, the horror I felt made my entire body stiffen. His face above his apron was flushed and sweaty, and perspiration ran in rivulets from his forehead.

"Lee," he said. "Listen."

I was between Dede and Devin Billinger; to see Dave, I had turned to the left and craned my neck, and Dede had turned to the right, also gazing up at him. Probably everyone else at the table was looking at him—at us—but I wasn't going to check.

"Lynn needs the car tomorrow," he said. "Can we postpone?"

It took a few seconds for me to realize it was a question that required a response.

I swallowed. "That's fine."

"Any other night this coming week is fine. I'm not on for Tuesday or Thursday, but if those nights don't work, Sandy owes me a shift, so I'm pretty open."

"Okay."

"Okay meaning which night?"

"I don't—I don't know." I could hear that my voice was deadened and emotionless.

"Is everything cool?" he said. "Are you . . ." He trailed off, and his eyes shifted around the table.

"I'm fine," I said.

When his gaze came back to me, he said—he sounded sarcastic, the only time I heard sarcasm from him—"All right then. Got it. Didn't mean to interrupt. See you around, huh, Lee?"

When he'd walked away, I turned back to the table. Looking at no one, with a shaking hand, I picked up another potato chip.

"Who's your boyfriend?" Aspeth said.

"He's not my boyfriend,"

"Are you sure? It kind of looks like he is."

"Aww, yeah," said Devin. He was responding to Aspeth and not to me, but the situation was unbearable. My mind raced: Would other people find out about this—would Cross Sugarman, who was Devin's roommate?—and what would they make of it? Which words would they use to speculate about Lee Fiora's link to the kitchen guy? But the real question was, what had made me imagine this *wouldn't* happen? Why had I assumed that Dave knew we were being circumspect?

"At least tell us his name," Aspeth said, and I felt hot and sick and desperate for the moment to pass.

Beside me, Dede said; "This tuna is totally rancid."

"You didn't see the sign?" said Devin. "It said, *Eat at your own risk.*"

"Hardy har," Dede said. 'That's so funny,"

Later, before our game, Dede came up to me in the locker room and said, "Are you going out with that guy?" When I said no, she said, "I'm sure he's okay, but you're an Ault student. Your life is here, not at a bowling alley in Raymond or wherever you were supposed to go with him. You can act like I'm being snobby, but I'm just telling you the truth. I don't think you want to separate yourself from the rest of our grade." I said nothing. "And you will," Dede continued.

"People will definitely talk if you're dating a townie." That's what Dede said to me in the locker room, later. But in the dining hall, she was the one who changed the subject. And I know that both times that day—sometimes I pretended otherwise, but Dede did not have a bad heart—she was trying to help. And even if she was wrong, even if she was only partly wrong, she wasn't telling me anything I didn't already believe.

After my game, I went by Sin-Jun's dorm room again and was glad that Clara wasn't there. I found Sin-Jun's passport where she'd said it would be and walked to the infirmary, my wet hair refreezing in the cold. I tried not to think about the exchange with Dave, tried to just be a body in the world, moving forward among the trees and buildings, beneath the darkening afternoon sky. From now on, I thought, I would pass over surfaces without leaving a mark, without entangling myself. After I'd been in a place, there'd be no evidence.

Partly I felt relieved that I wouldn't be going out with Dave the next night, or ever. Partly I felt angry at him for having approached me so publicly, for having made me act bitchy. (So all along, I'd just imagined that we were colluding in making our interactions occur on the side, at night, behind buildings? It had been happenstance on his part, not discretion—was that it?) And partly, of course, I felt ashamed, But my shame, being the largest and truest of my emotions, required the least attention; it was a rock in my gut and would remain with me.

No, it was relief that was most immediate. At that time in my life, no conclusion was a bad conclusion. Something ended, and you stopped wishing and worrying. You could consider your mistakes, and you might be embarrassed by them, but the box was sealed, the door was shut, you were no longer immersed in the confusing middle.

At the infirmary, I checked in with the same nurse who had been on duty when Mr. Kim and I had dropped off

Sin-Jun three days before. "You girls are good friends to her," the nurse said. "There's no way she'll get lonely with this many visitors."

I knocked on Sin-Jun's door, then turned the knob, and then I simply stood there, staring. They were both on the bed, writhing and clawing and panting—they were fully clothed, and if they hadn't been, I truly think I might have fainted—and Clara was on top. Because Clara was so much bigger and because I myself had never been part of such an arrangement with another person, the first thing I thought was, *Isn't she smashing Sin-Jun?* Clara was licking Sin-Jun's neck and Sin-Jun was gripping Clara's backside and the bed was shaking as they bucked against each other. Another thing I thought for a while afterward was that sex was always that frenzied. I'd have imagined, if I'd given it real thought beforehand, that it would be different to see two girls than to see a boy and a girl, but it really wasn't. I would like to say here that we are all voyeurs, but maybe what I should say instead is that I, clearly, am a voyeur. It was riveting to watch. Who'd have guessed? Even with Clara involved, it turned out, sex was sexy.

Clara got onto her knees, dropping her face from Sin-Jun's neck to her breasts to her navel and just at the moment she lifted Sin-Jun's shirt and exposed her bare skin, Sin-Jun turned her head to the side, opened her eyes, met my gaze, and yelped. Clara reared up, and both of them stared at me—Sin-Jun looked frightened and furious and Clara looked disoriented.

"I'm sorry," I said. "Sorry, I jus—"

"*Aigo!*" Sin-Jun cried. "*Nagar-ra!* Get out! Get out!"

"I'm sorry," I said again. I tossed her passport onto the floor and ran into the hall and out of the infirmary. How strange, I thought, that freshman year, when I'd been so consumed by the meaning of my preoccupation with Gates Medkowski, I'd had no idea my own roommate not only thought about kissing girls but actually did it. When the image of Sin-Jun and Clara came back to me later that day, as it did repeatedly, the feeling I had was that I'd seen it in a movie, that a scenario of such passion (what else can I call it?) certainly would never have played out anywhere on the Ault campus.

I didn't see Sin-Jun again before she left with her father, and I thought that maybe I'd never see her again, but I was wrong; she returned the next fall for our senior year. That summer between our junior and senior years, I received a letter from her, the address of my parents' house in Indiana printed in her careful script on a pale blue international envelope. My mother suggested I save the envelope for my scrapbook, forgetting, I think, that I did not keep a scrapbook.

You know I have love relationship with Clara, but it ends, the letter read. *I will not roommate with Clara next year. I will hope you don't tell no one what you saw.*

She signed the letter *Your friend always, Sin-Jun*, and she drew a smiley face next to her name. And when we saw each other again the following September, our relationship functioned, amazingly enough, just about as it had before she took the aspirin, which is to say we treated each other with affection and never spoke about anything of substance. But later—Sin-Jun was one of the few classmates I stayed in touch with after Ault—after she'd come out to the extent that it was clear to everyone except her parents she was a lesbian (she kept her hair short and spiky, she wore silver hoops up one ear), I did learn the whole story. She was the one who'd pursued Clara. We were sitting on a deck in Seattle, off the apartment Sin-Jun shared with her girlfriend, Julie, and Sin-Jun worked by then as a neurobiologist in a research lab outside the city. It was never that we'd had a breakthrough after which we talked candidly to each other; I think it was more that separately, in college and after, we grew up and certain topics came to seem ordinary rather than forbidden.

"But why Clara?" I asked.

"She was my roommate," Sin-Jun said. "'This was very convenient."

I almost laughed. By this point—she had been one of the first ones from our class—Clara was married and even had a son. She and her husband had met at UVA; apparently, he was from West Virginia, which was where they moved after the wedding so that he could oversee his family's coal mines. The photo of them that ran in *The Ault Quarterly* showed Clara, bosomy in a long dress and veil, standing beside a portly fair-haired guy in tails.

Sin-Jun had believed all along, she said, that Clara was straight. But she had also known that Clara was malleable, and the longer they were involved—it had started just after Christmas—the guiltier Sin-Jun felt. When she'd try to end the relationship, however, Clara would become hysterical. "She says she love me so much,' Sin-Jun said. "But I think she just love sex."

I did start laughing then—I couldn't help it—and Sin-Jun started laughing, too. Yet it is hard for me not to feel a certain admiration for Clara. I am not so sure that she was merely dumb or horny; I think maybe she was also a little brave.

I never talked to Dave Bardo after that lunch, and for the rest of my junior year, I avoided him completely. I even avoided making eye contact, and it wasn't that difficult. But near the end of spring term, I felt a burst of remorse, or maybe it was that the remorse I'd felt all along expanded. I began peeking behind the counter. By early June, his arms were tan—he must have been spending time outside—and he often seemed to be kidding around with other staff members. He was never looking at me, and it occurred to me that maybe there was a reason it had been so easy to ignore him for the past few months. By my senior year, he wasn't working any-more at Ault, though his sister, Lynn, had returned. Several times I was tempted to ask her where he'd gone—maybe he'd made it out to California, and liked it so much that he'd stayed—but I was afraid to remind her who I was.

I think now that it would have been better if Dave had known I was on scholarship; he might have understood, as opposed to agreed with, why I acted as I did. (Aspeth Montgomery could have gone out with him and gotten away with it, it could have been ironic. But my parents' car was barely nicer than his Chevy Nova.) Of course, I didn't imagine then that I could have had a real relationship with any guy. I thought that by virtue of being me I was disqualified.

None of which justifies how I acted. I was wrong, I screwed up—how else can I say it? But there was plenty I learned from Dave. Later, after all that happened between Cross Sugarman and me, I even saw Dave as practice for Cross, as preparation. He made me ready, as Conchita had once made me ready for a friendship with Martha; there are people we treat wrong, and later, we're prepared to treat other people right. Perhaps this sounds mercenary, but I feel grateful for these trial relationships, and I would like to think it all evens out—surely, unknowingly, I have served as practice for other people.

Or maybe I'm off base and Dave was nothing so reductive or symbolic as a path to Cross. Maybe Dave was just himself, and it was all supposed to turn out differently. If his sister hadn't needed the car that Sunday, and if we'd gone ahead on our date as planned—maybe it all hinged on that. I had envisioned the ways our dinner might go wrong, but what if, just as in the ether of my imagination there exists our awful date, our good date exists as well? We meet behind the dining hall. He's wearing a wool sweater, he's relaxed, we talk easily, He does the considerate things, like holding the door as we enter the restaurant, but none of the things that might freak me out: He's not wearing too much cologne, he doesn't slip on ice in the parking lot, he doesn't try using his own fork to feed me dessert. Even though it's not a fancy restaurant, there are candles on the table. The light flickers. The food is good, Neither of us is too talkative or too quiet, and maybe a few times we even laugh, and it's real laughter. I am thinking the whole night that what matters most is if we kiss at the end; I don't realize that what really matters is that I have entered this world, that I'll come to understand much earlier (much earlier, that is, in this imaginary life than in my real life) what dating is—not necessarily the biggest deal. Not obsession or nothing, love or disinterest. There is middle ground. In the winter, especially, sometimes it's just nice to dress up a little and go out into the night with another person.

7

Spring-cleaning

JUNIOR SPRING

MARTHA WAS NOMINATED to be senior prefect at a class meeting held during morning break in late May of our junior year, but I wasn't there because I'd been summoned to Dean Fletcher's office to discuss the fact that I was flunking math. I actually ran into Martha just after the first bell signaling the end of morning break had sounded—we were in the third-floor hall, she on her way to Art History and I on my way to Spanish—and she said, "What did Fletcher say?"

I shook my head. "I'll tell you later."

"Was it that bad?"

"No," I said.

Martha looked at me.

"It was kind of bad," I said.

"You're supposed to meet with Aubrey tonight, right?" Aubrey was my math tutor and—humiliatingly, in light of the fact that we were juniors—a freshman.

I nodded.

"Make him explain polar equations to you again. He needs to be clearer."

"Martha, it's not Aubrey's fault that I'm failing."

The second bell, the bell that meant *You should now be in your seat, with your notebook open and your pen poised*, went off.

296

Martha winced. "I want to talk about this more," she said. "But try not to worry too much."

I nodded.

"Seriously," she said. "I know you can pass."

I continued nodding.

"Say something."

"Like what?"

She laughed. "Okay, that counts. I better go." Then she was hurrying down the hall to Art History. When I pushed open the door to the Spanish classroom, the heaviness of the door and my own dread felt like the same thing.

But Martha hadn't mentioned the nomination. And, in fact, I first heard about it from Nick Chafee, who said at lunch, "What do you think of your roommate?"

"In general?" I asked.

Nick looked at me like I'd said something extremely peculiar, which I didn't think I had. "No," he said. "For being nominated."

"Nominated for what? You don't mean Martha was nominated to be senior prefect?"

"No, she was."

"Are you serious?"

"Dude," he said. "Calm down." This was something I hated being told, especially by a boy. My voice might rise half an octave. I thought of telling him, *but there's no need to take cover—I will not leap from my chair to embrace you, I will not even shriek with delight.* Though, if ever I *were* going to shriek with delight, this would be the moment.

Because being senior prefect, even being nominated for it, was not a small thing. Each grade had two prefects, a boy and a girl. (The school had had to make it both—it was a rule that started the spring before my freshman year—because when each grade had only one prefect, it was always a boy.) In addition to running roll call in the morning, the senior prefects led the disciplinary committee, and after graduation their names were engraved on white marble panels that hung in the dining hall, and the letters were painted gold. To me, the panels were the best part; they were also, as it happened, what had intrigued my own parents when I'd shown them Ault's dining hall the year before. Another bonus was that the senior prefects always got into Harvard. Two years earlier, when Driscoll Hopkins's early application had been deferred, everyone had been shocked, but then she'd been accepted during regular admission.

Martha's nomination shouldn't have been a surprise—she was smart and dependable and nice to everyone, plus she'd served as a class representative to the disciplinary committee since the beginning of junior year—but, in fact, it was astonishing. Because the thing was, Martha wasn't cool. She was exactly the kind of girl who got overlooked, not rewarded, by Ault. And being a prefect was Ault's biggest reward, a stamp of approval that would set you up, it seemed, for the rest of your life. (Your name would be on the wall of the dining hall *forever*. In *gold*.) Partly, being senior prefect was so desirable because, as with class prefectships for the earlier grades, you could not seek it out. You weren't allowed to simply run for election. Instead, you had to be nominated, but it would be tacky and transparent to have your close friends nominate you, so basically that meant you had to wait for a nomination to fall from the sky, and then to be seconded. And once you got nominated, you never gave a speech or put up posters. In fact, the word *campaigning* was used as an accusation, not unlike *ass-kissing*. This desperate aversion to seeming like you wanted anything, or worse, to going after it, stayed with me for years after I left Ault. When I graduated from college, my father told me he was concerned that I didn't express enough enthusiasm in job interviews, and the comment shocked me. Enthusiasm was a thing you were *supposed* to show? But wasn't it a little disgusting, didn't it seem the same as greed and neediness? Of course you wanted the job, I thought, and the interviewer should know that because why else would you have shown up in his office?

"Who are the other nominees?" I asked Nick,

"Aspeth," he said. "And Gillian, of course."

Both these nominations were predictable: Aspeth was the queen of our class, and Gillian Hathaway was the actual elected leader, having served as sophomore and junior prefect. There was something unobtrusively competent about Gillian in all ways: She was good at sports, especially field hockey and ice hockey; she was blandly attractive; she was intelligent enough; and most notably, she never, in class or at a meal or in a game, seemed nervous or uncomfortable. For my first few years at Ault, all of these qualities had impressed me, and then recently, just the month before, I had ended up at a lunch table with Gillian and her boyfriend, Luke Brown. It was seventh period, late for lunch, and I didn't get to the dining hall until two o'clock. They were the only juniors there, which made me worry that they'd scheduled a romantic rendezvous on which I was intruding. But their conversation suggested otherwise: First they talked for twenty minutes straight about golden retrievers versus labs—not about specific dogs, beloved pets from their childhood, but about the breeds: which was smarter and why it was they both suffered from hip dysplasia. (I had no idea what hip dysplasia was and didn't ask.) This discussion segued into one on skiing and whether you could feel the difference between real and man-made snow, and then one on how even though the snow tires on Luke's brother's jeep had different treads, he'd never had a problem with them. Besides the fact that I had nothing to contribute to any of these subjects, I couldn't speak because I was in a state of shock. Were they always so boring? How could you talk this way to a person you'd been going out with for a year? Didn't they want to discuss people, or things they were worried about, or the tiny events that had occurred since they'd last seen each other? Perhaps Gillian always seemed comfortable, I thought, because she was not particularly interested in the world, because she did not question her place in it. This possibility made me dislike her slightly, a feeling that was amplified a few days later at dinner when people were discussing the recent scandal over Massachusetts's governor having employed an illegal alien as a nanny. I heard Gillian say, with a laugh, "At this point, does anyone expect the liberals not to be total hypocrites?" She was oblivious to the possibility that perhaps not everyone present shared her views, and I thought, *You're sixteen. How can you already be a Republican?* Maybe the only reason I was already a Democrat was that one of my earliest memories was of my father heckling the TV during Reagan's inauguration, but still—I did not like Gillian Hathaway. And now, now that she was Martha's opponent for prefect, maybe I even hated her.

"So Aspeth, Gillian, and Martha," I said. "That's it for the girls? Only three?"

"The meeting was kind of rushed," Nick said. "You want to know the guys?"

"Yeah."

"Me."

"Are you serious?"

"Thanks, Lee. That's flattering."

"No, I just—I couldn't tell if you were kidding."

"Hey, John," Nick said. "Was I nominated for senior prefect?"

John Brindley, sitting across the table, looked up. "Chafee, there's no way I'm voting for you."

They both laughed, and Nick said, "I don't need your vote because I have Lee's. She says she wants to be my campaign manager, too. Isn't that right, Lee?" He elbowed me obviously, so John could see (at Ault, of course, there was no such thing as a campaign manager). Had we found ourselves alone, Nick would never have elbowed me, he'd never have touched me at all. Sometimes I felt flattered by this kind of teasing—it was, after all, a form of attention—and sometimes I resented the way that boys included me as a prop in their

300

exchanges with one another: the magician's assistant who climbed into the box, got sliced in half, and had to beam at the audience while, above her, the magician joked and gestured extravagantly.

"What other guys were nominated?" I asked.

"Let's see." Nick counted off on the fingers of his right hand. "Pittard, Cutty, Sug, Smith, and Devoux."

These nominations, like those for Aspeth and Gillian, were unsurprising. They were all bank boys, except for Darden Pittard, but he was our junior prefect, Gillian's male counterpart. He and Cross—Sug—were the likeliest to win. Certainly my own vote would go to one of them, either to Darden because I genuinely respected him, or to Cross because of my crush. What was certain was that I wouldn't vote for Nick Chafee.

After crew practice, Martha lifted weights, and when she got back to the dorm late that afternoon, it was almost time to leave for formal dinner. I was seated on the futon, reading, and Martha's back was to me as she inspected her closet for clothes to change into. "Did I send out my short-sleeved blouse to be laundered?" she asked,

"Which one?"

"The blue one."

"I'm wearing it."

Martha turned.

"I can take it off," I said.

"That's okay." She had turned back to the closet, and she pulled out a pink T-shirt with pink ribbon trimming the neck and sleeves.

I stood. "Really, Martha, I can change." Remarkably, though I wore her clothes all the time, this had never happened before. And I could have offered her something of mine, but she didn't wear my clothes, which was not a fact we discussed.

"Don't be ridiculous." She stuck her head through the

pink shirt, pulled it down, then raised one arm and sniffed her armpit. "Fresh as a mountain breeze." She took a skirt, white with green and darker pink swirls, out of the closet and held it waist-high in front of her, still clipped to the hanger. "This goes, right? So I want you to finish telling me what Dean Fletcher—oh, wow, Lee, this is adorable!"

She had noticed it, finally—the paper crown I'd made using her computer paper and her tape and my own markers. I'd drawn huge jewels in purple and green and red, and yellow lines around the base and the triangular tips, and in black I'd written, *Martha Porter, Senior Prefect and Queen of the World*.

She set the crown on her head. "Does it suit me?"

"Perfectly. You should wear it to dinner." In fact, I'd have been horrified if she wore it to dinner. It would be just what people would expect, evidence of our dorky-girls' glee at Martha's fluke nomination. "This is *so* exciting," I said.

"Well, it's nice that I was nominated. but I won't win."

"You might." Perhaps I should have been more vehement, but really, she probably wouldn't get it, and I didn't like acting fake with Martha. Acting fake with everyone else was okay only as long as you had one person with whom you were real.

"I'm predicting Gillian," she said. "Too many people don't like Aspeth."

"What if it's you and Cross, and you have to have lots of late-night meetings and hang out together all the time?"

Martha laughed. "I'm not the one who's in love with Cross. But did you know he was the person who nominated me? Weird, huh?"

Unlike Cross and me, Cross and Martha had a few classes together, and sometimes Martha told me things about him: *Devin knocked over Cross's Bunsen burner in Chemistry today and the table caught on fire*. Or, *Cross is going up to see his brother at Bowdoin for long weekend*. But I wasn't under the impression they had much direct interaction.

"And Conchita seconded the nomination," Martha added, This actually wasn't that weird—Conchita and I had rarely spoken since freshman year, but she and Martha had remained friendly.

"Maybe Cross likes you," I said in a voice that I hoped would not reveal how horrifying I found this prospect.

"Please." Martha grinned. 'We need to go to dinner," she said. She removed the crown and set it back on her desk. "Someday you'll meet a guy who loves you so much and you'll be like, why did I waste my whole time in high school mooning over that self-centered dork?"

"Okay, first of all," I said, and I could feel myself warming up for the conversation. Talking like this was sustenance for my feelings, it made Cross exist in my life even though we never spoke. "First of all, why do you think he's self-centered, and second, if I'm going to think I wasted my time, does that mean he'll never like me back?"

Outside, other students were also walking toward the dining hall, wet-haired, the girls wearing pastel blouses and flowered skirts and espadrilles; the boys in white or pale blue shirts and ties and blazers and khaki shorts. At Ault, evening was always the best time.

"He's just cocky," Martha said. "He knows he's good-looking, he knows he's good at sports, he knows girls like him. But so what? Big deal."

"I don't think he's cocky," I said. "I really don't."

'Well, he's sure not insecure. And what was the other question? Oh, yeah, do I think you and Purple Monkey will ever find love together?" Purple Monkey was what we called Cross whenever we were discussing him outside of our room. "Let me look into my crystal ball." Martha held her hands in front of her as if clutching something round. "Lee, you guys don't talk. If you want something to happen, you should try talking to him."

"But I don't think he wants to talk to me," I said. "I doubt he feels a major void in his life." The buoyancy was gone from the conversation, the sense of possibility that came from speaking hypothetically. I could feel myself sinking. And Martha did not contradict what I'd said.

Instead, she said, "You still have to tell me about the meeting with Fletcher. And don't change the subject this time."

Now that math had been introduced, I plummeted completely. We were only walking to dinner and even though it was a warm May night, even though the sun out beyond the athletic fields had turned the sky pink and orange, there would, when we got to the dining hall, be liver for dinner, I'd be assigned to a table of sophomore boys who would not bother to conceal their debate about whether Aspeth Montgomery was wearing a bra, Martha would not be elected senior prefect, Cross would never want me to be his girl-friend; things like weather or certain songs could make me forget it sometimes, but I was always still myself, "Fletcher said Ms. Prosek told him my average right now is a fifty-eight." I said. "And he asked if my parents talked to me after they got the letter at midterm, I told him they told me to study."

In fact, what my father had said was, "With a grade like that, I hope you're not actually going to class." When I explained that I had not missed a single day the entire year; he said, "What then, you're smoking dope beforehand?" After that, my mother forced him off the phone, got on herself, and said, "But, Lee, remember when Mrs. Ramirez told us you were the best math student she'd ever had?" Which was something I did remember, but, as I pointed out to my mother, that had been in fourth grade.

"The weird part with Fletcher—" I paused.

"What?" Martha said.

"He said, 'You know that you're an important part of the Ault community,' or some bullshit like that and then he was like, 'But we have some very serious concerns. If you aren't able to pull up your grade, maybe it's time to rethink whether Ault is the best place for you.'" As I said it, my voice cracked.

"Oh, Lee," Martha said.

I swallowed. We were passing the chapel, still forty yards from the dining hall. *Salad bar*, I thought. *Napkin. Ice cube.* When I swallowed again, I knew I wouldn't cry.

"They have no grounds for spring-cleaning you," Martha said.

"Oh, no," I said. "Fletcher never mentioned spring-cleaning."

Martha turned and, feeling her gaze, I turned, too. "Think about it," she said. "That's what he meant, even if he didn't use those words."

This time, I didn't feel the shakiness that came before tears; what I felt was a shock in my chest.

"I wasn't the one who was there," Martha said. "But I promise you, no teacher ever says, 'We're considering spring-cleaning you.' That's just what students say."

I thought suddenly of all the people who had been spring-cleaned since I'd been at Ault. My freshman year, it had been Alfie Howards, a fellow freshman who was always disheveled—papers spilled out of his backpack, his shirt fell out of his pants, his nose ran, and he arrived everywhere late. When other students were moving from breakfast to chapel in the morning, he'd be making his way *toward* the dining hall, headed against the sea of bodies. He probably shouldn't have been at Ault to begin with—he shouldn't have been living without his parents—but he was a fourth-generation legacy; for that reason alone, in spite of everything else, I was surprised when he was spring-cleaned. Also sharing Alfie's fate my freshman year had been Maisie Vilayphonh, a half-Finnish, half-Laotian junior whose parents were rumored to be spies. Maisie, I heard, had been at one boarding school or another since the age of seven; she spoke six languages; she once ordered a thousand-dollar foot-massaging machine from a catalog, left the machine in the common room after using it twice, forgot about it until the leftover water grew scum, then dumped the whole thing in the trash. This wasn't

305

the reason she was spring-cleaned. The rumor about that was that the school knew she was doing cocaine but they just never caught her at it, though her dorm head, Mrs. Morino, would drop by Maisie's room at random hours, wondering if Maisie had seen the Morino family cat, or wanting to make sure that Maisie knew there'd be evensong instead of morning chapel on Sunday.

That, actually, was the defining factor of spring-cleaning, what distinguished it from run-of-the-mill expulsion—that it happened not during the spring, as the name suggested, but over the summer, after the school year had finished. And it wasn't necessarily for one big reason—they never did catch Maisie snorting up—but more for an accumulation of smaller ones.

After my sophomore year, two people had been spring-cleaned: a freshman named Lenora Aiko, a girl from Hawaii who supposedly slept all day and stayed up all night, talking on the pay phone (and jumping in front of the booth whenever someone else tried to use it, insisting that she was waiting on a call), or else watching infomercials and preparing steak in the common-room toaster oven; and another girl, one of my classmates, though I'd hardly known her, a day student named Kara Johnson. Kara was pretty in an angular, even feral way, pale and skinny and smelling like cigarette smoke, always wearing black eyeliner and black jeans, though jeans of any color were forbidden in the schoolhouse. (Once I heard a teacher tell her to go to the dorm and change, and she said that she couldn't because she was a day student. The teacher told her to call her parents and have one of them bring her different pants, and she said she couldn't do that, either, because both her parents worked.) Kara and I were in the same Spanish class, and she was never prepared, had never done the translations or the reading, but would sometimes make stabbing attempts at proving otherwise. (I, on the other hand, always did my homework, even for math. It was just that I often did it badly.) A few times, I saw Kara outside the library just before curfew, presumably waiting to be picked up by one of her parents, and a junior or senior guy would be talking to her and you knew, you could tell just by their posture, that the guy cared a lot more about the exchange than Kara did. She seemed like someone who had a complicated life, who was often hung over or fighting with a boy or telling a lie, and, primarily because she was sexy, these circumstances contained a degree of glamour. But one of the nights I saw her waiting outside the library, she was by herself, and it was cold, and though it was not raining, there was something in her huddled form that reminded me of the times before our dog King was hit by a car that my mother and I would give him a bath—he was a Scottish terrier—and how with his fur plastered down King would look half his former size, he'd be shivering, and the sight of him like this was unbearably sad; the only reason that I helped my mother wash him was that I didn't want her to have to experience the sadness by herself. I don't think anyone really cared that Kara got spring-cleaned. She hadn't been friends with any girls, and though guys had chased her when she was in front of them, she didn't seem like someone they'd give much thought to in her absence.

In every yearbook, there was a page with the heading "Lost But Not Forgotten," which featured photos of the students who would have, but hadn't, graduated that year. The picture of Alfie—I saw this as a college freshman, when my Ault yearbook arrived that fall in the mail—showed him as a fourteen-year-old, the age he'd been when he'd left Ault; it was as if, unlike the rest of us, he'd never gotten older. The picture of Kara was slightly blurry and showed her turning, so three quarters of her face was visible—her almond-shaped eyes, her narrow foxlike chin and unsmiling mouth. There were four other people on the page: Little Washington, George Rimas, and Jack Moorey, who left, respectively, in April of our sophomore year and November of our senior year after being caught drinking, twice (for offenses related to alcohol, cigarettes, pot, and pharmaceuticals, as well as for breaking visitation—that is, for minor violations—you got two chances; for harder drugs, for cheating, and for lying, which were major violations, you got only one); and Adler Stiles, who had not returned after winter break of our junior year. People like Adler, the ones who left of their own volition, were enigmatic to me; I almost admired them. No matter how unhappy I was there, Ault was never a place I could turn my back on.

Martha and I had reached the dining hall, and the entrance was mobbed. The possibility that I could be spring-cleaned—that I could have anything, even that, in common with Alfie Howards or Maisie Vilayphonh or Kara Johnson—was utterly foreign. It was an idea I found impossible to absorb here, among so many people; I needed to think about it alone.

"I'm not trying to freak you out," Martha was saying. "But if that's what Fletcher meant, you should know."

"Yeah, of course."

"But they can't treat you like you're a bad seed," she said. "Because you're so not."

We'd crossed the threshold of the dining room, and it was time to split up and find our assigned tables. Martha was looking at me.

"Divide and conquer," I said, because one of us always said this just before formal dinner. And it worked, Martha smiled, and I smiled, too, so our moods would seem the same. But I don't think I fooled her. And already, that thing was happening where the scene before me pulled back, or maybe I was the one who shrank from it. It all became both huge and distant, something occurring far away—a blur of nicely dressed students making their way to tables covered by white cloths and silver serving plates with silver lids. Maybe several months from now, when I was enrolled at Marvin Thompson High School in South Bend, I'd be sitting on my bed one evening, doing homework, and this was the image

I'd remember, the precise moment when I first knew I'd lost my place at Ault.

At the library, on my way to meet Aubrey, I saw Dede through the glass door of the periodicals room. Her head was bent to look at a magazine, and I wasn't planning to stop, but then she looked up, *Hey*, she mouthed, and I waved. I made the mistake of holding her gaze, and she held up one finger, mouthed, *Hold on*, set the magazine on a table, and pushed open the door.

"Isn't it crazy about Martha? I was completely shocked." Her voice was upbeat and perfectly friendly.

"It's not *that* shocking," I said. "Martha would be a good prefect."

"Well, sure, she's 'responsible.'" Dede made air quotes, implying I had no idea what—that actually Martha wasn't responsible? That being responsible was hardly a qualification? "But it's not like she has a chance," Dede continued.

When Martha herself had said almost the same thing a few hours earlier, it had seemed only like the dreary truth; hearing Dede, the prediction sounded slanderous.

"You have no idea who'll win," I said.

Dede smiled a little tiny smile, and I felt like slapping her. Our antagonism had always contained a certain sisterly intimacy; once, during freshman year, when we'd been standing face-to-face arguing, Dede had reached out and actually pulled my hair, and the sheer immaturity of the gesture had made me burst out laughing. She'd said, almost shyly, "What? What?" but she'd started laughing, too, and then we hadn't been able to continue fighting. Dede and I were each other's opposites, I sometimes thought, and therefore uncomfortably similar—she faked enthusiasm, and I faked indifference; she glommed on to people like Aspeth Montgomery and Cross Sugarman, and I made a point of not speaking to them from one semester to the next.

"I'm sure you think Aspeth has it all wrapped up," I said.

"But, frankly, I'll be surprised if she wins." *Don't use the word* bitch, I thought—that would be going too far. "She's just—" I paused. "Basically, she's a bitch."

"Excuse me?" Dede said. "Am I in the twilight zone?"

"I didn't say *I* think she's a bitch," I said. "Let's not get into semantics." When I was at Ault, I thought that chalking up a disagreement to semantics sounded very smart. "Dede, I'm not trying to be rude, but your Aspeth worship is getting kind of embarrassing."

She glared at me. "You know what you are?" I could tell she was digging deep; searching for a particularly biting insult. "You're exactly the same as you were when we were freshmen."

Aubrey was waiting in the study room where we usually met; through a window, I could see him chewing on a plastic pen with his head tilted toward the ceiling. He wasn't doing anything weird, but his posture was so clearly that of a person who believed himself to be alone that I felt embarrassed on his behalf. I knocked on the window before opening the door.

Aubrey removed the pen from his mouth and sat upright "Lee," he said, and he nodded once. At all times, Aubrey comported himself with absolute seriousness. This might have been the way he was raised, or it might have been compensation for the fact that, at the age of fourteen, he was five feet tall and perhaps ninety pounds. He had puffy brown hair and a tiny ski-jump nose across which lay a sprinkling of tiny freckles. He also had tiny hands and, on his ring fingers, peaked fingernails. Whenever I watched Aubrey write out equations, I'd wonder, when boys had their growth spurts, did they always grow proportionally, or was there a chance some part of the body—for instance, the hands—didn't get the message and stayed as they were, vestiges of the smaller self? I was quite sure that Aubrey was smarter than I was, not just in math but in everything, and that he would eventually become, say, a stockbroker, and make enormous quantities of money.

After I'd sat in the chair next to him, while I was pulling out my notebook, math textbook, and calculator, I said, "How's it going, Aubrey?"

"I'm well, thank you. I'd like to see your homework for tomorrow."

I slid the notebook toward him—in pencil. I'd written, *Page 408, chapter review, all problems.*

Aubrey opened my textbook and read silently, nodding to himself. Then he turned to me. "Do you understand what they're asking for in the first one?"

I scanned the problem. "Kind of."

"Why don't you start, and I'll help if you run into trouble."

I continued to look at page 408, or at least to face in the direction of page 408. That I was bad at math was not a secret—from the time I'd arrived at Ault, I'd been a year behind my classmates. Most freshmen took Geometry; I and four other students took remedial Algebra. And this year, in Precalculus, I was the only junior in a class of sophomores. But still, no one, Aubrey included, seemed to have realized just how tenuous my grasp on math was. And Precalculus had been the worst year yet—it was not an exaggeration to say that I understood virtually none of what we'd studied since late September. I had spaced out during the first week or two of classes and never recovered. Yes, the situation was largely my own fault, but the problem was, everything built on everything else; from two weeks into the semester, it had been too late. The pages of my textbook were like a map of Russia with all the towns and cities written in Cyrillic. It was not that I didn't believe they made sense, just that I personally had no inkling of what they meant.

"Lee?" Aubrey said.

"Yeah, I'm not sure. I'm not exactly positive where I start here." I looked up and then out the window in front of us. It was dark, so I was looking at my own reflection; if it had been light, I'd have had a clear view of the entrance to the infirmary. One Sunday afternoon in the winter, I'd watched Aspeth Montgomery approach the infirmary, hesitate before the door, then turn around without entering. This reversal had consumed me for the rest of my session with Aubrey.

"The conic has its focus at the origin, right? And it has to satisfy these conditions." Aubrey pointed to where the textbook said, *parabola*, *directrix* y = 2. "So what do you want to do?"

A silence unfolded, and kept unfolding.

"You want to figure out what y is, right?" Aubrey said.

"Yeah."

"Like this—does that make sense?"

"Yeah." I nodded. "Definitely."

"And then you plug this in here."

"Okay," I said.

"Why don't you try the next one?"

For a while, I was looking at the problem, I really was. But then I found myself thinking about Gillian Hathaway, and about whether she and her boyfriend Luke said *I love you* to each other. How did you even know if you loved another person? Was it a hunch, like a good smell that you couldn't identify for sure, or did a time come when you had evidence? Was it like walking through a house and once you'd crossed a certain threshold, that was love and you would never turn back? Maybe you'd go into other rooms, you'd fight or even break up, but you'd always be on the other side of love, after and not before it. My interest in couples felt anthropological—even liking Cross, even wanting to hear from Martha that she could imagine me dating him, I myself could not imagine us together. Not as a daily presence in each other's lives, two people who had conversations and made out and sat next to each other in chapel. When I thought of Sin-Jun and Clara—and I did so often—what was hardest to wrap my head around was how they'd been a couple while living in the same room. How had they known when to fool around and

312

when to just sit at their desks doing homework? Hadn't it been either too intense, too tiring to always be around the person you wanted to impress, or else too familiar? Maybe in such close quarters you gave up hope of impressing them and sat there picking your earwax and not caring if you looked cute. But didn't you lose something there, too? If that was what people meant by intimacy, it didn't hold much appeal for me—it seemed like you'd be fighting each other for oxygen.

Aloud, I said, "Do you think Gillian is pretty?"

"Lee, please concentrate," Aubrey said.

"Gillian Hathaway," I said. "Not Gillian Carson."

"She's fine. If I were you, I'd start by isolating x on this one: And what information are they giving you about x?" But Aubrey was blushing, a hot shade of pink that blossomed in his face and spread down his neck.

"Really pretty or just medium pretty?" I said.

He turned to me. "I'm not doing your homework for you."

"I didn't ask you to."

"And if you don't grasp these concepts, you're not going to pass the final exam."

"Actually, it's better than that," I said. "If I don't pass the exam, I'll be spring-cleaned."

"What are you talking about?"

"It's when they kick you out but they wait—"

"I know what spring-cleaning is," he interrupted. I was slightly impressed—I hadn't known until after I came back for the beginning of sophomore year and Alfie and Maisie were gone. "Who told you this?" Aubrey said.

"Fletcher called me into his office today,"

"That's terrible."

"It wouldn't be your fault."

"I know," Aubrey said with such certainty that I wanted to rescind the exoneration. "What are you planning to do?" he asked.

I squinted at him. I was pretty sure he didn't have much

respect for me, but it still seemed like a shitty question. "Well, the school near my parents' house is called Marvin Thompson."

"No," he said. "Lee." He extended his small hand toward my arm, but then it just hovered there; I think he was afraid to touch me. He withdrew his hand and said, "I meant, what do you want to do about the exam? How do you want to prepare?"

"I'm not sure that it matters how I prepare," I said. "I mean, being realistic about it." This felt like a confession of sorts. "Do *you* think I can pass?" I asked,

He remained quiet for several seconds and finally said, "If you're willing to work very hard."

This was worse than if he'd just said no. Because I would put in the time, I would sit in a chair with my math book in front of me, but to actually work—the only choice I'd have would be to start from the beginning of the book. I'd always loved the part in movies when a project, or even a person's whole life, came together: the montage, set to uplifting music, where you saw the spunky multicultural kids set aside their differences and fix up the old man's house, straighten the hanging shutters, paint the outside, mow the lawn, and weed the flowerbed; or the twentysomething woman who finally lost weight, dancing through aerobics classes, mopping her brow while she rode a gym bike, with a white towel around her neck, and then at last she emerged from the bathroom all cleaned up, bashful but beautiful (of course, she had no idea how beautiful), and her best friend hugged her before she left for the date or party that would be her triumph. I wanted to be that person, and I wanted the in-between time when I improved myself to glide by just that smoothly, with its own festive sound track. But to really learn precalculus would be laborious and miserable. Plus, it still might not work. The only reason my average was as high as 58 was that in March, Ms. Prosek had let me do a special project for extra credit, and I'd made a timeline of women mathematicians through the

314

ages: *Hypatia of Alexandria, b.* A.D. *370, inventor of the astrolabe, died when Christian mob attacked her with broken pottery; Emilie du Châtelet, b. 1706, French aristocrat and author of* Institutions de Physique, *dated Voltaire.* I'd made the final woman Ms. Prosek herself, pasting a photo of her from the school catalog onto the poster board and writing next to it, *Valerie Prosek, b. 1961, precalculus teacher and inspiration to young math scholars everywhere.* Ms. Prosek had hung the timeline in her classroom, above the chalkboard, and she'd given me an A plus.

"If I were going to work very hard," I said, "where would I begin?"

"It wouldn't hurt for you to review some of the basics of graphing equations. I can create some problems for you." Aubrey wrote down several strings of numbers in my notebook, then pushed it toward me. The first one read:

$$3x - y = 5$$
$$2x + y = 5$$

This should not have been hard, I knew. He'd said himself that it was basic. But I had no idea what to do. And to admit my ignorance would be to truly reveal just how far behind I was.

"Actually," I said, "I'm thinking—I'm sorry I just made you write those up—but maybe it would be better for me to concentrate on the homework for tomorrow. Because that will already take me a long time, don't you think?"

Aubrey hesitated.

"I'll take those problems back to the dorm and work on them there," I said. "Thank you." I turned back to the textbook and read aloud the next problem: *Write out the form of the partial fraction decomposition . . .* Maybe this way, if Aubrey heard my voice, it would seem like I was participating. And it worked, I could sense him caving. All our sessions were like this—the warm-up, the persuasion, the part where Aubrey capitulated and just did my homework for me, after stating that he wouldn't. But even then, we went so slowly, with him narrating his progress, asking me questions, waiting while I made guesses, many of which weren't even in the right category—the answer Aubrey would be looking for was *an irreducible quadratic factor* and the answer I'd give was *seven*.

Though sometimes I needled him; or acted lazy, I had figured out early on how Aubrey liked me best: trying but not getting anything right. Or maybe: not getting anything right but trying. Either way, the other person's reaction was the only thing that ever counted to me—numbers were spiky and indifferent, but a person was warm and breathing, potentially swayable, I often messed up with people, it was true, but it rarely happened because I was reading them wrong; it was because I got nervous, or because I could see too clearly that I was not what they wanted. And, in fact, it was in falling short that I truly excelled. I might fail to be what the other person sought, but as a failure, I'd accommodate them completely—I could be obsequious or truculent, sad or earnest or utterly silent. If I'd had to guess, I'd have guessed that Cross knew I had a crush on him, and that in not trying to talk to him, in only every so often making eye contact with him and waiting a beat before looking away, I was acting just the way he'd think a girl who liked him but whom he didn't like back should act. And I might get spring-cleaned, but I'd be able to go out with everyone on my side—Aubrey, Martha, Ms. Prosek, and even Dean Fletcher, all of them rueful and sympathetic.

The housing meeting, which was the meeting I'd thought was occurring when my class had nominated senior prefects, happened the next day. At morning break, all the juniors assembled in the first few rows of the auditorium, and Dean Fletcher sat on the edge of the stage swinging his legs. He gave the same speech we'd heard the last few years—it was impossible to accommodate everyone, etc., etc., and he added that as seniors, we'd set the tone in the dorms. When the meeting was finished, Martha left the auditorium to check her mail, and I began filling out both our request forms; we'd already decided we wanted to stay in Elwyn's, the dorm we were in this year. As I pressed the paper against my thigh, writing Martha's name and then my own, it occurred to me that perhaps this was a futile act—if I were not returning to Ault, certainly there was no point in making a rooming request. But how could I not be returning? What things would I think about if I were not an Ault student? At Marvin Thompson High, the cafeteria floor was mustard-colored linoleum with black and gray flecks; the sports teams were called the Vikings and the Lady Vikings; there was an ongoing debate about whether to let the pregnant girls attend classes after they started to show.

"I've always thought that the rooms in Elwyn's smell like cat pee, but I guess that doesn't bother you and Martha."

When I looked up, Aspeth Montgomery was sitting to my right, sitting, in fact, so close to me that I felt the physical self-consciousness I usually experienced only with boys—did my pores look huge to her, I wondered, and was the skin around my mouth flaking because I'd forgotten my chapstick in the dorm and been licking my lips a lot? As my eyes met Aspeth's, out of nervousness, I licked my lips again.

"I've never noticed that," I said.

"Well, you lived with that squid in your room in Broussard's, too, before you got Little kicked out. You must be used to gross smells."

I said nothing.

After a beat, Aspeth said, "So I hear you think I won't make a very good senior prefect."

It had occurred to me that Dede might repeat my comments to Aspeth, but it had seemed too predictable—childish and vindictive in just the ways I knew Dede to be—and therefore I'd decided she wouldn't; people rarely did exactly what you expected.

"You're not denying it," Aspeth said, "God, Lee, you're

317

shameless." She leaned back, her left arm slung over the seat, and she did not seem angry but more amused; she hadn't had anything else to do before morning break ended, so she'd come over to needle me.

"Dede probably told you stuff out of context," I said.

"You think?"

"What do you want, Aspeth?" I asked. "Why do you care what I said to Dede?"

Aspeth seemed to reconsider me. She removed her arm from the seat back, sat up straight, and folded one leg over the other. "Does Martha really think she'll get elected?" she asked, and the lazy, teasing quality was gone from her voice.

"What are you doing?" I said. "Campaigning?"

An odd look crossed her face—a recomposing of her features to form the same expression they'd formed before—and it dawned on me that campaigning was precisely what Aspeth was doing.

"Martha won't win," she said. "This is what will happen. About half the class will vote for Gillian, maybe a little less. And a little more than half the class will vote for me, except let's say a tenth of the class will vote for Martha. You see what I'm saying? She'll get my votes. And that means Gillian will win."

I couldn't help smiling. "You just said yourself that those aren't your votes. They're Martha's,"

"You're missing the point. Do you want Gillian to be senior prefect?"

I shrugged.

"Of course you don't. Gillian's a fucking pill. But all these dimwits in our class will vote for her because she's been sophomore and junior prefect, and they're little status quo lemmings."

"Why don't you like Gillian?" I asked. Gillian and Aspeth were in more or less the same friend group, and I'd never heard of friction between them.

"Who does?" Aspeth said. "Gillian's a bore." During our

conversation, Aspeth had never once lowered her voice, and she didn't now, though dozens of our classmates were still milling around the front of the auditorium; for the fearlessness of her bitchery, I felt a surge of admiration. "The only person more boring than Gillian is Luke," Aspeth continued. "She probably falls asleep while he's boning her."

I felt a brief wish for Aspeth to ask what I thought of Gillian, so I could voice my assent; she didn't.

"Martha needs to drop out of the election," Aspeth said. "There's nothing at stake for her. If she had a shot at winning. it would be one thing, but I think we've established that she doesn't."

Again, I couldn't help but be impressed by the purity of Aspeth's condescension, her utter lack of interest in wheedling or bribery. Martha should drop out of the race simply because Aspeth was Aspeth; for the same reason, Aspeth should be elected.

"Maybe you should talk to Martha yourself," I said.

"Why? I just talked to you." Aspeth unfolded herself—she had the longest legs of any girl in our class, fantastic legs, and she was wearing a khaki skirt that ended six inches above the knee—and stood; apparently, her business with me was finished. She seemed about to walk away, but then she took a step toward me and leaned over. Her honey blond hair fell in front of my face, and when she pressed one finger against the rooming sheet still on my lap, I could feel her fingertip on my thigh, through the paper. "I'd give the cat pee thing some thought," she said. She turned to look at me, and our faces were so close, how could I not have thought of kissing her? She tapped her finger a few times, smiled knowingly, and said, "Just some friendly advice." Then she was gone, the smell of her shampoo lingering in the air. I actually knew what kind of shampoo Aspeth used because Dede used it, too, though its scent didn't cling to Dede's hair like it did to Aspeth's. When I was at Ault, that shampoo was the smell of popularity; after I graduated, it became the smell of Ault

319

itself. One afternoon after work, in my early twenties; I was at a CVS and I held a bottle toward a friend and said, "I think this is the best-smelling shampoo in the world," and she gave me a bemused look and said, "So buy some." And I'd thought by then that I'd outgrown my Ault self, but still, the suggestion was revelatory; paying for it at the cash register, I had the same residually fraudulent sensation you experience the first time you buy alcohol after turning twenty-one.

After lunch, as Martha and I were leaving the dining hall, I saw Ms. Prosek thirty yards in front of us, walking by herself. I grabbed Martha's elbow and stopped walking. "Hold on." I said. "Just let her get a little further ahead."

At exactly that moment, Ms. Prosek glanced over her shoulder. Seeing us, she motioned for me to approach.

"Did she just hear me?" I asked.

"She couldn't have."

"That was totally weird."

"Catch up with her. She's waiting for you," Martha pushed me forward a little. "You'll be fine." After I'd walked a few steps, she added, "Take deep breaths."

"I was hoping I'd run into you," Ms. Prosek said when I was alongside her. "How're things?"

"They're okay." As we walked, I snuck a look at her.

"I know about your conversation yesterday with Dean Fletcher," she said, "if that's what you're wondering. I'm curious about how you're feeling."

I didn't say anything—I honestly didn't know what to say—but when my self-consciousness about the silence overrode my confusion about how to respond, I said, "Fine."

Then it was Ms. Prosek's turn not to talk.

The problem was, Ms. Prosek was not just the teacher whose class I was bombing, whose flunking grade might result in my expulsion—she was also my adviser, and, until quite recently, even for the first several months after my math grade had plunged, our relationship had been nothing but chummy. I'd gotten to know Ms. Prosek freshman year because she was the thirds basketball coach. She didn't seem personally offended when we lost a game, as some of the other coaches did, but we somehow got her to promise that if we ever won, she'd do three back handsprings right there on the court—she'd been a college gymnast—and she did; it was the day we played against Overfield. Afterward, when she was standing there a little unsteadily, with her hair askew and the other team gawking at us, Ms. Prosek said, "I definitely should have worn a different bra." On the days when we weren't playing the same school as JV and varsity, instead of riding the bus we rode in a van that Ms. Prosek drove, and on the way back to campus, she'd take us to McDonald's.

There were two things I admired deeply about Ms. Prosek, and they reinforced each other. The first thing was that she seemed liberal—she was, though I did not completely understand the meaning of the word at the time, a feminist—and she was neither belligerent nor apologetic in the expression of her views. She once drove a van of students into Boston for a pro-choice rally (I didn't go because I was a freshman and I thought maybe I wasn't supposed to) and she wore no makeup and, on Sundays, she wore a blue bandanna that pushed back her curly hair. The second thing about Ms. Prosek that impressed me was that she had an extremely handsome husband. His name was Tom Williamson, he worked in D.C. as a speechwriter for a Democratic senator, and he wasn't around much except on the weekends, but sometimes he'd just materialize for formal dinner in a coat and tie, or you'd see them running together, and girls would elbow one another: *There goes Mrs. Prosek's cute husband.* Ms. Prosek herself was attractive but not beautiful, maybe not even what most people would call pretty, and it filled me with wonder—that she was not beautiful and he loved her, that she was smart and opinionated and he loved her, that it seemed, from the way you'd see them talking or touching in

321

a casual, not particularly romantic way (his arm around the back of her chair with his fingers just grazing her shoulder, his head tilted toward her as she said something while they made their way down the crowded steps outside the dining hall after dinner) like maybe he even loved her a lot and like she really loved him back.

"I won't lie," Ms, Prosek said. "I'm worried about you. Do you and Aubrey have a study plan?"

"Kind of. But I guess I don't understand if the exam is only a week away, why did Fletcher wait until yesterday to threaten me with spring-cleaning?"

I wanted her to refute that Dean Fletcher had made any such threat. Instead, she said, "Are you telling me you would have done things differently if you'd known what the consequences were?"

"No," I said, and I could hear how defensive I sounded.

"Lee." Ms. Prosek set her hand on my shoulder. I stiffened, and she removed her hand. We had reached the entrance of the schoolhouse and stopped walking, as if we'd agreed ahead of time not to carry the conversation inside.

I looked at her with what I hoped were widened, receptive eyes; the stiffening had been involuntary.

"Just focus on the math. I want you to be really familiar with the exponential and the logarithmic functions. Okay? Let's cross those other bridges when we come to them."

Easy for you to say, I thought, and it was unpleasant to feel animosity toward Ms. Prosek. Starting in the fall and continuing into March, I'd gone over to her house on Sunday afternoons, after her husband had left for D.C. for the week. (Though once he'd still been there and he'd answered the door and said, though we'd never met, "Hi, Lee," and I had felt excited enough to take flight.) Ms. Prosek and I would review the material, and she'd be making soup or vegetarian chili and she'd give me some. When we talked about math, I tried, out of respect to concentrate, but often I got distracted just as I got distracted with Aubrey. I was completely attentive, however, when the subject wandered to a recent chapel talk or an article in *The Ault Voice*, or to speculation about other students and teachers. Ms. Prosek never expressed her own views, she often shook her head when I was critical of someone, but she was usually smiling as she did so, and I could tell she found me interesting. Maybe, after all, it wasn't her cute husband or her politics or her sportiness that made me like her—maybe it was only that she found me interesting and that in her presence, even more than in Martha's, I *felt* interesting, And then one afternoon, shortly after spring break, she seemed subdued, she kept steering us back toward math when we swerved away, When I'd arrived, she'd said she had a headache, and I thought that was why, but after perhaps half an hour—I was in the middle of explaining why I thought Mr. Corning was in love with my old dorm head Madame Broussard—Ms. Prosek said, "Lee, I want to tell you something. I had to send a letter to your parents. I could get away with not sending one last semester because you'd just gotten the C on the midterm, and things were looking up. But now I'm really concerned."

I wanted to reassure her that I didn't have the kind of parents who would freak out over such a letter, but I wasn't sure that was the point. And still, then, I didn't feel real panic about my grade. What I felt was shame that I'd been gossiping so casually, that I'd made myself so at home here at her dining room table. I'd imagined that she was charmed by me, when really I was a bad student eating up her free time, making inappropriate comments about her colleagues.

"Your grade last semester was a D," Ms. Prosek said. "That doesn't leave you any wiggle room, If you flunk for the semester, you flunk for the year. And you're flunking now. You have a forty-nine."

I had known I was doing badly, but a forty-nine was worse than I'd realized.

"I'll make a deal with you," she said. "And I'll offer the same option to all the students, but—" She didn't finish

323

because she didn't need to—*you're the one I'm doing this for*. The deal was to work on a project for extra credit, and that was what I made the timeline for. And Ms. Prosek did laugh when she saw that I'd included her on it, but things weren't the same between us. In her apartment the afternoon that she'd told me I had a forty-nine, she had not, as she usually did when I left, confirmed that we were on for the following Sunday. And I could have asked in class that week, but I didn't—I didn't want to burden her—and because I hadn't asked, I didn't go the next Sunday. In class the Monday after that, we made eye contact as I was sitting down, and she pressed her lips together as if she were going to say something, but she didn't; anyway, other students were around. I still saw her almost daily, of course, but outside of class, it was only in passing, or in a group—when it got warm in April, she had all of her advisees over for a cookout.

Standing in front of the schoolhouse, I said, "But, I mean, I'm not a bad seed. Am I?"

"Of course you're not a bad seed."

"I know I'm not great at sports, or I'm not, like, an *asset* to Ault. But I don't break rules. It just seems like maybe I should get the benefit of the doubt. I don't see why this exam has to be the difference between if I stay or not."

She sighed. "I don't know why you have the idea you're not an asset to the school. You have just as many supporters as anyone else. Beyond that, I hope you understand that no one is trying to be punitive. But, Lee, you're already a year behind most of your classmates in math. The school has requirements, and in order to get a diploma a year from now, you need to fulfill them. And what guarantee do we have that the same situation won't arise in calculus? At a certain point, I don't think it's fair to you to keep putting you in over your head."

"This won't happen with calculus," I said.

"No?"

"If I had it to do over, it would be different," I said. "I know it would."

She was quiet again, and then she said. "I think it would, too. I think we let this get away from us. But you have to realize that our concerns are academic, not personal." She was squinting into the sun and because of this, it was difficult to discern her expression when she said, "I really don't think they'll spring-clean you."

The first thing I thought was, *They?* Maybe when it came down to it, she could not save me, but wasn't it a lie to act like she couldn't prevent the situation from arriving at that point? Surely, if she wanted to, she could give me a D; she could fudge and never discuss it, even with me.

The second thing I thought was that I'd have to tell Martha—contrary to what she'd said, apparently teachers did use the expression.

Classes ended that Friday, and for the week before that, we hadn't been doing much anyway; in Latin, Mrs. Pfaff brought in Rice Krispie treats her ten-year-old daughter had made, and in Spanish, we watched Mexican soap operas. In the dorms, some people had already started packing, which I hated doing—I saw the naked walls and cleared-away surfaces as unkind reminders of just how fleeting it all was, just how illusive the idea that any of it belonged to us.

After classes ended, I saw Aubrey every night, even Saturday, and I found myself practically looking forward to our meetings. Without classes, the days seemed stretched beyond use, like old rubber bands; it was good to have a few hours of structure. Also, the weather was pretty then, which always made me feel crazier. I heard about other students swimming down in the river, jogging together, riding their bikes into town for ice cream. To participate in such activities would have been like flaunting something; even if I wasn't really studying, it would look better later on, after I'd failed the exam, to have stayed in the dorm.

On Wednesday evening, the night before my math exam, on the terrace outside the dining hall, we voted for senior prefects. No faculty members were there, only Gillian and Darden, who distributed the pieces of paper themselves. Afterward, they were the ones who'd tally the votes.

"I can totally imagine Gillian stuffing the ballot," I said to Martha as we walked back to the dorm.

"She'd get kicked out," Martha said. "It's not worth the risk."

"Who did you vote for?" I asked.

"Aspeth, of course. She's such a natural leader."

"Ha ha," I said. "But I actually meant who did you vote for for guys?"

"Oh. Darden. Did you vote for your lover Cross?"

"Martha," I hissed. Jenny Carter and Sally Bishop were walking behind us.

"Sorry, I meant Purple Monkey. Here, I'll make it up to you. Get on." She had stepped in front of me and was squatting, her back to me. "Climb aboard," she said over one shoulder.

"Get on your back?" I said uncertainly.

"I'm taking you for a ride on the Marthasaurus."

"Are you drunk or something?"

"Not unless someone spiked the juice dispenser at dinner. Get on."

I turned back to look at Jenny and Sally, then waited for them to pass us. "Hi," I said, and they both smiled. "I think I'm too heavy," I said to Martha.

"Have you not seen this?" Martha flexed one arm—she was wearing a tank top, red cotton with a scalloped neckline—and her bicep rose. She was an inch shorter than I was and thinner as well, but she was definitely stronger.

"Okay," I said. "Get ready." I stepped forward and draped my arms over her shoulders. As she rose, she reached around to catch my legs, and my leg sockets locked into her arm sockets. She staggered a little, and I made an involuntary whoop, but then she steadied herself.

"Where do you want to go?" she said. "You name it."

326

"Boston?"

Martha made a snoring noise.

"Okay, fine. How about Bombay?" I tried to say it in an Indian accent.

"Much better."

"How about Mother Russia?" I tried, with about the same degree of success, to use a Russian accent, and Martha laughed. "To my dacha!" I cried and knocked my knees against Martha's sides. "Vamonos!"

She tried to gallop, but she was laughing too hard. She stopped and bent over, with me still on her back, and just stood like that with her shoulders shaking. Being able to feel her laugh made me laugh, too.

"To fin de siècle Paris," I yelled, and Martha said, gaspingly, "I think you just spit in my hair."

This was definitely the weirdest I had ever acted in public at Ault; it was still light out, and people were standing on the steps outside the library, throwing a football on the circle. To my surprise, none of them seemcd to be paying attention to us. Martha righted herself, and I said, "Am I strangling you?"

"Yes, but it's okay."

In the courtyard, just outside the entrance of Elwyn's, I slid off. "Thanks for the ride," I said. "And by the way, you're so strange."

"I know. I blame my parents."

"I'm not kidding," I said. "You're nuts."

"Lee, everyone is nuts. I promise."

"I don't believe you," I said, and she said, "But I'm right."

Who knew what would happen, as we walked up the steps of Elwyn's, with the election or the math exam? The probable outcomes were not in our favor; we were hovering in that thin space before resolution, when the cards still might, but probably would not, fall in our favor. Usually, I just wanted to learn the ending. At that moment, however, the suspense didn't bother me so much. It was a warm spring night; at least for a little while longer, it was almost nice not to know how it would all turn out.

After chapel, when everyone was walking en masse to the schoolhouse for roll call, Aubrey materialized beside Martha, and me and said, "I have something for you." He looked at Martha, and she said, "I'll leave you two alone. Just find me inside, Lee."

Aubrey passed me a manila envelope with my name written on the outside in capital letters.

"Is it the answers to the exam?" I asked.

He looked appalled.

"I was kidding," I said. I pulled out a card, handmade, that said on the front, in spindly boy letters, *GOOD LUCK!* Inside, it said, *I hope that you do very well on your exam, Lee! From, Aubrey.* He had not, as a girl would have, decorated the page with stars or flowers or balloons.

"It didn't take me long." He was blushing. "Do you have any final questions?"

"I don't think so. But thank you—I appreciate the card, Aubrey." I did appreciate it, and I also felt a little baffled by it. It was the kind of thing I would make for someone else, what I would spend an evening on instead of math homework; but no one had ever made a card like this for me.

"When you're isolating a variable, remember to go one step at a time. You'll only become confused if you attempt to solve for both variables simultaneously."

We were just inside the study hall. Because he was a freshman, Aubrey had an assigned desk for roll call; my classmates and the seniors stood in back, or sat on the wooden boxes covering the radiators along the far wall.

"Thanks for all your help, Aubrey," I said.

He didn't move immediately.

"I guess this is it, huh?" I said.

He still didn't move and, because I didn't know what else to do, I extended my hand. Roll call was starting. We shook.

I remained near the door listening to announcements—
the Minority Student Alliance was having an end-of-the-year
dinner in the activities center Sunday night, and also Mrs.
Morino hoped we'd all congratulate Adele Sheppard on the
good citizenship award she'd just received from the Raymond
Long-Term Care Center where she'd been volunteering every
week since sophomore year. When Mr. Byden stepped forward—he stood just behind the prefects during roll call, and
when he had an announcement, he usually went last—I felt a
sudden quickening of my heartbeat. He was going to say
who'd won the election; I was sure of it. The year before, he'd
made the announcement at formal dinner, but I realized
elections must have been held earlier, because formal dinner
was now finished for the year.

He cleared his throat "As you know, prefect elections for
all grades were held yesterday. I'm pleased to share the
results." As he went through the younger grades, I scanned the
room for Martha, and I saw her leaning against the far wall. I
tried to catch her eye, but she was watching Mr. Byden.
I looked around for other nominees and saw Darden standing nearby. He had a mild, pleasant smile on his face, an
utterly agreeable expression, and I knew he knew he hadn't
won; I felt a pang for him, to have to be here in front of everyone acting like a good sport. "Finally," Mr. Byden said, "for
the rising senior class—" Before he got any further, a few
people around me hooted. Mr. Byden smiled dryly. "For the
rising senior class," he repeated, "please congratulate your
new prefects, Cross Sugarman and Martha Porter."

The room exploded. All around me people seemed to be
shouting and giving high fives—why, I wondered, was it
acceptable, once the decision had been made, to show that
you cared about it, but wrong to have done so beforehand?—
and I was clapping, too, but I did not feel elated. The truth
was, I did not even feel happy. I felt stunned. Martha had
won? Martha? It had been easy to root for her because she was
my roommate, because even if no one else recognized it,

Martha was great—because we were underdogs, both of us. Except that, apparently, *we* were not.

I looked again at Darden, who was still clapping heartily, still smiling, though a muscle in his jaw, a little below his ear, was twitching.

"Darden." He didn't hear me, and again I said, "Darden." He turned.

"I'm sorry you didn't win," I said. Was this disingenuous, given that I had voted for Cross?

He shook his head. "No big thing. Hey, pretty cool about your roommate, huh?"

I tried to smile. "It's crazy." Darden and I stood there for a few seconds, both of us with our fake grins, and then at the same time we turned toward the back of the room. It was easy to locate Cross because of his height, but so many people were surrounding Martha that I couldn't even see her. Up on the platform, Mr. Byden had started speaking again, but I don't think any seniors were paying attention.

If I had been a good friend, a good person, I'd have pushed my way through our classmates and thrown my arms around Martha. And that, the instant of congratulating her, would have been manageable. My fear was of what would come next—her giddy disbelief, the welling nakedness of her feelings. Also, how I might have to reassure her that she did deserve this. Or worst of all—that maybe she'd just be *happy*. Maybe she'd simply want to luxuriate in the moment, guess who had and hadn't voted for her, anticipate what the role of prefect would be like. And these would not be unreasonable impulses—who could you be your smug and exuberant self with if not your roommate?—but I did not feel like I had the ability to stomach them. I walked out of the room; I didn't look around, so I don't know if anyone saw me.

Downstairs in the math wing, I entered an empty classroom—not Ms. Prosek's but the one across from hers—and didn't turn on the lights. I started paging through my textbook. It was far too late, but it felt good to be doing something.

It was then eight forty-five. We were to pick up the exam from Ms. Prosek's classroom at nine o'clock, take it to the study hall or to our room, and return it by noon; in a little more than three hours, it would be over, my fate would be sealed. Afterward, I'd do something for Martha—make her a card or get her flowers from town. And by that point, she'd be calmer. She herself was about to take a history exam, which would certainly dilute this moment, and maybe after that she'd talk out her election with someone else, the person she was walking back to the dorms with. By the time we met up again, she'd be able to hand her reaction to me as a tidy package: a single square of lasagna in a sealed Tupperware container as opposed to a squalid kitchen with tomato sauce splattered on the counters. And I wouldn't have had to be there while she got it in order.

When Martha had been chosen by Mr. Byden to be on the disciplinary committee, I'd been pleased for her—it wasn't a really big deal, in a way it was the distinction of a goody-goody, but it was still a distinction, and I congratulated her sincerely. And other things—the summer before our junior year, when she started going out with her brother's friend Colby, the choreography of their attraction had enthralled me; for a couple weeks, I'd spoken to Martha nightly on the phone, interpreting Colby's behavior, advising her, as if I knew anything at all about the minds of boys. For several days after she told me they'd kissed, I felt intermittent bursts of joy and it would always take me a minute to remember that it was not to me but to Martha that something good had happened. And I was always glad for Martha when she got good grades—she studied hard, and she deserved them.

But being prefect—it seemed a little arbitrary. Before Cross had nominated her, it hadn't been a thing we'd ever dis-cussed, a thing she'd even, as far as I could tell, considered. And then it had just worked out, without her really trying. And finally—what if I had been nominated for senior prefect? What if I'd gone to the meeting that day instead of to the dean's office and my presence there had made someone, maybe even Cross, think, *Why not Lee?* And what if I had been the wild card instead of Martha? Maybe people secretly liked me, too, or respected me, or saw me as an alternative to Gillian or Aspeth. It was not impossible. Because, really, wasn't this turn of events as much a defeat for the two of them as a victory for Martha? If I had been elected, I would be Cross's counterpart, we'd talk to each other every day, standing side by side at the desk in front of the entire school. With evidence that people believed in me, I'd be different, confident; I'd finally be able to relax. And certainly I would not be spring-cleaned—how could Ault spring-clean a senior prefect?

Yet these were grubby thoughts; just to have them in my own head was embarrassing. And now I knew myself to be generous with encouragement only when I either did not want the thing the other person sought or did not believe the person would really get it. It was the opposite of what I aspired to—in the moment of truth, I wanted to be loyal and forthright, reliable, humble, trustworthy. Instead, I was greedy and envious.

Roll call had ended. I could hear people in the halls of the math wing. It struck me that being spring-cleaned might, in an awful way, be easier than watching Martha become prefect.

It was eleven-thirty when Martha got back to the room, and I was lying on the futon, on my stomach, eating stale tortilla chips. I was hanging my head off the end of the futon so the crumbs would spill onto the floor, and the position was making blood rush to my face. Also, because I had given up on my exam after about fifteen minutes and then spent more than an hour sobbing, I felt dehydrated and slightly hoarse. "Hi," I said. "Congratulations on being prefect." This wasn't how I'd planned to say it—I'd planned to overcompensate and shout, *I was looking for you everywhere!*—but there it was; I'd said what I'd said.

Martha looked at my desk, where the exam lay folded open to the second page, then looked back at me. "What are you doing?"

The question seemed rather broad. "I'm having a snack," I finally said and held out the bag of chips. "Want some?"

She picked up the exam and flipped through it. I had signed my name under the Ault oath on the first page, which was the same one that appeared on every exam: *With my signature, I hereby verify that I have neither given nor received any help on this test . . .* On the next page, I'd completed the first problem, which Ms. Prosek clearly had started with so as to put us at ease. I had written a few numbers under the next problem, and then, though it had nothing to do with what the problem was asking, I'd written out the quadratic equation, just in case I'd need it later. After that, from the second page to the seventh, I hadn't written anything. As she got closer to the end, Martha's expression vacillated between confusion and dismay.

"Okay." She turned her wrist to look at her watch, then set the exam back on the desk. "You're not turning it in like this."

"I'm not?"

"Jesus Christ, Lee, what's wrong with you? Do you not understand what's at stake here? First of all, sit up."

Obediently, I sat.

"Wipe your mouth," she said. When I did, crumbs came away on my hand.

She picked up the exam again. "Come over here," she said, and when I was standing in front of her, she pointed to the desk chair. When I was seated, she set the exam in front of me, open to the second page. "You know some of this, right? Here, where it asks you to write the equation—you know how to do that, don't you?"

I blinked.

"It's like, you see that directrix y equals two—Lee?"

I looked up at her.

"What's going on?" she said.

333

"I can't do these." My voice was a little flat but not wobbly, definitely not tearful.

"But you did the first problem."

"Look at it, Martha. That's not precalculus. It's algebra."

"So you're giving up? You're just going to turn in all these pages blank?"

"There's no point in doing more."

"What about partial credit?"

"I don't think you understand," I said. "I don't know how to answer these problems. I could write stuff, but it would be gobbledygook."

"I don't believe this."

Based on her tone, I wasn't sure if she literally didn't believe it or if she just meant that she was disgusted.

"Move over," she said, and I had never heard her sound more irritated.

I shifted so I was sitting on only half the chair, and she sat on the other half. She picked up a piece of loose-leaf paper set on top of my dictionary, saw that it had writing on one side, and turned it over. (The writing was a list of vocabulary words for Spanish, a study sheet I was planning to use, but I didn't dare protest.)

"Give me your calculator," she said.

She started with the second problem, writing out the equation in pencil on the loose-leaf paper. Briefly, I thought that she could not be doing what she appeared to be doing. But she was. It soon became clear—she definitely was.

"I'm not sure this is a good—" I began, and she said. "Don't talk to me. We have less than half an hour."

When she'd gone on to the third problem, she said, "Start copying. And get me more paper."

I opened the desk drawer—because of the way we were sitting, we both had to lean back—and pulled out a spiral notebook. After I'd passed it to her, I said, "But won't it look suspicious if too many are right?"

"You'll get a C or a C minus. There's no way I can finish

the whole thing, and anyway, I'm putting in some mistakes."

After that, we didn't speak. There was only the sound of our pencils, and once, after she'd messed up on something, Martha saying "Fuck" before she started erasing. She was the one who kept checking her watch, and it was less than five of noon when she said, "You need to take it over." She'd gotten to the top of the sixth page.

I stood, clutching the exam, and when I reached the door, I couldn't help glancing back. "Martha—"

"Just go," she said, and she was looking at the wall in front of my desk. "Turn it in."

When I returned to the dorm, Martha had gone to lunch, and she stayed away from the room for the rest of the afternoon, until after dinner. When she finally came back, I stood as she entered and said, "Martha, thank you so much."

She held up her hand and shook her head. "I can't, Lee. I'm sorry, but I just can't."

I was quiet. "Okay, then," I said, "well, it's really great that you're senior prefect. I'm so proud to have such an accomplished roommate." The oddest part was that by that point in the day, it was true. The morning, when I'd bolted from roll call, seemed like months ago; by the afternoon, the idea of Martha as senior prefect had already become ordinary.

"Thanks." Martha seemed extremely tired. For the last several hours, during her absence, I'd had visions of her celebrating her victory, possibly with Cross—turning cartwheels, or being sprinkled with confetti. These possibilities now seemed highly unlikely.

"You don't seem that excited," I said.

"It's kind of been a long day."

We looked at each other. It was very hard not to thank her again, or to apologize.

"I think you'll be a really good prefect," I said. "You'll be fair."

Then Martha's face crumpled, and she started crying. She

335

lifted one hand to her eyebrows as if she were shielding her face from the sun, except that her head was bent toward the floor.

"Martha?"

She shook her head.

I crossed the room and set my palm on her back. What could I say, what else could I do? We just had to wait it out, to let more time elapse from the moment of Martha writing the answers to my exam. Because, I could see, that's what this day was to her—not the day she'd been elected senior prefect but the day she'd cheated. And I don't even think it was the fact that she had so much to lose, though she did: If we were caught, she wouldn't be senior prefect, of course, but that would be because she'd be expelled; we both would. And how titillating it would seem, given that Martha was also a member of the disciplinary committee. But fear of the consequences, I was fairly sure, wasn't the reason she was crying.

It turned out Martha had won the election, as they say, by a landslide. It had been close with the guy nominees but not close at all among the girls. I didn't know what this meant— that Martha was cool after all? That coolness had turned out to matter less than I'd believed? After we graduated, the letters of her name were carved into the marble in the dining hall, then painted gold.

I'm also not sure what it means that I felt no guilt at all toward Ault as an institution, or toward anyone specific—not Ms. Prosek, certainly not Dean Fletcher—except for Martha herself. The next day on the way out of chapel, someone tapped my shoulder. When I turned, Ms. Prosek whispered, with an enormous smile on her face, "Seventy-two." I just nodded, feigning neither surprise nor pleasure. I could feel in that moment how she would forgive me, how now that I'd passed, things between us could go back to the way they'd been before. But what was the point, after the precariousness of our bond had been revealed? It was one thing for a person who didn't really know me to act distant, but it was quite

336

another for someone to get to know me and then to back away. And besides, I wasn't sure I still respected her. It seemed like she could have stood up for me more forcefully, or talked to me more directly, but she had acted in the Ault way, all avoidance and decorum. And maybe I shouldn't have been surprised—after all, during those afternoons at her apartment, I, not Ms. Prosek, had been the outspoken one. The next fall, I requested a sixty-two-year-old physics teacher named Mr. Lithrow as my adviser.

Aubrey—poor Aubrey with his priggish, infinite patience—continued to tutor me through Calculus, and my math grade never dropped below a C senior year. Also that year, Aubrey did not grow. He did grow later—after I was in college, when I was a sophomore and he was a senior at Ault, I received a copy of the alumni quarterly that included a photograph of him with other members of the lacrosse team, and he looked to be at least six feet. He was handsome, though his features contained no trace of their earlier delicacy; it was as if a man had burst from inside his boyish self, complete with stubble.

His handsomeness seemed to me ironic because of something else, something that happened the day I graduated from Ault. After the graduation ceremony, all the faculty and then, adjacent to them, all the seniors lined up on the circle. And then all the other grades got in an opposite line, like two teams shaking hands after a game, except with twenty times as many people. In this way, every senior said good-bye to every non-senior, no matter how well or not well you'd known each other; after the juniors had passed by the seniors, the faculty went, too. The whole process took several hours, and there was much hugging and crying. When Aubrey got to me, I wrapped my arms around him—I was still considerably larger than he was—and thanked him profusely; the bizarre fact of finally graduating had made me hyper. He nodded solemnly, said, "I'll miss meeting with you, Lee," and, passing me a sealed envelope, added, "Read this later." Because I wasn't curious about what it said, and because I was distracted, I didn't read it for several days. What it was was a card—another card—with a black cap and gown on the cover, and the words *Congratulations, graduate!* inside. Underneath, Aubrey had written *I would like to express that I have very strong feelings of love for you. I do not expect anything to happen and you don't have to write back, but I wanted to say it. Good luck with your life. You are extremely attractive.* It was the nicest card I ever got, and I never responded. For a while, I meant to, only I had no idea what words a girl whom a boy had an unrequited crush on would use in a letter to that boy. But I kept the card; I have it still.

And as for Martha—I never understood when I was at Ault why she liked me as much as I liked her. Even now, I'm still not sure. I couldn't give back half of what she gave me, and that fact should have knocked off the balance between us, but it didn't, and I don't know why not. Later, after Ault, I reinvented myself—not overnight but little by little. Ault had taught me everything I needed to know about attracting and alienating people, what the exact measurements ought to be of confidence and self-deprecation, humor, disclosure, inquisitiveness; even, finally, of enthusiasm. Also, Ault had been the toughest audience I'd ever encounter, to the extent that sometimes afterward, I found winning people over disappointingly easy. If Martha and I had met when we were, say, twenty-two, it wouldn't have been hard for me to believe she'd like me. But she had liked me before I became likable; that was the confusing part.

In the first month of our senior year—we'd gotten the biggest and best room in Elwyn's, with three windows facing the circle—Martha and I broke two full-length mirrors in the span of a week. There was a radiator beneath the windows, and we set the first mirror on top of it, between two windows, and a breeze came through the screens and knocked the mirror onto the floor. So we went into town, bought another mirror, put it in the same place, and managed to be surprised

338

when that one also fell and shattered. Martha nailed the third mirror to the back of the door, and we left it there when we graduated from Ault.

But I remember the day the second mirror broke, how we'd run into each other in the gym after practice and walked back to the dorm together, and when we opened the door of our room, we saw it at the same time. "Shit," I said, and Martha said, "How stupid are we?"

She lifted the mirror and propped it against, but not on top of, the radiator. It was cracked in dozens of places, and a few pieces had fallen out altogether and remained facedown on the rug, jagged shards shaped like Tennessee or North Carolina. I was standing behind Martha, and we were reflected over and over in the remaining pieces of glass; her eyes and nose and mouth were as familiar to me as my own.

"Fourteen years of bad luck," I said, and it seemed an unfathomable stretch—not just in length, though it did seem long, but in terms of how much our lives would change during that time. In fourteen years, we would both be thirty-one. We'd have jobs, and we might be married or have children, we might live anywhere. We would be, by any definition, adult women.

Martha was the closest friend I'd ever had; I was, as always, preoccupied by the present moment (I was hoping to borrow her yellow wrap-around skirt for formal dinner); and I was too young then to understand how simple facts of geography and time can separate people. These are reasons I shouldn't have wondered what I wondered next, as I looked at our reflections in the splintered mirror—whether anything, even bad luck, would be enough to keep us bound to each other over all the years to come.

8

Kiss and Kissing

SENIOR YEAR

CROSS SUGARMAN CAME BACK to me in the fifth week of our senior year. It was a Saturday, and Martha was staying with a cousin up at Dartmouth, trying to figure out if she wanted to apply there early. It was nearly three when the door to our room opened; I had gone to bed hours before. I think Cross must have just stood there for a minute, his eyes adjusting from the light of the hallway to the darkness of the room. This is when I woke up. Seeing a tall male figure in the threshold made my heart quicken—of course it did—but I knew by then that the weird things that happen at boarding school usually happen at night. Plus, since none of the dorm rooms had locks, I'd become accustomed to people barging in.

I must have stirred, because Cross said, "Hey." He said it in that hoarse tone that's half whisper and half real-voice, different from actual talking, less in volume than in meaning.

"Hey," I said back. I still wasn't sure of his identity.

He took a step forward and the door shut behind him. I sat up on the bottom bunk, trying to make out his face. "Can I lie down?" he said. "Just for a minute."

That was when I realized who it was, but I remained disoriented from sleep. "Are you sick?" I asked.

340

He laughed. At the same time, he kicked off his shoes and eased into my bed, under the covers, and I found myself scooting toward the wall. There was a particular instant in our shifting when I could smell him—he smelled like beer and deodorant and sweat, which is to say that to me, he smelled great—and I thought, *Oh my God, it's really Cross.* It seemed the unlikeliest possibility in the world.

The way we settled was that I was lying on my back, looking at the bottom of Martha's mattress, and he was lying on his side, looking at me. The alcohol on his breath could have conjured up bus stations and old men with dirty clothes and bloodshot eyes, but because I was seventeen and a virgin and because I lived nine months a year on a campus of brick buildings and wooded hills and lovingly mown athletic fields, it conjured for me summer dances at country clubs. lives with wonderful secrets.

"I like your bed," he said.

How had this happened? Why was he here? And what if I did something wrong and he left?

"Except," he added, "it's kind of hot. Hang on." He pushed back the covers, raised his torso as if doing a sit-up, crossed his arms, lifted his sweater and T-shirt over his head, and tossed them away. "There. Much better." When he lay back down and pulled up the covers again, relief washed over me—I'd been afraid he was leaving altogether, but now (his shirt was off!) it seemed he was settling in. "So," he said, "this is what it's like being Lee Fiora."

Since our freshman year, we had scarcely spoken and I'd imagined a thousand conversations for us. And now I knew, I was finding out, that none of them had been right at all. "Yeah," I said. "it's probably not as exciting as being you." Immediately, I wondered whether the comment had sounded flirtatious or insecure.

"Oh, I'm sure that being you is *way* more exciting." (So: I had been flirting.) "All the time," Cross continued, "I ask myself, why isn't my life half as cool as that girl Lee's?"

"A lot of people ask themselves that," I said and when Cross laughed, it felt like the best thing that had ever happened. I was finding the situation strangely manageable, perhaps because of its strangeness: because we were alone together, because it was the middle of the night, because I had never predicted or tried to plan for it. Then he said, "Hey, Lee."

"What?"

Perhaps four seconds had passed when I understood that I hadn't been expected to say anything; I had been expected to turn my head, and if I had, he would have kissed me. The knowledge felt both impossible and definite; simultaneously, I was glad that I hadn't turned and fearful that I had blown my only chance.

He sighed, exhaling beery breath. (I liked his beery breath—I like it still, on grown men, because of Cross.) "So Martha is at Dartmouth, huh?"

"How do you know that?"

"Let's see. Maybe because I talk to her about ten thousand times a day."

This was true, because of their being prefects. Over the summer, I had wondered whether, when we all returned to school, their new connection would affect my own contact with Cross, but it hadn't seemed to. They ran roll call together, of course, and a lot of times when I was with Martha, sitting at a table in the dining hall or walking out of chapel, Cross would approach, but their exchanges were usually quick or else so long that they went off somewhere together. In these moments, I felt a vast and sickening jealousy, and then a loathing for myself for being jealous of my closest friend, who was herself completely unjealous.

And yet in bed with Cross, it was hard not to think that maybe his link to Martha *had* affected his contact with me—maybe he'd been reminded of me, all those times when he'd spoken to her and not even glanced my way.

"You know what I think?" Cross said. "I think Martha tells

you all the secret prefect business. I bet you know everything that goes on at the disciplinary meetings."

"Of course I don't," I said. "That would be a violation of the rules."

"Yeah, whatever."

"Do you tell Devin everything?"

"Devin doesn't care. But you're probably interested in that stuff."

"Why would I be interested if Devin isn't?"

"You just are," Cross said. "I can tell. You think I don't know you?"

"I don't see how you could since you haven't talked to me in, like, four years."

"Try three. In fact, less than three years because that surprise holiday was in the spring."

I think maybe my heart stopped, just for a few seconds. He remembered—he didn't even try to conceal that he remembered—and he knew that I remembered, too.

I might have tried to prolong, or to amplify, the admission, but he said, "For instance, I'm sure Martha told you all the details on Zane."

Arthur Zane, a junior, had been busted a few weeks before, in the first month of school, not for drinking or drugs but for breaking into the headmaster's house late one afternoon while everyone else was at practice and trying on Mrs. Byden's clothes. The break-in part of the story was what got announced at roll call; the clothing part they had tried to keep quiet.

"I doubt I know any more about Arthur than anyone else," I said. (He had even put on Mrs. Byden's panty hose and lipstick. And though he'd left the school, he hadn't technically gotten kicked out—it was his first disciplinary offense, and besides, Arthur was third-generation Ault—as much as encouraged to find a place where he'd feel more comfortable. "What does that mean?" I'd asked, and Martha had said, "It means Mr. Byden was terrified Arthur would be the first student in the history of Ault to come out of the closet." Both Martha and I assumed then that cross-dressing was the same as gayness, and also that Arthur was the only gay person we knew—at that point I still didn't recognize Sin-Jun as actually gay.)

"You're not a very good liar," Cross said. "Has anyone ever told you that?"

I felt the comers of my lips turn up.

"But here's the real question," he continued. "Was he caught in a black strapless dress or a red sequined one?"

"Mrs. Byden would never wear a red sequined dress," I said. It was true—she mostly stuck to long pleated skirts and cropped wool jackets.

"So you're going with the black strapless? You're positive you don't want to change your answer?"

"Wasn't he just wearing a brown corduroy skirt and a blouse?"

"You're *so* busted," Cross said. "Martha totally tells you everything. I knew it."

"She tells me nothing."

"She tells you everything."

"Okay, fine," I said. "But if Mrs. Byden did have a red sequined dress and a black strapless dress, any self-respecting transvestite would have picked the sequins." Saying this, I felt a twinge of guilt—calling Arthur a transvestite wasn't the cruelest remark I could make about him, but it wasn't particularly nice, either. But what strikes me now is that I had no idea how much I'd give away in the service of flirting. This was just the beginning! For years and years, there would be so many things I'd do for a guy that I wouldn't do in my usual life—jokes I wouldn't normally tell, places I wouldn't normally go, clothes I wouldn't normally wear, drinks I wouldn't normally drink, food I wouldn't normally eat or food I would normally eat but wouldn't eat in front of him. I am twenty-four, and I and the guy I like are with a group of people and the person driving is drunk and the seat belts are buried in the seat and I ride along anyway because, apparently, what I want from the guy is worth more than everything else I want or believe. It must be, right?

Cross was silent. I wondered if, after all that, he hadn't even found my transvestite joke funny. Then I wondered if he had fallen asleep.

That was when, not unlike the way he had that rainy evening in the taxi three years before, he began to stroke my hair. He set his fingers against the top of my forehead and ran them back, smoothing out my hair against the pillow, then set his fingers against my forehead again. Over and over, back through my hair, the glide of his fingertips—I think that maybe nothing else in my life ever felt that purely, un-complicatedly good. I couldn't speak because I was afraid if I did, I might start crying, or he might stop doing it. I shut my eyes.

After a long time, he said, "You have nice hair. It's really soft." He ran his knuckles along the line of my jaw, over my lips. "Are you awake?"

"Sort of," I murmured. It was an effort to speak.

"Can I kiss you?"

My eyes flapped open.

I was, of course, obsessed with kissing; I thought of kissing instead of thinking of Spanish verbs, instead of reading the newspaper or writing letters to my parents or paying attention during Indian sprints at soccer practice. But to imagine it and to have Cross next to me wanting to kiss were different. I didn't know *how* to kiss. Kissing terrified me, as an actual thing you did with another person, and there was no one it would be more humiliating to kiss badly than Cross.

He had propped himself up on one elbow. "Don't be nervous." He leaned down and kissed my cheek. "See?"

His lips when they finally touched mine reminded me of the skin of a plum.

"You can kiss me back," he said.

I pursed my lips toward him; we were kissing. It was

harder work than I had imagined, and less immediately pleasing. In fact, it felt intriguing more than enjoyable—the shifting, overlapping wet and dry parts of our mouths and faces, the mild sourness of his mouth (it seemed so *personal* to be tasting Cross's mouth), and also the way it was hard not to be conscious of the moment as it happened, not to want to pause and acknowledge it, even if only by laughing. I didn't find kissing funny, but it didn't seem that serious, either, not as serious as we were acting like it was.

He rose and twisted over me so that his legs were on either side of my hips and he was balanced on his knees and the palms of his hands. He had an erection, I realized, and I was slightly shocked. I'd heard, of course, that all boys wanted was sex, that they masturbated endlessly, and that any of them would do it with any girl, even if she was ugly. But I existed outside this world; no one ever tried to do anything with me.

Except that now, Cross was trying. And was his erection because of me or was it just the situation? And if it was me—was I supposed to have sex with him? It didn't seem like that would be a very good idea.

Over my nightgown, he gripped my breasts, squeezing one, then pressing his face to it, sucking the nipple through the cotton. I did actually laugh then—it felt ridiculous, like I was nursing him—but Cross didn't seem to recognize the noise as laughter, which was probably for the best. "Do you like this?" he asked.

If I had liked it a lot, I wouldn't have been able to admit it. But because I liked it only fine—definitely I didn't like it better than having my hair stroked—I said quietly, "Yeah."

He leaned down to reach for the hem of my nightgown—it was white and calf-length, those were the kinds of nightgowns girls wore at Ault and as he started to push it up (was he planning to take it off me completely?) I stiffened.

"It's okay," he said. "I want to make you feel good."

"Why?"

"Why?" he repeated. "What kind of question is that?"

346

So I'd said the wrong thing; really, it had only been a matter of time. "Never mind," I said.

I thought he'd press me, that he'd say, *No, what?*; I had so little idea of how it all worked. Instead, he ran his hand over my abdomen, my left hipbone, down to my thigh, then back to my abdomen. My nightgown was bunched around my waist, over my underwear, and I knew what would happen next—it was all a combination of suspense and not suspense.

He used two fingers, and I bucked against his hand, as if I were trying to help him find something inside me. Everything was damp and hot. Abruptly, I was at his mercy, I could sense how things had shifted and I wanted it more, but it felt so good that I almost didn't care. I couldn't tell how long it lasted, only that it made me feel wild with greed, ravenous and ecstatic. Then it ended and we were kissing again, and the kissing was easier this time, it was something we were coming back to. And then slowly we grew calmer, I understood that he wasn't going to try to have sex with me (and how could this have disappointed me, when I had already decided I didn't want it?), and he lay with his head on my chest, over my heart; his legs must have been dangling off the end of the bed. His body was heavy against mine, almost too heavy, but not. I could adjust to it. This was also something I didn't know until later, how some guys will never rest their full weight against you, and how with Cross it made him seem sure—sure I was strong enough and sure that I would want it, which I did. I put my palms on his shoulders and my hands made a hushing noise as I rubbed his back.

After a long while, from outside, we heard a car drive past. The car might have been the night watchman, patrolling the campus—it was after four o'clock—or it might have been a teacher coming home very late or leaving very early. Whoever it was, it imposed reality; the moment broke. "I should go," Cross said. Neither of us spoke, and he didn't move right away. I looked down at his head. Slightly, very slightly, it rose and fell as I breathed.

When I woke the next morning, there were a few seconds before I opened my eyes when I remembered that something good had happened, but I could not remember what it was. Then I thought, Cross. I opened my eyes. The room was light —it was a little before nine, and Sunday chapel, which was mandatory, would be at eleven—and it all seemed so ordinary: the desks and posters, the futon and the trunk that served as a table, covered by magazines and pens and cassette tapes and an open bag of Chips Ahoy and a rotting orange; There was no evidence of Cross anywhere—I had thought that if he forgot his shirt or sweater, I wouldn't say anything, but he'd remembered to take both—and I began sliding into that familiar state of distrust and disorientation. It was like when I was supposed to meet someone in the library, and I'd arrive and they wouldn't be there, or I'd get to their door in the dorm and the moment before I knocked, I'd think, *Did I imagine we had something scheduled?* Sometimes I couldn't even return phone calls, because I'd talk myself into believing I had made up the other person's call in the first place.

But Cross *had* been there. I knew he had. I rolled over and my body was sore, and the soreness was proof. And it seemed I should feel glad about what had happened—I had finally kissed a boy, that boy had been Cross—but the more that sleep, and the night, slipped away from me, the stranger the incident seemed. Who had been the girl who let Cross stick his fingers inside her, then writhed and whimpered beneath him? Certainly it could not have been me. I wanted to talk to Martha, but she wouldn't be back until the evening.

Most people skipped breakfast on Sunday mornings, but Martha and I always went. We went around nine and ate slowly and a lot and shared several newspapers with the handful of our classmates who'd also showed up. Among the regulars was Jonathan Trenga, who would lay claim to the serious sections of *The New York Times*—his parents both were lawyers in Washington, D.C., and no matter what was going on in the world, which unpronounceable countries were at war, what drug or energy or market crisis was unfolding, Jonathan was not only conversant in the subject but had a strong opinion about what needed to be done. Once I had asked, "But are you a Democrat or a Republican?" and Jonathan said, "I'm socially progressive but fiscally conservative," and Doug Miles, a football player who also came to Sunday breakfast but only ever read the sports section and ignored everyone, lifted his head and said, "Is that like being bisexual?" Which I actually thought was funny, even though I was pretty sure Doug was a jerk.

Then there was Jonathan's roommate, Russell Woo, who also didn't talk much but had a more benign presence than Doug. For reasons I couldn't pinpoint—it wasn't much more than glances—I had the idea Russell was in love with Martha, which I mentioned to her on a weekly basis, as we left the dining hall, and she always denied. I knew little about Russell except that he was from Clearwater, Florida, but sometimes I wished he were in love with me so that I could visit him there on spring break.

The other seniors who showed up regularly were Jamie Lorison, the boy who our freshman year, in Mrs. Van der Hoef's class, had given his presentation on Roman Architecture just before I gave mine; Jenny Carter and her roommate, Sally Bishop; and, on the days she'd gotten up early to study, Dede. On these days, she wore her glasses and her navy blue sweatpants, which I found curious because she was so vain the rest of the time, and even though not many people saw you on Sunday morning, it wasn't like *no one* did.

I never dressed nicely for breakfast, but I didn't dress nicely the rest of the time, either. That morning, after I'd washed my face and brushed my teeth—on Sundays, I rarely showered—I pulled on jeans and a long-sleeved T-shirt and a fleece jacket. Then I stood in the room, fully dressed, feeling Martha's absence. I'd have gone to breakfast alone without much thought if not for what had happened the night before.

But was it appropriate now to go as if everything was ordinary? *Was* everything ordinary? Maybe it was, after all.

I walked outside, and the farther I got from the dorm, the more strongly I felt it: Everything wasn't ordinary. My unease was rising around me like smoke, By the time I reached the dining hall, I was choking on it; I couldn't go inside. What if, by coincidence, today was the one Sunday Cross went to breakfast? And what if he saw me like this, in the light, in the daytime (why had I left the dorm without showering, why was my natural impulse to be such a slob?) and what if he felt surprised to remember I wasn't prettier, what if he decided he'd made a mistake? Or maybe what had happened was not, to him, even a big enough deal to count as a mistake. That was the thing I wanted to know the most, if it meant something or nothing. I turned around and began walking toward the dorm, walking more and more quickly, and as I hurried—it felt important, suddenly, not only that I not run into Cross but that I not run into anyone, not even a teacher—I actually missed my old self, the self I had been until the night before. I had gone to Sunday breakfast with Martha and talked or not talked to the other students, I had gotten seconds on pancakes, and it hadn't mattered. For the first few weeks of this year, my senior year, I'd felt the calmest I ever had at Ault. There hadn't been pressure, I hadn't been answering to anyone, trying for anyone. Or I had—all along, of course, I'd been trying for Cross—but in the moments when I'd needed to think he couldn't possibly notice, I'd been able to. It had all been acrobatics in my head. And now something mattered, there was something for me to ruin.

In the dorm, I climbed back in bed because the covers were protection, my own closed eyes were protection. Horizontal and cocooned, I could relax, I could even remember fragments of the night before and feel a tiny happiness again—his voice, his hand in my hair, how nothing had made him hesitate except (and then I cringed, thinking about it) when I'd said, *Why? Why do you want to make me feel good?* It was mainly that it needed to be dark again, I realized, the bright and unforgiving day had to pass: meals where you chewed food, computer screens, shoelaces, and all the small terrible conversations, even the ones you weren't participating in and just had to listen to, waiting for them to be over. But in the night you could dispense with everything disagreeable or irrelevant. It was you and the other person, your warm skin, how good you could make each other feel. (*Had* I made Cross feel good? I could have tried harder, probably, except that I wouldn't have been sure how.)

I was in bed when the bells rang for ten o'clock, and I still thought I would go to chapel, or at least I hadn't decided against it, but then the bells rang for eleven o'clock, and I couldn't pretend to be surprised. So I was skipping chapel—a first for me.

It was two in the afternoon before I got out of bed again, and that was mostly because I needed to pee. I ate a column of saltines, plucking them from their opaque wrapper, and opened my history textbook and sat on the futon, looking around the room and thinking of Cross. By five, Martha still wasn't back, which meant I couldn't go to dinner. In the common room, I put on water to boil, and I was standing next to the stove when Aspeth Montgomery walked through. She didn't live in Elwyn's, but she lived in the dorm next door, Yancey's, and sometimes dropped by our dorm to visit another senior named Phoebe Ordway.

"Did Sug come to your room last night?" she said. I would not have been more surprised if she'd asked to borrow my sports bra.

"Did what?"

"When he said he was going to, it was like three in the morning. I was just like, first of all, have some manners. I'm sure they're sound asleep. And besides that, Martha will freak out if you break visitation. I mean, great idea—maybe you can *both* get busted, and Mr. Byden can shit in his pants. Are you making ramen?"

"Cross was coming to see Martha?" I said uncertainly.

"Oh, so he didn't? Good." She started walking again. "Forget it then."

Normally at this juncture in a conversation, I'd have given up, and especially with Aspeth, who made me feel awkward before I opened my mouth. But my interest was intense. "I don't understand where you guys were at three in the morning," I said.

"We were playing poker. A bunch of those guys came over, and Devin and Sug got smashed, of course, and Sug announces he's going to meet with Martha. It's like, do you think maybe you're taking the prefect thing a *little* too seriously?"

But Cross had known that Martha was at Dartmouth, he'd been the one who'd brought it up. It was possible he'd forgotten and remembered only in the doorway, when he saw her empty bed. But I felt almost sure that he'd known all along. (I never asked him this. I had plenty of chances, and certainly I wanted to know, but I couldn't ask because what I'd really have been asking was a bigger question, and I was always afraid that I already knew the answer. You only ever try to pin a person down because they are not yours, because you can't.)

"Your water's boiling," Aspeth said, and by the time I'd moved the pot, she was walking up the stairs to the rooms. "Don't get an MSG headache," she called.

Of course Aspeth knew how to play poker—probably five girls on campus did, and it was utterly unsurprising that she was one of them. She was probably good, too, she probably beat the boys and laughed her Aspeth laugh as she took their money. And the worst part was that if I were a boy, Aspeth was the kind of pretty, bitchy, unattainable girl I myself would like; certainly I wouldn't find a so-so girl and then stare hard inside her to see all the ways she was worthwhile.

The wrongness of what had happened between Cross and me—I could feel it now. Not a moral wrongness, but a screwup, a thing that needed explanation: a bird in the grocery store, a toilet that won't stop running, that moment when your friend has come to pick you up and you open the door and realize it's not your friend's car at all; the person driving is a stranger, and now you must apologize.

My meeting with Mrs. Stanchak was the last period of the day. I had met with her before—at Ault, college counseling started in the spring of your junior year—but this was supposed to be a definitive meeting, the one at which I presented her with the list of colleges where I was applying.

When I was seated in the chair beside her desk, she opened a manila folder, pulled her glasses down on her nose—the lenses were rectangular, with blue plastic frames, and they were attached to a chain around her neck—and peered at the top piece of paper. Still looking down, she said, "How's this year going for you, Lee? Off to a good start?"

"Pretty good."

"How's math?"

"I have a B minus right now."

"No kidding?" She looked up and smiled. "That's fantastic. You're still meeting with Aubrey?"

I nodded.

Mrs. Stanchak was in her early sixties, married to Dr. Stanchak, who was head of the classics department. She had the kind of hair I wanted when I was her age—it was about three inches long, almost white, and fanned off her head as if she'd been riding in a convertible, though it appeared she used no gel. She was a little plump, and her face was deeply lined and tan, even in the winter. During vacations, she and Dr. Stanchak traveled to places like China or the Galapagos Islands. They'd had three sons go through Ault—the youngest had graduated at least ten years before—and in the pictures I'd seen, the sons were all fair-haired and incredibly handsome. I liked Mrs. Stanchak, in fact there was something about her I liked quite a bit, but whenever I was in her office,

I thought almost continuously, even during the times I myself was speaking, of how people always said that she was who you got assigned to if Ault wasn't planning to get behind your college application. The other counselor, Mr. Hessard, was in his forties, a tall, sardonic English teacher—Mrs. Stanchak didn't teach any classes and worked only part-time as a counselor—and he himself had gone to Harvard, while Mrs. Stanchak had gone to the College of Charleston in South Carolina, which was not a place Ault ever sent anyone. (You knew where all the faculty had graduated from, and what degrees they'd received, because it was listed in the school catalog.) Apparently, the talk about Mr. Hessard versus Mrs. Stanchak circulated every spring, just before juniors found out which counselors they'd been assigned to, and every spring, the other teachers tried to squelch it; in history class, when Dean Fletcher heard people discussing it, he said, "Not that bullcrap again," and Aspeth, who was in the class, said, "Fletchy, I'm shocked by your language."

But then, when we got divided, Martha got Mr. Hessard, as did Cross, as did Jonathan Trenga, as did pretty much all the other kids in our class who seemed either smart or adored. The only remotely smart person who got Mrs. Stanchak was Sin-Jun, but I wasn't sure Ault cared where Sin-Jun went to college just as long as she didn't try to off herself again before graduation. The weird part of the assignments was that it actually surprised me not to get Mr. Hessard. Sure, I believed the worst of myself but—not really. I was always waiting to be proven wrong.

Mrs. Stanchak jotted something down before turning to me. "Let's have a look at your list."

I passed it to her, and she scanned it. She didn't make any affirming noises as she read.

Finally, she said, "My main concern is that you're not giving yourself a whole lot of safeties. A place like Hamilton, I'd say that's a good bet for you. But when we're talking about Middlebury or Bowdoin, those could be trickier."

354

"What about Brown?"

"Lee." She reached forward, touched my forearm, then leaned back and pushed her glasses up on her head, nestling them in her fluffy hair. "You're going to love college. Do you know that? *Love* it. And that's because there are more wonderful schools out there than either of us can count But if you listened to some of the people here, you'd think there were about eight good schools. Am I right?"

She was exactly right. The number was eight because Penn and Cornell were barely Ivies, but Stanford and Duke might as well have been.

"That's just silly," Mrs. Stanchak said. "I know you know it's silly, too."

"So you don't think I can get into Brown?"

"You know what I'll say? I'll say apply to Brown. Go ahead. Why not? But I want you to look at other places, too. Did you order a catalog from Grinnell like we talked about? Grinnell's a fabulous school. And Beloit, too."

"What state is that in again?"

"Grinnell is in Iowa, and Beloit's in Wisconsin."

"I don't want to go to school in the Midwest," I said. "I like it better here."

"Lee, I want you to feel comfortable with the decisions we make. But I need you to work with me, and that might mean taking a second look at some places."

"What if I write a really good essay for Brown?"

She sighed. "Lee," she said—never had my name been uttered with more sympathy—and I could feel a hardness form in my throat, a welling behind my eyes. "You almost flunked precalculus," she said. "You're up against kids from here, your own classmates, who have straight As and board scores of 1600. And then you're up against the top students from schools across the country. And we haven't even touched the issue of financial aid. I'm not going to set you up for disappointment. Lee?"

I didn't speak.

"Wherever you go, that school will be *lucky* to have you," she said, and I burst into tears. In the first gush, I thought of Cross—I had been thinking of him for most of the day anyway, for most of the time since he'd left my room a little less than thirty-six hours before—and it felt like I was crying, simultaneously, because I hadn't heard from him, because maybe our interaction had been random and singular and he'd never touch my hair again or lie on top of me, because I hadn't even really appreciated it while it was happening, and, finally, because Cross, being a prefect, would probably go to Harvard and Mrs. Stanchak was trying to separate us by sending me far away to Wisconsin. Desperately, I thought that I just needed one more chance from Cross and that if he gave it to me, I'd understand the situation. I'd be grateful to him without showing my gratitude in a way that was sickening.

Mrs. Stanchak passed me a box of tissues and said, "Take as many as you like." My tears did not appear to faze her at all. (Later, when I told Martha about crying in Mrs. Stanchak's office, she said, "Oh, I've already cried twice with Mr. Hessard. It's like a rite of passage.") "It's a tough time," Mrs. Stanchak said. "I know."

For at least a minute, we sat there listening to me sniffle. During this time, I managed to have a fantasy that Mrs. Stanchak would ask what I was really upset about, and when I told her, she would respond by saying something about Cross, and the situation, that was wise and true. I think adults forget just how much faith teenagers can have in them, just how willing to believe that adults, by virtue of being adults, know absolute truths, or that absolute truths are even knowable. But then, outside Mrs. Stanchak's window, I saw Tig Oltman and Diana Trueblood walking with their hockey sticks to the gym, and I remembered how it was probably unwise to confide in anyone at Ault besides Martha. There wasn't anything in particular about Tig and Diana that reminded me of this fact, nothing about them I especially didn't trust, it was just that—they existed. They wouldn't literally be able to hear, but if you had a moment of vulnerability at Ault, someone always found out. Once a thing left your head, you lost your privacy.

I glanced again at Mrs. Stanchak, who was waiting patiently, and I suddenly doubted that she had great truths to impart. "Sorry for this," I said.

"Don't be sorry," she said. "Don't worry about me. What I want you to think about is you."

It occurred to me to tell her that I did little else.

She passed me the list of colleges. "I want you to rework this," she said. "Take a few days, and give it some thought. Talk it over with your parents. Take a long walk. And let's try not to get too hung up on labels. Will you try that for me?"

"It's not like I want to go to Brown just because it's prestigious," I said. The expression on her face implied both that she did not believe me and that she did not fault me for lying. But I was lying only partially. "I want to go to Brown because it attracts interesting people," I said. "And because it's in the Northeast and it doesn't have distribution requirements." I wanted to go to Brown because if I went to Brown, it would mean I was a person who deserved to be there. And also: because if I was a person who deserved to be there and if this was somehow official, then it would mean everything was going to turn out okay.

"Those are great reasons," Mrs. Stanchak said. "And you know what I want you to do, and I'm giving myself the same assignment? I want you to come up with five other schools that also fit that description. Now, remember that the federal financial aid forms will be available in November, and your parents need to get them in, in January. And you know you're not applying anywhere early—we're clear on that?"

I nodded. It was slightly surreal to speak so openly about money when I was accustomed to considering it the worst possible topic. It was like going to the gynecologist, which I started doing in college—how embarrassed and apologetic I'd feel about the fact that my vagina was in the doctor's face and how it was both liberating and just weird to remember that there really wasn't anything to hide, that exposing my vagina was why I was there.

"You can sit here awhile if you want to get collected," Mrs. Stanchak said.

"That's all right." I stood. In equal parts, I was mortified that I had started crying, and I wanted to leave her office while I still looked teary, because maybe Cross would see me and think I had been crying about something that mattered and then I would seem intriguing. "Thank you, Mrs. Stanchak," I said.

"Thank *you*, Lee. Do you know why I'm thanking you?"

I shook my head.

"Because you're the one who's going to get yourself into college."

That morning, I'd received a note in my mailbox from Dean Fletcher reprimanding me for missing Sunday chapel and instructing me to report to the dining hall at five p.m. for table wipes, which was basically predinner cleanup. After soccer practice, I walked with wet hair from the gym to the dining hall. I'd never received table wipes before, and I was possibly the only senior who could make this claim, including Martha. As I headed around the circle, the air smelled like burning leaves and the campus was shot with that amber light you see only in the fall, and I felt, as I often did at Ault, both as if I were undeserving and as if the beauty around me was not really mine.

Just before I stepped from the outer hall into the dining room, I heard Cross's voice, felt a wave of shock, and considered turning around. I shouldn't have been shocked at all—in addition to being the senior prefect, Cross was one of the three dining hall prefects, and apparently this was his night on duty.

I entered the dining room, where about twenty students were wiping the tables and setting down cloths. Cross was holding a sheet of paper and a pen and laughing while he spoke to two sophomore guys. Even when I was three or four feet away, he did not seem to notice me. "Excuse me, Cross," I said.

He looked over, and so did the two sophomores. "What can I do for you?" Cross asked, and his voice was not entirely friendly.

"I have table wipes." I gestured toward his piece of paper. "At least I think I do. I got a notice from Fletcher."

Cross looked at the paper. "I didn't realize you were a delinquent," he said, and his tone was more relaxed. "You guys should get to work," he said to the two boys. "And no sloppiness." One of them made that jerking-off gesture as they walked away. "Hey!" Cross said. "A little respect there, Davis." But he was laughing with them.

When they were gone, he said, "You wanted an excuse to talk to me?"

"No! I skipped chapel."

"I was just kidding." He glanced down at his watch. His hair was wet, too, and as we stood there, I had the bizarre notion that we'd just showered together. My face flushed. "Listen," he said. "Dinner doesn't start for forty minutes, and we already have plenty of people here. You can leave."

"Are you sure?"

"I'll check your name off the list if that's what you're worried about."

"So I just go?"

"Unless you don't want to."

"No, I do. I mean, I don't not want to. Thank you." I turned, and as I did, he touched me very lightly in that place between your hip and your back, and I knew something more would happen between us. Not just that I wanted it to, but that it would come to pass. It was because he set his hand so low. If it had been higher, it might have meant, *No hard feelings?* or even merely, *See you around*. But like that, at the base of my spine, even I could recognize in it something prospective and vaguely territorial. I looked back, but he was already talking to someone else.

"The fact that he let you leave isn't a bad sign." Martha was standing in front of the full-length mirror, brushing her hair, while I sat on the futon. "You don't understand this because you've never had table wipes, but they're kind of humiliating. Especially for seniors. So it's not like, oh, he didn't want to be around you so he told you to go. It's more like he was being nice."

"He didn't say anything about the other night," I said. "Not a word."

"What was he supposed to say? Other people were there."

"Maybe he doesn't remember since he was drunk."

"He remembers." Martha set down her brush and lifted her perfume bottle. She squirted some into the air in front of her, then walked through the mist—it was a trick I'd picked up from Dede freshman year and passed on to Martha. "It actually doesn't sound like he was all that drunk. A lot of guys can't, you know, get it up when they've had a lot to drink."

"Really?"

"Alcohol depresses your central nervous system."

"Has that ever happened with Colby?" Martha and Colby had been together for more than a year. He was a junior at UVM, and they spoke once a week on the phone, on Mondays, and wrote to each other and spent time together on vacations and she'd had sex with him (her first time) six months into the relationship, after they'd gone to a clinic for him to get tested for AIDS because he'd had sex with two previous girlfriends. He was tall and nice and liked Martha, but he was also pale and had a beaky nose and was, at least in my opinion, rather humorless. When Martha was home, they did things together like go for fifty-mile bike rides, or take turns reading aloud their favorite parts from *The Odyssey*. I did not feel jealous.

"Colby doesn't drink that much because of crew," Martha

said. She looked at me. "You really shouldn't be stressing."

"I'm not." I propped my legs on the trunk and looked at my calves in black opaque tights and my feet in black dress shoes. I wondered if my shoes were cheesy. Lately, a lot of girls were wearing chunkier heels.

"What do *you* want to happen?" Martha asked. "Seriously."

I wanted to be the person Cross told things to. I wanted him to think I was pretty, I wanted him to be reminded of me by stuff I liked—pistachios and hooded sweatshirts and the Dylan song "Girl from the North Country"—and I wanted him to miss me when we were apart. I wanted him to feel, when we were lying in bed together, like he couldn't imagine anywhere better.

"Can you picture him being my boyfriend?" I asked.

Martha was putting on her jacket, with her back to me, when she said, "No," and because she couldn't see my face, I don't think she realized how startled I was. By the time she turned around, I was straining not to seem surprised or hurt. "I'm sure if you want to hook up with him again, you can," she said. "But the sense I get, just from little comments he makes, is that he's really into this being his senior year. I doubt he wants to be tied down. And also, just, you and Cross?" She made a face like she'd smelled something bad. "Do you see it happening?"

"If you can't imagine Cross and me going out, why'd you just tell me to think about what I want?" I tried to speak in a normal, curious voice. These were, hands down, the worst things Martha had ever said to me, but if she knew I thought so, she'd feel terrible and stop being honest.

"I'm not saying to be passive. That's what makes me worry about you, that it seems like you're leaving it all in his hands. You definitely should express what you want, and if he can't deal with it, it's his problem."

"But why should I go after something you're so sure I won't get?"

"I'm not sure of anything. How could I be? But you've had

361

a huge crush on Sug for almost the entire time you've been here. He came over, you guys fooled around, and now there's an opportunity, and you owe it to yourself to see what happens. And it's not like I'm skeptical because I don't think you're good enough for him. If anything, you're too good. I'm just not sure he realizes that."

"So what should I say to him? And when?"

"He's not that hard to find. Go to his room during visitation,"

"I would never go to Cross's room."

"Then wait until you see him around campus, and tell him you want to talk to him."

"To say what?"

"Lee, there aren't magical words." Martha stepped into shoes exactly like mine, and my resentment of her flared. Most of the time I loved having her as my roommate, I loved the clarity and closeness of one single best friend. But at rare moments, for exactly the same reason, I felt trapped by my reliance on her, flattened by her pragmatism and bluntness. If I had ever made Dede into my best friend and if I'd then had this conversation with her (and if, of course, Dede herself hadn't harbored a crush on Cross for years), then in this moment Dede would scheme and bolster. She wouldn't deflate me like Martha was doing.

And besides, why was it right, why was it so goddamn reasonable, for Martha to have a boyfriend and me not to, for her to be senior prefect and me to be nobody? I literally wasn't anything, not a chapel prefect or yearbook editor or sports captain (Martha, also, was captain of crew). The summer after our junior year, I had gone through a class list to try to find anyone similarly undistinguished and had come up with only two other people: Nicole Aufwenschwieder and Dan Ponce. Both of them were less than boring—they were practically invisible.

In the dining hall, before we split up to find our separate tables, Martha said, "Divide and conquer," and I detested her for being both ordinary and lucky, when most people at Ault were lucky and lucky, or ordinary and ordinary.

When Cross came the second time, I believed it was because waves of desire were rolling off my body and across the courtyard between our dorms. It was a Saturday morning—it was around one o'clock, I think, because Martha had already gone to bed. She usually stayed up later than I did, studying, then woke me when she'd turned out the light so we could talk. When Cross showed up, this had happened already and we'd both gone to sleep,

He was all the way in the room this time before I awakened, crouching over my bed with his hand on my arm. "Lee," he was whispering. "Lee—it's me." I opened my eyes and smiled, and it wasn't a smile where you choose it or not. Before he even climbed into bed, he leaned down and kissed me on the mouth and then we were kissing and kissing and I realized that this was what kissing was, *this* was why people liked it—the perfect sliminess of each other's tongues. I wasn't sure of the exact moment he lowered himself onto me.

When I felt his erection, I squirmed around under him until it was between my legs, I wrapped my legs around his waist. He jerked against me so strongly that I thought he might tear through my underwear (though, really, who cared about my underwear?). He took off his shirt, and his skin was warm and soft and smooth.

I think he might have heard Martha first, the straining springs of her mattress above us. She didn't say a word, but Cross and I froze, and then she was climbing down the rails of the bunk bed. She walked out of the room.

"Is she pissed?" Cross asked when the door shut. In this moment, clearly, she was not his co-prefect; she was my roommate.

And if she was pissed, I didn't care. Being like this with Cross was everything I wanted. What is there to say? Sometimes in your life, you're selfish; you just are.

"Don't worry about it." I said.

Then we stopped speaking. At one point, I heard myself make the kind of moan that I'd heard in movies, and I could not believe that such a noise had been dormant inside me, all this time.

After a while, I said, "Why didn't you talk to me in the dining hall on Monday?" and he said, "I talked to you," and I said, "Not really," and he said, "Your cheeks were all blushed," and then I didn't ask him any more about it. And much later, when it was not yet light but it was less dark, closer to morning than to night, and I could feel that he was about to leave, I said, "You're not going to tell people about this, right?"

He was quiet for a few seconds. "Okay."

"When we see each other in school, we can just act normal," I said.

"What does acting normal mean?" He sounded amused maybe, or maybe skeptical.

"I won't come up and kiss you good morning at breakfast." I said. "If that's what you're afraid of."

Again, he was quiet, and then he said, "Okay."

"Or it's not like I expect you to bring me flowers." I had meant for the example to sound absurd—of course Cross wouldn't bring me flowers—but it didn't sound absurd enough. It would have been better if I had said, *It's not like I expect you to buy me a diamond necklace*.

"Anything else?" he said.

"I'm not trying to be weird."

His voice contained no trace of amusement when, at last, he said, "I know."

In the morning, as we were getting dressed, Martha said, "I don't think it's a good idea for him to come over like that."

"I'm sorry. Are you totally annoyed?"

"Waking up to the sound of you and Sug making out and then having to go sleep in the common room isn't my preference, no." (This seemed rather small of her, I thought, it seemed blind to the fact that this was the first guy I'd ever kissed. Didn't I get any allowance, or just some time to learn how to act? And anyway, wasn't it all part of boarding school, that you listened to your roommate huff and pant with some boy?) "But the real problem," Martha continued, "is that if he ever got caught here, I could be implicated. I can't tell him what to do, but I *am* responsible for myself."

I said nothing.

"Is he planning to come back?" she asked.

"I don't know," I said, "but probably," and saying it made me feel so good that it almost overrode the unpleasantness of the exchange with Martha; I didn't smile, but it was only because I was trying not to.

"Can you understand why this puts me in a weird position?" she said.

"Yes."

"Technically, I should turn you in just because I know you're breaking visitation. No one would really expect me to, I don't think, but I do talk to Mr. Byden or to Fletchy practically every day. And they assume that I'm being honest. You're not the one having all these meetings with them and looking them in the eye and talking about school integrity."

"Martha, I already said yes, I can understand why this puts you in a weird position."

Martha sighed. "I know you like him a lot."

Neither of us spoke.

"Are you saying he *can't* come over?" I finally asked.

"Don't make me be your mom. That's not fair."

"But that's what you're saying, right? That you'd rather he never set foot in here again?" Had Martha always been this rigid?

"Wait a second," she said. "I have an idea. You can use the day student room."

Immediately, I felt resistant, though it was hard to say why. Every dorm had a day student room, smaller than a real room

365

usually, with only one bed and a desk or two. The day student room in our dorm was three doors down from ours, and the only day student affiliated with Elwyn's was Hillary Tompkins, a junior who wasn't around much.

"Would I have to ask Hillary?" I said, and Martha actually laughed.

"Maybe you could ask Fletchy, too," she said. (Before this year, I thought, she had always called him Dean Fletcher, and she'd called Cross Purple Monkey, not Sug. Now she sounded like Aspeth.)

"I guess that means no," I said.

"I doubt Hillary would care," Martha said. "Anyway, it won't be that frequent, right?"

Why did she think it wouldn't be that frequent?

"Are we having a fight?" Martha asked.

"No," I said quickly. Then I said, "We couldn't be. Martha and Lee *never* fight." I'm not sure this is what anyone else thought of us, but it was what I thought; as seniors, Martha and I were one of only four pairs of girls in our grade to have stayed together for the three years you chose your roommate. Boys stayed together, but girls usually didn't.

"But I've heard Martha is kind of a bitch," Martha said.

"Actually, Lee is the horrible one," I said. "She's totally insecure, and she complains all the time. And she's so negative. I can't stand negative people."

"When life gives negative people lemons, they should make lemonade," Martha said.

"Negative people should turn that frown upside down," I said. "Hey, Martha?"

She looked at me.

What would someone else have said? *Your friendship means so much to me. I love you.* Martha and I had never said *I love you* to each other; I thought girls who did, especially girls who said it all the time, were showy and hollow. "I'm glad you're not mad at me," I said.

* * *

It was like I had been walking down the sidewalk in a suburban neighborhood and then I stepped on a certain square of pavement and the square fell away and I was falling through infinite blackness with white stars glittering all around me. I was waiting to find myself slammed back onto the same sidewalk where I'd started, blue jays resting on a telephone pole, the sprinkler running in a yard across the street, and me with perhaps a cut on my knee or a bruise on my forearm—proof that *something* had occurred, but that what had occurred had been less than I imagined it to be. But it never happened. I just kept falling.

Partly, it had to do with the fact that on the nights Cross came, I didn't get much sleep. Things always seem strange then. Also that I was eating less. I wasn't eating nothing, it wasn't like I was anorexic, it was just that food, like almost everything else, now seemed beside the point. Certain foods I was ravenous for, like avocado, which I craved so badly I rode Martha's bike to town, bought four, let them ripen on the windowsill, peeled the skin off with Martha's pocketknife, and ate them like apples. Vanilla ice cream also—these foods seemed somehow pure, thcy would slide down my throat instead of getting caught in my molars. Casserole, on the other hand, made me want to vomit.

My grades actually improved. It was because I did my homework, I could focus because homework wasn't my entire life, in fact it didn't really matter and was just something I had to do to act normal. So I sat down and opened my books and did the reading or memorized the equations—whatever it was—whereas once I had sat down and then looked at the ceiling and started thinking about things like if I should give myself a middle name when I went to college, or if I had chronic body odor, would anyone tell me?

The third time Cross came over, he was half-lying on me, our arms were already tangled (it surprised me how sloppy hooking up was, and how this was one of the good parts: how your bodies did not become sleek and precise, as in a synchronized swimming routine, but how they remained your bodies—your arm still hurt if the other person's weight was distributed the wrong way, your nose could bump his collarbone, and this clumsiness made me feel at home, like Cross and I were friends) when I said to him, "We can't stay in here. We can't—" and then he cut me off by kissing me and I said, "No, Cross, really—" and then we were kissing more and then I heard Martha roll over, and I said, "Just follow me. Get up and follow me."

Stepping into the brightly lit hall was terrible. I had pulled him out of bed, tugging him across the room, but when I'd opened the door we'd lost physical contact and to be in the light, not touching at all, was hideous; I missed him, and I also felt self-conscious because he was behind me. Was my hair sticking up in back, and really, did Cross even know what I looked like in the light? I certainly wasn't about to turn around, face-to-face, and show him.

"Wait up," he mumbled as he followed me, and then I opened the door to the day student room. The room had one window, with the shade up, and light from a lamppost outside made it possible to see. On the bed was a sleeping bag and I lay on it, and then I sat up and reached for Cross and he was on top of me again, his khaki pants and belt buckle, the buttons down his shirt, my face at the side of his neck, just below his left ear, his stubble and how good he smelled and how warm he always was and how much I liked to be with him. I already recognized, even then, the sadness of another person lying on top of you. They will always leave (what's someone going to do, just lie there forever?) and that's the sad part. You can always feel the imminent loss.

It seemed to me, and it kept seeming like this for a long time, that this was what it was to love a boy—to feel consumed. I'd awaken in the morning, without him, thinking, *I love you so much, Cross.* Knowing that other people would not consider what went on between us to be love—of course they wouldn't—only made me more certain. When he arrived at night, tapping my shoulder in the dark, then the two of us walking down the hall to the day student room, then finally being in bed again, our bodies overlapping, my arms around his back—that was one of the times when not telling him I loved him required willpower. Also when he was about to leave. I loved him so much! Later, with other guys, I'd think, *Do I? Is this what it feels like? Does love feel different with differ-ent people?* But with Cross. I never wondered. There was nothing about him I didn't like. The other guys, guys in my future, were maybe also tall but as slim as girls, they listened to classical music and drank wine and liked modern art, and they seemed to me like sissies. Or we had enough to say to each other to fill an evening, we could go to a baseball game, but it never stopped being an effort. Or their fingers were— not stubby, but not long and sure. If I kissed these guys, I'd wonder if it would turn out to be an obligation, if I was moving forward into a situation from which I'd later have to extricate myself. It's not that they were *unattractive*, they weren't boring. But I never thought of what Cross wasn't, I never had to explain or defend him to myself, I didn't even care what we talked about. It was never a compromise.

Or maybe for him it was. But it never was for me.

If people asked, which not many did, I said I was staying on campus for long weekend to work on college applications. Really, I was staying at school because school was the place of Cross. He was leaving, of course—I knew, not because we'd talked about it but because I'd listened to a conversation in the dining hall, that he and a few other guys were going to Newport to stay with Devin's mother and stepfather—but at least school would be the place he'd been and was coming back to, whereas Martha's house in Burlington, where I'd gone every long weekend since freshman year, would only be a detour; all I'd be doing was waiting to leave.

Martha was taking the bus, a bus I'd been on with her many times, and just before she caught the one from Ault that would transport her and other students into Boston and leave them off at South Station, she stood facing me in the room. "Are you sure you don't want to come?" she said. "I promise I won't distract you."

"It's better for me to stay here," I said. "But tell your parents hi."

Martha looked at me. "You're okay, right? Nothing's wrong?"

"Go," I said and hugged her. "You'll miss the bus."

I was relieved as I watched the buses pull away. In the room alone, I lay on the futon, not reading, not sleeping, not even shutting my eyes, and I thought of Cross. I thought of him otherwise, of course, but it was while I was doing things, and when I tried to think of him at night, I usually fell asleep; but lying alone on the futon was almost like meditating. Everything that had happened between us, every comment he'd made, each way he'd touched me, I could now think about for longer than the thing had taken to occur.

For a while, I was glad it was getting dark, glad that campus was mostly empty—the only people who stayed around for long weekend were the ones who didn't get invited somewhere, or were too poor to travel, or both. There was a long weekend every term, and as a freshman, I'd stayed on campus for all three, though it was hard to remember how I'd spent them—reading magazines probably, and waiting for it to be time to go to a meal, and feeling isolated. But maybe this was the beginning of my luck, maybe from now on, I'd get what I wanted most, though I wasn't sure I'd ever want anything more than I wanted Cross.

He had been coming over for three weeks by then, and we'd almost had sex. A few nights before, we'd both had all our clothes off, and his penis had been jabbing at me not so it hurt but so it felt like something I wanted. I had opened my legs to him and neither of us had spoken because if we did, it could only be to acknowledge what was happening.

Finally, I said, "Do you—"

He was kissing my shoulder. He did not say anything but I could feel him listening.

The moment stretched. He propped himself up to look at me. My hands had been set on either side of his rib cage, but I became self-conscious and pulled my arms in, as if to block a ball from hitting my chest. He moved my arms, first one, then the other, and set them at my sides. I liked this about him, how he didn't let me get away with things. If it was like we were starting from the beginning every time, it wasn't that I was testing *him*. It was more like needing proof: *You want to be here; you want to touch me.* In these moments, when I was stiff or bashful, he'd say, "No shyness," and burrow into me, and shyness seemed such a generous word for it.

"Do I what?" he said. He was smiling.

What could I ever say to equal Cross's face above mine, Cross's smile? Down below, the stabbing was milder now, but both of us were still moving.

He settled back onto me and said, "You have the softest hair in the world," which was a compliment I loved. Because I couldn't control it, it seemed true, not like if I were wearing perfume and he said I smelled good.

He was nudging my legs further apart, starting to enter, and I felt the first flash of not actual pain but anticipatory pain. But I didn't know I was resisting until he said, "What?" Then he said, "It's cool," which I thought for a split second was his way of reassuring me that it was okay if I didn't want to go through with it. But that wasn't what he meant—he was still easing my legs open with his own.

"I just don't think—" I said, and then he stopped. It was good he stopped, and also a letdown. I wanted to say that I was sorry, but I knew I shouldn't. "It's not that I don't want to," I said.

"Does that mean you do want to?"

In a small voice, I said, "Yes."

"Then what's wrong?" He asked it softly, not accusingly.

I didn't say anything.

"Are you afraid it'll hurt?"

I sometimes wondered if Cross knew just how in-experienced I was; this question indicated that he did, or at least that he knew I was a virgin.

"I'll go really slow," he said.

"We don't even have a condom."

"I know you hear all this sex ed stuff, but I can pull out. I'll be careful."

It wasn't really because of not having a condom. But it was hard to say what it *was* because of. And it was hard to believe this moment was existing—that Cross was trying to persuade me to have sex and I was declining. It did not feel, as I might have imagined, satisfying; instead, it felt weird and precarious.

"We could do other stuff," I said.

He didn't reply. But the energy had changed, with that single comment. I'd been at the top of the teeter-totter, perched in the air, and then I'd thudded to the bottom; I was squatting on the ground, calling up to Cross.

"I want to make you feel good." I said, and I didn't even realize until the words were out that they were the same ones he'd uttered the first time he'd come to my room. If he had said, *Why?*—he'd have to have said it on purpose, a further echo of our earlier conversation—I'd have thought he was great. I'd have wanted us to watch bad movies together, to go bowling together, to eat too much and tell embarrassing stories. I'd have thought we had the same sense of humor, which—there was enough Cross gave me, more than enough; it's not a complaint—we didn't.

"I want to make you—" I couldn't say the word *come*.

"Come?" he said.

I was quiet. In all the times we'd hooked up—he visited every three nights or so, five times so far, and in the time between his visits I always convinced myself that the time before had been his last, he wouldn't be returning—he had never come. I had held his penis only once, and it had been another moment in which I'd had no idea what I was doing. All those years of reading women's magazines, and I couldn't even remember the fundamentals of a hand job—I had simply run my curled fingers up and down the length of it. I'd been lying on my side, and he'd begun rubbing my thigh and hip and then his fingers slid down and into me and it had seemed confusing (surely, this notion would strike other people as laughable), it had seemed chaotic even, for both activities to be happening at once. I'd wondered if he was trying to let me know he'd had enough of my hand. I let it fall away from him and rolled my body toward his, and he said, "You like to be close, don't you?" I was always yanking away the sleeping bag if it got wedged between us, or making sure we touched at all points if we were spooning. And it seemed like these were things he wanted, too, but the truth was that there was almost nothing about Cross or Cross with me that I knew for sure. I'd considered asking Martha about the fact that Cross had never come, but I feared that the explanation would reveal an inadequacy in me so humiliating that it was better not to share it even with her—wasn't it a joke how fast high school boys usually came? Also, I suspected that both Martha and Cross were people who'd disapprove of disclosing intimate details. If it would bother only one of them, I might have told Martha, but imagining the double force of their censure stopped me.

"What are you saying?" Cross asked.

I didn't reply, but I understood how now I had to go through with the thing I had not even been certain I was proposing until I had heard in his voice that that was what he took my proposal to be. I had to go through with it not because he would make me, not because he was *trying* to show me that I was testing his patience but because I actually was testing his patience. And anyway, I had been the one to bring it up.

"Here," I said, and I shifted so he'd shift, too. He rolled onto his back, and I got onto my knees and let my hair hang in front of my face —as if it might veil how my stomach looked from this angle—and scooted backward. It was very different to be naked above Hillary Tompkins's sleeping bag, out in the dark but not pitch-black air, than it was to be naked beneath it. I was straddling him above the knees. Then it was like when you had to do a presentation in class and you felt like you needed some official sign to begin, like a whistle in a race, but instead everyone was just waiting for you and the most official thing that would happen would be that you'd say *okay* a few times: "Okay. Okay, the French and Indian War, also known as the Seven Years' War, began in 1754 . . ."

I even said, "Okay." Then I crouched down, and as I did, I thought of how probably there were women who did this in daylight, their asses exposed, bobbing toward the ceiling, and how I would never, ever be one of them. I had hoped, without realizing I was anticipating such an event in my own life, that it would feel different from what it was: something bigger than you'd ever under normal circumstances put in your mouth going into your mouth. It seemed difficult to breathe. I didn't like it—I definitely didn't. But then, in its uncomfortableness, I felt a sort of nobility—a kinship with all the girls who'd done this before me for the boys they liked (I thought of Sophie Thruler, Cross's girlfriend from freshman year), an affection for myself for being willing to do it, an affection for Cross for being a person I would do it for. It made me feel like an adult, like drinking wine would later, before I liked the taste of it.

He set his hands on my shoulders, lightly, and occasionally, he'd reach for one of my breasts, he'd swipe it—I had not thought of him as guarded before, but he definitely was the most unguarded I'd ever seen him—and he was gasping and moaning in a ragged, sometimes high-pitched way that startled me. I wondered, did all boys make noises like this? And I felt glad that it was Cross, who could never disgust or offend me, whom I was first seeing this way. If it had been another boy who seemed less cool or less experienced, I might have judged him, chalking up such a reaction to his uncoolness or inexperience.

In the middle—until then, I'd been doing with my mouth pretty much what I'd done the other time with my hand, a steady up-and-down motion—I actually did remember a tip from a magazine: *Treat his penis like a delicious ice cream cone.* I slid my mouth off and began to lick the sides, nodding and turning my head. Less than a minute had passed when Cross shuddered once and then the hot milky liquid was all over my chest. If he'd come in my mouth, I would have swallowed it; I definitely would have. He reached for me, pulling me back up to him, and when I was lying against his chest, he petted my back, squeezed my ass and arms, kissed my forehead. He said, "That was a great blow job," and I felt prouder than if I'd gotten an A on a math test. Was it possible that I had a particular gift? If I did, it would be like with haircutting (except better) and the fact that I didn't find the act particularly enjoyable would be irrelevant. When you were really good at something, you just did it, because it was a waste not to. In the next second, of course, I wondered if Cross was only trying to make me feel good, but in the second after that, I thought that if he were, Cross trying to make me feel good was in itself a reason to be happy.

That episode had been earlier in the week. The first night of long weekend, while I was lying on the futon, the memory still felt bright and thick; I didn't sense yet how over the next few days I would return to it until it was frayed and diluted, a mental exercise rather than a physical interaction with another person.

It was completely dark—it had started getting dark at four-thirty—and it occurred to me just to go to sleep for the night, but then I'd probably awaken at eleven p.m., disoriented and hungry. I stood and turned on a light and pulled down the shades, and I felt the first ache of loneliness, the first inkling that staying on campus might have been a mistake. I turned on Martha's computer and clicked on my college essays folder and, inside that, the file titled "Brown app." Then I sat looking at the single, incomplete paragraph I'd written the week before: *My most unusual quality is that I am from the Midwest yet I have lived in New England for the last three years . . .* I wished that at that moment, instead of facing a computer screen, I was making out with Cross, and that he was reaching up my nightgown or inside my underwear.

For no particular reason, my back hurt, and I also was thirsty; I definitely wasn't in the mood to work on an essay. I shut the file and folder and put the screen to sleep; after dinner, possibly, I'd feel more inspired.

The only other seniors in the dining hall were Edmundo Saldana and Sin-Jun, and they were sitting at a table with a couple of juniors—three black boys (there were four black boys in the whole junior class) and Nicky Gary, a pale girl with strawberry blond hair who was rumored to be a born-again Christian, but the weirdest part was that her parents weren't even born-again; just she was, on her own. The boys were Niro Williams, Derek Miles, and Patrick Shaley. At other tables, there were slightly larger representations of sophomores and freshmen, and at a fourth table were the few teachers on campus for the weekend.

What surprised me as I looked around, what I had forgotten since freshman year, was how Ault on long weekend wasn't really Ault—it wasn't full and hurried, there weren't people I felt fascinated by and felt self-conscious in front of. Instead, it was cleared-out buildings. There was nothing that would surprise or entertain you over the next few days. (I used to fear, and I wasn't completely wrong, that this was what the rest of the world was like. Hardly ever did it matter if you brushed your hair before driving to the grocery store, rarely did you work in an office where you cared what more than two or three people thought of you. At Ault, caring about everything was draining, but it was also exhilarating.)

When I sat down, Niro and Patrick were talking animatedly about a video game, and no one else was talking about anything. Sin-Jun and I spoke briefly—she also was working on applications and had just decided to apply early to Stanford—but our conversation petered out quickly, and a few minutes later, before I was finished eating, she stood to leave. Sitting there with Edmundo and Nicky and the junior boys, I thought that I definitely should have gone to Burlington with Martha. I felt an old, unpleasant sensation of not mattering to anyone present, and it seemed difficult to believe the feeling could return so abruptly, though I couldn't have said where it was returning from. And then I realized how much my idea of myself had changed. Probably it had changed slowly, starting with Martha becoming my friend in the spring of ninth grade, and perhaps it hadn't changed again significantly until the previous May when she got elected prefect and I became the prefect's roommate. And it had shifted once more over the last few weeks, after I first kissed Cross. I felt—not cool, it was hard to imagine I'd ever feel cool, but I felt like a person I myself would have been intrigued by as a freshman or sophomore. Meaning, maybe, that a current freshman or sophomore could be intrigued by me. Except that I had never seen any evidence for such a possibility, and furthermore, intriguing people didn't stay at school for long weekend; at the very least, they went to Boston.

And then there was the fact that no one knew Cross and I were fooling around. Or officially they didn't, but I also became aware in this moment how much I'd been counting on the secret getting out, because at Ault, secrets always did. Cross's roommate Devin had to know, or maybe a girl in my dorm had been walking down the hall to the bathroom at just the moment around quarter of five in the morning, when Cross was leaving. (Cross had to be the one who leaked the information; I couldn't.) It wasn't that I'd been disingenuous when I'd asked Cross not to discuss what was happening. It was just that I'd assumed people would learn of the basic facts without explicit discussion.

The possibility existed that Niro and Patrick and Edmundo didn't care, of course, but it seemed likelier they didn't know. Because surely if they knew, they'd somehow show it, surely they would at least look at me for a beat longer when I sat down. After the first time Cross had come over, it had felt so uncertain, and I had imagined that if people caught wind of it, all they'd think was, *Her?* But it was lasting, it had become something Cross was choosing rather than something arbitrary. And this knowledge did not change the way I acted, but certainly it affected the place in the social order where I saw myself; now my regular behavior felt gracious and charming. I could have let Cross's interest in me go to my head, but look—I was as humble as ever. I didn't suddenly sit next to Aspeth Montgomery in chapel, or expect to be invited to Greenwich with her.

"Can you pass the ketchup?" Derek Miles asked.

I blinked at him.

"It's right there," he said.

I handed him the bottle. He had no idea. It definitely wasn't school-wide news, so the only remaining question was whether it was news at any level—senior news, news among Cross's circle of friends. Did Aspeth Montgomery know? If she didn't, nobody did. And, no, I thought, she didn't. She didn't because if she did, she'd tell Dede, and if Dede knew, she'd confront me; she wouldn't be able to stop herself.

When I walked back to the dorm, the only light was the one I'd left on in my room. I slept twelve hours that night and did the same for the next two nights, waiting for Cross to come back. On Sunday, Mrs. Parnasset drove a van to the Westmoor mall and left it there for the afternoon. Sin-Jun and I went to a movie about a suburban family whose young son died, and everything about the movie reminded me of Cross, or, more accurately, made me think of him and then keep thinking of things about him that had nothing to do with the movie at all. Sunday dinner was cold cuts; the temperature that night fell below freezing for the first time since the previous winter. Then it was Monday again; Cross, and everyone else, returned to school.

We had sex a few days later because it was inevitable, because now that he was back on campus, I wanted everything and all of him, because I loved him, because I was afraid of losing him, because it felt good or at least because everything up to that point had felt good and it was what came next. The reality, of course, was that the pain made me clutch his arms just below the elbows and arch my head until the crown of it was pressed against the mattress. I was surprised he didn't offer to stop, but maybe it was good because if he had, I'd have accepted the offer, and I'd just have been postponing the pain. He had brought a condom, and afterward, he went into the bathroom and got wet paper towels to wipe the blood off my thighs. The paper towels were warm, and I thought how at the sinks in Elwyn's, the hot water always took so long to come out and how he must have waited for it.

Both of us were sweaty and then, as we lay there, clammy; Hillary's sleeping bag was plaid cotton, not one of those nylon ones that's supposed to wick away moisture. But our clamminess didn't really matter, or my belly against his hip—things that I might once have been self-conscious about, I no longer was. At least in the dark, there wasn't much I felt like I was hiding from him anymore. It was as if for my entire time at Ault up to this moment I'd been in a frenzy, a storm of worry, and now it was all finished and I felt only a profound calm; it was hard to believe the sensation would not be permanent. Actual sex wasn't as different from more casual fooling around as I'd imagined, but it wasn't exactly the same, either—afterward, you felt like something had finished instead of just tapering off. And now with every reference in magazines or movies or conversations, I could nod, or at least, when listening to other people, I wouldn't have to avert my eyes lest they look into them and see that I didn't really understand. I could disagree, even if I never did so aloud.

379

He stroked my hair, and there was nothing I wanted to say or wanted him to say; there was nothing I wanted except for this: The soreness made me unsure how soon I'd be able to have sex again, but it wasn't a bad soreness. It was like after hiking, because of a thing you were glad to have done. Two days later, I picked up my first packet of birth control pills from the infirmary, which made me feel so unlike myself that I would not have been surprised, when I looked in the mirror, to see a forty-year-old divorced mother of two, a cowgirl, an aerobics instructor on a cruise ship in the Caribbean. The real part was being in bed with Cross.

Before and after I was involved with Cross Sugarman, I heard a thousand times that a boy, or a man, can't make you happy, that you have to be happy on your own before you can be happy with another person. All I can say is, I wish it were true.

In November, I began attending his basketball games; he never came over the night before a game. I sat high up in the bleachers, often next to Rufina, who went because Nick Chafee played, too. The Saturday night games were crowded—I'd get Martha to go with me to those—but during the afternoon ones, other students had their own games, so most of the spectators were parents who lived nearby, random teachers, or JV players. The reason I was free to go was that all seniors got one sports cut and I was taking mine that winter. The strangest part was that I had actually played basketball myself for the last three years, but when I watched Cross, it was like a new game; it was almost like sports were new to me, and I could understand for the first time in my life why people liked them.

For home games, they wore white uniforms with maroon trim; Cross, who played center, was number six. He wore black high-tops, and his legs were long in the long white shorts, his arms pale and muscular in the jersey.

During my own basketball games, I had always, I realized,

been half-asleep, paying attention less to the other team than to whether my shorts were riding up, or whether the chicken nuggets from lunch were churning in my stomach. But during Cross's games, I was alert to the sport itself: the squeak of the players' shoes, the refs' whistles, the way the players and coaches would protest after calls they didn't like. At the Saturday night games, the people in the bleachers around me would chant: "Let's go, Ault!" or, if Cross was running the ball down the court, they'd say "Sug! Sug! Sug!" I never cheered at all—under the bright lights, among the excited crowd, I always felt tense and slightly nauseated—and at first I was amazed by how much everyone seemed to care. Or maybe, by how little they concealed that they cared.

And then I realized that here, in sports, it was okay to show that something mattered to you. Maybe because it didn't actually matter, it was okay to invest yourself—investing yourself was almost ironic—but then you really had invested yourself and you really did care yet it was still okay. They'd get angry—I once saw Niro Williams get a technical foul for setting the ball against the court and walking away instead of passing it to the ref—and it was okay to be disappointed and it was okay to try. You could grunt or trip, you could twist your body and make fierce expressions when you were trying to rip the ball from someone else's hands and all of it—it was fine. When they played Hartwell, Ault's rival, the teams were within a couple points of each other the whole game, and then Hartwell got eight points in the last minute and a half. When the buzzer sounded, I looked at Cross and was astonished to see that he was crying. I looked away reflexively, then looked back; his face was scrunched-up and red, and he was roughly wiping his eyes and shaking his head, but he wasn't dashing to the locker room or otherwise trying to hide it. Darden Pittard stood in front of him, and then Niro joined them, and Darden was talking—it looked like he was saying something nice—with his hand set on Cross's upper arm.

381

Sports contained the truth, I decided, the unspoken truth (how quickly we damn ourselves when we start to talk, how small and inglorious, we always sound), and it seemed hard to believe that I had never understood this before. They rewarded effortlessness and unselfconsciousness; they confirmed that yes, there are rankings of skill and value and that everyone knows what they are (seeing those guys who were subbed with two seconds left before the end of a quarter, I'd think how girls' coaches were never that heartless); they showed that the best things in the world to be were young and strong and fast. To play a great game of high school basketball—it was something I myself had never done, but I could tell—made you know what it was to be alive. How much in an adult life can compare to that? Granted, there are margaritas, or there's no homework, but there are also puffy white bagels under neon lights in the conference room, there's waiting for the plumber, making small talk with your boring neighbor.

Once, also in the fourth quarter of a close game, Cross made a shot from behind the three-point line, and when the ball went through the net, his teammates surrounded him, patting his ass, holding up their hands for him to slap. No one in the bleachers glanced at me like they did at Rufina when Nick scored (even teachers glanced at her; I'm not sure they knew they were doing it). Cross didn't belong to me, and seeing him on the court, I understood that even if he'd been my boyfriend, he still wouldn't have belonged to me.

I don't know if Cross himself realized I went to his games. I didn't mention it because I feared it would seem like a violation of our agreement, either clingy or just too public. And he never talked about the games, though if they'd won and if he came over (he never came over when they lost and only sometimes came over when they won), he was pushier than usual, the way you're led to believe guys are when you're eleven years old—that they'll pull at your clothes and grope you and mash against you. But the fact was that I always wanted to be mashed and groped. Later on, when I tried to imagine how I might have ruined things, that would occur to me—that I'd so rarely resisted, that I hadn't made it hard enough for him. Maybe he felt disappointed. Maybe it was like gathering your strength and hurling your body against a door you believe to be locked, and then the door opens easily—it wasn't locked at all—and you're standing looking into the room, trying to remember what it was you thought you wanted.

As a freshman, I had gone home for Thanksgiving, but never after that—only three weeks elapsed between Thanksgiving break and Christmas break and the plane fares were high. ("We love you," my father said once, "but not that much.") At Martha's house for Thanksgiving, as in other years, we stayed up late watching movies, woke at eleven a.m., and ate pumpkin pie for breakfast. On the twin beds in her room were two-hundred-count percale white sheets and white duvets that I always worried about getting a pen mark on, and in the cupboards and closets were extra of everything—towels and toilet paper and boxes of cereal; there was even a whole extra refrigerator in the basement. I often wondered, while visiting the Porters' house, if my exposure to their way of living would be fleeting or if one day I would live in a house as nice as this, if it would be as easy for me to be generous to other people as it seemed for them to be generous to me. It actually appeared true that it didn't matter if Mrs. Porter had to make an extra serving of lobster bisque because I was there, or if they had to buy an extra ticket to the choral performance at their church (that I would pay for my own ticket, let alone for my own portion of lobster bisque, was not a possibility anyone considered). There were other kids at Ault I had a feeling about, kids who came from poorer families than I did and would probably grow up to make a lot more than I would—they'd be surgeons, or investment bankers. But making a lot of money didn't seem like something I'd be able to control;

383

I'd gotten as far as Ault, but I wasn't sure I'd get any further. I wasn't smart or disciplined the way those kids were, I wasn't *driven*. Presumably, I'd always be aware of lives like these without living one; I couldn't confuse familiarity with entitlement.

On Thanksgiving itself, Martha's cousins came over, and Ellie, who was eight and inexplicably fond of me, squatted behind me on the couch, braiding my hair. When that got boring, she took grapes from the cheese platter and tried to persuade me to open my mouth so she could throw them in, and I actually did a few times, when the adults and Martha and Martha's brother weren't looking; I liked Ellie because she reminded me of my own brothers. Mr. Porter carved the turkey wearing an apron that said *Kiss the cook*, though as far as I could tell, Mrs. Porter and her sister had been the ones to prepare everything. Then we all ate too much; after dessert, I started eating mashed potatoes again and, uncharacter-istically, so did Martha.

It was a good Thanksgiving; I felt lucky to know Martha's family, to be Martha's roommate. But under all of it, still, all the time, I thought of Cross.

Martha's acceptance from Dartmouth came on December fourteenth and I made her a sign and when people congratu-lated her, she acted much the way she had when she'd been elected prefect: slightly embarrassed, as if what they had just said instead of congratulations was that they'd seen her taking out the trash that morning in her bathrobe. The next day Cross got into Harvard, and when he came over two nights after that, his reaction to his college acceptance was detached politeness. When I congratulated him and he said "Thanks"—that, in fact, was *all* he said—I felt how I was not a person with whom he'd discuss something as ordinary and personal as college. What kind of roommates he'd end up with, what he'd major in, whether he'd have a shot at playing basketball there—it was likelier that he'd talk to Martha than to me about such topics. The things he did tell me were self-contained and anecdotal: that as a three-year-old, he'd flunked the entrance exam at a private school because he said that an elephant had five legs (he'd thought the trunk counted); that when he was eleven, he'd gone trick-or-treating in his building in New York and a woman on the first floor had answered the door in a black teddy and high heels (she hadn't even had any candy, so she'd given him and his friend an open bag of Oreos). These stories made me feel protective and adoring and also far away from him.

Ault's service of lessons and carols was the night before Christmas vacation started, and Cross and Martha were two of the three Wise Men. The senior prefects always played the Wise Men, and then a third senior, an outstanding senior, was selected to join them; to no one's surprise, this year it was Darden Pittard. When everyone stood to sing "We Three Kings" the three of them walked down the aisle of chapel wearing robes and crowns, bearing their gifts (Martha had been assigned the frankincense). Later that night, when Cross and I were lying in Hillary Tompkins's bed, I said to him, "You looked handsome in your crown." This was not the sort of thing I usually said, but we wouldn't see each other for two weeks, and I was pretty sure I could get away with it. We had already had sex twice that night, and there was between us that air of extra generosity and affection that arises when you're about to be apart. "I bet you didn't know I'm an actor, too," I said. "In fourth grade, my class put on this play about Christopher Columbus coming to America, and I was the star."

"You were Queen Isabella?"

"No!" I punched his shoulder, "I was Columbus."

"Really?"

"Why is that so hard to believe? I was good. I wore pantaloons."

"I'm sure you were good." Cross said. "I just thought a boy would play Columbus." He pressed his lips against my ear. "But your pantaloons sound very sexy."

Later, I remembered this as our best night. Not because it was remarkable but because of its unremarkability—for all the ways it wasn't fraught and loaded, for how we got to have sex but also, sort of, we got to be friends.

The next day classes ended at noon, and I boarded the bus to Logan in front of Mr. Byden's house. As the bus pulled away, I looked out the window and thought, *No, no, no.*

At the airport, in line to check my bag, I felt more aware of myself as a prep school student than I did at any other time. My age, my clothes, the books in my backpack, probably even my posture—these all were markers, signifiers of my membership in a subculture I felt I belonged to only when I was away from it. When I was through the line, I walked to the bathroom, passing the terminal's long wall of paned mirrors, my reflection a cubed giant wearing my clothes.

What I usually did next was get ice cream and eat it standing in front of a magazine rack, reading, and then just before my plane boarded, I'd buy one magazine—an especially fat issue, which I'd purposely not have read in the store. There'd be other Ault kids in the terminal, of course, and if we passed, we acknowledged one another, usually without speaking, but I didn't hang out with them. As a freshman. I'd been too intimidated—a bunch of students always sat in the back of a restaurant that sold clam chowder and doughnuts, smoking and talking noisily—and now that I was older, I was still intimidated, at least by the smokers, but I also wasn't particularly interested; I *liked* eating ice cream and reading magazines by myself.

But I had gotten no farther than the entrance to the ice cream shop when I felt a tap on my shoulder. I turned.

"When's your flight?" It was Horton Kinnelly, Aspeth's roommate, who was from Biloxi. "You should come back with us." She nodded her head toward the doughnut and clam chowder restaurant. Over the entrance, I noticed for the first time that neon orange lettering spelled out the words *Hot n' Snacks.*

"That's okay," I said before remembering myself—Horton looked at me, but we both pretended I hadn't tried to decline the invitation—and adding, "Okay, sure. You're just in there?"

She nodded. "Me and Caitlin and Pete Birney and some other people. Have you ever talked to Pete Birney? He's totally cracking me up."

"I'll come over in a second."

As soon as she'd walked away and I'd stepped into the ice cream shop, I realized that I wasn't buying anything. Because then what—I'd sit there eating in front of them? Or I'd shove it down beforehand? And what did Horton want with me anyway? Over the years, my path had crossed Aspeth's many times, but it had virtually never crossed Horton's.

I entered Hot n' Snacks and saw them sitting, as I'd known they'd be, in the back—not just Horton and Caitlin Fain and Pete Birney but two or three other Ault students, laughing in a haze of smoke. I approached their cluster of chairs, which surrounded two small tables pushed together. Simultaneously, everyone looked up at me. "Hey, Lee," Horton said, and I thought she'd find a chair for me—being Horton, she was the hostess—but then she turned back to Pete. I carried a chair from another table and set it down between Suzanne Briegre, a junior girl with long straight black hair, and Ferdy Chotin, also a junior, who still had braces but was nationally ranked in tennis. They both did something more than nod and less than smile. Everyone was discussing a woman in a movie who had worn cowboy boots and a cowboy hat and nothing else. (Listening to the conversation, I thought, was that what Cross wanted, a girl in cowboy boots and a cowboy hat? Her skin would be taut and tan, and she would never be confused about the mechanics of a blow job. A nervous chant started in my head: What was he doing with me, what was he doing with me, why were we together?)

Meanwhile, I was observing my schoolmates with a kind of awe, how they had so many sets of behavior in their repertoire. On campus, they attended chapel and turned in papers; here, they lit cigarettes and acted irreverent. And it wasn't even like all of them were cool, not definitively cool like Horton was. I knew for a fact that Caitlin planned not to have sex before marriage, but here she was, hanging out, casually violating a school rule, showing another side of herself, when I was always me. I didn't have the impulse, just because I could get away with it, to act any differently at the airport than I did at Ault. And the only time I'd ever smoked was sophomore year at Martha's house, when we decided to smoke one cigarette each, but Martha stubbed hers out after two puffs, proclaiming it disgusting; I'd kept going, but only for practice. I'd been practicing, I saw now, for a situation like this. But the practice had been a long time ago and incomplete and I wouldn't take a cigarette if it was offered to me because in the daylight, in front of classmates I hardly knew, it would be almost as bad as kissing in public.

"She wasn't a brunette," Horton was saying. "Her hair was bleached blond." They were still talking about the woman in cowboy boots and a cowboy hat.

"Not all of it,' Ferdy said slowly, grinning.

"Horton,' Pete said—Pete was a junior who'd won Assassin the year before—and when Horton looked at him, Pete tapped his temple. "We're not talking about up here."

Horton looked at Pete for a second, then made an expression of distaste. "You're a foul man, Mr. Birney," she said, and the guys started laughing.

"We're just kidding," Pete said. "Don't be pissed. Are you pissed?"

Horton glared at him without saying anything, then finally, in a small voice, she said, "Maybe."

"Maybe!" Pete exclaimed, and I almost thought he liked Horton, but it might have been just more of his repertoire—that he could flirt enthusiastically with her when they were in the same place, but that he'd have shown no less enthusiasm with another pretty girl. They started talking just to each other, and I wished I were eating ice cream alone and wondered if I'd been sitting there long enough that I could leave without attracting attention.

At that moment, Horton leaned across the table, extending a pack of cigarettes. "Want one?"

I shook my head. "No, thanks."

"Because of your parents?" Horton said. She had stuck a cigarette in her own mouth and held a pink plastic lighter to the tip of it. The lighter looked both cheap and cool in its cheapness. But how had Horton known that? What made it not simply tacky? "I always tell my parents the restaurant was so full that I had no choice but to sit in the smoking section," she said.

"Or," Suzanne said, perking up, "you say that your friends were smoking but you weren't. Then it's like you're being honest by telling on your friends."

I smiled weakly.

"Horton," Pete said. "If you give me the one you just lit, I'll light you another one."

"Okay, *that* makes a lot of sense."

"No, it does. Here's why—"

I stopped listening to them. He wanted his mouth to touch where her mouth had touched. He wanted them to be passing something between them, fingers grazing, leaning into each other. In some ways, boys were easier to read than other girls—with boys, it was pursuit and lust, it was effort. With so many girls, it just seemed to be about receiving, or not receiving, rather than trying. It was saying *yes* or *no*, but not *please*, not *come on, just this once*.

I had been at the table less than ten minutes then, and I waited fifteen more before I stood to leave—to catch my plane, I said. Everyone wished me Merry Christmas, and I waited to see if Horton had anything to say, but she didn't; it appeared I had been summoned, I had been sanctioned by her, for no particular reason. Or I had been summoned for a particular reason that no one would ever articulate—because now I was linked to Cross. There were a lot of moments I could point to that indicated that no one knew; that afternoon in the airport, Horton's invitation to join her table, was one of the few times I thought maybe everyone did.

In the enclosed space of the car, riding from the airport to our house, I thought that surely my mother could sense the difference in me—not necessarily that I'd had sex, but something in that direction. But if she were to ask, I'd tell her nothing. I had never been a girl who confided much in her mother, mostly because my mother had never seemed altogether certain what to do with the information I did share. "Mary McShay kissed a fourteen-year-old boy at the Y this summer," I told my mother on the first day of sixth grade.

"Did she?"' my mother asked mildly. "Fourteen sounds a bit old." But that was all she said—she didn't want to know more about the boy, or the nature of the kiss (it had indeed involved tongue), or whether I had plans to kiss fourteen-year-old boys myself. I think it was a mixture of my mother's shyness and her distraction, though the things that distracted her were always motherly, like the fact that she needed to take the lasagna out of the oven; it wasn't as if her mind was consumed with matters unrelated to our family. Basically, I didn't consider my mother to be much of a resource, not like Kelli Robard's mother, who listened to the same radio station we did and knew brands of clothing and the names of the cute boys in sixth grade. My mother was a benevolent but uninformed presence. In fourth grade, when I'd asked her what a hunk was, she'd said sincerely, "It's a big piece of cheese."

And yet she regularly surprised me by what she did know, or at least intuited, but would not comment on unless pressed. My mother was in many ways what I aspired to be— someone who didn't spill and opine, not because she successfully stifled her urges to do so but because she didn't have those urges in the first place.

In the car, she said, "I'm so happy to have you safely home. Dad called to say there was weather on the East Coast, and I'm sure glad you weren't delayed." The highway and my parents' Datsun and my mother herself all looked exactly as they had in early September, when I'd left. This was both reassuring and disorienting—the sameness seemed at times to cancel out Ault, or make it seem like something I had dreamed. "How did things end up with math?" my mother asked.

"I didn't know everything on the final, but I'll probably get a B minus for the term."

"Honey, that's fantastic."

"Or maybe a C plus."

"I know you're working so hard."

The observation felt untrue, but I didn't correct her.

"Last night I made cookies for Tim and Joe to take to their teachers, and I tripled the recipe and just made a mess of things. I thought, well, that's where Lee gets it. It wouldn't be fair to expect you to have a head for numbers when I don't."

"I assume we're going to the Pauleczks' for Christmas Eve."

"Lee, we are and I know you don't like to, but—"

"No, it's fine."

"Well, honey, Mr. Pauleczk has been such a supporter of Dad's, and I just think it's important—"

"Mom, I said it's fine." The Pauleczks were in their sixties, and Mr. Pauleczk owned a bunch of motels between South Bend and Gary and had always bought the mattresses for them from my father. For years, we'd gone to their house before midnight mass, for dessert and hot drinks, but neither Joseph nor I had eaten or drunk anything since my sophomore year, when I'd found a long gray hair in a slice of chocolate cherry cake, (Joseph was fourteen, just three years younger than I was, but Tim still ate at the Pauleczks' because he was only seven and didn't know better.) After that, just the smell of the Pauleczks' house made me feel like gagging, Mrs. Pauleczk always asked if Ault was a Catholic school, and when I told her it wasn't, she'd say, "Episcopal?" then turn to my mother. "Lee's school is Episcopal, Linda?" Her tone would imply that perhaps I'd concealed this dirty secret from my parents until Janice Pauleczk herself had set things straight. My mother in her mild, laughing way always said something like "They have Lee going to church six days a week up there. You can't do much better than that!"

But this year—really, who cared what Janice Pauleczk thought? And how big a deal would it be to sit for a few hours in their living room? Now I had happiness somewhere else. Cross kissed me at night, and that made tolerable all the parts of my life that had nothing to do with him. It occurred to me that I'd probably been a lot crankier before Cross, I'd been so much more dissatisfied. If you knew where your happiness came from, it gave you patience. You realized that a lot of the time, you were just waiting out a situation, and that took the pressure off; you no longer looked to every interaction to actually do something for you. And wanting less, you were more generous—definitely, this Christmas, I planned to be more generous with everyone I saw in South Bend and especially with my family.

We were passing the Kroger near our house, the dry cleaner's and movie rental place. This, also, always happened in South Bend—I was struck by how homely it was, how accustomed I'd become to Ault's bricks and flagstones and Gothic tower, its marble mantels and blond-haired girls. Outside of Ault, people were fat, or wore brown ties, or seemed to be in bad moods.

We pulled into the driveway, and I saw from the car that my mother had attached a sign to the storm door, the sign partly blocking the wreath that hung on the real door: *Welcome home for Xmas, Lee!* In the corners of the sign, she'd drawn sprigs of holly. "That's so cute," I said.

"You know I'm not much of an artist. I asked Joe to make one for you, but he went over to Danny's so that's what yours truly came up with."

"You're the next Leonardo da Vinci."

"More like the next Leonardo da Nobody."

And I felt it then, in the ordinariness of our words—a kind of rising pressure that would, surely, result in an explosion if we did not open the car doors. She knew I'd had sex. She also knew: It had been with someone who didn't love me. My mother wasn't mad, but she thought that I deserved better. Oh, sure, Ault was a fancy place and I'd always been impressed by it, but didn't I understand that I was special, too? I'm not that special, Mom, I said, and she said, *Yes, you are, Lee. You might not see it, but I do*. We weren't actually speaking, we weren't even looking at each other as we climbed from the car and I retrieved my suitcase from the back seat, and then we were speaking, but it was to debate whether I needed help carrying the suitcase into the house, and the debate lasted several seconds longer than the time it would have taken to walk from the car to the front door. "I don't want you hurting yourself," she said, and I replied, "I'm strong."

Once the moment was over, I might have decided that I'd been making up our exchange except that that night, after I'd already said good night to her—my brothers and I kissed our parents on the cheek every night before bed—she returned to my room. She was wearing her red terrycloth robe over her nightshirt (for as long as I could remember, she'd worn a gray Notre Dame nightshirt that came down to her shins; unlike my father, she had no particular fondness for sports, so either he'd given it to her or she'd found it on sale at the mall) and she was carrying a single roll of toilet paper, I think to take to the downstairs bathroom. She stood in the door to my room and said, "Did you bring home your nice shoes?"

"Yeah, of course."

She continued to stand there. "You would know how to use a rubber, wouldn't you, Lee?"

"What are you talking about?"

"A condom—I guess that's what everyone calls it now."

"My God, Mom."

"They've taught you is all I'm asking."

"Yes," I said. By they, she must have meant Ault, did Ault teach sex ed? Which they did, in a series of four nighttime meetings that occurred in the winter of your sophomore year. The meetings were called Human Health, or H.H., which most people pronounced in two heavy breaths. I had gone out of my way never to pronounce it at all, so as not to embarrass myself either by panting in front of other people or by looking like a spoilsport for not panting in front of other people. Neither of my parents, meanwhile, had ever provided any real sex education except that once, when I was ten and they'd had friends over for dinner—perhaps the friends had remarked on how boys would soon be after me—my father had roared, "She's staying a virgin until she's thirty! No ifs, ands, or buts about it. And, Lee, don't let anyone tell you oral sex isn't sex."

"Terry!" my mother had said, but I think she'd felt constricted on behalf of the guests more than on my behalf. Neither of my parents had seemed to imagine that I knew what either virgins or oral sex were.

Standing in the doorway of my room, clutching the toilet paper, my mother said, "You know I'm not accusing you of anything."

I just wanted her to leave. Her talking about it in her ratty robe—it made sex seem, frankly, disgusting. And not even intriguingly disgusting, just disgusting in a daily way, the way of the household. It was like the smell of someone else's shit lingering in the bathroom while you brushed your teeth.

"I trust you, Lee," my mother said.

"Mom, I get the point."

"But I'm not stupid. I know things are different than when I was your age."

If I spoke, I would say something like, *Good for you*.

"Just be careful," she said, then paused, then added, "if you decide to share yourself." (My mother was so awkward! How had it taken me until this moment to realize just

394

how awkward she was?) "That's all I'm trying to say, honey."

"Okay, Mom."

"Let me tell you good night again," my mother said, and she stepped into the room to kiss me.

When she was gone, I could breathe, I could think a thought without trying to insulate her from it, and I also knew that it had been unfair of me to have acted like what she was saying was strange and off-target. And that she was a mother who would go along with such a charade, instead of calling me on it—that made my own behavior worse. Or maybe she'd wanted to pretend, too. Maybe she didn't want to know, she'd have been as horrified as I would have if suddenly I'd started describing Cross. Really, we did not share a vocabulary that would allow for such a conversation; it was far too late to tell her anything.

When I went down to the kitchen on the morning of the twenty-fourth, Joseph said, as I poured my cereal, "Remember to save room for Chez Hairball tonight," and my mother said, "That was years ago."

"Hey, Linda," my father said.

She looked at him. "What?"

"Have yourself a hairy, hairy Christmas," my father said.

At midnight mass, because it was midnight, because the church smelled like incense and the carols reminded me of being younger, because outside it was cold and dark, I wished that Cross were in the pew next to me so we could hold hands or I could lean against him. I wouldn't have grabbed him in an obvious way anyone else might notice; I just wanted him to be there, so I could feel sure of him. I pictured Cross with his brother and sister and parents in Manhattan—his family was probably the kind that had a tree with only white lights and glass ornaments—and how all of them probably drank scotch together and gave one another not tube socks and plastic key chains but leather wallets and silk ties.

Then Christmas passed, New Year's passed. I had no

friends left in South Bend and stayed at home with Tim eating pizza and watching movies he'd selected. Joseph was going out with his friends, and my parents went every year to a party across the street. Before they left, my mother exclaimed festively, "Get pepperoni on it!" which was one of her comments that sort of seemed funny and sort of made me want to cry—my mother's sense of what was extravagant and celebratory, her attention to whether I was celebrating, her kindness to me. Then, finally, it was the night before I was supposed to go back to Ault; to me, that had been the real countdown.

It was a Saturday and a girl in Joseph's class was having a fifteenth-birthday party at a roller-skating rink. At ten o'clock I went with my father to get Joseph, because my father had asked if I wanted to and though normally I'd have said no, I was leaving in less than twenty-four hours., And besides, hadn't I planned to be more generous this vacation?

The rink was twenty minutes from our house. My father pulled up to the entrance of the wide, low building. The parking lot was enormous and half-empty, and a few boys loitered in front of the glass doors, wearing hats but not coats.

"You see him?" my father asked. Before I could answer, he said, "Dammit," and stuck the car into park without either moving it from in front of the entrance or turning off the engine. "I told him to be waiting."

"I'll get him," I said. If our father went to retrieve Joseph, the mortifying part would be our father's tone more than what he said, his grumpiness, and how you'd sense that other kids felt sorry for you because you had a father who sounded mean; how could they understand that what he really was, was a father who didn't care how he sounded? Which was a form of meanness, but far from the most extreme kind.

Inside, it was dark, with a disco ball flickering over the rink proper. I stood at the edge, watching people sail past, and at first I didn't see Joseph. Then I turned and spotted him on a bench tying up his regular shoes, another boy next to him. I walked over. "Hurry up. Dad's waiting."

"He said ten-fifteen."

"It is ten-fifteen. It's after ten-fifteen."

"And what does it look like I'm doing? Don't be such a bitch."

"Fuck you," I said, and when the other boy's eyes widened, I wondered if I seemed like our father. But Joseph and I were peers, it wasn't like I was bullying him—this was just standard bickering.

Joseph turned to his friend. "You need a ride?"

"Nah, I'm going to Matt's."

"All right. See you later, man."

When we were out of earshot of the other boy, I said, "You definitely wouldn't have offered him a ride if you knew what a bad mood Dad is in. Where does that kid live?"

"In Larkwood."

"That's twenty minutes from our house."

"First of all, it's ten minutes, which I'm not surprised you don't know because you don't even live here. And second, the Petrashes drive me everywhere. We owe their family big-time."

"We owe their family big-time?" I repeated. "Have you been watching Mafia movies?"

We were outside, and I was a stride behind him, which was why he reached the car first, and how he opened the door to the front seat.

"You're not sitting there," I said.

"Oh, really?" He slid in. "Hi, Dad," I heard him say. "Sorry I'm running late."

I knocked on his window, and he glared at me and mouthed, *Get in back.*

I shook my head.

He unrolled the window. "Dad says get in back," he said. "You're acting like an idiot."

Briefly, I considered the feasibility of walking away, calling a taxi, and asking the driver to go directly to the airport. But it actually wasn't feasible at all, I didn't have my wallet, or my plane ticket, or the clothes and books I needed to take back to Ault. I opened the back door and got in, and I was stiff with fury.

"Trouble with the lock back there?" my father said. His tone was cheerfully sarcastic, his bad mood apparently having vanished.

"Joseph should not be sitting in front," I said.

"It's fair this way," Joseph said without turning around. "You were in front on the way out."

"Yeah, exactly. The way out to get you, you dickhead."

"Oh, did Dad need help steering? I bet you helped him a lot. You're a really good driver from what I hear." He laughed—the joke being that though I'd turned seventeen the previous June, I still didn't have my license—and my father laughed, too.

"Tell you what, Flea," my father said. "When we get home, I'll park, Joseph and I will go inside, and you can sit in front for as long as you like."

They laughed uproariously then, and I hated them. I hated them because they thought I was someone to mock and insult, because of the way they brought out the worst in me and it felt so familiar, it felt like the truth—it made my life at Ault seem like pretense. *This* was what I was, fundamentally: a petty, angry, impotent person. Why did I even care who sat in front?

I didn't speak for the rest of the ride, and they chatted about the birthday party—Joseph disclosed far more information to our parents than I ever had—then the conversation segued into the basketball team at the rival high school to Joseph's. All the names they mentioned belonged to kids I no longer knew, or hadn't known to begin with. About half-way through the ride, my father looked in the rearview mirror, made eye contact with me—I averted my gaze immediately— and said, "I must say, Joseph, I've never found your sister's contributions to the conversation so fascinating." They both laughed, Joseph especially.

At home, I stepped out of the car while the engine was still running, slammed the door, and walked into the house. In my room, I removed my coat and climbed into bed with my clothes still on, without brushing my teeth or washing my face, and I cried hot tears of rage that resulted not in that high gulping but in sustained periods of silence marked by thick hissing outbursts. My mother knocked perhaps fifteen minutes later, murmuring my name, and when I pretended to be asleep, she opened the door but did not enter the room. But she said, "Good night, honey," so maybe she knew I was faking.

Of course I'd turned out like I had—being part of this family, you were always about to be made fun of, someone's mood (my father's mood) was always about to change, and there was no situation you could trust or settle into. Their mockery was both casual and slamming, and it could be about anything. So no wonder—no wonder I never wanted Cross to see me naked.

I hated them because they thought I was the same as they were, because if they were right, it would mean I'd failed myself, and because if they were wrong, it would mean I had betrayed them.

Probably I had started thinking seriously about the Valentine's flowers months before—even as a sophomore and junior, I'd wondered each year if there was any chance, if there was the remotest of possibilities, that Cross would send me one, and apparently there never had been—but after we got back from winter break, I was fixated.

Every year, accompanied by notes, I received one pink carnation (friendship) from Sin-Jun and one white carnation (secret admirer) from Martha, whose note would say, in her undisguised handwriting, something like, *From your red hot mystery man*. As a sophomore, I'd also gotten a pink one from

Dede, which immediately made me wish I'd sent one to her, and I'd gotten a pink one from my adviser Ms. Prosek, who was one of the few faculty members who participated in the exchange; a lot of them openly disapproved of it. I had never gotten a rose, which stood, of course, for love, and cost three dollars to the carnation's dollar-fifty. The exchange was a fund-raiser, organized by ASC, the Ault Social Committee, a club overseen every year by pretty junior girls who planned the dances and ran spring carnival. And therein existed the flower exchange's most predictably flawed and titillating aspect: Whoever you sent a flower to, whatever message you wrote on your note, the ASC girls saw it. They processed all the forms, and it was only natural that the closer the giver or receiver of a particular flower was to their social nucleus, the greater the interest that flower held for them. There was, therefore, nothing truly secret about sending a secret admirer carnation.

Around midnight, as February 13 became February 14, ASC members (they had special permission to be out after curfew, they had work to do!) delivered the flowers to each dorm in large brown buckets, the flowers giving off cold air like the food in the refrigerated section of a grocery store, the notes stapled around the stems but never stapled in such a way that someone for whom the note was not intended couldn't still open it and read a good chunk of the contents. The idea was that you'd have flowers awaiting you in the morning; the reality was that in most dorms, the flowers were pawed through by twelve-fifteen. Usually, they were pawed through by someone like Dede, a person unsure how many flowers she'd get and unable to conceal this anxiety. A person like Aspeth, on the other hand, could stroll into the common room just before chapel the next morning to pick up her bounty, and it would be impossible to say whether she'd waited so long because she wanted everyone to see how many she'd received or because it really wasn't that big a deal to her. My freshman year, Aspeth had received—I feared these figures would remain with me long after I'd forgotten the date of the Battle of Waterloo or the boiling point of mercury—six pink carnations, eleven white carnations, and sixteen red roses, twelve of which were from a sophomore named Andy Kreeger, who had never before spoken to Aspeth.

By early February of my senior year, I was giving so much thought to the flower exchange that when the form showed up in my mailbox, it was surprising that it had arrived at a moment when, in fact, the flower exchange was *not* foremost in my mind. Once the form was in my possession, it felt immediately incriminating, as if, instead of being the generic form given to everyone, it was one I'd already filled out. I quickly stuffed it in my backpack.

In the room that night, Martha said, "I swear it feels like I was just doing this for last year. Doesn't it feel like that?"

"I guess so," I said. I paused. "Do you think I should send one to Cross?"

"If you want."

I was composing my next thought—I felt tightly wound, and inarticulate, on this subject—when Martha added. "I probably will."

"Will what? You mean you'll send Cross a flower?"

She nodded.

"What color?"

She started laughing. "Red, of course. Lee, what do you think?"

It wasn't funny to me. And it seemed surprising that she couldn't guess this.

"So you'd send him a pink one?"

"Do you not want me to? If you don't, I won't."

This was how she always disarmed me, with her openness and her flexibility. She let me choose, and then I was the one who had made the choice.

"No, of course you should," I said. "Since you work together so much, and since you're friends." What was I doing reassuring her about Cross, how had we arrived at this point?

Abruptly, I did not want to be having the conversation anymore.

The night the fire alarm went off—this was also in early February—Cross and I had fallen asleep, and I heard the terrible screaming siren and opened my eyes in a panic, first because I didn't understand what was happening and then because I did. Already, Cross had scrambled out of bed and reached for his clothes. In the not-fully-dark darkness, his penis was swinging, his thighs and chest were pale. The truth was that I had never really looked at his naked body, that even when given chances, I'd averted my eyes (I was not at all sure that a penis was a thing I wanted to see), and I wouldn't have been looking at this moment if the room had been light or the alarm hadn't been wailing, These distractions, the fact that he was distracted, allowed me. Then our eyes met, and he said, "Get up"—I think he might have been shouting, but his voice was barely audible over the alarm. I stood. I had my nightgown on already; sometimes, though he didn't like it when I did, I'd pull it on again after we'd had sex. He fastened his pants, shrugged on his shirt and sweater. He reached for the doorknob, then looked back at me, and yelled, "Come on." In the threshold of the door, he hesitated, turning his head both ways down the hall. To the right was Martha's and my room, two other rooms, the bathroom, a fire escape door that led I didn't know where; to the left were more rooms and the staircase to the common room. From behind Cross, I looked into the hall, and remarkably, no one was in it yet. Cross took off. He went right, dashing down the hall and pushing through the fire escape door, and I thought, *Oh my God!* and then I realized the fire alarm was already going, he couldn't set it off, and the door had not yet swung shut behind him when Diana Trueblood and Abby Sciver emerged from their room, both of them wearing fleece sweatshirts over their nightgowns.

What I felt, standing there, was abandoned. It seemed

402

nothing so much as rude for Cross to have sprinted away like that, without saying good-bye, without kissing me quickly or even touching my shoulder or my cheek.

The hall had become crowded, and over Diana's and Abby's heads I made eye contact with Martha—she had exited our room, seen me, turned around and come out again, this time carrying my coat and running shoes. When she handed them to me, Martha raised her eyebrows: *Where's Cross?* I shook my head: *We didn't get caught.*

Outside, the siren was immediately quieter, as if the sound were wrapped in a blanket. The air was icy. We stood in a cluster in front of the entrance to Elwyn's, our breath visible, and some girls were barefoot and then someone spread a sweatshirt on the ground, and all the barefoot girls crushed onto it, pressing into one another. Mrs. Elwyn called out our names and checked us off on her list, and girls complained and swore in hoarse voices, but there was also a certain festivity to the moment—fire drills were always a little bit festive.

Groups similar to ours stood in front of the entrances to other dorms. All the dorms on our side of the circle had emptied into the courtyard, and you could look into the rooms where the lights were on and the shades were up and see people's posters, the sweaters on the top shelves of open closets. Among the boys outside Barrow's, I searched for Cross and I found him, in his puffy black coat—so he'd made it all the way back to his room with time to spare. He was talking to Devin and some other boys, and I felt a momentary confusion. Had we really just been lying in the same bed, did we even know each other at all? He was only forty feet from me, but there might as well have been a deep lake between us.

There was, in the swiftness with which he'd slipped from the dorm, something almost offensive. He'd made it out unseen only by a matter of seconds, which still meant he'd made it out unseen; it was the same as if he'd been sleeping all night in his own bed. What I wished was that he'd been as disoriented as I had, that he hadn't thought to use the fire door (only I would not have thought to use the fire door) and he'd come down the main staircase with me, both sheepish and aloof as the other girls looked at us, and then he'd slunk over to his dorm, and maybe he wouldn't be caught by a teacher, or maybe I did want him to be caught, I wanted both of us to be—we wouldn't get kicked out because breaking visitation was a minor offense, but everyone would know. My regret surged and billowed, as regret does in the middle of the night; everything had happened so quickly, the chance to have caused a different outcome was still so recent. Later, after we were allowed back inside, after I'd gone to sleep in the room with Martha and awakened in the morning, I thought that in the moment of standing outside our separate dorms, it *hadn't* been too late. I could have gone to him, I could have created a reason or just created a scene; I could have wept. It was like being drunk, how you so rarely feel drunk enough to do the thing you want to, you still feel pinned back by your own sense of the rational or the proper, but the next day, hung over, you realize just how drunk you were. You had a window of opportunity. If you had used it, you probably would have embarrassed yourself, but in not using it, you wasted something irretrievable.

As the alarm blared, it was so cold and most people weren't wearing coats. Some of the girls around me had started howling up toward the sky, like wolves. "Let us back inside," Isolde Haberny cried to no one in particular, and Jean Kohlhepp said—she wasn't crooning, she said it plainly—"I just want this to be over with."

Now I think, *Jean, Jean! You got your wish.* The fire drill is finished, but so is everything else. Did we believe we could pick and choose what passed quickly? Today, even the boring parts, even when it was freezing outside and half the girls were barefoot—all of it was a long time ago.

I didn't pay much attention at curfew two nights later when I saw Hillary Tompkins, Hillary whose sleeping bag I thought of as my own, with Cross's dried cum all over it. Hillary was rarely in the dorm at night, but I knew there was a big test in AP Chemistry the next morning, and if I assumed anything, I assumed Hillary had stayed over to study.

Then she raised her hand during announcements, and when Mrs. Elwyn called on her, Hillary said, "Yesterday in my room, I found some underwear, and they were *not* clean."

Other girls laughed, and Hillary was almost smiling, but she also seemed sincerely irritated. "I threw them away," she continued, "so if they were yours, I guess you have one less pair of underwear. I have no idea how they got there, but please try to have some consideration and don't throw your crusty underwear into other people's rooms."

Gina Marquez, a boisterous junior, cried, "Hear, hear!" and started clapping, and almost everyone else clapped, too. My face was burning, and tremors of anxiety shot through my chest. I glanced at Martha, who was not applauding and not smiling. But she also was not looking at me, her eyes were not wide with sympathy. Martha was the kind of person who would never leave her underwear around, whereas I was the kind of person who thought I wouldn't but actually would. The fire drill, Martha's posture seemed to say, was no excuse.

"Was it a G-string?" Gina called, and Mrs. Elwyn said, "Settle down ladies."

It wasn't a G-string. The underwear were white with moons and stars; the moons were blue slivers, and the stars were small and yellow.

I had decided well ahead of time that I wouldn't, on the eve of Valentine's Day, stay up late and go digging through the bucket of flowers. I'd just go to sleep and in the morning, whatever would be there would be there. After all, it was especially unseemly for a senior to show eagerness.

I had sent pink carnations to Martha, Sin-Jun, and, in the end, also to Cross. I couldn't take the risk of sending him a white carnation or a rose, but I also couldn't bear to send him

405

nothing. On the card, I wrote, *Cross, Happy Valentine's Day! Love, Lee.* Surely this would release the pressure of my longing a little.

And then at three o'clock in the morning, I awakened for the fourth time, amidst swirling repetitive dreams about the flowers—that he had sent me none, that he had sent me some but I had not been able to find water to put them in, that he had sent a dozen roses to Aspeth and each of them had been grotesquely huge, an eight-foot bouquet. I went to the bathroom and when I was washing my hands afterward, looking at myself in the mirror above the sinks, I knew what I would do, what I'd been planning to do all along.

The common room was light—its lights, like the hall lights, always stayed on through the night—but silent. There were two plastic buckets, and the sight of them made my heart lurch; how unsettling it was for the question I had wondered about for so long to actually be answered. My fingers trembled as I approached, and I looked around the common room, just to make sure no one was lurking. When I was standing with the buckets in front of me, I reached for one flower, then another and another. I was handling them— gently at first, planning to leave no evidence of my search, but soon I was shoving through them, pushing aside the ones with someone else's name on the front of the note. Which had been, so far, all of them. By the time I found the first with my name, my search had taken on the quality of a binge. And that note was only from Martha—the note was around a rose—but I didn't bother to open it because I recognized her handwriting. In the whole rest of the first bucket, there was nothing for me.

I moved on to the next one, which contained about half as many flowers; this time, I checked the roses first. And then I saw one with my name, the letters all in caps, in blue ink, and I felt a crazed glee, a balloon of exhilaration. I was ripping it open, and it was taking way too long—it must have taken less than a single second—and I was thrilled and hot and shaking with gratitude, thinking *Finally, finally, finally*, and these feelings spilled over into the point of recognizing that the flower was not from Cross but from Aubrey—from Aubrey? *Aubrey?*—and so at the same time, the traces of my earlier happiness were making me think, *Maybe Cross is my boyfriend now, maybe I convinced him over the last few months, it took a while but he saw that I had good in me*, while, because I had realized the truth—it was like line sprints in basketball, how on the last one down the length of the court you were going so fast that you couldn't stop immediately even though the drill was over—I also was thinking, *Why the fuck would Aubrey send me a rose?* But he was only a sophomore, and a boy, and probably didn't understand the way the flower exchange worked. The card said, *You have made a lot of progress in math. Good job! From, Aubrey.*

My own delight, born and killed off in front of no one, was humiliating; it was humiliating that I was someone who cared so much about things so small. And this disappointment was a good check, but still, after digging through the remaining flowers, I managed to be disappointed again to find that Cross had sent me nothing. No one had besides Martha and Aubrey—not even Sin-Jun. As with a binge, I had the wish then to undo what had just happened. Even if the results were the same and I'd still receive only two flowers, why couldn't I get up in the morning like a normal person, remember that it was Valentine's Day as I was passing through the common room on the way to breakfast, calmly pull out my flowers, put them in a vase back in my room, and forget about the whole thing?

It turned out to be worse than I thought. I discovered in the morning that Martha had gotten seven flowers—certainly in the past, before she'd become prefect, she'd never gotten more than four—and one was from Cross. She put all of ours in the same vase, and we didn't discuss them at all, except that she said to me, "Your note was funny." But she didn't ask if Cross had sent me a flower, or tell me he'd sent one to her.

The way I found out was by looking through her notes myself, when she was out of the room. The flower he'd given her was a pink carnation, as all of hers were. But still. It wasn't that Cross hadn't sent flowers; it was that he hadn't sent flowers to me.

The next thing that happened—this was near the end of February—was that Cross hurt his ankle. After Valentine's Day had passed without comment, except that he'd said when he came over the next time, "Thanks for the flower," a period of eight days went by without his visiting. When I saw him in the dining hall on the eighth night, I passed within three feet of him and stared straight ahead. I don't know if I was trying to show him that I cared or that I didn't, but either way, it worked; he awakened me in the night and we went to Hillary's room and said nothing, either of us, about his absence. I didn't have the feeling it had anything to do with the carnation I'd sent; the carnation, it turned out, hadn't seemed to have much significance one way or the other.

I wondered if the balance between us was shifting. Not that things had ever really been balanced—I was in love with him, and he was unreadable to me—but that imbalance had had its own patterns, and also its own clarity.

I'd been having the sense lately that I ought to pull back a little. I skipped three of his basketball games in a row, and that was why I wasn't there the day he tore his ankle ligament. They were playing Armony, whose center was six six. Cross went up for a layup, got fouled—Armony's center blocked his shot—and came down on his ankle. He ended up having to go to the hospital, where they wrapped his ankle and put him on crutches; obviously, with less than three weeks left until spring break, he was out for the season.

I found out all of this hours later, when I pieced together the sequence of events from the conversation at dinner and from Martha, who'd been apprised of the incident by Mr. Byden because they'd decided to delay a disciplinary committee meeting scheduled for that night. Listening to my classmates at dinner, I felt an initial spike of fear that he'd been seriously hurt. When I realized he hadn't, what I felt was a sense of territoriality—didn't the misfortune belong to me, too? "Is he back from the hospital?" I asked. It was the first thing I had said, and only the two people sitting closest to me turned. One of them was Dede and the other was John Brindley, who'd also been in the taxi that time freshman year,

"I'm pretty sure he's back in the dorm by now," John said. "Are you gonna go by?"

I was uncertain at first that he was even talking to me. Given my link to Cross, it was a perfectly reasonable question. But given that that link was invisible, the question was bizarre. Why on earth would I go by Cross Sugarman's room? We hardly knew each other.

"Why would Lee go see Sug?" Dede said, and John looked between the two of us. *What have you heard?* I longed to ask. If he'd been a jerk, a guy who liked to make innuendos, surely he'd have revealed more. But John was nice, and it was possible that the question was just arbitrary.

"No reason," he said, and I said, trying to sound low-key, "I might go by." I felt Dede staring at me and did not meet her gaze.

And then there occurred a period after dinner when I *was* planning to go. John's question had given me permission—after all, he was the one who'd thought up the idea of my visiting. At eight fifty-five, because visitation started at nine, I brushed my teeth and sprayed on perfume and then I looked at myself in the mirror and sat down at my desk. How could I go to Cross's dorm? Who knew who'd be there—presumably Devin would—or what if Cross was just hanging out in the common room, maybe he'd ordered pizza and was watching TV and the other guys sitting around wouldn't understand why I was there, and there was a good chance that neither would Cross. So either he'd be not outright rude but aloof, or else he'd be polite, he'd try to make me feel comfortable, and his trying would be the worst part—the effort of it all. And what were the chances of his being a little woozy but clearly glad to see me, of scooting over and then, when I sat next to him on the couch, resting his arm around my shoulders, of neither of us needing to explain anything except that I'd ask how his ankle was? The chances were infinitesimal. I bent over in the chair and leaned my forehead against the heels of my palms. To long for him like this—it was excruciating. And it was excruciating that he was always so close by. For the whole year, it had been like this, the proximity of our dorms, the knowledge that I literally could, in less than a minute, get up and walk out of the room and find him and touch him, but that really I couldn't do this at all—it made me crazy. No crush is worse than a boarding school crush; college is bigger and more diluted, and in the office, at least you get a break from each other at night.

It was unbearable to know that to act would be to mess things up, to know that my own impulses were un-trustworthy. I just wanted it to be the middle of the night and for him to come over (certainly, on crutches, he would not be coming over for some time) and to lie on me and for me to stop wanting everything I wanted when he wasn't around. When I think of Cross now, a big part of what I remember is that sense of waiting, of relying on chance. I couldn't go to his room—it was decided. And that meant that in order to convey to him my concern about his injury, I would have to run into him in the hall when few or no other students were around, and when I did, I'd have to quickly intuit his mood to find out if adjustments were to be made so that we could keep seeing each other.

I realize now: I ceded all the decisions to him. But that wasn't how it felt! At the time, it seemed so clear that the decisions *belonged* to him. Rules existed; they were unnamed and intractable.

I went to the play with Martha, and when Cross came

onstage—the play was *Hamlet* and after he'd had to quit basketball, he'd been assigned the part of Fortinbras, which previously Mrs. Komaroff, the drama teacher, had simply cut—everyone laughed. We weren't really supposed to see him as Fortinbras; the point was that it was Cross Sugarman on crutches, in an ancient mink coat. He had, at that point, not been to my room for nine days.

The roles of Hamlet and Ophelia were played by Jesse Middlestadt and Melodie Ryan. Jesse was a senior from Cambridge, thin and flush-cheeked and jumpy. He was someone girls liked without having crushes on him—I was always glad when I ended up at his table in the dining hall because he talked a lot *and* he was entertaining—and someone that I was surprised guys seemed to like, too. Melodie was a junior with long curly blond hair, a widow's peak, and big blue eyes. I knew she was considered very attractive, and what I always thought of when I saw her was how as a freshman she'd gone out with a senior named Chris Pryce and how, according to rumor, the two of them had had anal sex. It was never clear to me whether they'd done so once, or repeatedly; either way, whenever she came onstage, I'd think, *But doesn't it hurt?* I kept wondering if she'd wanted it, too, or if she'd just been accommodating Chris.

In the scene before Ophelia drowns herself, Melodie and Jesse kissed, and I felt jealous of them, of how, because of their parts in the play, they'd had to become comfortable kissing so publicly, how during the weeks of rehearsal they'd had that kiss to count on. Every day, they'd known they would touch another person, and it didn't depend on anything external; it didn't matter what they did or didn't do.

I should have signed up for drama, I thought, but for that also, it had become too late.

The same day that I got rejected from Brown and accepted by Mount Holyoke and the University of Michigan (at that point, I'd already been accepted by Beloit, rejected by Tufts, and had a rejection yet to come from Wesleyan), I ran into Cross outside Dean Fletcher's classroom. The last period of the day had just ended, and both of us were alone.

"Hey," he said. "Congratulations on Michigan."

I couldn't imagine how he knew.

"You think you'll go?"

"Probably." I definitely would and the reason I would, which I'd discuss with no one except Mrs. Stanchak and my parents, was that tuition would be a lot cheaper than at a private college, plus they were offering partial financial aid. Mount Holyoke was closer to Boston, but it wasn't that close, and by then I knew without having to say it to myself or to anyone else—it was all ending. The parts of Ault that didn't have to do with Cross were ending and the parts that did, and if I wasn't a girl he talked to in front of other people. I certainly wasn't a girl he'd travel across the state for, or host in his dorm at Harvard. All of which made a conversation about college seem, between the two of us, utterly irrelevant. Hours before, when I'd opened the three letters, I'd cared a great deal—I'd cried, of course, over Brown, before growing bored with my own tears—but with Cross in front of me, it just seemed far away. It was March, and we attended Ault, and our lives after this were as distant as a bazaar in Morocco.

I gestured toward his crutches. "Are you in pain?"

He said, "Not really," in a way that made me think the opposite had to be true. His tone was upbeat; I couldn't imagine Cross complaining bitterly about anything that truly bothered him, and, honestly, I had difficulty imagining what *would* bother him, though surely there were things that did. For the first time, it occurred to me that maybe it had been rude, maybe I'd been somehow neglectful, not to get in touch with him right after his injury. I had a flashing memory—why hadn't I thought about this before?—of how nice he'd been when I'd fainted at the mall our freshman year.

"I'm sorry this happened," I said.

"I don't blame you."

"No, but I mean—"

"I know what you mean. I'm joking."

Looking up at him, I wanted, once again, to say how much I loved him. How could I want to say it even in daylight? From outside, there was the sound of a boy yelling something, and then another boy yelling back. It was three in the afternoon, that lull after classes and before practice. I cannot say that I was surprised when he cocked his head toward Dean Fletcher's classroom. "You want to go in there?"

My pulse quickened, and I could feel the heaviness in my belly that was both excitement and anxiety. Very quietly, J said, "Sure."

The door to the classroom wasn't all the way shut, and he pushed it open with the tip of his right crutch, then shut it again, still using the crutch, from the other side. It was a gray day, and gray light came through the windows; Cross did not turn on the overhead lights: It was a classroom with a long rectangular table, and he pulled two chairs out from the table, facing each other, and after he'd sat in one, I thought the other one was for me; then I saw that he meant it to be for his foot. I hovered to one side, waiting to be directed, and I hated my own giggling passivity. Did he say what he said next because he knew I wanted to be told what to do, or had he decided already, before we entered the classroom?

Either way: I said, "Am I supposed to sit in your lap?" and he said, "If you want to" (of course, I asked, "Am I hurting you?" and he said, "No, not at all"), and I thought that things were okay, that he just wanted to hold me like I wanted to hold him, but we had been kissing for less than a minute when he murmured, "If you gave me a blow job now, that would be so great."

It was a hardwood floor, and my knees ached almost right away. And I didn't want to lean the weight of my upper body against his thighs because—because as long as this was supposed to be, for him, an enjoyable experience, he deserved to enjoy it entirely; my posture didn't need to be his concern.

And now there was no doubt: I had seen his penis, I was seeing it at this very moment. So strong was my own wish for him not to see my body that I had at times imagined he shared it; clearly, he did not. Why was taking off your clothes not embarrassing to other people? His pulled-down corduroy pants and boxers didn't seem remotely sexy; they made me think of him shitting. And which students would sit on this chair tomorrow having no idea Cross's bare ass had rested against it? And the warm, sour, thrusting weight in my mouth, the pressure of his palm on the back of my head—this was what I had missed in the last few weeks, this was what I was being denied?

With a great groan, he pulled out of my mouth and came all over my sweater (it was tan wool, with cables); while he was still not paying attention, I rubbed at the cum with the back of my sleeve, already imagining asking Martha to send out the sweater with her other dry cleaning. I stood and stepped away, wanting to leave—in my dorm, he was always the one who made us part, and I was the one who would have let him stay forever—and the unpleasantness of the moment felt like something to hold on to; if I could keep it, I would never again be at his mercy.

He had pulled up his pants but not yet buckled his belt. Still seated, he said, "Come here," and I was skeptical and irritated and I stepped closer doubtfully, and then he wrapped his arms around my waist and pressed his face to my breasts and hugged me tightly and my eyes filled with tears. There was nothing to do but rest my hands behind his shoulders, to touch his hair with my fingers; he always said how soft my hair was, but the truth, which I never told him, was that so was his.

Spring break was pretty much like Christmas break had been, except that the house was empty during the day because my brothers' vacation had already occurred. In the quiet, I sat around watching television and not showering and a few

414

times, in especially pathetic moments, opening my parents' Ault directory, which I was pretty sure they had never used for anything, to look at Cross's listing. This was, of course, a thing I had already done so many times on campus that the sight of his typed name and home address had long ago lost their potency.

When I saw family friends, which I tried to do as little as possible, they congratulated me on Michigan, and in accepting their good wishes, it became real to me that that was where I'd spend the next four years. On the Saturday before I was to return to Ault, my mother and I drove to Ann Arbor, where it was thirty degrees and the sidewalks were still icy. We wandered around the cold campus and she bought me a hooded sweatshirt, even though I told her I didn't need it. We drove back to South Bend in the evening, because my father had said it was fine with him if we stayed overnight at a hotel but it wasn't going to be on his nickel.

He was the one who took me to the airport, and I was, again, overwhelmingly relieved to be leaving. He hugged me by the car, gave me a five-dollar bill to buy lunch, then drove away. After I checked my suitcase, I walked through the terminal crying. When you go to boarding school, you're always leaving your family, not once but over and over, and it's not like it is when you're in college because you're older then and you're sort of supposed to be gone from them. I cried because of how guilty I felt, and because of how indulgent my guilt was. Standing in a store that sold bottled water and birthday cards and T-shirts that said *Indiana* in ornate writing, less than twenty minutes away from my family's house, I missed them so much I was tempted to call my mother at work and ask her to come wait with me for my plane; she'd have been alarmed, possibly frantic, but she'd have done it. But then she'd know what she'd probably only suspected—how messed up I really was, how much I'd been misleading them for the last four years.

It would be better once I got on the plane, better still back on campus. But while I was in their city, it just seemed like such a mistake that I had ever left home, such an error in judgment on all our parts.

I received the note from the headmaster's office more than a month after spring break. It was on Mr. Byden's official stationery, with the crest of Ault at the top, though the note itself, hardly seeming to warrant such formality, was only two lines long: *There's something I'd like to discuss with you. Please ask Mrs. Dershey to set up a time for us to meet.* A cold dread came over me. So this was what it was like to be busted—of course, in the end, I'd been caught. And it did not feel romantic or adventurous in the least. It was twelve-fifty p.m., and I was alone, when I'd always imagined that Cross and I would be caught together. Maybe I'd been ratted on and Cross hadn't—maybe another girl (Hillary Tompkins would be my first guess) had said she'd seen me with an unidentified boy.

I walked upstairs from the mail room and headed straight to Mr. Byden's office; it would be best just to know the damage. And also to get some reassurance—probably I would not be kicked out, but that was the first thing I wanted to confirm.

When Mrs. Dershey saw me, she said, "About the article, right? Wait just one moment." She stood and knocked on the door to Mr. Byden's office. I looked out the window, which offered a view of the grassy circle. Directly across the circle from the schoolhouse was the dining hall, and I could see people leaving lunch. Feeling just as I had when I'd learned my junior year that I might be spring-cleaned (how abruptly your life could become derailed, and how sickeningly familiar it seemed when it did), I located Martha walking with Sin-Jun; though I couldn't make out their faces, I recognized Sin-Jun's black hair and Martha's shirt, which was a pink button-down.

"Lee," Mrs. Dershey said. "He can see you right now."

Mr. Byden was at his desk. "Come in, come in," he said.

"Don't be shy. If you'll just have a seat there while I finish up one piece of business."

Mr. Byden tried to make himself accessible to students—my sophomore year he'd dressed up as Santa Claus for the last roll call before Christmas, and he taught an elective on ethics every spring—but he still intimidated me, and I'd managed to avoid ever having a real conversation with him. He knew my name because he made it a point to memorize all the new students' names within the first month of classes. Whenever we'd passed each other since my freshman year and he'd said, "Hello, Lee," or, "Good evening to you, Lee," I'd been tempted to tell him he could forget me, that it was okay if he used the space in his brain to retain, say, the phone number of some rich old alum.

I sat facing his desk, in a chair that had blue-and-red-striped brocade fabric and wooden arms. Another chair just like mine was a few feet away, and behind me—I surveyed the room while Mr. Byden wrote—were a couch and a low cherry table and several more armchairs. There was also a fireplace, with a white marble mantel, and above it a portrait of Jonas Ault, circa 1860. I had never been in Mr. Byden's office before, but I recognized the portrait from the school catalog. Jonas Ault, as we heard in chapel every year on Founder's Day, had been the captain of a whale-hunting ship, the rebellious youngest son of a wealthy Boston family. One night before he departed for a sea voyage, his young daughter Elsa pleaded with him to stay at home, and Ault refused. While at sea, the men encountered a storm so severe that Ault swore, as the ship rocked and waves crashed over the gunwales, that if he made it back to shore alive he would give up the whaling trade. He and all his men survived, but when they returned to port, he learned that three days prior Elsa had died of scarlet fever. In her memory he founded Ault School. (Not Ault Academy—that's what my parents sometimes called it, but the correct name was Ault School.) Though the story possessed a certain romantic doom that appealed to me, what

I always wondered was, why did Ault found a school for boys in memory of his daughter? Even if she'd lived, she would have had to wait until she was 104 years old before she was allowed to attend.

"Allrighty," Mr. Byden said. "I appreciate your prompt response. If you'll bear with me, I've got a few questions for you, and then I'll more fully explain why I called you in. Does that sound acceptable?"

"Yes," I said. Then I added, "sir." I meant it to be respectful, but coming out of my mouth, the word sounded almost sarcastic. The Southern students I knew pulled off *sir* and *ma'am* effortlessly.

"You came here as a freshman, correct?"

It wasn't the question I'd expected; I nodded.

"And how would you characterize your Ault experience? Just in the broadest terms, and keep in mind that there's no right answer."

This, I knew, was never true.

"I like it here," I said. Meaning, *Don't kick me out. Preferably, don't even bust me.*

"Tell me about the highlights."

Maybe I *wasn't* in his office because of Cross. Because surely this couldn't be the way most busts began. And, as I considered it, it occurred to me that if I were going to be busted, it would probably be not by Mr. Byden but by Mrs. Elwyn, or possibly Dean Fletcher.

"Just tell me what comes to mind first," he said.

I glanced out the window and saw several seniors, including Martha and Sin-Jun, lying on the circle. Since spring break, even before it had become truly warm, there'd almost always been seniors sitting or lying in a group on the circle; it was like a massive volunteer effort they were completing in shifts. I hadn't once hung out there because I knew it would make me feel conspicuous and like I was wasting time. It had never bothered me to sit in the dorm, listening to music, staring into space, but wasting time alone felt less like wasting time than like keeping my despair in check.

I looked back at Mr. Byden. The highlight of my Ault experience, as I saw it at that moment, was Cross. "The highlight of my Ault experience has been my friends," I said.

"There's something about living in the dorms, isn't there?" Mr. Byden said. "A real closeness that develops."

"And Martha and I have roomed together for three years, which is nice."

"Believe me, I know all about you and Martha. I hear great things about the two of you."

From whom? I thought.

"How about academics?" Mr. Byden said. "There was a bit of a problem with precalculus, was there not?"

I felt a new flare of panic—maybe this was what our meeting was about, I thought, maybe after all these months, they'd figured out I'd cheated—but Mr. Byden was smiling. His expression seemed to say, *Math—isn't it pesky?*

"Things have been better this year," I said. "I've been able to stay on top of it."

"And you're off to the University of Michigan if I'm not mistaken."

I nodded.

"A fine institution," he said. "One of the really outstanding state schools."

I smiled at him without saying anything. With people outside of Ault, you pretended that you were lucky to go to the University of Michigan and maybe, depending upon whom you were comparing yourself to, you really were; but Mr. Byden and I both knew that within Ault, it wasn't lucky at all.

"Do you feel prepared for college?" Mr. Byden asked.

"Yes, definitely. I've gotten an excellent education." This, in fact, was true.

"Any favorite classes?"

"Eleventh-grade history with Dean Fletcher was great. And tenth-grade history, with Mr. Corning. I liked environmental science pretty much, too. I had Mrs. McNally for that. Really, all my teachers here have been good. It's just that I haven't always been so good at the subjects."

Mr. Byden laughed. "Nobody's perfect, right? But I know you've contributed a lot to this place, Lee, in your own way."

What on earth did he want from me, I wondered, and at that moment, he said, "I'll get to the point. *The New York Times* is planning a feature on the school."

"Wow."

"Well, it's certainly an opportunity, but media attention is always a double-edged sword. It's smart to approach any situation like this with a degree of caution, especially in this day and age, when the general public isn't all that enamored with the idea of prep school. The *Times* is a first-rate paper, of course, but sometimes the media tends to simply reinforce existing stereotypes instead of taking the time to tell the real story. Do you know what I'm saying?"

"I think so."

"All of us at Ault are awfully proud of the school, and when the *Times* comes here to do the interviews, we want them talking to kids who can convey that pride. I'm not saying, if you'll pardon the expression, that we want to feed them a line. What we're looking for are students who can provide a view of the school that's balanced as well as truthful. My question for you is, can I persuade you to be one of those students?"

"Oh," I said. "Sure."

"Terrific. Now, the angle of the story as it's been described to me is the changing face of American boarding schools, with Ault functioning as a stand-in for Overfield, Hartwell Academy, St. Francis, et cetera. What they're saying is, these places are no longer enclaves for the sons of the wealthy. We have girls, we have blacks, we have Hispanics. Despite their reputation, boarding schools are mirrors of American society."

"So I would be speaking as a girl?"

"As a girl, or on behalf of any of your affiliations."

420

I wondered if he thought there was more to me than met the eye—that I was Appalachian maybe. "Are there specific things I should tell them?"

Mr. Byden grinned. I still think of that grin sometimes. "Just the truth," he said.

Cross had visited only once since spring break, about two weeks before my conversation with Mr. Byden. Upon returning to school, I'd expected him the very first night, because that was what *I* wanted; I forgot, over and over, that the fact of my wanting something wasn't enough to make it happen. As the days passed, I expected him less while thinking about him just as much or more—the first thing that occurred to me when I awakened in the morning was that another night had passed without a visit. During the day, as much as possible, I kept an eye out for him. He was off crutches and at breakfast, or at chapel if he skipped breakfast, or at roll call if he'd skipped chapel—he was guaranteed to be at roll call, since he and Martha ran it—I'd register what he was wearing, and then for the rest of the day I'd always be scanning for the red-and-white-striped button-down, or the black fleece vest; it was like his clothes gave the day a personality. I didn't talk to him at all but it reassured me to see him; if he was at a lunch table two away from mine, then at least he wasn't down by the boathouse having outdoor sex with Aspeth.

At first, my fear had been that Cross was using spring break as a cutoff point and that he would never visit again. If he did come by, therefore, it would be disproportionately reassuring, it would represent more than a single visit. And then he did come, and everything wasn't okay. I could feel how off we were immediately, how I was stiff and overly attentive and he was distant. We had sex, and he didn't come for a long time—longer, it seemed, than ever before—and afterward I could sense that he wanted to leave. He didn't, though, and then we both fell asleep, and when I awakened it was because he was tapping me to say good-bye. He was out of bed, dressed already, and it was only a little after three. I shouldn't have let myself fall asleep, I thought, or at least I should have woken up when he did, so I could stop him before he climbed out of bed. Not by persuading him logically, but by distracting him physically—by giving him a reason to stay.

He was leaning over me with one hand set on my shoulder. I folded back my arm and reached for his hand, and he let me take it, squeezed my own hand once, then dropped it. "It's still early," I said. I wasn't whispering and my voice was whiny, and gravelly from sleep.

"I've got to leave." That's all he said; he didn't give a reason.

My questions clamored forward. *Where have you been? What did I do? Are you coming back? Please come back because I don't think I can stand it if you don't.* Had this visit been probationary, I wondered, and had my behavior disappointed him?

"Okay?" he said, and he pulled the sleeping bag up around my shoulders and patted the top of my arm once more. Of course it wasn't okay. But he left anyway, and when I was alone, I thought of how many times I'd wondered if things were awry between us, if I was displeasing him or he'd lost interest. All those times, I'd suppressed my impulse to ask, and I was glad I had because maybe asking would have hastened the end. And because—I understood this now—you really didn't need to ask. When it was over, you knew.

The reporter from *The New York Times* was named Angela Varizi. Hearing the word reporter, I had imagined a man in his fifties, gray and balding, in a dark three-piece suit, but when I entered Dean Fletcher's classroom, which was where she was meeting students for interviews, she looked younger than thirty. She was sitting at the head of the table, and when she stood to shake my hand, I saw that she had on jeans—a violation of Ault's dress code when worn in the schoolhouse—and cowboy boots and a white button-down shirt. Her straight hair was pulled back in a ponytail, and she had a gap between her front teeth. She definitely wasn't beautiful, but there was something open and intense in her face—she did not seem apologetic about the fact that she wasn't prettier. When she shook my hand, her grip was firm.

I was missing my second-period class in order to be interviewed. I knew, from a memo Mr. Byden had sent out, that Angela Varizi had met Mario Balmaceda, a junior, before me and that after me was Darden Pittard.

"Have a seat," Angela Varizi said.

An image flickered through my mind of giving a blow job to Cross in this same classroom and I winced, though I couldn't have said if it was with disgust or longing. I sat on the side of the table opposite where we'd been that day.

"Will anyone else be here?" I asked. "Not other students, but will there be a teacher to make sure I don't say anything bad?"

Angela Varizi laughed. "Do you often say bad things?"

"Sometimes I do."

"I like you already," she said. "And the answer is no. Either the administration trusts you guys, or they vetted you so I don't get to talk to any malcontents. Now let's get some of the nitty-gritty stuff out of the way first. You're a senior, aren't you, and you've been here all four years?"

"Yeah."

"Remind me where you're from."

"South Bend, Indiana."

"Gotcha. I'm meeting with so many of you that I'm starting to get your profiles confused, but now I remember you."

Who had provided Angela Varizi with a profile of me, I wondered, and what exactly had it said?

"You're the one going to the University of Michigan, aren't you? Congratulations."

"Well, I applied to Brown, but I nearly flunked precalculus last year, so I didn't really expect to get in."

She nodded, jotting something in her notebook. "You're writing that down? Has the interview started?"

"Lee, whenever you're talking to a reporter, you're being interviewed."

"I thought reporters used tape recorders."

"Some do, but a lot of us who work for newspapers choose not to. We often have such tight deadlines that there isn't time to transcribe tapes."

"Sorry to have so many questions," I said.

"Ask them at any time. And you can call me Angie, by the way. Now let me ask, how do your parents feel about you going to the University of Michigan?"

"They're happy. I'll be a lot closer to home."

"Are they Michigan alums?"

"No. My dad went to Western Indiana and my mom started college but then she didn't finish because they got married."

"What do your parents do?"

I paused. "I'm sorry to keep being like this, but I don't really understand what my parents have to do with the article."

"Here's the deal. You and I will talk and talk, and then the article will come out, and I'll have quoted you for a paragraph or two. You'll think, why did Angie leave out all my other brilliant insights? But a lot of what I'm asking is for context—it won't be in the article, but it'll inform the article, if that doesn't sound completely pretentious."

"My mom is a bookkeeper at an insurance company. And my dad is in sales."

"What does he sell?" Angie's head was down, and she was writing again. Her voice was neutral; it seemed as if she would react the same to anything I said.

"Mattresses," I said. "He sells mattresses."

She didn't gasp, or clasp her chest. Instead, she said, "And he works, what—in a chain or in an independent store?"

"It's a franchise, which he owns."

"Gotcha. And tell me about siblings."

"My brother Joseph is fourteen, and my brother Tim is seven."

"Will they go to boarding school as well?"

"l don't think so. Joe is already the age that I was when I started here. And it's just not that normal for people where I'm from."

"So why did you go?"

I'd developed two standard answers to this question, which I varied depending upon my audience; I decided to give Angie both. "This is a much better school than the public high school I'd have gone to in South Bend," I said. "The resources here are incredible—the caliber of the faculty and the fact that the classes are so small and you get all this individual attention and your classmates are really motivated." As I said it, I imagined this being the remark that Angie quoted—it was definitely my most eloquent so far. "The other reason is that I had a sort of dumb thirteen-year-old's idea of boarding school," I continued. "I'd gotten it from TV shows and *Seventeen* magazine, and I thought it sounded really glamorous. So I did research and applied. My parents thought it was weird, but when I got in, they let me go."

"Just like that? They didn't need more convincing?"

"No, they needed convincing. But our next door neighbor, my mom's best friend, Mrs. Gruber, is an elementary school teacher and she thought this was a great opportunity and went to bat for me. In the end, my parents said I could decide."

"All this when you were thirteen years old?"

I nodded.

"Not bad. You must have been a lot more mature than I was. Now let me ask you this. It's no secret that boarding school is awfully pricey."

I could feel myself blushing, my heart rate picking up speed. It seemed impossible that she would ask what it appeared she was about to ask. It would just be so—*obvious*.

"Ault is, what, twenty-two thousand a year?" Angie continued. "What I'm wondering is how much of a factor the cost was for your parents when they were deciding to let you go."

My cheeks were burning.

"Does the question make you uncomfortable?" Angie asked.

"People here don't really—" I paused. "Money isn't discussed."

"Talk about the elephant in the living room!"

"But that's why," I said. "People have so much, so it's like nobody needs to mention it."

"Do you see differences between people who have it and people who don't?"

"Not really. We never use cash for anything. For your textbooks, or if you're taking the bus into Boston, you just fill out a card with your student number."

"And then your parents pay the bill?"

"Yeah."

Our eyes met. She wanted me to say something she already knew. And I didn't yet understand that just because you can recognize what another person wants and just because that person is older and more powerful than you are, you don't have to give it to them. "It's a little different for me," I said. "The thing is that I'm—I'm on scholarship." In four years, the only people I'd ever talked about this with were Mrs. Barinsky, who worked in the admissions and financial aid office, and Mrs. Stanchak. I'd never even discussed it with Martha. Martha knew, I assumed, but not because I'd said anything. "My parents pay for my expenses," I continued. "But they only pay, I think this year it's four thousand in tuition."

"Gotcha." Angie nodded several times and again, I felt a stir of confusion, I was nearly certain she'd already known. "That's a real tribute to you."

"For all I know, the school regrets its decision to let me in

426

here in the first place. I did really well in elementary school and junior high, but after I got here, I started to have academic problems."

"Were you inadequately prepared?"

"Not exactly. It was more that I just stopped feeling like I could do it. I was so—so un-outstanding here. It wasn't like anyone expected me to be a star."

"I want us to grapple with the issue of financial aid a little more. I sense this isn't your favorite topic, but stay with me. I'm wondering if you think the faculty shows favoritism toward wealthy students."

"No, not really."

"Not really?"

"There's one young teacher who's friendly with these guys in my grade who all went to the same school in New York before they came here. They're called the bank boys, and they're all pretty, you know—rich. The teacher gives them rides to McDonald's, or he took them to a Patriots game one time, and people thought that was kind of weird because most of the class didn't even know about it until after it had happened. But I don't think the teacher is friendly with the bank boys because they're rich. He coached most of them in soccer, and that's how he knows them."

"Why are they called the bank boys?"

"Because all their dads work for banks. I mean, not really all of them do, but that's what it seems like."

"Would that be *bank* and *boys* with big Bs or little Bs?"

I stared at her. "You're putting this in the article? Please don't."

"Let's keep talking and see what else we come up with. I'll tell you a story. I did my undergrad at Harvard."

I thought of having told her about my rejection from Brown and felt embarrassed,

"You said there aren't differences between students who have money and students who don't, but that doesn't jibe with my own experiences," she said. "I'm from a working-class family in New Jersey, and in college I had to take out tons of loans. And the kids at Harvard, especially the boarding school kids, had an attitude about money that I had never seen. Freshman year, my roommate bought a black wool coat with a black velvet collar. It was beautiful. I didn't care much about clothes, but I positively coveted this coat. And a week after she bought it, she lost it. She forgot it on the T. And you know what she did?"

I shook my head.

"She went back to the store and bought another one. Just like that. But the real kicker was, I made a comment about charging things to Daddy, just teasing her, and she was enraged. And it took me a long time to figure out, okay, what she's really doing is inflicting her discomfort with herself onto me."

I looked out the window. Sunlight fell through the branches of a nearby beech tree.

When she spoke again, Angie's voice was softer. "Does that story ring any bells?"

"One time, when I was a sophomore—" I said and then stopped.

"Go on. This might feel weird. Lee, but I'd argue that it's awfully important."

"Sophomore year, I had a teacher for English who people didn't like very much. I was walking with other students after class one day, and one of them, this girl, said something about the teacher being LMC. She was talking about the teacher's clothes."

"What does LMC mean?"

"That's what I was wondering. So later I asked my roommate, and my roommate, who would never say something like that, seemed kind of embarrassed. She said she wasn't sure but she thought it stood for lower-middle-class." Martha had known that was what it stood for; I could tell that she'd just felt self-conscious explaining it to me. When I'd told her why I was asking, she had said, "Aspeth is so ridiculous."

428

"Unbelievable," Angie said.

"People here aren't obviously snobby, but their idea of what's normal—well, another thing I remember for some reason is you can take the bus to Boston on Saturdays if you don't have a game. And the dean gets on before you leave campus to say all school rules are in effect, and then he meets the bus when it comes back at the end of the day and randomly searches people's bags. One time last year, the bus was about to pick us up in Boston, and I ran into some girls by Fanueil Hall. They were girls from my dorm. We were all at a clothes store, and one of the girls was taking stuff off the racks and carrying it up to the cash register without trying it on. I said to the other one, 'Doesn't she want to see if it fits?' and the girl said, 'She's just buying stuff to wrap the alcohol in.' She didn't say alcohol, but that's what she meant. It was probably a hundred dollars' worth of clothes."

Angie shook her head. "What kind of alcohol had she bought?"

"Probably vodka. That's the one you can't smell on people's breath, right?"

"I take it you're not a drinker yourself."

"No."

"Do you think being here on scholarship makes you less likely to violate school rules?"

I thought of Cross and felt a little injured—why exactly did Angie think I was less likely to violate school rules? But all I said was, "Possibly."

"How about other scholarship kids? Do they drink or smoke?"

"I don't really think of people as scholarship and not-scholarship."

"You don't know who's receiving aid and who isn't?"

"You know. But nobody discusses it."

"Then how do you know?"

"You can tell by people's rooms—whether or not they have stereos, or if the girls have flowered bedspreads, or if they have silver picture frames. Just the quality of their stuff. And their clothes—everyone orders clothes from the same catalogs, so you'll see lots of people in an identical sweater, and you know exactly how much it cost. And things like, you can send your laundry to a service or you can do it yourself in the dorm machines. Or even some of the sports, how much the equipment costs. Ice hockey is a really expensive sport, but something like basketball isn't that much."

"Is it safe to assume you don't have a flowered bedspread or silver picture frames?"

"I have a flowered bedspread." I had asked for it for my birthday freshman year. As for silver picture frames, as for everything else—Martha was my beard.

"There's another thing," I said. "Probably the biggest clue about who's getting financial aid and who isn't is race. Nobody ever talks about it, but it's just sort of known that people from certain minorities are almost always on scholarship."

"Which minorities?"

I hesitated. "You can probably guess."

"You're not going to offend me, Lee."

"Well, blacks and Latinos. That's basically it. People from other minorities, like Asians or Indians, usually aren't on scholarship, and blacks and Latinos usually are."

"So how can you tell if a white student is on scholarship?"

"I doubt there are that many of them who are," I said. "That many of us." For a moment, I couldn't think of anyone in the senior class besides me, and then I remembered Scott LaRosa, who was from Portland and was captain of the boys' ice hockey team. He had a pale meaty face and a Maine accent, but he also was big and confident. In our class, I couldn't come up with anyone else.

"Why do you think so few white students receive financial aid?"

"We don't add diversity to the school. And there are plenty of white kids whose parents *can* pay."

"It seems like you've spent a lot of time here feeling left out"

Once, this observation might have made tears well in my eyes—she *understood*—but now it just seemed like part of the conversation. And besides, though I wanted Angie Varizi to like me, I was not entirely sure that I liked her.

"Of course I've felt left out some of the time. But that's to be expected, right?" I smiled. "I'm kind of like this nobody from Indiana."

"Do you feel different from your family when you go back home?"

Out the window, a breeze rose, and I could hear the leaves in the beech tree rustle. "It would be depressing if I did, right?" I said. I was quiet, and then I said, "You know how we were talking before about why I came to Ault? And I said two reasons? Well, there's another one I didn't say. It's kind of hard to explain, but it's probably the main reason." I took a deep breath. "When I was ten, my family went on vacation to Florida. It was a big deal, like neither of my parents had been before. It was the summer, and we drove down. We were staying on Tampa Bay, and one day, we were driving around and sightseeing, or maybe we got lost, but we ended up in this neighborhood with huge houses. It wasn't like a new development—the houses looked old-fashioned. A lot of them were white shingled, and they had bay windows and porches with rocking chairs on them and big green lawns and palm trees. In front of one house, a boy and girl who were probably brother and sister were playing soccer. I said to my dad—I was at the age where you don't really understand the difference between something costing a thousand dollars and a million dollars—I said, 'We should buy a house like this.' I thought they were pretty, and I thought my family would be happy in one. And my dad started laughing. He said, 'No, no.'" I had, I remembered, been sitting in the front seat beside my father; my mother had been in back with my brothers, because Tim was an infant. I'd felt close to my father in this moment, believing I'd come up with a good idea. "My dad said, 'Lee, people like us don't live in these houses. These people keep their money in Swiss bank accounts. They eat caviar for dinner. They send their sons to boarding school.' And I said to him"—Had it all really hinged on this, had this been the reason I'd become who I was, the reason I'd enrolled at Ault? In a way, it couldn't have been because it was far too small. But maybe it always comes down to small reasons, incremental turns, conversations you almost didn't have, or heard only part of—"I said to my dad, 'Do they send their daughters to boarding school?'"

"Wow," Angie said.

"By the time I applied to Ault and other places, I doubt my parents remembered that conversation. And I didn't remind them of it, obviously."

"You were ready to trade up," Angie said.

"I'm not sure I'd put it like that. I mean, I was ten at the time," I could tell that we were near the end of the interview. During parts of it, my heart rate had sped up, my cheeks had flushed—there was something exciting about talking to her, as if I had waited a long time to say these things. But thinking of my family in the car together, none of us knowing that in four years I would leave home, made me feel sad and emptied out.

"Listen, Lee," Angie said. "You've given me a lot of great information. I can't thank you enough for your candor." She passed me a business card, and the part that said *The New York Times* was in that fancy script just like at the top of the newspaper. "Call me if you have any questions."

When I left the room, I passed Darden Pittard in the hallway. "What am I in for?" he asked.

"It was kind of weird," I said.

"Good weird or bad weird?"

Five minutes earlier, I'd have said good weird, but an odd feeling was expanding in me. I had told Angie Varizi a lot about myself, and it was hard to say why, except that she'd asked. "I don't know," I said. "Just weird."

* * *

During the break between third and fourth period, I found Martha in the spot where we often met, by the community service bulletin board in the mail room. Other students buzzed past us.

"How'd it go?" she said, "Was the guy nice?" She unwrapped a granola bar and broke it in two, holding a piece toward me, I shook my head.

"It was a woman," I said. "I guess she was nice, but I feel like maybe I said too much. She asked all about tuition-type stuff." The strange part was, the more I thought about it, the less I could remember what I'd said.

"Really?" Martha's mouth was full, which made her voice garbled, but I could tell from her raised eyebrows that she was surprised. She swallowed. "Why would she want to know about that?"

"I have no idea."

We looked at each other. Surely there was a conversation Martha and I could have had somewhere along the way about the differences between us, but given that we hadn't, it was too large to embark upon now.

"That seems random," she said.

"Do you think I should be worried?"

Martha smiled. "Nah. I bet you were her favorite interview of the day."

When it was over, you didn't need to ask, you knew, and yet— you could still be caught off guard; your sense of the situation could be at odds with your wish for a particular outcome. That Saturday night when I was sitting on the edge of one of the tubs in a T-shirt and shorts shaving my legs, Martha walked into the dorm bathroom. "I thought you might be in here," she said.

"Hey. The dance isn't over, is it?"

"No, but it was kind of hot and boring. So you know Aspeth?"

"You mean Aspeth we've gone to school with for four years?"

Martha bit her lower lip. "She and Sug are good friends, right?"

"Martha, what are you trying to say?"

"They were dancing together. A lot."

A jittery sensation began to rise from my stomach to my chest. "Do they not usually dance together?"

"I guess I've never really noticed. There was just something obvious about it tonight. Neither of them was dancing with anyone else. And then they were by the snack bar and he was leaning against that railing"—I knew the snack bar, I knew the railing; I had walked through the activities center many times, but only during the day, when it was quiet and dusty-looking—"and she was leaning against him."

"Facing him?" I asked.

"No, no. They were both facing out. I think he had his arms around her waist." Until this moment, Martha had remained standing by the tile wall. Now, she came and perched on the tub next to me. "I'm sorry, but I thought you'd want to know."

I looked at my half-shaven legs.

Martha said, "Aspeth is dumb," and there were many things that Aspeth Montgomery was, but dumb had never been one of them.

After that, I was on the lookout. And it was true that Cross and Aspeth were often together, but maybe no more than they ever had been. It was late May, and as the weather got nicer, seniors were outside on the circle constantly, an even bigger group—after lunch and during free periods and on the weekends—and more than once, as I walked by and pretended not to look at the flock of them, I could make out Aspeth shouting, "I do not!" Or another time: 'That's so gross!" Why didn't I ever join them? I wanted to, but there would be that one unbearable moment after I approached when I stood on the fringes of the group, and they would shade their eyes and look up and wonder why I was there. There was something I would have to say, there was a place in the grass I would have to sit, a posture I would have to sit in. For other people, these decisions seemed effortless, not decisions at all; for me, they had never stopped being decisions.

I couldn't tell anything for sure, though, and I thought that by remaining vigilant, I was protecting myself. Then, in the year's last issue of *The Ault Voice*, next to an editorial titled "Plaid Shorts Should Be Allowed in the Schoolhouse," Low Notes included the line, "C.S. and M.R.: Sugar daddy is singing a new melody." New issues of *The A. V.* were distributed once a month at roll call, and those roll calls were unusually quiet, as most students read during the announcements; several teachers always admonished us to put the papers away, and no one did. I, too, read during roll call but I'd taken to avoiding Low Notes in public because I was always terrified—or maybe I was hopeful—that there'd be a mention of Cross and me, and that someone would observe me reading it. This meant that it was not until that evening that I read the line and even before I really comprehended it, I felt flooded with a hot nauseated blend of shock and recognition. I was astonished, and also, I was not really surprised at all. And Martha, as usual, wasn't around—she was at a meeting—and she didn't return to the dorm until curfew. The moment curfew ended, I whispered, "I need to talk to you."

In our room, I picked up my copy of the paper and held it out to her. "Look at this."

I pointed, and her eyes moved over the page. It seemed to be taking her longer to read it than it should. Finally, she said, "Who's M.R.?"

"Melodie Ryan. Who Cross was in *Hamlet* with, I've never heard anything about this, but they must have—I don't know. He hasn't been here for more than a month, Martha," I said, and I burst into tears.

She patted my back.

"It has to be, right? But maybe it's not because Melodie is spelled I-E and this is just with a Y. So is it?"

Martha looked distressed. "I don't know."

"Has he said anything to you? Is he going out with Melodie Ryan and everyone knows and I don't? Is he going out with Aspeth?"

"If Cross has a new girlfriend, I don't know it, either. But, Lee, before you tear yourself apart, remember how silly Low Notes are."

"But they're usually right." I wiped my nose with the back of my hand.

"Remember that one about Katherine Pound and Alexander Héverd, and no one believed it at first? But it was true."

"But it can just mean Melodie and Cross hooked up," Martha said. "Not that they're a real couple."

I started crying harder—to me, hooking up was being a couple. Apparently, I had persuaded Martha that the Low Note was right, and it hadn't been hard to do.

"You need to talk to Cross," Martha said. "You're allowed to ask him stuff, Lee. And, at this point, what is there to lose?"

But the next day was Friday and it seemed to me inappropriate to corner Cross on a weekend. Because (yes, I was nuts, and I also think there's a decent chance I'd operate on this logic again, given the opportunity) what if he and Melodie had something planned and I interrupted it? Or just ruined his mood before a romantic evening? I hated the idea of being a pain in the ass, the kind of girl who always wanted to *talk*. Talking to him was, of course, exactly what I wanted to do, but not in a cornering way, not tediously.

On top of that, it wasn't just any weekend—it was the weekend Angie Varizi's article was supposed to run in the *Times*. She had warned me that it might be bumped at the last minute, depending on breaking news, but if everything proceeded normally, it would appear on Sunday.

Looking back on this period, I feel both a retroactive dread and a sense of protectiveness for myself as I was then, for how distraught I felt about Cross, how earnestly sad at the prospect of graduating from Ault. I feel the way you do watching a movie in which a teenage girl is in the house alone at night, in a storm, and the electricity goes out, or a movie in which a young couple share a romantic dinner and emerge from the restaurant into a snowstorm that seems to them beautiful, then climb into their car to drive home along curving roads. The same way you want to yell, *Get out of the house! Stop the car!* what I want to say to the younger me is, *Just go. If you leave now, your memory of Ault will be unspoiled, You will think that your feelings about the school are complicated, but you still will possess the sweet conviction that it was the place that wronged you and not the other way around.*

Over the course of the weekend, I kept forgetting and remembering the article. On Sunday, Martha and I awakened around eight, a little early, but it wasn't because of that. Walking to the dining hall, we were discussing what shoes we'd wear for our graduation ceremony, which was a week away. At Ault, you wore not a cap and gown but a white dress, and the boys wore khaki pants and navy blazers and straw boaters. Then we started talking about how the year before, Annice Roule had tripped on the stairs leading up to the stage when she went to collect her diploma.

The usual handful of students was in the dining hall, but the weird thing was, they were all sitting at the same table. The freshmen and sophomores and juniors had joined the seniors Martha and I always sat with—Jonathan Trenga and Russell Woo, Doug Miles, Jamie Lorison, Jenny and Sally. The other weird thing was that no one was speaking, All their heads were ducked, and I realized that they were reading.

"Are they reading *my* article?" I asked Martha, and then, from ten feet away, I could see that they were—two or three of them were clustered around each copy of the paper. "Holy shit," I heard Jim Pintane, who was a junior, say. When we reached the table, some of them looked up, and then all of them looked up. For a long moment, no one spoke.

Finally, in a cold voice, Doug Miles said, "It's the infamous Lee Fiora."

Everyone at the table was still staring at me.

"I must admit," said Jonathan, "I didn't know you had such strong opinions." His tone was harder to gauge—not unfriendly, but not friendly, either.

"What does it say?" I asked slowly, and when no one answered, Martha said, "This is ridiculous." She grabbed one of the newspaper sections. "Come on," she said.

As I followed her to another table, Doug called, "Hey, Lee."

I turned around.

"Didn't anyone ever tell you that you don't piss in your own pool?"

We sat at another table, side by side, without getting our food. My heart hammered, and my fingers were trembling. The section Martha had taken was open to the second page of the article, not the page where it started. Martha flipped backward. The article started on the front page, I saw the front page of the front section. The headline was BOARDING SCHOOLS CLAIM TO CHANGE, STUDENTS TELL DIFFERENT STORY. Below that, in smaller letters, it said WHAT IT'S LIKE TO BE WHITE, MIDDLE-CLASS— AND AN OUTSIDER. A large photograph featured, oddly enough, the nonwhite Pittard brothers sitting on a couch in a dorm common room. Darden was demonstrating something with his hands and his brother Eli, who was a freshman, was laughing. But the first paragraph was not about the Pittards; it was about me:

Among the cliques in Lee Fiora's senior class at Ault School in Raymond, Massachusetts, is a group of male friends known as the "Bank Boys"—so named, as Miss Fiora explained, "because all their dads work for banks. Not really all of them do, but that's what it seems like."

The clique's appellation is one of the few references, however oblique, that Ault students make to money. In general, at this school, whose small classes, pristine grounds, and state-of-the-art facilities come with a $22,000 price tag, and at other elite schools across the Northeast, the subject is taboo. Thus is created an environment which, according to Miss Fiora, defers to the rich and shortchanges everyone else—including Miss Fioro herself. "Of course I feel left out," Miss Fiora, who receives a financial aid package which covers approximately three quarters of her tuition, recently told a visitor to Ault. "I'm a nobody from Indiana." Miss Fiora is white; for non-white students, particularly African Americans and Hispanics, she feels that the difficulties of life at Ault are only compounded.

It went on and on. Angie Varizi had me expounding on race (presumably because no one else, no one who wasn't white, had been willing to), saying I suspected that Ault regretted the decision to give me a scholarship, telling the anecdote about the girls buying clothes to hide their alcohol. She had me giving a rundown on how to spot scholarship students based on their possessions and their behavior. And, of course, she had me sharing the story of the house in Florida. Throughout the article, my own comments were juxtaposed with hearty endorsements of the school from Mr. Byden, Dean Fletcher, a sophomore named Ginny Chu, Darden Pittard, and recent graduates. Another student who was not named said about me, "She's not the most popular person in our grade. Not everyone thrives in a place like this."

I read the article, in its entirety, only once, and it was that time in the dining hall. Sometimes as I read, I murmured, "Oh my God," and Martha patted me. By the end of the article, her hand was set on my arm.

The mess I had made (had I been the one who'd made this

439

mess?) was so awful that it was hard to absorb or quantify. The person I was as of this moment, the person the article made me, was the precise opposite of the person I had, for the last four years, tried to be. It was the worst possible mistake I could have made.

"Okay," Martha said. "We have a week left and then we're out of here forever. So you'll just live your life like normal. Let other people freak out, and, yes, they will. But it's not your problem."

"I'm going back to the room."

"Listen to me," she said. "We're getting breakfast."

In the kitchen, we picked up trays, filled our glasses with milk and juice, received plates of steaming pancakes. I felt dizzy with regret. I had been an idiot, I thought. Why on earth had I told Angie Varizi my secrets, what good had I imagined would come from it? This was how it always was with me—I wasn't able to tell that something was happening (that I was, for Angie's benefit, digging my own grave) while it was happening. Every single thing about the article was humiliating. Being on scholarship was bad, being unhappy was worse, and admitting to either one was worst of all. I had been indiscreet. That's what it was. How much better it would have been to fuck up in a normal, preppy way—to get caught the week before graduation smoking pot, or skinny-dipping at midnight in the gym pool. To make politically charged complaints to a *New York Times* reporter, on the other hand, was just tacky.

When we carried our trays out to the dining room, we passed three freshmen, girls whose names I didn't even know, and where normally I'd have looked right past them, I couldn't keep from making eye contact. I wanted to be able to tell from their expressions whether they'd read the article yet, but their faces were blank. What I felt in that moment looking at them was what I continued to feel until graduation—the suspicion, but not the certainty, that other people were scorning me, the sense that their scorn was not unjustified, and also the knowledge that maybe they were not thinking of me at all.

I realized already that this would be, in the context of Ault, a very big deal. Yet at the same time, to most students, it was someone else's big deal. Only to me was it personal. Maybe when kids went home over the summer, people would say to them: *Is your school really that snobby? Was that girl as unhappy as she seemed?* But it would be a topic of conversation; it wouldn't be their life.

I went to bed before dinner Sunday night—I just didn't want to be conscious anymore—and at one-fifteen, when I'd already awakened eight or nine times and couldn't stand it any longer, I rose, changed into a T-shirt and a pair of sweat-pants and left the dorm while Martha snored softly. It had rained that day, and the courtyard was dark and shiny. I could have gone through the basement, which was Cross's usual route, but I was wholly unafraid of getting caught; I have always believed that extreme circumstances protect you from ordinary dangers, and while I recognize my belief as illogical, I have not yet been proven wrong.

At first, the common room of Cross's dorm appeared empty, But when the door shut behind me, a head rose from the couch in front of the television. It was Monty Harr, a freshman. The sound to the TV was off, and Monty's face looked gray.

"Where's Cross's room?" I asked.

He blinked at me.

"Cross Sugarman," I said. "Which room is his?"

"At the end of the hall on the left," Monty finally said. He was rubbing his eyes as I walked away.

There was a poster of a basketball player on the door, a guy in a green uniform leaping through the air with a blurry crowd behind him. I knocked, and when no one responded, I turned the knob and opened it. The light was on inside, and someone was sitting at a desk. At first, because I was looking for Cross, I thought it was him, but the person looked up and I saw it was Cross's roommate, Devin. Over the last four years, Devin had gone from skinny to almost fat and he had blond hair, dark eyebrows, and a pug nose.

My bravado, or whatever had propelled me across the courtyard, dwindled. "Hi," I said in a quiet voice. I looked around the room; both the beds were unmade, and the only light came from a desk lamp and a lava lamp set on the windowsill. No one was there besides Devin.

A grin had spread across his face. "It's the woman of the hour."

"Devin, please." I tried to remember if we had spoken to each other since I'd assassinated him in ninth grade. Not much, but still—weren't we both people? Might not my palpable desperation elicit sympathy from him just this once?

"Please what?" he said. "I have no idea where he is, if that's what you're asking. Anyway, isn't it kind of late for a young girl to be out by herself?"

"I know what time it is."

"After that article today, I'd be careful about giving Byden a reason to toss me out."

"You don't get kicked out for breaking visitation the first time," I said.

"Forgive me." Devin smirked. "I didn't realize you've never broken visitation before."

"Fuck you," I said, and maybe my mistake was being the one to make things definitively ugly.

"I'm tempted to say fuck you, too, but I think my roommate's got that taken care of."

I turned to leave, and Devin said, "A quick question."

I paused (of course I did) in the threshold.

"Are you fish or cheese?"

I didn't have the slightest idea what he was talking about.

"You have to be one," he said. "So which is it?"

Still, I simply looked at him.

"For the list. You know, we're keeping a list, we're checking

442

it twice." He was actually singing, and it occurred to me for the first time that perhaps he was drunk or stoned. He opened his desk drawer, saying as he did, "You're one of our missing seniors. Your roommate, too, as a matter of fact, so it'd be great to kill two birds with one stone tonight." From the drawer, he'd removed a rumpled school catalog. He opened it, flipped to the back, and passed it to me. This was where the class lists were, and in the spaces between people's last names and the place they were from—between, for instance, *Deirdre Danielle Schwartz* and *Scarsdale, New York*—it said, in capital letters, written with a red marker: *FISH*. They didn't all say *FISH*; some said *CHEESE*. And they weren't all written with red marker—some were in black or blue ballpoint pen. Also, they weren't next to everyone's names; they were next to some girls', and no boys'. I glanced several times between the catalog and Devin; I wasn't sure what I was reading, but I wasn't uninterested. Aspeth, I saw, was *CHEESE*; Horton Kinnelly was also *CHEESE*; Hillary Tompkins was *FISH*.

Finally—not because he wanted to give me the gift of an explanation, I think, but just because he was frustrated by my lack of understanding—Devin said, "It's what you taste like. All girls are one or the other. Get it?"

A question formed inside me, but before I asked it aloud, the answer formed itself, too: *No, not when you kiss them. Not then.* Knowing what the list represented, it seemed like I ought to throw the catalog across the room. But the problem was, I was still curious. The list was so—it was so weirdly attentive. It was something I myself might have kept, in a parallel universe. "How long have you been working on this?" I asked.

"Oh, I'm not the only one. God, no. Personally, I sub-scribe to the idea that it's better to receive than to give if you know what I mean. But it's a collective effort passed down from generation to generation.' Naturally, it gets updated every year."

"What a classy tradition."

"Listen." His eyes narrowed. "Before you get on your high horse, you might want to know who this year's custodian is."

I didn't say anything.

"Do you not believe me?" he asked, and I sensed because of the way, he said it, by how much he hoped I'd challenge him, that he was telling the truth.

"Given that he's the custodian," Devin continued, "I'd say it's pretty ungenerous of him not to fill in certain blanks. But therein lies the paradox."

"Maybe he respects other people's privacy," I said, and Devin laughed so heartily, and so spontaneously, that I felt sure he wasn't just trying to torment me.

"Chivalrous Sug—that's how you see him, isn't it? That's great. It's classic."

I needed to leave—for real this time, because there was nothing to gain from staying.

"Let it be said"—here, Devin sounded genuinely admiring—"that no one ever played Ault better than Cross Sugarman. It's practically obscene."

Leave, Lee, I thought, and heard myself ask, "What's that supposed to mean?"

"Just that you've got to hand it to him. He gets the grades, he gets the positions, he gets the girls, but most of all, he gets the respect. I bet you hardly know the guy."

Perhaps this was what I'd been waiting for—an insult that was undeniably true, "You're an asshole," I said, and I stepped into the hallway, letting the door close behind me,

My parents finally reached me the next morning; they had called repeatedly on Sunday, but whenever another girl in the dorm knocked on our door, I asked her to tell them I wasn't there. This was considered poor dorm-phone protocol, necessitating a return trip downstairs to the common room, but nobody said no—I could see how other people deferred to the dubious celebrity the *Times* article bestowed on me. By right after Sunday chapel, which I'd skipped for the second time ever, everyone knew. I hadn't left the dorm for the rest of the day, but I had seen it in girls' faces. "Were people talking about it at lunch?" I'd asked Martha, and she had said, "Sort of." Which had been gentler than saying yes.

The way my parents got to me was by calling at six-fifteen a.m. on Monday morning. Abby Sciver knocked on our door, waking us up, and I could tell from her bleary expression that she'd just awakened, too, presumably because of the phone's ring. "It's your dad, Lee," she said, and it was far too early to ask her to take a message, or to have my father believe that I was otherwise occupied.

It wasn't just him. He was on one phone, and my mother was on the other. At the same time, he said, "What kind of crap is this?" and my mother said, "Lee, if you feel like a nobody, I wish you wouldn't feel that way because you're so special."

"Mom. I don't—it's not—please, will you guys not overreact?"

"I just have one question for you," my father said, "and that's why have you been lying to us for the last four years?"

"Go easy, Terry," my mother said.

"I'll go easy when she answers me."

"I wasn't lying," I said.

"You asked us to make sacrifices for your education, and we made them. We bought your books and your plane tickets, and why do you think we did that? Because you told us it was worth it. You said you loved it up there living in a dorm and going to your brilliant classes. And now you say, no, here's my misery and here's how the school treats me and I've been given every advantage but it wasn't what I wanted. Well, I don't know what the hell you wanted, Lee."

Listening to him, I found it hard to locate the center of his anger. People at Ault were angry at me for making critical remarks in a public forum, but my father's displeasure was, obviously, personal.

"Dad and I know you have lots of friends," my mother

said. "For heaven's sake, Martha is president of your class, and she's just crazy about you. And Sin-Jun, and the Spanish girls—"

"Mom, you don't have to name all my friends."

"But, Lee, what the lady wrote about you just isn't true. That's what I've been telling Dad. It's not your fault if you trusted the media because your headmaster told you to."

"And we're supposed to come see you graduate in a week?" my father said. "Your mom and I are supposed to take off from work and pull your brothers out of school so they can say, 'We never got behind your daughter, but thanks for all the checks you wrote. You know what I say to that? Thanks but no thanks."

My father had never understood, and I had never really tried to get him to, that the checks he wrote were utterly insignificant, practically symbolic in their tininess. I think he'd genuinely convinced himself that if he pulled me out of Ault, Mr. Byden would have to, say, trade in his Mercedes.

"So are you not coming to my graduation?" I asked.

"Of course we're coming," my mother said.

"You're lucky it's over," my father said, "because if it wasn't, it still would be over for you. No way would we send you back for another year."

"Lee, just think how nice it will be to go to college closer to home. You had a big adventure in high school, and now you can know, well, maybe where you're from isn't so bad."

"I never thought where I was from was bad."

For the first time, the phone line was silent.

"Have a lot of people said stuff to you about the article?" I asked. Who that my family knew read *The New York Times*?

"Mrs. Petrash told us her mom called them first thing yesterday morning," my mother said. "That's how we knew to get it. Do you know that woman is over eighty; but her eyesight is sharp as a tack. And, Terry, who left a message?"

"I didn't hear any message. And with all due respect, Linda, I'm not real interested in Edith Petrash's eyesight right now."

446

"What do you want from me, Dad?" I wasn't fighting with him, and I didn't feel hostile. Mostly, I felt ashamed. I understood—this was the reason I'd avoided their calls the previous day—that I had failed them. My father was right that I had lied. But lying was not the real transgression; rather, my failure resided in my inability to lie consistently. We had made a deal, the three of us—*if you let me go, I will pretend that going was a good idea*—and I had violated the terms of our agreement. In the end, the way I betrayed my parents stayed with me longer, and felt far worse, than the way I betrayed Ault.

"I want you to stop being so impressed by bullshit," my father said.

"What Dad means is that being rich doesn't make you a better person."

"Good luck getting her to believe that, Linda," my father said. "You really think Lee'll listen to two simpletons like her parents?" Then, in the voice of his I disliked the most, he added, "Sorry we couldn't buy you a big house with a palm tree, Lee. Sorry you got such a raw deal for a family."

At roll call, Cross was wearing a navy blue polo shirt, but the brightness of daytime, the brutal energy, always stalled me. I'd approach him after formal dinner, I decided, but he wasn't there. The new dining hall prefects from the junior class had been elected the week before (how quickly, really even before you graduated, you became obsolete—for a little while, because you were a senior, the school was yours and then it wasn't yours at all anymore), and Cross must have skipped the meal altogether, now that he could. As people were leaving, I walked over to Devin and tapped his shoulder. He turned around. "Where is he?" I asked.

Devin regarded me disdainfully. "The last I knew, he went to shoot hoops."

As I walked to the gym, the fading sunlight was yellow and the air smelled like cut grass. Though I'd imagined that Devin might have misled me and I'd find the gym locked for the night, the door swung open when I pulled it. Climbing the stairs leading to the basketball court, I could hear the pound of a ball against the floor.

He was alone. For a few seconds, I stood in the doorway, as he must have once stood, unobserved, in the doorway to my room. He dribbled up the court, and shot from the three-point line. The ball dropped through the net, and I began clapping.

He looked up from retrieving the ball. "Hey."

As he walked toward me, his face was red, and beads of sweat rested on his forehead and ran in streaks from his hair-line down his neck, and down his arms and legs as well. I was wearing a cotton skirt and a linen blouse, but all I wanted was for him to embrace me. Of course, he wasn't going to—it was still light out, we were standing up, he was holding the ball. And besides, he hadn't touched me in more than six weeks.

"I came by last night." I said.

"Yeah, Devin told me. Sorry I missed you." As we regarded each other, he seemed to realize that I was waiting for more. "I was down the hall in Thad and Rob's room," he added. I had never known him to lie, but it seemed so much likelier, it seemed so heartbreakingly logical, that where he'd really been was with Melodie Ryan.

And then I couldn't help it—I'd wanted to ease into the conversation, to not seem overwrought—and I asked, "Did you see Low Notes?"

I often imagined that my own unseemly frames of reference would elude other people, but Cross said, "Yeah, I saw them."

"And?"

"*The A. V.* is written by a bunch of losers."

I looked down at the floor, the painted lines and blocks against the shiny wood. "But is it true?" I said, and my voice caught. I had never wanted to cry in front of Cross, because girls who cry—especially girls who cry while having

448

talks—are so ordinary. "Is she your girlfriend?" I asked.

"I don't have a girlfriend," Cross said.

I blinked several times—no tears had actually fallen—and said, "Right. How foolish of me."

He said nothing, and I understood that whatever I had to say, I'd have to say outright; he wouldn't tease it from me.

The knowledge, unfortunately, wasn't much help—I still couldn't say what I wanted to because it was lodged inside me like a bowel movement and all that was coming out was hot stuttering air. "I guess the big question," I said, "is am I fish or cheese?"

"Oh, Jesus."

"No, I'm really curious." I made my voice earnest.

"Devin's a prick," Cross said, "And letting him upset you is a waste of time."

"If he's a prick. why do you room with him?"

"He wasn't always this way. He's bitter now because he's going to Trinity."

So Cross had also been experiencing roommate tension this year; all along, we could have commiserated. Surely there were other, ordinary things we could have talked about if only we'd known—how annoying it was to wait in line to take a shower every morning, for example.

"Anyway," Cross said, "that's trash talk. It's what guys say in the dorm when they're showing off."

"But you're the custodian of the list."

"The what?"

"Devin said—"

"Lee, Devin's full of shit I don't know how much more plainly I can put it." Even saying this, Cross wasn't angry; he hadn't yet made the investment that being angry would require, and I had the strong feeling that he wanted to go back to shooting baskets. "Frankly," he said, "I'm having a tough time seeing what this conversation is about."

I probably knew then that this was my one chance, which made it harder, not easier, to say what I meant. "I just don't understand what you were doing with me," I said. "I mean ever. Sometimes I try to see this all from your perspective, and none of it makes sense. You come into our room and you're all drunk and maybe you knew I'd had a big crush on you or maybe it was just random. And I'm this dorky girl but I cooperate. I melt at the slightest touch. So we fool around, whatever. But then you come back. That's what I don't get. God forbid you ever talk to me at dinner, but you keep coming back for the whole year." Actually, not for the whole year—not much past spring break. And wasn't I only able to say this because he'd stopped coming? It felt like I was trying to salvage something, but wasn't it all already finished?

Cross shifted the basketball so he was holding it against his right hip. "Saying that I never talked to you at dinner— you're acting like I tried to hide something."

"Well?"

"Are you for real? Lee, people knew about—about"—I think he was hesitating to say *us*—"about what was going on," he finally said. "You're crazy if you think nobody knew. And regardless, you're the one who set the terms. You can't deny that."

"What are you talking about?"

"You said let's not tell people about this, don't kiss me at breakast. It never seemed like you wanted a boyfriend."

"So is that why you didn't send me a flower on Valentine's Day? Because I told you don't send me flowers, was that it?"

"That's exactly what you told me."

"You would never have been my boyfriend," I said.

His jaw tensed, which meant that at least I was getting to him. "You wouldn't have," I said. "I'm sure of it."

"That must be nice to be sure of things."

Simultaneously, I had the impulse not to contradict him—just to let his comment sit there so that later I could cling to its implication—and I had the impulse to destroy it for the lie it was.

"I'm not sure of everything," I said. "But I'm sure

of this. You would never have been my boyfriend."

For a long time, we watched each other. Finally—not meanly—he said, "Yeah, you're probably right," and I began to cry. (When I went over the conversation, and over and over and over it, thinking of that part continued to make me cry. It never made things any better to remember that I had forced the admission.)

"Lee," he said, and his voice was pleading. "Lee, it was—there were a lot of things that were good. You were funny. That was one of the things."

I wiped my eyes.

"You were—this will sound weird, but you were business-like. It was as if you expected me to come back and were trying to plan for it."

I had been *businesslike*?

"You'll be happier in college," he said.

I blinked at him.

"I just think you're that kind of person."

"Is this about the *Times* article?"

"No. Well, not exactly. It's not like anything you said in the article surprised me."

To be talking about something other than us and whether he'd ever touch me again seemed a waste of time. And yet I was intrigued.

"Your mistake wasn't expressing your ideas per se," he said. "It was expressing them in *The New York Times* instead of writing an editorial for *The A.V.*, or giving a chapel talk. In the *Times*, you're just giving ammunition to people who want to think prep schools are evil, which isn't what will make anything change on this campus."

"So you think things *should* change?"

"Some things, sure. On the whole, Ault does a good job, but there's always room for improvement." Of course he thought this—what a balanced perspective!

"Were you appalled that I said all that stuff to the reporter?" I asked.

451

"You could have chosen a different forum. That's my only point. That, and that I think it's good you're going to a big school, somewhere less conformist than Ault. Which isn't to say you're as weird as you think you are." (How bizarre this conversation was turning out to be, what surprising remarks were emerging from Cross's mouth.) "You confuse being weird and spending time alone," he continued. "But anyone who's really interested in anything spends time alone. Like basketball for me—look at what I'm doing right now. Or Norie Cleehan and pottery, or Horton and ballet. I could give twenty other examples. If you want to be good at something, you have to practice, and usually you practice by yourself. The fact that you spend time alone—you shouldn't feel like it's strange."

But I'm not practicing anything, I thought. Or, if I had been: What was it?

"Also," he said, "and this gets back to the article, if you feel like there are differences between you and other people, how much you want to play them up is really your decision. Obviously, not in every case, but in most cases. Even Devin will say *kike* this or *Jew you down* or whatever. And I don't say anything, because what would getting pissed off achieve? He's just talking."

"Wait a second," I said. "You're Jewish?"

"On my dad's side. Which is technically the half that doesn't count, but with a name like Sugarman—"

"Sugarman's a Jewish name?"

"It's the English version of Zuckerman."

Cross was *Jewish*? Never once had this occurred to me. But he was so popular, he was senior prefect. (Did other people know? Had that always been part of the reason Dede had liked him?)

"I'm just saying that—" His tone softened. "That I bet things would be easier for you if you either realized you're not that weird or decided that being weird isn't bad."

The gym was quiet. I was so flattered and so embarrassed that I couldn't make eye contact with him.

452

I heard him swallow, and then—all this time, he had been holding the basketball against his right hip—he leaned down and set the ball against the floor. When he was upright again, he said, "Lee—" and when I dared to glance at him, he was looking at me in a way that was both predatory and tender (I do not think it's an exaggeration to say that my life since then has been spent in pursuit of that look, and that I have yet to find it a second time in just that balance; perhaps it doesn't, after high school, exist in that balance) and it was because whatever he was about to do was exactly what I wanted while also scaring the hell out of me that I folded my arms and said, "I'll have to take this all under advisement". I knew immediately that I'd sounded sarcastic, and I did nothing to correct the impression. I guess that I had meant to sound that way, because this was the most terrifying thing in the world: that he knew me—he did know me, after all—and that knowing each other, we were going to kiss.

(And this is how I know that it's all just words, words, words—that fundamentally, they make no difference. *I wouldn't have been your boyfriend*, he was saying, and, *it ended between us because of this*, and I was saying, *no, this*, and a good way through that conversation, he'd still have kissed me. Our relationship, for as long as things were good, and in that moment when they could have been good again, was about the irrelevance of words. You feel what you feel, you act as you act; who in the history of the world has ever been convinced by a well-reasoned argument?)

And after I'd folded my arms, after I'd used that terrible tone, his stance—inclining slightly forward—reversed. He exhaled through his nose, then crossed his own arms. "Okay," he said. "You do that."

It still wasn't too late. (Of course it wasn't too late! But it was so hard to believe that just because he'd have kissed me thirty seconds before, he still wanted to now. Look how easily I'd dissuaded him, or maybe it was that I'd misinterpreted his original intent.) No, it wasn't too late, but, as with the fire drill, it felt too late. And so, deciding that the moment had passed just like that, with me helpless in its tide—I let the sarcasm come surging in.

"But enough about me," I said, "How about Melodie—fish or cheese?"

"Jesus Christ, Lee."

"Aren't we friends? I don't mean Melodie and me, I mean you and me. And don't friends share secrets and closeness? But you've never told me any secrets at all. I feel kind of shortchanged."

"Don't be like this."

"Like what?" I laughed, briefly and bitterly. "Don't be myself? I thought we just established how funny and businesslike I am."

"Act however you want, but don't bring Melodie into it."

It injured me that the weight of what he'd just said rested on her rather than on me.

"So you admit you're—well, if you're not officially going out with her, I'm not sure what to call it. Fucking her? Or I guess, since it's Melodie, I should say butt-fucking her."

"This is ridiculous." He scooped up the basketball and walked toward the hoop. Over his shoulder, he said, "I doubt you've ever talked to her, but she's actually a very nice person."

"You're right," I said. "I haven't talked to her." The fact that he'd walked away was by far the worst thing that had happened in the conversation. I raised my voice. "I can't comment on her niceness, but I do think she's attractive. She might even be attractive enough for you to associate with in public."

He had begun dribbling in front of the basket, his back to me; at this, he stopped, turned to the side—I could see that with his upper teeth, he was biting his lower lip—threw the ball so it slammed against the door I'd entered, and glared at me. "You want to know?" he shouted. "You really want to know? Fish! That's what you taste like!"

The door he'd hit the ball against was still reverberating; otherwise, the gym was absolutely quiet.

"I can't believe you just said that."

"You asked me!"

"Yeah, I guess I did," I said, and I knew that I was stunned partly because I could hear it in my own voice.

"Lee," he said. "I didn't mean to—"

I shook my head, cutting him off. I was about to cry again, but I wasn't crying yet, and I wanted to use the time I had left. In a very tight voice, I said, "When I was in junior high, I used to think I would turn out to be one of the guys, and boys would say, 'Oh, you're so great.' but they wouldn't date me. I thought I wasn't pretty enough. But then I got to Ault and first of all, I'm not really friends with any guys. And then, with you this year, I thought, if Cross will keep hooking up with me, maybe I'm okay after all. But time passed and I never became your girlfriend. And so then I thought, not only was I wrong, but my life turned out the opposite of how I expected. Meaning, it wasn't my appearance—that's not the bad thing about me. It's my personality. But how do I know which part? I have no idea. I've tried to think about if it's one thing in isolation or everything together, or what can I do to fix it, or how can I convince you. Then I thought, maybe it *is* my looks, maybe I was right before. And I never figured it out. Obviously, I didn't. But I've spent a lot of this year trying. And the reason I'm telling you all this is that I want you to know no one in my life has ever made me feel worse about myself than you."

Was this a pathetic thing to tell him? Was it even entirely true? It doesn't matter anymore. It's what I said. Then I said, "So I guess I'll go now," and I walked out of the gym.

"Lee!" he yelled.

It's hard to say if I should have turned back. The fact is, I didn't, and he didn't chase me, and he called my name only once.

* * *

In the phone booth in Elwyn's, I lifted the receiver from the hook. On one of my thighs I'd set Angie Varizi's business card, which I glanced at as I dialed, and on the other thigh I'd set the roll of quarters I would use to pay for the call. On the second ring, a famiar voice said, "This is Angie Varizi at *The New York Times*."

"This is Lee Fiora," I said.

She hesitated.

"From Ault," I added.

"Of course. Good to hear from you, Lee. Forgive me if I seem distracted; but I've got a million and one things going on today."

I opened my mouth before it occurred to me that I was unsure what to say.

"Do you want some extra copies of the article?" she asked.

"No. That's okay."

"What can I do for you?"

"The article—" I stopped. "Why didn't you tell me it would be like that? I thought I was just telling you stuff for context."

"Lee, unless you specifically identify your comments as off-the-record, everything you say when you're being interviewed is fair game." Then she said, "No, you can leave it here." To me, she said. "So are people giving you a hard time?"

I didn't say anything.

"Is that your problem? Or is it theirs?"

"I'm graduating in less than a week," I said. "And I'm this person who aired the school's dirty laundry." (I aired the school's dirty laundry and there was proof. There's still proof—go to a library, find the microfiche from the month and year I graduated.)

"You're in a really insular community," she said. "But I've gotten a ton of terrific feedback for the article, including from other boarding-school graduates. It might be frustrating now, but I'm confident that you'll look back and know you did the right thing. This'll be something you really feel proud of."

Listening to her, I realized how foolish I had been to call—I had imagined she might say something that would actually make the situation better.

"Your classmates are defensive," she said. "It's hard for anyone, and especially for the privileged, to see themselves objectively. I'll tell you a story. I did my undergrad at Harvard. When I was a freshman, I had a roommate who bought a beautiful black wool coat with a black velvet collar. Now, less than a week—"

The automated voice of the phone company requested that I insert another ninety cents. Angie was still talking; perhaps on her end, she couldn't hear the voice. The pack of quarters on my lap was two-thirds full, but I simply sat there listening, motionless, until the call got disconnected.

There was a special dinner on Wednesday for the faculty and the seniors, welcoming us into the alumni association. In our room beforehand, I sat on the futon, dressed but paralyzed, and Martha said, "We're not even talking about it. Just follow me." Walking to the terrace outside the dining hall, I fought the impulse to clutch Martha's arm. At first, it wasn't so bad, it was almost possible to pretend this was an ordinary event at which I felt ordinarily skittish, but when I got in the buffet line, I heard Hunter Jergenson, who was two people in front of me, say,"—then she could have left. No one was holding her hostage, so it's not like—" and then Sally Bishop jabbed Hunter in the back. "What?" Hunter said and turned around, and our eyes met. Three days had passed since the publication of the article, but if anything, people seemed to be talking about it more. I'd heard that Mr. Byden had been flooded with calls from alumni, that the admissions office was being contacted by students who'd registered to come for the following year and were having second thoughts, that on Monday Mr. Corning's second-period class abandoned their review session to discuss the article.

When we'd gotten our food, Martha and I went to sit on a

low stone wall. After we'd eaten, we threw away our paper plates, and as we passed Horton Kinnelly on the way back from the trash can, she said, "You're going to the University of Michigan, aren't you, Lee?"

I nodded.

"That's what I thought," she said and kept walking.

I looked at Martha. "What did that mean? Does she think that because I didn't get into a better college, that's why I insulted Ault?"

"Lee, it's not worth thinking about."

"I'm going back to the room."

"But the juniors are about to come sing to us." Martha's eyes searched my face. "Want me to go with you?"

Of course I wanted her to go with me. I also wanted, as I'd wanted before at Ault, to be a different person—this time, to be a person for whom it was perfectly fine to stand there and watch the juniors sing. "You should stay," I said.

On the edge of the terrace, Mrs. Stanchak, my college counselor, stopped me. "I think you're very brave," Mrs. Stanchak said, and I began to weep. All around me I could hear my classmates talking and laughing. It was a warm evening in early June. Mrs. Stanchak enfolded me in a hug, and I shook against her.

I had cried plenty of times at Ault, but never this publicly; my eyes were shut, and I feared that I couldn't open them ever. Then I felt another pair of hands on my back, a familiar voice saying, "Let's get you out of here."

At some point as we walked down the terrace steps and onto the path leading to my dorm, I realized the person with me, his arm still set against my back, was Darden Pittard. I realized this in a factual way; I was too distraught to consider the oddness of it or the way it looked. I simply accepted his presence and it was a moment, I thought later, when perhaps I knew what it felt like to be someone else, a person who experienced life without dissecting it.

At the arch leading to the dorm courtyard, I was still crying fresh tears, and my shoulders were heaving. "You want to keep walking?" Darden said. "Let's keep walking." He guided me past the dorms, and at the schoolhouse we sat side by side on steps outside the entrance. Across the circle, our classmates ate dessert on the terrace. "You just need some time," Darden said. "But you'll be fine. You'll be totally fine."

Eventually, I stopped sobbing. I thought—I had never thought this about a guy my age—that Darden would be a good father. We watched as juniors emerged from the dorms and the library and walked toward the terrace.

"She was trouble," Darden said.

At first, I didn't know who he meant, and then I did.

"I can't really blame her." It was the first thing I'd said in at least fifteen minutes, and my voice was croaky. "Unless you tell the reporter something is off-the-record, everything you say to them is fair game."

"Whatever. She had an agenda. She wanted me to be an angry black guy. She had us all pigeonholed before we set foot in Fletcher's classroom."

"But you're *not* angry." I glanced at him. "Are you?"

"No more than most people."

"So why—why did I fall for Angie's act when you didn't?"

"Because you're white."

I looked at him to see if he was joking; he gave no indication that he was.

"Black people who live in a white world learn to be careful," he said. "You learn not to make waves." The only time I had ever heard anyone, including Darden himself, discuss his race was the time sophomore year in Ms. Moray's class when he and Dede and Aspeth had gotten in trouble for their Uncle Tom skit. "Or let me put it this way. You don't make waves unless there's a reason, and it better be good. Because once you do, that's it. You're a troublemaker, and they never think of you any other way."

"Then the opposite must be true, too," I said, "Mr. Byden must love you now. He probably wants to make you a trustee."

459

Darden laughed.

"Did he say anything to you? He hasn't said anything to me."

"In passing," Darden said. "Nothing major."

"He's probably so mad at me." I'd been a little surprised, actually, not to hear from Mr. Byden at all; leaving roll call the previous morning, I'd made eye contact with him, and he'd simply looked away.

"If it's weighing on you, write him a letter this summer," Darden said. "For now, let it blow over."

On the terrace, the juniors had assembled. "I don't want to make you miss the singing," I said.

"I'll live,' Darden said.

Then we could hear them—not the specific words, but the sound of a piano, and voices. It sounded farther away than it was.

"I can't believe we're graduating," I said.

"I'm ready." He smiled, and it seemed to me a sad smile. There was so much I didn't know about Darden.

We stopped talking and just listened to the music, the lyrics we couldn't decipher. When the song had ended, every senior got a white balloon, and they walked onto the circle and released them, all at the same time. The sky was darkening, and the balloons as they floated up were like dozens of tiny glowing moons; people stood on the grass with their necks craned, watching the balloons until they vanished. That wasn't the last year Ault released balloons, but it was the second to last. They stopped because it was bad for the environment, which isn't something you can argue with, at least not persuasively. It's just that—the balloons were so pretty. I'm not saying they should have kept the tradition. But they really were pretty. And it seems like a lot of other things stopped around then, too, like my classmates and I were at the tail end of something. We still listened to music from the sixties and seventies, but kids a few years younger than us, including my brothers, had their own music. And clothes, too. Through my

460

senior year, I wore floral dresses that came to my shins, sometimes with a belt of fabric at the waist, sometimes with puffy sleeves, with a square neck, or a lace collar, or a corduroy Peter Pan collar. Everyone wore these, even the prettiest girls—I wore them *because* the prettiest girls wore them. A few years after college, I gave away all the dresses, though it was hard to imagine who would want them—someone's grandmother, maybe. By then, teenage girls wore short skirts, fitted shirts and sweaters, and in the years after that, they wore really short skirts and really fitted tops. And technology—I guess e-mail existed when I was at Ault, but I had never heard of it. No one had voice mail, either, because we didn't have phones in our rooms, and certainly no student had a cell phone. When I think of how a whole dorm would share a pay phone, how most of the time when our parents called either the phone rang and rang without getting answered or else it was busy, it feels as if I'm remembering the 1950s. And I know the world always changes; it just seems like for us it changed kind of fast.

"Darden," I said. The balloons were long gone, and our classmates were dispersing. Sitting on the steps with him, I felt untouchable, protected from both the judgment of others and time itself—as long as Darden was next to me, we were still at Ault, our futures hadn't happened yet—but I knew that I had to let him leave. It was partly because I wanted to find out the answer and partly just to keep him there that I said, "Did you ever hear that Cross Sugarman and I—that we were—"

"I heard something about it," Darden said. "But nothing big."

"You heard, like, that we were—what did you hear?" (Darden was so dignified, and I was so awkward and insatiable.)

"That you were hanging out for a while. Something like that. I wouldn't sweat it."

I couldn't correct him. To tell him that he was comforting me in the wrong way, in the opposite of the way I wanted—it

461

would cast a shadow over the fact that just prior to this he had understood exactly what I needed.

"Anyhow," Darden said, "that was months ago. And no one but a fool believes everything they hear in this place."

Did he mean that he was willing to act like it wasn't true? Or just that he was ready for the conversation to be over? Probably that, the latter.

We stood. "You're okay?"he said.

When I nodded, he hugged me. It was the kind of hug he and Aspeth might exchange after walking back from the library to the dorms for curfew, a hearty hug but a throwaway hug. At least, hypothetically, a throwaway hug; for me, it was the first time I'd been hugged by any boy at Ault besides Cross.

"I'm sorry that I screwed up," I blurted out.

He shook his head. He didn't say I hadn't screwed up (he probably thought I had—also, of course, he was probably the one who, in a factual and not cruel way, had made the comment to Angie Varizi about my not being popular). Instead, Darden said, "I know you are."

Martha came to find me in the library. Since everyone else was outside all the time, the library was where I'd been hiding when I couldn't stand to be in our room anymore. Seniors were exempt from exams, so there was no work. All that was left was graduation itself and, after that, senior week, during which we'd drive from party to party in Dedham and Lyme and Locust Valley. Because it was the very last part of Ault, and because how could I not, I actually was planning to attend the whole thing.

The past few days had been sunny and endless and I had felt afraid of everyone and despairing about Cross. I'd spent most of the time trying unsuccessfully to pack. Every June before, when we'd had to remove our posters and unscrew Martha's futon and stack our books in boxes that we stored in the dorm basement, the chore had depressed me—all the space in the room, the blank walls. It reminded me how ephemeral our lives at Ault were. This time, I would fold three sweaters and stick them in a box and then I'd need to get out of the room, and I'd peer out the window, and if the coast was clear, I'd race outside and sprint past the chapel and the dining hall to the library and go into the periodicals room, which was empty and dark and cool, and I'd read magazines, and sometimes in the middle of an article, I would look up and think, *I have ruined everything.* During my time at Ault, I'd always felt I had things to hide, reasons to apologize. But I hadn't, I saw now. In a strange way, it was as if all along I'd anticipated what would happen with *The New York Times*, I'd known how it would end.

When she entered the periodicals room, Martha was breathing heavily, as if she'd been running. "Scoot over," she said.

I was sitting on the floor, my back against a wall. I shifted, and she sat down next to me.

She said, "You know how tomorrow's chapel will be the last one for the year?"

I nodded.

"Apparently, some seniors were looking for a student to give a talk refuting what you said in the article. I guess they've found someone."

"Who?"

"That's the part I don't know. The rumor was that they were trying to find either a minority or a white person on scholarship."

"Good luck. So which seniors?"

"I don't know that, either."

I looked at her.

"Who you'd expect," she said. "Horton Kinnelly. Doug Miles."

"And is this the part where you tell me I should go?" I said. "To build my character or something?"

"Not to build your character. But I do think you should go because it's the last chapel."

463

"Martha, probably half the senior class will skip."

"I don't think so." She shook her head. "People are getting sentimental."

I thought of Darden and said, "Not everyone. Not you."

"Just wait. I'll be bawling at graduation."

We were quiet, and I could hear the sound of a saw outside; adjacent to the chapel, the maintenance crew was building the graduation stage. Because the ceremony was supposed to be held outside, all the seniors were obsessed with whether the sunshine would last. I could truly say that I didn't care—in fact, a part of me would have been grimly satisfied if it rained and we had to move into the gym.

And similarly, a part of me was relieved to know that I would, perhaps implicitly or perhaps not implicitly at all, be scolded in public. This seemed the Ault way, to be held accountable. Already, over the years, I had gotten away with too much.

"I sure blew it, huh?" I said,

Martha was quiet, and then she said, "Well. it's not like it was an accident."

I stiffened. *Not you, too, Martha*, I thought. It would be more than I could take, though I realized in that moment that she had never said to me anything like, *You weren't wrong*, or, *This wasn't your fault*. What she'd said instead was, in essence, *You can't let it bother you*. Not to be confused with *I'm on your side*.

"You're not stupid," she continued. She did not seem particularly accusatory; she seemed to be musing. "In fact, you're probably the most careful person I know about what you say."

"Are you suggesting I wanted this to happen?"

"I don't see it as that black-and-white."

Sitting there, so close together, I hated her a little bit. But this was not the same as thinking she was completely wrong. Maybe the reason I'd had a premonition about how it would all end at Ault was that I would cause it to end that way. Because how was it possible that I'd lasted four years without

464

ever truly exposing myself, and then blown it in the last week? Could it have been that secretly I had craved the opportunity to say to everyone at Ault, *You think I think nothing. But when I do not speak, I am always thinking. I have opinions about this place, about all of you*. Maybe. Maybe that's what I'd wanted, but if I'd wanted it, I'd wanted it on my own terms. I had imagined that Angie Varizi could make me seem articulate and persuasive, not bitter and isolated, not vulnerable.

"Are you mad at me because I made you look bad in front of Mr. Byden?" I asked, and as I said it, the idea occurred to me for the first time. "Are you the one who told him to have *The New York Times* interview me?"

Martha said nothing and then she said, "I don't think anyone is to blame. It's the way the situation played out. I made a choice to suggest you, he made a choice to have you do it, you made a choice to tell the woman what you told her."

It was so terrible I almost couldn't think about it—that Martha had imagined she was giving me a present. She had wanted to be nice, to provide me with the chance to stand out that I'd never been able to provide for myself. I felt guilt bordering on nausea, but I also felt angry, angrier than before. One, because she should have told me—possibly I'd still have said what I said, but I'd have understood that I was meant to praise the school. And two, because there was another thing I was mad at Martha for, it had been simmering for the last few days or perhaps for the last few months, and in the same moment, there in the library, I understood exactly what this murky resentment toward her was, and I understood that I would never be able to express it. I resented her for having said, back in October, that she didn't think Cross would be my boyfriend. She had made it true! If she'd said she could picture it, it didn't mean it would have happened. But by saying she couldn't, she'd pretty much sealed that it wouldn't. Had she not understood how literally I took her, how much I trusted her advice? She had discouraged me from being hopeful, and how can you ever forgive a person for that? And how

465

could I ever tell her any of this? It would be too ugly. For me to have messed up, to have done a thing that required *her* forgiveness, was not atypical, For her to be the one at fault would unbalance our friendship. I would not try to explain anything, and who knew if I could have explained it anyway? The mistake I had made was so public and obvious, and the one she'd made was private and subjective; I was its only witness. No, I would not tell her anything; I would be good old incompetent Lee, lovably flawed Lee, a golden retriever who just can't stay out of the creek and keeps returning to the house with wet, smelly fur.

"So you think I betrayed the school?" I said, and I could tell I sounded cranky, but cranky was (Martha would never know this) something we could recover from—cranky was a far cry from what I actually felt.

"That's not what I said."

"You might as well have." (I did wonder, was it possible that there'd be nothing left to miss? Finished with Ault as an institution, finished with Cross, finished with Martha.)

"I think you told the reporter what you meant to tell her," Martha said.

"Martha, were you brainwashed by being prefect? When did you decide that it should be against the law to criticize Ault?"

"Exactly. That's my point. You had criticisms, and you expressed them."

"So now I should deal with the consequences?"

She did not reply for a long time. Then, at last, she said, "Yeah, kind of."

"Then what are you doing here? Why are you warning me about the chapel talk when it's exactly what I deserve?"

"You're my best friend, Lee. I can disagree with your choices and still care about you."

Well, aren't you complex? I thought. I didn't say it; instead, I pulled my knees toward my chest, folded my arms across the top of them, and set my head facedown on my arms.

"Are you crying?" she asked.

"No."

Martha touched my shoulder. "Forget what I'm saying. I'm just—I don't know what I'm talking about."

"It's what you think." I said.

"Yeah, but who cares what I think?"

I raised my head and looked at her.

"I don't want you to remember it like this," she said. "Just because it's the end, I mean—the end isn't the same as the most important."

I said nothing.

"What you should remember is stuff like—okay, how about this? That Saturday morning in the spring when we got up really early and rode bikes into town and ate breakfast at that diner next to the gas station. And the eggs were kind of undercooked, but they were really good."

"It was your birthday," I said. "That's why we went."

"That's right. I forgot that part."

"You were sixteen," I said. Again, in the quiet, we could hear the saw.

"That morning," Martha said, "that was what our lives were like at Ault."

The humiliating part is that I went to look for him a second time. Or a third time, if you counted going to his dorm room in the middle of the night and finding only Devin. I had never been to his room before that week, and then I went twice in four days. It was early evening, before dinner, and I walked through the common room and down the hall. I nearly collided with Mario Balmaceda, who was coming out of the bathroom and looked at me with a confused expression, and I did not stop to apologize or explain myself. At the end of the hall, I knocked on the door—the poster of the basketball player was still up—and then without waiting I opened it. No one was in the room. It was still light outside, and shadowy inside, and I could hear the tick of an alarm clock sitting on a white plastic crate next to one of the beds.

In my imagination. he'd been reading in bed and he'd sat up when I entered and I'd crawled onto his lap and wrapped my legs and arms around him. And at first I'd be weeping and he'd stroke my hair; he'd murmur to me, but of course it would quickly turn sexual. And it would be urgent—we'd clutch and bite, we'd want it the exact same amount. Maybe I'd give him a blow job, on my knees on their dirty rug, and I'd be wearing a shirt on top and nothing on the bottom, and he'd wind his legs around me and dig his heels against my ass; because of me, he'd be in agony.

Except that he wasn't there, and that looking at his room, the unfamiliar objects—I didn't even know which bed was his—I realized how absurd it was to have assumed, or just to have hoped, that he'd be in the same mood I was, waiting for me. Quickly, the shift was occurring from disappointment at his absence to terror that he'd appear before I got out. I would seem—this would be the word he'd use, or other people would—*psycho*. That is, as annoying as a girl who cried, but also aggressive.

He wasn't waiting for me, he wasn't looking for me. It would have been a lie to say the only reason I wanted to see him was to smooth over the earlier ugliness, but that was one of the reasons, and had it been so far-fetched to think he might want the same? Now I think it was far-fetched, that my impulse was feminine, and that the masculine response (maybe I just mean the more detached response) was to realize that our final interaction had been overblown and unfortunate but that we each understood well enough where the other stood. Another exchange would be reiteration, not clarification.

I shut the door and hurried down the hall. Back in Elwyn's, it took a few minutes for my heartbeat to settle. But then it did, and I realized all at once that nothing had actually happened. It felt like I was recovering, but from what? I was by myself; the fan in the window was whirring, the room was cluttered with half-empty boxes. "It's over," I said. "Everything with Cross is finished." If I said it out loud, maybe I would finally stop being so hopeful.

The person giving the chapel talk always sat to the left of the chaplain, and the next morning, that seat was occupied by Conchita Maxwell. I cannot say I was completely surprised. As she climbed the steps to the pulpit, I saw that she was wearing a black linen skirt and a white blouse; she had long ago stopped dressing eccentrically and had grown out her hair. She cleared her throat and said into the microphone, "The article that appeared in last Sunday's *New York Times* has left many people in the Ault community feeling angry, hurt, and misrepresented. I am one of those people. As a Mexican American, I took special exception to the article. In no way did it reflect the experience I have had for the last four years, in this place I have come to call my home." Listening to her, at first I felt hostile, but eventually, I felt sad and then not even that—more just a distance from the whole situation. Hearing the talk, which relied heavily on rhetoric and was not particularly well written, reminded me of reading someone else's history term paper about a subject I was not interested in, and, not even on purpose, I found myself tuning out. What I thought of was Conchita and me as freshmen, of teaching her to ride a bike behind the infirmary. How long ago that seemed, how far I felt from her now; I couldn't remember talking to her even once during our senior year. And, with graduation, we were about to be cut loose from each other completely—the distance between us would be physical and definitive, and perhaps we'd never speak again. It seemed an impossible thought—so often did we all come together at Ault that I had begun to believe life contained reckonings rather than just fade-outs— and yet I also saw then that as more and more years passed, the time Conchita and I had known each other, the time I had known any of my classmates, would feel decreasingly significant; eventually, it would be only a backdrop to our real lives. At some cocktail party years into the future, in an incarnation of myself I could not yet fathom, I would, while rummaging for an anecdote, come up with one about a girl I'd known at boarding school whose mother took us out for lunch one day while the family bodyguard sat at the next table. In the telling, I would feel no pinch of longing or regret; I would feel nothing true, nothing at all, in fact, except the wish that my companions find me amusing.

When Conchita had finished, there was the customary moment of silence—you never applauded after a chapel talk—and then we stood to sing the hymn, It was the last all-school chapel service of the year; another service would be held graduation morning, but only for seniors and parents. Always before breaks, including summer vacation, the hymn we sang was "God Be with You till We Meet Again," and this was what we sang that day. We sang all four verses—at Ault, we always sang all the verses of all the hymns—and when we got to the third one, to the lines that went "When life's perils thick confound you/Put His arms unfailing round you," tears welled up in my eyes. Not again, I thought, but after a moment I happened to glance around and then I understood that Conchita's talk had little to do with what most people were feeling in this moment and that, in at least one sense, I was not alone; the chapel was filled with crying seniors.

Then there was graduation, which was anticlimactic in the way of any ceremony. My family stayed at the Ramond TraveLodge, the same place my parents had stayed in the fall of my junior year, and the first thing they told me when we met in the school parking lot on Saturday night before walking over to Mr. Byden's house for dinner was that right after they'd checked in, Tim had taken such a huge shit that he'd clogged the toilet and they'd had to switch rooms because it was over-flowing. "He's six!" Joseph was shouting. "How can a six-year-old take a dump that size?" Tim, meanwhile, was blushing and smiling as if he had accomplished something great that modesty prevented him from acknowledging directly. At first, my father ignored me, but everything was so hectic that ignoring me was impractical; he downgraded his anger to talking to me curtly. On Sunday, at the graduation itself, Mr. Byden shook my hand in an entirely neutral way (Joseph told me our father had threatened to confront Mr. Byden and somehow I'd known he wouldn't). My parents and brothers sat with Martha's parents and brother at the ceremony—at last, my mother's wish to meet Mr. and Mrs. Porter was realized—and my family left that afternoon, the trunk of the car weighted down with all the possessions I'd accumulated in the last four years.

For graduation, Tim gave me a pair of socks with water-melons on them ("He chose them himself," my mother whispered), Joseph gave me a mix tape, and my parents gave me a hundred dollars in cash, which I spent helping buy gas for the people from whom I got rides during senior week—Dede a few times, and Norie Cleehan and Martha's boyfriend Colby. The last party was in Keene, New Hampshire, and Colby drove down from Burlington to get us and then kept driving south to drop me off at Logan Airport before they returned together to Vermont. Hugging them both—I had never hugged Colby, and I never saw him again after that—and pulling the suitcases from the trunk and checking that I hadn't left my plane ticket wedged in the back seat, I felt desperate for them to leave and for it all to be done with; I just wanted to be alone. And then they drove away, and I was. I was wearing shorts and a T-shirt, and both the airport terminal and then the airplane itself were frigidly air-conditioned. Flying to South Bend, I was freezing, and exhausted from drinking a lot and sleeping not that much over the course of the last week, from saying good-bye to so many people, from the friendli-ness—in the end, only a few classmates had been conspicuously unfriendly to me that week, After the plane landed and I walked through the terminal and collected my luggage and went out to the curb, where my mother and Tim were waiting, the air was a hot thick blast, and Ault was absolutely behind me. I had no reason to ever go back, no real reason—from now on, it was all optional.

Of course, I did go back, for both my fifth and tenth reunions. Do you want to know how everyone turned out? They turned out like this: Dede is a lawyer in New York, and I get the idea, though she's grown more modest with age, that she's very successful. The summer after we were sophomores in college, I received a card in the mail with a Scarsdale return address. On the front of the card was a picture of Dede in an over-the-top college coed outfit—a pleated skirt, an argyle sweater-vest over a button-down shirt, wire-framed glasses, and a stack of books in her arms—and under the picture, it said, *The problem with a Know It All* . . . and inside, when you opened the card, it said . . . *is that she thinks she Nose everything.* Below that, it said, *Yes, I have finally done it! My nose job was completed at 4:37 p,m. on June 19. Fewer pounds, fewer ounces. The most welcome arrival of my life!* After that, I always liked Dede, I liked her unequivocally, as I never had at Ault. I see her now when I go to New York, we have dinner and talk about men. She makes me laugh, and I don't know if it's that she's funnier or if I just wasn't willing to see, at Ault, how funny she was.

Like Dede, Aspeth Montgomery lives in New York, and she owns an interior design boutique, which always disappoints me a little to think about—it just seems so insignificant. I was right about Darden (he's also a lawyer), who became an Ault trustee at the age of twenty-eight. Sin-Jun, of course, lives with her girlfriend in Seattle and is a neurobiologist. Amy Dennaker, whom I never lived with after freshman year in Broussard's, is a conservative pundit; I don't usually watch those Sunday morning political shows, but sometimes when I do, if I'm in a hotel, I see her arguing in a business suit, and she always seems to be enjoying herself. I heard that Ms. Prosek and her cute husband got divorced a few years after I graduated. I hope that it was she who left him, or at least that it was mutual; basically, I just don't want him to have left her.

She no longer teaches at Ault, and I'm not sure where she's gone. Meanwhile, Rufina Sanchez and Nick Chafee are married; they married two years after she graduated from Dartmouth and he graduated from Duke. In equal measures, this sounds suffocating to me—high school sweethearts and all that—and I envy it; I think it must be nice to end up with someone who knows what you were like when you were a teenager.

I haven't seen Cross since we graduated because during our fifth reunion, he was living in Hong Kong, working for an American brokerage firm, and then he was planning to come to our tenth reunion—he lives in Boston now—but his wife went into labor the night before. Recently, Martha and her husband, who also live in Boston, met Cross and his wife for dinner, and Martha called me afterward and left a message saying, "He keeps golf clubs in his trunk. I'm not sure why I'm telling you this, but it seems like the kind of thing you'd appreciate." I know what Cross looks like now, because there was a picture from his wedding in *The Ault Quarterly*. He's balding, and he has a handsome face, but it's handsome in a different way. Because I knew it was him in the photo, I could discern his earlier features, but if we'd passed on the street, I'm not certain I'd have recognized him. His wife's name is Elizabeth Fairfield-Sugarman.

Martha is an assistant professor of classics, tenure-track. I was the maid of honor in her wedding, but the truth is that we talk about twice a year and see each other less than that.

And as for me: Cross had been wrong, and I didn't particularly like college, at least for the first few years—it seemed so vast and watered-down. But then as a junior I ended up getting an apartment with another girl and two guys, though I knew only the girl ahead of time and knew her only a little. One of the guys wasn't around much, but the other one— Mark, who was a senior—and the girl, Karen, and I made dinner together most nights, and watched television afterward. Upon moving in with them, I thought at first that they were both kind of LMC, but somewhere along the way, I forgot that I thought this. I learned to cook from Mark, and that summer, a few weeks before he moved out, he and I became involved; he ended up being the second person I ever kissed, the second person I had sex with. (Once, I had imagined that the first boy you were involved with was your initiation, that after him the switch had been flicked and you dated continuously, but, at least in my own case, I had been wrong.) After the first time Mark and I kissed, I was talking to Karen about it—I didn't know for sure if I liked Mark—and I brought up Cross. I was planning to say he was someone I *had* been certain about, but before I could, Karen said; "Wait a second. The guy you dated in high school was named Cross Sugarman?" She began to laugh, "What kind of person is named Cross Sugarman?"

I actually didn't—I don't—particularly like talking about Ault. I don't even really like reading the quarterly, though I always at least page through it. But if I give it real attention, my mood plummets; I remember my life there, all the people and the way I felt. In college, or after, in the course of ordinary conversation, someone might say, "Oh, you went to boarding school?" and I'd feel my heart thickening with the need to explain what the person did not truly care about. By my sophomore year at Michigan, if the subject arose, I would make only the most superficial remarks. *It was okay. It was hard, I was lucky to go.* These conversations were a lake I was riding across, and as long as we didn't dwell on the subject, or as long as I didn't think the person would understand anyway, even if I tried to explain, I could remain on the surface. But sometimes, if I talked for too long, I'd be yanked beneath, into cold and weedy water. Down there, I could not see or breathe; I was dragged backward, and it wasn't even the submersion that was the worst part, it was that I had to come up again. My present world was always, in its mildness, a little disappointing. I've never since Ault been in a place where everyone wants the same things; minus a universal currency, it's not always

474

clear to me what I myself want. And anyway, no one's watching to see whether or not you get what you're after—if at Ault I'd felt mostly unnoticed, I'd also, at certain moments, felt scrutinized. After Ault, I was unaccounted for.

But I should say too that I don't scrutinize others the way I once did. I did not, when I left Ault, carry my vigilance with me; I've never paid as close attention to my life or anyone else's as I did then. How was I able to pay such attention? I remember myself as often unhappy at Ault, and yet my unhappiness was so alert and expectant; really, it was, in its energy, not that different from happiness.

And so everything has to turn out somehow, and other things have happened to me—a job, graduate school, another job—and there are always words to describe the way you fill up your life, there is always a sequence of events. Although it doesn't necessarily have a relationship to the way you felt while it was occurring, there's usually some satisfaction in the neatness of its passage. Some anxiety, too, but usually some satisfaction.

On the night of my graduation from Ault, there was a party at a club in Back Bay, a place Phoebe Ordway's parents belonged—they were the ones giving the party. My own parents had already left for South Bend, but other parents were there early on, for dinner, and then they took off and my classmates, many of whom had been openly drinking in front of parents, stayed and danced and cried. I drank beer out of green bottles, and got drunk for the first time, and it felt great and dangerous. Great like I was wearing a cape that made me invisible; so I could observe everyone else without being observed—at one point, Martha was dancing with Russell Woo (I did not dance at all, of course) and I sat at a round table for eight by myself, utterly unselfconscious. And it felt dangerous because what was to stop me from just walking up to Cross, there in a group of people near the bar, and doing exactly what I wanted? Which was to wrap my arms around his neck and press my face into his chest and just stand there forever. I had had four beers; no doubt I was less drunk than I believed myself to be, and that's what stopped me.

A little before midnight, Martha said she was exhausted and wanted to leave. I was in the middle of a long conversation with Dede, who was smashed and was saying in a strangely beneficent way, "You were always so sad and angry. Even when we were freshmen, you were. Why were you so sad and angry? But if I'd known you were on scholarship, I could have lent you money. You were dating that kitchen guy last year, weren't you? I know you were." I was not completely listening to her—I was watching Cross as he moved around the room, danced, left, came back, talked for a while to Thad Maloney and Darden. I stayed at the party so I could keep watching him. Martha and I were both supposed to spend the night at her aunt and uncle's in Somerville, but when Martha left, I stayed. I thought that because I was drunk, maybe everything would be different, that as the night waned, Cross would eventually come to me. But instead, when the DJ played "Stairway to Heaven" as the last song of the night, Cross slow-danced with Horton Kinnelly and then the song ended and they stood side by side, still close together, Cross rubbing his hand over Horton's back. It all felt both casual and not random—in the last four minutes, they seemed to have become a couple. And though they had not interacted for the entire night, I understood suddenly that just as I'd been eyeing Cross over the last several hours, he'd been eyeing Horton, or maybe it had been for much longer than that. He too had been saving something for the end, but the difference between Cross and me was that he made choices, he exerted control, his agenda succeeded. Mine didn't. I waited for him, and he didn't look at me. And that was what the rest of senior week was like, though it surprised me less each time, at each party, and by the end of the week, Cross and Horton weren't even waiting until it was late and they were drunk—you'd see them entwined in the hammock at John Brindley's house in the afternoon, or in the kitchen at Emily Phillip's house, Cross sitting on a bar stool and Horton perched on his lap.

It was at Emily's house—this was the last party, in Keene—that I opened the note from Aubrey, the note where he declared his love for me. It was three-thirty in the morning, and I was standing in a field where Norie's car was parked, searching for the toothbrush in my backpack, when I found the card. I was very moved, not only because what he'd written was so sweet but also because—even though it was from Aubrey, tiny and prissy Aubrey—it meant the *Times* article hadn't made me untouchable; Cross Sugarman wasn't the only Ault boy who had ever noticed something worthwhile about me.

But not the last night of senior week, the first night—the night at the club in Back Bay: When Martha told me she was leaving, I didn't yet understand that Cross and Horton were together, and I wanted to stay.

"But I only have one key to my aunt's," Martha said. "How will you get in?"

"I'll figure something out," I said.

"I got a room at the Hilton, and you can crash there," Dede said.

"Thanks," I said, and Martha looked at me incredulously. "I'll call you in the morning," I told her.

I ended up sleeping in my skirt and blouse, sharing a bed with Dan Ponce and Jenny Carter; Jenny slept between Dan and me, and Dede and Sohini Khurana slept in the other bed. We turned off the light at quarter of four, and I woke at seven-thirty and left immediately. I didn't feel as bad as it seemed like I ought to, I couldn't *not* stand up or walk, and so I thought maybe the alcohol hadn't really affected me after all.

I boarded the T at Copley and rode to Park Street, where I knew I had to change to the Red Line to get to Martha's aunt's house. But Park Street confused me—while at Ault, I'd ridden the T only a handful of times—and I went down a set of stairs, then up again. The upper level was crowded and very green, and everyone around me was rushing. Not the Green Line—that was what I'd just gotten off of. I went back downstairs, to where it was red and a little calmer but not actually quiet. I was standing there in my clothes from the night before, clogs and a long skirt and a short-sleeved blouse, and as I gazed down at the track, it moved a little, then moved again in another place. Mice, I realized, or maybe small rats—they were skittering all over the track. almost but not quite blending in with the chunky gravel.

I remembered it was Monday. And rush hour—that was why the station was so crowded. Around me on the platform, people passed by, or stopped in a spot to wait: a black man in a blue shirt and a black pin-striped suit; a white teenager with headphones on, wearing a tank top and jeans that were too big for him; two women in their forties, both with long ponytails, both wearing nurse's uniforms. There was a woman with a bob and bangs in a silk skirt and matching jacket, a guy in paint-speckled overalls. All these people! There were so many of them! A black grandmother holding the hand of a boy who looked about six, three more white guys in business suits, a pregnant woman in a T-shirt. What had they been doing for the last four years? Their lives had nothing at all to do with Ault.

It's true that I was hung over for the first time, and still naïve enough not to understand what a hangover was. But these people, making their way through the morning, all their meetings and errands and obligations. And this was only here, in this station at this moment. The world was so big! The sharpness of that knowledge went away almost as soon as I'd boarded the T, but it has returned over the years, and even now sometimes—I am older, and my life is very different—I can feel again how amazed I was that morning.

Acknowledgments

My amazing agent, Shana Kelly, believed in this book before it existed and has helped me immeasurably with her encouragement, hard work, and level-headed intelligence. Also at William Morris, Andy McNicol has, with gusto, gone to bat for *Prep* and for me. At Random House, I truly have the best editor in the world: the wise and hilarious Lee Boudreaux. At every stage, Lee has known what's in this book's best interest, has allowed it to be itself, and has shown such enthusiasm. I am similarly indebted to Laura Ford, who rooted for the book early on and is a patient hand-holder and generally terrific person, as well as to Lee's and Laura's Random House colleagues Holly Combs, Veronica Windholz, Vicki Wong, Allison Saltzman, and my all-star publicity team—Jynne Martin, Kate Blum, Jen Huwer, and Jennifer Jones—who floored me with their creativity and dedication.

I have learned a tremendous amount from my teachers, including Bill Gifford and Laine Snowman. Most recently, at the Iowa Writers' Workshop, I was privileged to study with Chris Offutt; Marilynne Robinson; Ethan Canin, who was a wonderful adviser; and Frank Conroy, who cares so much about writing and whose beliefs have been so inspiring to me. I also learned from my challenging, insightful Iowa classmates, especially Susanna Daniel and Elana Matthews, who are my dear friends, and Trish Walsh, who always told me to just keep writing.

During the time I worked on this book, I received financial assistance from the Michener-Copernicus Society of

America. In addition, I literally was given a home by St. Albans School, and welcomed—so welcomed, in fact, that here I still am—by St. Albans's students, teachers, and staff.

I have been able to support myself without working in an office only because of assignments from various magazine and newspaper editors, including Rory Evans, who has been a mentor since I was seventeen years old. Bill Taylor and Alan Webber, the founding editors of *Fast Company*, hired me for my first and only full-time job and continued to give me incredible writing opportunities after I moved on.

I am deeply grateful to my other friends, readers, and combinations thereof: Sarah DiMare; Consuela Henderson Macpherson, Cammie McGovern, Annie Morriss, Emily Miller, Thisbe Nissen, Jesse Oxfeld, Samuel Park, Shauna Seliy, and Carolyn Sleeth. Matt Klam was a much-valued advocate and a sender of wacky and excellent e-mails. Field Maloney provided smart and timely editing advice. Peter Saunders brought my hard drive back from the dead and performed other feats of technological wizardry. Matt Carlson makes me happy in many cities.

Finally, of course, there's my family: My aunt Dede Alexander has been a stylish and attentive presence for my entire life. My other aunt, Ellen Battistelli, is my most faithful reader, has at times been my only reader, and is my kindred spirit in neuroses. My sister Tiernan gracefully suffered the indignity of being the main character in pretty much everything I wrote until the age of eighteen. My sister Jo talked through many aspects of *Prep* with me, including names and titles, and—when not coming over to my apartment, sitting an inch away from me, and chatting Jo-ishly—kept insisting, correctly, that I needed to finish the book. My brother, P.G., was himself in high school during the years I was writing about Lee Fiora's high school experience, and he sagely advised me on math, sports, and matters of the heart. Lastly, for their great love, I thank my parents. I am very lucky to be their daughter.